Radwa Ashour (1946–2014) was [...] and scholar. She was the author of [...] memoir, and criticism, including the novels *Granada* and *Specters*. She was a recipient of the Constantine Cavafy Prize for Literature and the prestigious Owais Prize for Fiction.

Kay Heikkinen is a translator and academic who holds a PhD from Harvard University and is currently Ibn Rushd Lecturer of Arabic at the University of Chicago. Among other books, she translated Naguib Mahfouz's *In the Time of Love* (AUC Press, 2010).

*

"Radwa Ashour was a powerful voice among Egyptian writers of the postwar generation and a writer of exceptional integrity and courage. Her work consistently engages with her country's history and reflects passionately upon it . . . She will surely occupy an important place in the story to which she attended with such sensitivity and conscience."
—*The Guardian*

"Rich, challenging and indisputably important . . . a grand narrative of Palestinian life since the Nakba . . . Read this book. Then read it again, and then lend it to your friends, the bloke in the corner shop, his grandma and her poodle. They'll all thank you for it."
—*Electronic Intifada*

"One of the most influential writers in the Arab region."
—*Egypt Independent*

"Ashour writes beautifully, balancing her own talent for evocative language."
—*The Daily Star*

"Gives new insight into the known and hidden chapters of Palestinian history. It is also a celebration of Palestinian popular culture, of unsung heroes, big and small acts of resistance, creativity and resilience in the face of overwhelming odds."
—*Jordan Times*

The Woman from Tantoura

Radwa Ashour

Translated by
Kay Heikkinen

hoopoe
AN IMPRINT OF AUC PRESS

This edition published in 2019 by
Hoopoe
113 Sharia Kasr el Aini, Cairo, Egypt
200 Park Ave., Suite 1700 New York, NY 10166
www.hoopoefiction.com

Hoopoe is an imprint of the American University in Cairo Press
www.aucpress.com

Dar el Kutub No. 13058/18
ISBN 978 977 416 900 7

Dar el Kutub Cataloging-in-Publication Data

Ashour, Radwa
    The Woman from Tantoura / Radwa Ashour.— Cairo: The American
University in Cairo Press, 2018.
    p.   cm.
    ISBN 978 977 416 900 7
    1.   English Fiction
    I.   Title
    832

1 2 3 4 5   23 22 21 20 19

Designed by Adam el-Sehemy
Printed in the United States of America

For Mourid Barghouti

1

Cast Ashore

HE CAME OUT OF THE sea. Yes, by God, he came out of the sea as if he were of it, and the waves cast him out. He didn't come floating on the surface like a fish, he sprang out of it. I followed him as he walked toward the shore, his legs taut, pulling his feet from the sand and planting them in it, coming closer. He was bare, covered only by white pants held around his waist by a rope, drops of water shining on his face and shoulders. His hair was plastered on his head, chest, and arms, wet and shining. I was standing in front of him on the shore, but when I recall the scene I see myself on the threshing floor, among the stalks of wheat, spying on him while he was unaware of me. I know that the threshing floors were on the east side, separated from the sea by the houses of the village and the railroad, and that I was standing on the shore. I was tempted to run away, but I did not run.

I was the one who spoke first. I asked him his name and he answered, "My name is Yahya, from Ain Ghazal."

"What brought you here?"

"The sea!"

His face reddened in a blush that I caught like an infection from him; shyness overcame me, and then him, too. I threw him a stammered goodbye, and then turned away.

As I was going I turned my head and did not see him, so I was sure that he could not see me. I ran to my friends and found them as I had left them, as if nothing had happened, chattering, and playing in the sand.

I told the story. It seems my words came tumbling out fast; they stopped me and asked me to start over. I did, and they began to wink at each other and laugh. I said, "What's so funny?" I got up, shook the sand from my dress and went toward the house.

I didn't go into the house. I bypassed it and went to the Indian fig bushes behind the rear courtyard. I began to pick the fruit and went on until I filled the large basket that we left nearby. I carried it into the house, got a knife and a large plate, and crouched near the basket. I grasped the fruit between the thumb and index finger of my left hand, avoiding the circles of spines. With a single, quick blow I cut off the upper end with the knife and then the lower; then I split the rind lengthwise with the edge of the knife, pulling it back a little. Next I put the knife aside and freed the fruit from its spiny covering with my fingers and put it on the plate. Usually I would do that with a speed that astonished my two big brothers, as they could never succeed in peeling it, despite their love for the fruit. The spines would get stuck in their fingers and they would curse and swear while I watched them, laughing. When my mother would see me absorbed in peeling the figs, she would say, "Bless you, you're as fast as always!"

The sea was the border of the village, lending it its voices and colors, suffusing it with its scents, which we would smell even in the aroma of the large, flat stone-baked bread loaves. I don't remember when I learned how to swim just as I don't remember when I learned how to walk or talk. In later years I headed for coastal towns. I said, "The sea in Beirut or Alexandria is the same sea," but it wasn't. City sea is different: you look at it from a high balcony or you walk along an asphalt path and the sea is there, separated from you by a ditch and a fence. And if you decide to go to it you come as a stranger, sitting in one of the coffee shops on the shore, or carrying with you strangers' gear—an umbrella, a chair, perhaps a towel and swimsuit. It's a limited visit; you come as a guest, then you pick up your things and leave.

Like most of the houses in the village, our house was entwined with the sea. I would go to it carelessly, almost unnoticing, two steps in the water meaning to wet my feet and then a wave would surprise me, wetting my whole garment. I would jump back to the sand and in the flash of an eye it would turn me into a sand creature, then another jump and I would dive into the water all the way. I would swim and play, alone or with the other girls and boys. We would share in digging, then "Me, me, me . . . ." I would go down into the deep pit and they would spread sand over me until my body disappeared, leaving only the head rising excitedly from its warm, sandy burial place. A grave surrounded by the laughter and devilment of the young. At other times I would shout at the top of my lungs like someone struck by madness, "Hun-*ter*! Hun-*ter*!" I would crawl on the ground and jump and crawl again, in my hand the copper vessel that I had secured between the rocks as a trap for fish, in which the poor thing had been caught. I would lift the silver fish by its tail and say teasingly, "My fish is always the biggest and the best." In a flash the thought would occur to me: Was it luck or my skill in scattering moistened crumbs in the bottom of the vessel, which I would cover with cloth, making holes in it that allowed the fish to slip inside when it was tempted by the food?

In our sea there is a sugar spring, a spring of sweet water fixed among the salty waves. Yes, by God, a sugar spring, and right beside it was the newlyweds' plaza. We would hold our weddings on the shore; the young man would appear after his friends had bathed him and helped him into his new clothes. They would sing to him, "The handsome one comes from the bath . . . may God and his name be with him . . . the handsome one comes from the bath . . . God and his name be with him." He would appear on a horse curried as if it were the groom. We would jump as if we had grasshoppers inside us, jumping from the groom's street to the bride's rock to all the aunts absorbed in preparing the food, and singing:

> Say to his mother, rejoice and be glad,
> Place myrtle on the pillows and henna on our hands.
> The wedding is here and the couple is smiling,
> The home is my home and the rooms are all mine,
> We are engaged, let my enemy die!

We slip in among the young men who have left the beach and gone to dance the dabka. We stand next to an old man lost in the ecstasy of singing, who has begun before anyone has arrived, just singing alone, fascinated by his own voice and the verses he is repeating.

The wedding spreads over the seashore, and expands. It is festive with the women's trills and ahazij songs, the dabka circles, the aroma of grilled lamb, and the torches. The call and response of the ataba and ooof songs escape from the men's chests and reverberate, yes, by God, they escape and hover as if they might reach the Lord on his throne above, or fly beyond the neighbors to nearby villages to entertain the residents of the whole coast, from Ras al-Naqura to Rafah. Then the riders come, competing in galloping and dancing. Each is on the back of his purebred mare, digging up the sand of the beach with her hooves, her body and legs swept away as she approaches, turning, the young man on her back leaning lightly forward as if he were flying like her. The scene takes our breath away. We forget the sea. Perhaps the sea, like us, is absorbed in watching and forgets itself in calm, or is gradually overcome by sleepiness after the long evening. Like the sea, we give in to the gentle torpor. We don't notice until our mothers take us away, and we follow them like sleepwalkers. We settle into our beds, not knowing if we are in the house or on the beach, if what we see or what rings in our ears is the real wedding or a dream in our sleep.

The sea resides in the village. As for the train, it has set times, appearing and then disappearing, like the night-haunting ghoul. We are disturbed by the roar of its engines as it approaches, the earth's shaking as it passes, the friction of the wheels on the rails, its whistle bursts, the hiss of the brakes because it is stopping. The train passes through the town daily, and has a station in the east, in Zummarin. Sometimes it carries local people like us; mostly it is ridden by English soldiers or settlers with business in Haifa or Jaffa, who come and go by train. My two brothers ride Abu Isam's bus once a week, going to Haifa at the beginning of the week and returning at the end, to spend Thursday and Friday night with us.

Less than a month after I met the young man who sprang from the sea, we were visited by the sheikh of Ain Ghazal. He drank coffee with my father and asked for my hand in marriage for his nephew.

My mother said, "His name is Yahya."

I muttered, "I know his name is Yahya."

My mother didn't notice. She continued with what she was telling me.

"Your father wants to know what you think before he gives him the answer. He said to them that the alliance honors us, and God willing, good will come of it. Your father agrees, but he says, if Ruqayya accepts we will only read the Fatiha now and we'll hold the marriage in a year, when she will be fourteen." My mother said that she had objected and said, "Why would we marry her to a young man from Ain Ghazal?" and that my father said, "The people of Ain Ghazal are our maternal cousins, they have married our daughters before. And the boy has a good mind, he's educated and he's studying in Egypt." "When he said Egypt I shouted, 'Will you send your daughter away, Abu Sadiq?' He said, 'I won't send her away. The boy will finish his studies before the marriage is consummated.' I objected again, 'As long as the boy is studying in the university he won't work as a fisherman or a farmer, and he won't live here or in Ain Ghazal. He'll get a job in Haifa or in Lid, and he might go farther away, his job might even take him to Jerusalem, and frankly I don't want to send my daughter far away. It's enough that the two boys are away in Haifa and that I don't see them more than a day and a half each week. If she's going to leave the village let her marry Amin. The father's nephew unseats a groom riding to his bride, as they say. Amin is better for her, and Beirut is closer than Cairo.' He said, 'He won't stay in Cairo, he will return to Ain Ghazal. And if he gets a job in Haifa you can take the train and reach your daughter in less than half an hour.' I said, 'And if the Jews close the road to us?' His face got red, and he scowled and said, 'God forbid! Enough talk! We're buying the man, not the location of his work. The boy is nineteen and educated, the family brings honor and distinction, his uncle is the sheikh of Ain Ghazal, an upstanding man with a reputation like gold. Ask the girl, and if she agrees, may God bless it.'"

"What do you think?" My mother was directing the question to me.

I did not say, "Even if he were working at the ends of the earth . . . ," rather I said, "I agree."

My words came out clear, in a loud voice. She scolded me, "Good God, where's your shame! Say, 'Whatever you think,' say, 'It's for my parents to decide!'"

On the next visit the sheikh of Ain Ghazal came with his brothers and with a large group of his most important relatives and of men of their village. They were received by my father, my uncle, my brothers, and the elders of our village. They read the Fatiha. The formal proposal was made with Yahya pursuing his university studies in Egypt. My mother and my aunt were absorbed in preparing the feast, for which my father had slaughtered two lambs. My mother was coming and going, repeatedly whispering in my ear, "You'll have a bad reputation among the women, they'll say you're a lazy, good-for-nothing bride. Look lively, show them what you can do." I slipped out of the house and headed for the sea, sitting cross-legged and staring at the boy as he approached, wet and golden. I recalled the scene and then recalled again, against the background of the sound of the waves and the women's songs and trills of joy coming from the direction of our house:

She lowered her eyes, her hand held out for their henna,
Such a small gazelle—how could her family sell her away?
O Mother, O Mother, prepare my new pillows,
I'm leaving home without even a family's farewell!

2

The Night-Haunting Ghoul

I IMAGINE MY MOTHER DURING those days. I recall what she said, and what she did not say. I hear her as she repeats to one of the neighbors what she has already said to my aunt: "I said to him, 'You're sending your daughter all the way to Haifa, Abu Sadiq!' He said, 'You'll take the train.' Good God, I'll travel from one town to another to see my daughter? And what if she goes into labor in the middle of the night? What if she gets sick, God forbid? Besides, how will I take the train, and who will tell me how to take it, and how to get off, and how to get from the station to her house? And how can I take the train when most of the passengers are English soldiers or Jewish settlers? Even if they left me alone and no one bothered me, how would I dare ask any of them a question? They might not understand me when I ask, they might make fun of me, they might intentionally mislead me so that I get off at the wrong station and get lost between towns. I might find myself in one of the companies they call 'settlements,' what would I do then? Knock on the Jews' door and tell them to bring me back home? Why did Abu Sadiq choose the hard way and say, 'Accept my choice'? Why shouldn't my daughter live near me, so I wouldn't have to do anything to go see her except put on my sandals and put my scarf back on my head? She would put on the coffee when she sent for me and I would arrive before it boiled! And he says, 'Take the train'!"

I don't know if this anxiety that possessed my mother was the normal anxiety of a woman who had never left her village, or if it was complicated and deepened by a reality weighed down by fears, a reality that led her as it led others to take refuge in all that was familiar to her and associated with her. The distance separating her from Haifa—which was twenty-four kilometers, no more and no less—seemed like a rugged road surrounded by dangers, more like Sinbad's voyage to the land of Wak Wak, or like going to the hiding place of the ghoul lying in wait for Shatir Hasan. These fears were not solely caused by the probability that her expected son-in-law would live in Haifa; after all, the young man was studying in Cairo, and neither she nor anyone else knew what work he might find, or where. In fact, God would spare her the trip to Haifa and its twenty-four kilometers; the young man would not work in Haifa and her daughter would not live there. My mother would live and die without taking the train. She would never visit Haifa, and no mount or automobile would take her to Ain Ghazal or to any of the other neighboring villages, except for al-Furaydis.

She would go there in a truck.

I tell my grandchildren tales about their great-grandmother, to amuse them. I tell them about their great-grandfather too. I say, "He used to love to tease her. Was it an old habit he had acquired when they were little, since he was her cousin and only four years older, or was it something new that came after marriage? I don't know. He would intentionally pick a fight with her and she would take his words seriously. He said, 'Take the train.' Of course he was toying with her, because Abu Isam's bus went from the village to Haifa every morning and came back in the evening, and no soldier or settler rode it. There were two Dodge cars that could be rented, that would take anyone who wanted not only to Haifa but also to Acre or Nazareth, or to Jerusalem or Jenin or Safad, or to Jaffa or even Gaza, usually to greet the pilgrims returning from

Mecca by way of Suez. But he said, 'Take the train.'" The grandchildren laugh and I join in, even though my awareness of the irony is like a lump in my throat. They don't need to get used to traveling from town to town to see their grandmother or to visit their uncles or to attend a wedding or a funeral; they've never known any other way. I have not gotten used to it. Even after all these years, I have not gotten used to the movement of airplanes, which sometimes seems to me like a sky that the sky itself hides behind. I mutter to myself, "God rest you, Mother. If God had lengthened your life you would have known another time, and it would have taught you to know distant cities thousands of kilometers away from you. You would have stumbled over their names and clung to them, because the children are there." Did I say I have not gotten used to it? I take it back. I have become accustomed. No one can resist being tamed by time.

I said to my granddaughter Huda, commenting on a silver ornament the size of a chick pea that she had put on the end of her nose, "If your great-grandmother saw you now!" She looked at me questioningly, not knowing if the comment showed admiration or implied criticism. I smiled and said, "I was a lot younger than you, maybe four or five at the most, when the Nawar came to our village." She stopped me: "The Nawar?" "The Gypsies," I explained. Then I continued, "They set up their tents in the village square, and there was a woman with them who put a basket of seashells in front of her, the kind that are small and spiraled. She would say, 'Blow on them and give them back to me and I will read your fortune.' That seemed very exciting, and she herself seemed different, arousing curiosity by those green marks on her face. There was a little round mark on the end of her nose and others more like two horizontal lines under her lower lip, and there was a crescent earring, not placed as usual—a pair with one in each ear—but fastened on the side of her nose. Her accent was different and so was her garment; it was different from our mothers' long dresses. She said that she could read the unknown and uncover hidden things, and that it was possible for her to tell us what would happen to us when we grew up. Everyone ran to his house; one came back with a stone-baked loaf, one carried an egg, one brought dates. She read our fortunes, but even after we learned our good luck, we didn't disperse but stayed in a circle around her. Then I found myself pulling on the edge of her dress and pointing to the green marks on her face and asking her, 'How did you color that, Auntie?'

"She laughed, 'I didn't color it!'

"'Were you born like that?'

"'That's a tattoo, and we inscribe it whenever we want. It beautifies the face. Do you want one like it?'

"'Yes, I do.'

"'What will you give me in exchange?'

"I flew to the house and came back with a copper pot that I gave to her. She made the tattoo for me. I went home and when my mother saw the tattoo she stood screaming at me, threatening to beat me. When she found out about the copper pot she made good her threat and beat me with a stick until my brothers rescued me from her. For years I didn't understand why my mother was so angry, and why she kept saying, 'Now people will think you are one of the Nawar girls.'"

What did Anis say? He was my grandson who lived in Canada, and he had been following what I told his cousin. He said what would never occur to me, nor cross my mind: "It's clear that Great-grandma was racist. What she said about the Gypsies is racist talk, it's not right, and beating children is also unacceptable." He added, in English, "It's politically incorrect!"

I burst out laughing and laughed a long time, until the tears rolled down my cheeks. I said as I was wiping away the tears, "Your poor great-grandmother! God rest her soul and bless her and her time."

I wait for Maryam to return from the university. I wait for her to finish studying her lessons. I wait for the calls from the children. I wait for the six a.m. news broadcast, and for the news at eleven at night, and then for the news at six the next morning. The hours pass slowly, in loneliness, as if I were moving about in a cemetery. The summer comes, or more precisely a certain summer month comes, and the house comes to life. We have to organize comings and goings to avoid traffic congestion, and the conflict of temperaments and desires. "What will we cook tonight?" What the girl wants, the boy won't like. One smokes ceaselessly and one can't stand the smell of cigarettes, one wants to watch a soccer match and another wants the news, while the third group wants to watch movies. One calls from an inner room, "Lower your voices a little, I want to sleep," and one asks for help from the kitchen because he has caused a minor disaster, with no great consequences. I say, "A madhouse!" and notice the confusion of Mira's face, my granddaughter who wears glasses, who reads a lot, and who takes everything that's said seriously. I explain, "I'm joking, your being here is as sweet as honey for me."

We laugh, we laugh between the jokes, the silly stories, and the recalled foolishness. We fill the gaps of months of absence with the stories of what happened to them, or to me, or to others of our family and friends who live in Ain al-Helwa or in Jenin or in Tunis or who stayed in the area of al-Furaydis, or who are scattered among the villages nearby, those we know and see from time to time and those we never meet, whose stories reach us and which we repeat, so they become part of the shared fabric of the family.

My neighbor, a young woman, a doctor to whom Maryam introduced me, asked me, "Your oldest granddaughter is in college, when did you get married?"

"Before I was fifteen."

"God forbid, you were a child!"

I changed the subject as I didn't think it was appropriate to present the story of my life, with a full accounting, to a neighbor who had met my daughter less than two weeks before, and then had surprised me with a visit, saying that she wanted to meet me. There was plenty of time for us to become closer, to become friends, and for her to know some of my story—or to be satisfied with polite neighborliness, "Good morning" and "How are you?" when we met by chance in the elevator or at the door of the building, each going her own way and knowing no more of her neighbor than her name and the broad outlines of her life.

After the month of vacation, which might be a week more or less for one reason or another, I say goodbye to the children. The schedule of arriving flights is exchanged for another one, for departures to Abu Dhabi, to Toronto, to Paris, to Lid via Larnaca or Athens, to Nablus via Amman and the bridge. We go to the airport, then we go again, then we go a third time and a fourth and sometimes a fifth. Weeping has been worn out, maybe because the tears have become ashamed of themselves, there's no place for them. The children kiss my hand and move away with unhurried steps, not turning around so I can see their faces one more time. The grandchildren, Noha and Huda and Amin Junior and Anis and Mira, follow their families with hurried steps, turning their necks again and again: "Goodbye, Teta." I look at their smiling faces. I wave. They wave.

I hold Maryam's arm as we come home together. A space of calm to recover the usual rhythm, to contemplate, to bathe, to put the house in order, to repair my relationship with the plants which I'm convinced get angry, like children, if you neglect them.

Usually it all takes two weeks, after which the house regains its cleanliness, the window glass and the wooden shutters and the doors, the carpet and the curtains and the furniture. And I spoil the plants, seeking to please them until they are satisfied.

Afterward I return to my usual daily schedule: I listen to the news broadcast at six. I wake Maryam. We have breakfast together. She goes to her university and I go to the sea. I cross the Corniche and go down to the beach. I take off my shoes, I go across the sand until the end of the wave reaches me and wets the edge of my dress. When I go up to the paved road, I walk for an hour or more. Then I go home. I boil coffee, and I drink it in the company of the plants on the balcony.

It's strange; after the children have left, with the first sip of the first cup of coffee I make myself, my mother's voice always comes to me, crying in disapproval, "You are sending your daughter all the way to Haifa, Abu Sadiq!" I smile and murmur the Fatiha for her spirit.

3

Fickle February

IN OUR TOWN WE CALL grass "spring," because the spring is when the year turns and its season arrives, when it clothes the hills and the valleys. Classes and types and denominations of color, intense or coarse, deep or delicate, soft or light and vivid, all an unruly and unfettered green, and no one is sad. In its expanse grow the wildflowers, scattered wherever they please. But despite their red or yellow or gradations of purple, they can never be anything other than miniatures plunged in the sea of green.

All alone the almond tree ruled over spring in the village, the undisputed queen. None of the surrounding trees dared to contest it. Even the sea was jealous of the almond tree in the spring, even the sea foam was jealous, for what was its poor white compared to a heart like a carnation, taking one stealthily to a frank crimson? The almonds flower and steal our hearts, and then they capture them entirely with their delicate, deceptive fruit, stinging and sweet. We don't wait for it to harden, we stretch our hands to pick what's close. We climb the branches and take what we want. We eat in the trees or carry it as provisions in our pockets, or lift the ends of our garments to hold them, and then fly home.

My mother says, "February can't be tied down." She says, "February is fickle and stubborn, it huffs and puffs and has the smell of summer." The winds are active and the waves high and the cold still lingers, cutting to the bone as if we were in the depths of winter, but we know that March is only two steps away. Then the almond flowers, as if opening the way and giving permission, followed by the apricot blossoms, and afterward the trees are covered as they rush to compete, first with their flowers and then with the early fruit. Then we know that April has planted its feet on the earth, and that May will follow it, to set the wheat on the threshing floors and the fruit on the trees.

So why did they choose these four months for war, for strikes, and for killing people without number?

I didn't know all the details, what happened in Haifa on any given day, how many were killed by the powder barrel the settlers rolled down Mount Carmel on such-and-such a street, or in what village they invaded the houses by night, pouring kerosene on the stores of flour and lentils and oil and olives, firing on the inhabitants. But like the rest of the girls in town I knew that the situation was dangerous, not only because we heard some of what went from mouth to mouth, but also because there was something frightening in the air, something on the verge. On the verge of what? We didn't know. The madafa that served as a town hall for the men was almost never without meetings, where they would stay until late at night. Sometimes my father would wake us, asking us to prepare something to eat and a bed for guests, saying, "It's late, they will spend the night with us. Offer them whatever there was for supper, and get up early in the morning to prepare breakfast because they are traveling." So we would make a quick supper and prepare a bed, and get up early in the morning to make breakfast for the men who were traveling.

My father and the men of the village must have known about the partition resolution when it happened, and in those meetings of theirs they were making their arrangements to confront it. (The coastline from south of Acre to south of Jaffa, including our village, was included in the Jewish state

18

after the partition.) But I don't remember that I heard about it or that the topic was brought up among the women of the village, or among the girls like me. The first news that alerted me was what happened in Haifa at the end of the month of December, since one of the neighbors told my mother about fights in Haifa between the Jewish and Arab workers in the oil refinery. The neighbor said that the Jews threw a bomb from a fast-moving car and killed and wounded many of us. She said that on the very next day the Palestinian workers rose against the Jewish workers, armed with sticks and knives, taking vengeance and killing anyone they could. Before dawn the Jewish soldiers attacked Balad al-Sheikh and a neighborhood on its heights where the refinery workers from Ijzim and Ain Ghazal and other neighboring villages lived with their wives and children. They descended on the residents with axes and knives and bombs and rifles, and left behind them corpses everywhere. Some say they killed sixty residents and some say that hundreds were killed.

My mother got up hurriedly and I followed her. She went to the house of the headman and asked me to go into the madafa and call my father. He came.

"What is it, Umm Sadiq?"

"Have you heard about what happened in Haifa?"

"I heard."

"Aren't you going to go to see your boys?"

"God protect them, if one of them had been hit we would have heard the news from a hundred sources. Be calm. What happened, happened in the oil refinery, and it's far from where they live and from the school and the bank. Go home, women don't come to the madafa like this to talk to the men at the door!"

"But the boys . . ."

He cut her off. "The boys are fine, God willing, and they'll come at the end of the week. And if they can't come because of the situation, they'll come at the end of the week after."

We went home. My mother was crying and saying over and over, "O Lord, O Lord, protect her and me and my boys and deliver them, O Almighty, O Munificent." Her voice would choke in tears and then rise in lament: "*Yaammaa*, apples of my eye, they're shooting at you so far away and nobody even knows, *yaammaa*, oh my beloveds!" I shouted at her, "Your weeping is a bad omen, Mama. It's forbidden! Our Lord will be angry with you and afflict them tomorrow with what spared them today." I said it in a decisive tone, as if I were scolding her. The words stuck in her mind and she calmed down, and then turned toward the sky and said, "Forgive me O Lord, I'm not opposing your decree. Protect Sadiq and Hasan, restore them and bring them home safe and sound from distant lands. Be kind to us, O Lord." It was as if God had heard her and shut the door as she finished speaking, and she considered it an agreement. She looked at me suddenly, as if she had finally realized that I was walking beside her, and said, "By God, by God, I will not give you to the boy from Ain Ghazal if he doesn't promise to live far away from Haifa. We'll record the condition in the marriage contract!"

While we waited for Thursday my mother hid her fears in her breast, afraid to break the implicit agreement between her and the Most High, as if what I had said about the omen was not from my own mind but rather an inspiration from Him, telling her His will and conditions. The poor thing kept the conditions and followed the path with determination, not crying or complaining or referring to the subject, just growing paler day by day. When Abu Isam's bus returned from Haifa the tears began to flow silently from her eyes. Then a boy came from the direction of the highway, bringing her good news and saying that they had arrived in a car that left them at the entrance to the village, at the place we called "the Gate." "I saw them with my own eyes." My mother got up, washed her face and changed her dress and went out to the courtyard of the house. My father joined her. She saw them

coming from afar but she stayed calm, as if she were waiting until she could be certain beyond any doubt. When they
came within two steps of her, so that her hand could touch
them, she let out a ringing trill of joy—at which my father
slapped her face with his hand, a resounding slap followed
by a shout of anger, "Have some shame, woman! A hundred
men were martyred in one week and you are trilling!" Silence
fell, all movement stopped. My brothers stopped walking, I
was nailed to the ground. My mother seemed thrown into
confusion, not knowing what to do about the first slap she had
ever received from her cousin. Then the scene resumed: my
brothers began walking toward the house. They kissed their
father's hand before moving to their mother's arms, waiting
to enfold them.

My father said, "Come with me to the madafa, to give the
men the news from Haifa."

My mother asked, whispering, "And supper?"

My father asked, "Are you hungry?"

"We'll eat and then we'll go to the madafa."

"You won't die of hunger; follow me to the madafa. After
that you can eat however you like."

The madafa in the headman's house was where the men
met to talk, to spend the evening in company, to discuss recent
events and sometimes to solve disputes; and there the men
sat in a circle around the radio to listen to the news. Women
did not enter the madafa and the only news that reached
them was what the men kindly told them, which they then
exchanged among themselves. When it all happened the roof
collapsed on everyone's head, with no difference between the
men and the women, the old and the young, or even the nursing infants dependent on their mother's milk for their very
life. I said there was no difference; I take that back, and I look
at it again. There was a difference. Yes, there was a difference.

A few weeks after my mother's joyful trill and the slap
that followed it, the refugees arrived in the village. Qisarya

was located on the sea like us but it was south of town; it fell and the residents were forced to leave, and our village hosted some of the families. Our share of the guests was a widow with two children, a four-year-old boy and a girl a year younger than I. My new friend Wisal, the first of the refugees I met, told me about the scenario that all of the coastal towns, and others, would live through three months later. The scenario was not identical in every detail but it was the same in the general outlines. My friend told me that the Jewish troops laid siege to the town, attacked it, and drove the people out of their houses.

"My mother said, 'Where will we go? We have no one to support us, no one who can take us to another town or arrange a way for us to live.' She insisted on staying in the house. We stayed, and we learned that others did as we did. A week after they entered the town, they took us out of the houses and destroyed them and forced us to leave. They did the same with the Muslims and the Christians."

I found that strange, and I asked, "Are there Christians in your town?"

"Yes, Muslims and Christians and Jews."

"And Jews?"

"Yes."

"In the 'company,' or in the town?"

"In the town."

"Many?"

"No, a few."

"Did they drive them out?"

"They came to give them the village, so why would they drive them out? Are there Jews in your village?"

"There was one man, then he moved to Zummarin, their 'company' in Zummarin that's called Zikhron Yaakov."

"Is it large?"

"Oh yes, it's large. East of the village. It's about an hour's walk away."

"They built a 'company' in our town too, they can get there in a ten-minute walk. They built it in the town territory, on farmland. They built it a few years ago; its name is Sdot Yam. I haven't visited it."

"I haven't visited Zummarin either, but my father visited it, because there was a problem, and the police station and the government are there. There are people in the village who sell fish there and sometimes eggs, and sometimes they buy clothes there because they're cheap. But my father says that since the big strike in '36 there has been a decision: we will not sell to them or buy from them. Sometimes they come to swim in the sea. Or there's a problem, so the headman of the 'company' visits the headman of the village. When will you go back?"

"My mother says we'll go back soon. I don't believe her."

I introduced my friend to the girls of the village. I took her to the Sugar Spring and the Newlyweds' Beach and the islands and the castle built on one of them. She did not find it wonderful. She said, "Our village is bigger. The houses are bigger and there are more streets and we have more gardens. And we have ruins."

"There are ruins in our village too!"

I took her to the tower to see for herself.

She didn't wonder at it. She said, "We have more and better ruins. Marble pillars as white as milk and veined with a strange color, like smoke. And if you dig in the sand you'll find tiled floors and pictures, as if the inside of the earth were built and paved and decorated with pictures."

"How's that?"

"Once a young man from our town dug and found a colored drawing of a swan, made of small stones stuck together. After that he said to the young men, 'Dig more,' and they found pavings with pictures of pelicans and ducks and flowers and tree leaves, in colors. One of the old men of the town said that these are ruins from the time of Byzantium and maybe before, and no one knew the meaning of 'the time of Byzantium.' The old man told them that there must be important finds among them, and if the Jews knew about them they would take the village. So no one saw anything and no one knew—they kept it quiet."

"In our village too, there's a good swimmer who said he dove into the sea and found a big ship, not one of the new ships that broke on the coast but an old ship, with strange colored things in it. He didn't tell anyone but my brother and my brother told me, and I haven't told anyone but you. Maybe that's the reason they didn't come to our village."

"By God we didn't tell anyone and we didn't inform them, but they came into the town and occupied it."

She looked as if she was about to cry. I said, "When you return safely I'll come and visit you there." Then I amended, "If Yahya allows me to."

"Who is Yahya?"

I smiled. "The groom, from Ain Ghazal. His father and uncles came and asked for me four months ago, and they recited the Fatiha with my father."

"When is the wedding?"

"My father said, 'Let her reach fourteen before we write the contract.' Yahya is studying in Egypt, in Cairo, have you heard of Cairo?"

I said it proudly, emphasizing the word "Cairo" by repeating it and pronouncing it on a higher tone that the rest of the words, anticipating that my friend would be impressed.

She didn't look impressed. She said, "I won't get married until after we go back home. How could the proposal happen . . . and where would we receive all the important family members, when we are like this, without a home?"

The proverb of my mother's was right: February is fickle and stubborn, it huffs and puffs and has the smell of summer.

And what a summer!

4

How?

MY FATHER, LIKE THE REST of the men of the village, listened to the radio in the madafa. I never saw this apparatus as I was not allowed into the madafa except as a little girl, and the radio had not yet arrived then. But I would hear my father saying to my mother, "I heard such-and-such on the Jerusalem broadcast, Cairo radio announced such-and-such." Or he would comment on what my brothers told him, saying, "It's strange that they didn't announce that on the radio."

On their next visit after the episode of the slap, at my father's request, my brothers brought with them two big cardboard boxes. He opened the first and took out a large wooden apparatus and placed it in the front part of the house, near the entrance. Then he opened the second and took out a black box, which he said was the battery; the radio doesn't work without it. He connected it to the apparatus and then turned a button on it and a sound came out of it. He sighed in satisfaction and said, "Now I can listen to the news every morning in peace."

The apparatus seemed exciting because of its large size and because of the noises that emerged from it: a strange crackling and then the clear voice of someone speaking, as if he were with us in the house. At first my mother was confused, and then she adjusted her scarf on her head, as if it were likely that the voice of the strange man which had suddenly entered the house meant that he was present in it, and could see her. After that came a woman's voice, singing. My father cut her off with a movement of his fingers, turning a button on the apparatus, and she was followed by another man, speaking.

I said to my father, "Can we hear songs on the radio?"

"Yes, but we didn't buy it to listen to songs, we bought it to know what's happening in the country!"

It didn't occur to me for a moment that what my father said was a choice of what he would hear. I didn't connect it with his will or preference but rather with the function of the apparatus. Songs, like dabka circles and the call and response of ataba and ooof songs, were for weddings and special occasions; the radio was like the madafa in those days, reserved for learning of events and news as they happened. With the large wooden apparatus and the men's voices (it was not a single voice that was emitted from it, but multiple voices that could be distinguished easily), new expressions entered the house. Some were clear and familiar: the Arab kings and presidents, the Zionist gangs, Jaffa/Tel Aviv; some were obscure, as when the speaker referred to the Supreme Arab Authority or the Liberation Army or said "Hagana" or "Irgun," expressions which would require an explanation from my father. My mother and I would attend to his words, and then when the explanation went on my mother would get up and turn to her work, since she was not following the thread or had become lost in the details, or because she was bored by the talk. New names were to enter the house which would be repeated afterward by the townspeople, who fastened on some and feared them or who were anxious about others, but who in either case were preoccupied by what these names said and did. It was certain that there was a relationship between them and what was happening to us, even though it was obscure for me at the time.

The big wooden apparatus occupied a prominent position in the house, attracting the attention of visitors. The voices that emanated from it as long as my father was in the house were just as prominent, but my mother didn't pay much attention to them. Perhaps those voices weighed on her, with their words that she always said she didn't understand. Did she really not understand them, or was she averting additional fears that she had no power to bear? She would sit with her sister, exchanging complaints and cares. She would say to my aunt, "I said to him, 'Why should the boys stay in Haifa?' He disapproved and said, 'Do you want them to sit at home with you?' I said, 'They can work the land, or supervise the fishing boats, we have not one but five boats, they can keep track of them with the captains of the boats.' He scolded me, 'Did I send them to school to till the earth or sell fish?' And what's wrong with tilling the earth? What's wrong with selling fish?" My aunt would soothe her, and the soothing would give her an opening to set out her own complaints: "Thank God for Abu Sadiq, God protect him and bless him, he fills up the house for us. Abu Amin is like a bird, you don't know when he'll alight and when he'll up and fly away. In '36 we said it's a revolt and it has its demands, and we're afraid of the English. But afterward? He said jihad, is it endless jihad? By God I'm tired, Zeinab, Sister, I'm tired. A day at home and a thousand away. And he says that Amin has to study. Does he have to study at the ends of the earth, and the little boy and I have to stay alone? He's a strange one, Abu Amin! The village is here, our Lord is kind and blesses us, why should he drag himself all over the place?" They exchange roles, Zeinab complains and Halima calms her, then Halima complains and leaves it to her sister to provide relief. The talk continues: "Zeinab, Sister . . . , Halima, Sister. . . ."

Did my mother and my aunt ever imagine, as they spent their evenings together every day, that what had happened to the people of Qisarya could happen to them? Judging by myself and by what they said every day, I think that Qisarya probably seemed far away, another town that we had never seen where a disaster had befallen the inhabitants, so we had to sympathize with them and help them. The reality was that the distance between us and that other town was no more than half the distance between us and Haifa. Twelve kilometers, ten minutes by car. The men and maybe some of the women must have been aware of this fact. I can't remember, for example, when I learned that the men were organizing themselves to confront the danger, or that they were buying weapons or that they had formed a committee to organize guards for the village. But I remember that we girls began to watch the men as they were training with target practice on the roofs. They would put an orange on a box or a pile and aim at it. I heard my father say something, I don't know in what context or why, I don't remember. He said, "Weapons come to them from everywhere, and we go barefoot to get rifles, sometimes from Sidon and sometimes from Damascus and sometimes from al-Mansura. Old rifles, rifles that don't even work unless luck is with us!"

But 'fickle February,' for all it brought with it, was gentle and kind compared to the months that followed. When the almond trees flowered the whole village knew that war was breaking out here and there, and that weapons were now as needed as a drink of water, necessary to stay alive. Talk about buying arms had begun to be common even among the women of the village. The names of Zionist gangs and their leaders, names that were strange and hard to pronounce, started to circulate among them: they knew who Hagana was, and Stern, and Etzel, and Ben-Gurion. Then the news about Muhammad al-Huneiti, commander of the Haifa militia, reached the town: he and his companions had fallen into an ambush as they were returning from Lebanon with two truckloads of weapons, and two weeks later Haifa fell. None of us, girls or boys, noticed that the almonds had turned green on the trees.

It was at night when we heard a knock on the door. My mother sprang up in alarm, for who would come at such a late hour except to deliver bad news? She rushed to the door and I followed her, and there were my two brothers, covered in dust, their hair matted. They had come from Haifa on foot, through the woods and by winding mountain paths. My father did not say, "Let's be off to the madafa to give the men the news of Haifa." The news had reached them two days before, two days in which the house had nearly caught fire from the burning feelings of everyone in it. My mother ceaselessly lamented her boys, who had not appeared since the fall of the city, saying that her heart told her that she would not see them again. Her fears would spread to me and I would leave my own fears aside and chide her, repeating to her that it was a bad omen and she was tempting providence; but unlike the previous time she did not listen to my words and was incapable of making any agreements with the Lord of the universe who ordered all things. She continued to weep, in anticipation. My father seemed like a minefield, with one mine after another exploding in my mother's face or in mine, because scheduling the guard shifts and the training for the young men who had not yet received it was not enough of an outlet for his anxiety over the fate of his boys and the fate of the country.

How had Haifa fallen? The question would be repeated over the length and breadth of the country. Had the British handed it over to the Jews? How? What had happened to the garrison? What had happened to bring the people out to the port collectively, to leave the city? Now I can't pluck apart the threads to know what I heard from my father or from my brothers after their return, or what came to me from the talk the girls had heard from their fathers and shared among themselves, or what my uncle told me later in Sidon, or what I gathered in later years of my life. But I know that the fall of the district capital was like a bolt of lightning in the village, a bolt that strikes the earth and the sky and causes a convulsion that encompasses everyone, as if they are waiting to see if the sky would fall on the earth and cleave it in two, or if the disaster would pass and the universe would remain as it was.

Haifa fell, and two weeks later Abd al-Qadir al-Husayni was martyred. The whole village, not just the madafa, seemed to be a house open for mourning. It was an extended mourning, as Abd al-Qadir's funeral—which I would not imagine or see in pictures until years later—would be held in Jerusalem after the mourners had heard the details of the massacre at Deir Yassin. Qastal fell and Abd al-Qadir was martyred defending it, and at dawn of the following day the attackers moved on neighboring Deir Yasin and slaughtered any of the residents they could. Three days later Safad fell, and after three more days, Jaffa. And three days after the fall of Jaffa, Acre fell. What happened in Safad? Its residents were twice our number and the people in our village said that it was inaccessible, located on four hills, and that the people were resolute—what happened that Safad fell in one night? Why did the garrison withdraw from it? And the Jordanian task force and the Syrian detachment, why did they withdraw? Where did the Liberation Army go? What dislodged the people from their houses? And could Acre possibly fall? How could Acre fall when it was Acre? These were not my questions, because I was only a girl of thirteen hearing what was repeated in a village that seemed like a time bomb, where the people were aware of the ticking that brought them closer to the explosion. But would it explode among us or among them? The young men were sure that it would explode among them. They said, "We have prepared ourselves and the rest is up to God." They said that the Arab armies would enter the battle, that the Arabs would not let Palestine be lost. My father repeated what they said although he seemed less impulsive, or more precisely he seemed both impulsive and restrained by apprehensions which appeared only in his explosions. Since my brothers' arrival from Haifa my father had included them in the guard duty shifts. Neither of them was trained in carrying arms; they trained for three days and then took shifts like the rest of the young men, one of them stationed at the school behind the railway east of the village, and the other toward the jail on the south side near the beach.

It's hard for me now to convey the feelings of the townspeople, perhaps because then I was living in a state that my years did not permit me to comprehend. Perhaps I wondered like everyone else, when would our turn come? Perhaps like them I was clutching at straws, like the young men repeating that Ain Ghazal and Ijzim and Jabaa that were smaller than Safad and Jaffa and Acre, and that were guarded only by their inhabitants, had endured and turned away aggression time after time, and that like them we would turn away any attempt to capture our village. Will we be able to? I cut off the question and go to the sea. I crouch on the beach, watching the scene with my eyes.

The rocky islands were firmly anchored in place, and I was accustomed to the clamor of the waves and the movement of the sea foam and the spray. The sky would be clouds upon clouds, piled like thick blankets of dark blue or grays slipping into black, lightened suddenly by a spot of silver. The sea beneath would resemble the sky, divided between a deep, blackish blue and clearings of white. The waves would rise to the sky as if they were calling to it, speaking to it, or protesting that they were there; they would scud before it in a broad blessing of pure silver, dissolving gradually and mixing with a light gray blue that caressed the shore.

Or the sun would be setting, hanging in the rounded shape of an orange, as if when it descended a little it would not set in the west but rather would settle full and safe on one of the islands. The sky behind it had a strange color, descending gradually, easily, from a clear red to dark orange to an ambiguous color, neither brown nor the color of lead, which stealthily met the sea behind the islands. It left it for the sun to color the water in front of it, making it whatever color it pleased, making it a wondrous mirror, pink here and silver there, and making lines and clear spaces of leaden gray, the water rolling peacefully between the one and the other.

I did not think about what had been. I did not think about what was to come. Even the son of Ain Ghazal seemed far away, farther than the disc of the sun that was suspended before me.

5

My Uncle and My Father

MY UNCLE ANNOUNCED THAT HE was leaving. The house blazed.

They were close, more devoted than was usual even in a village where brothers were close to each other, close in where they lived and worked and in how they managed their lives. When they married they contracted for their brides on the same day and held the wedding on the same night, my father taking Zeinab and my uncle, two years younger, taking her sister Halima. My mother would say, "They're like two peas in a pod." Neither would do anything unless the other did it too. Even when they joined the rebels in 1936 they came and went together, and patrolled the village together. The day the British searched the house looking for weapons, and poured the oil in the gas and the gas on the olives and the flour and the lentils, they were looking for both of them. They asked for them by name and said they had information that they were hiding weapons. They had hidden the arms in the boat and the boat had been put to sea. My mother laughs, though it was not funny then, when the British soldiers invaded the house looking for the arms, and everyone knew the consequences: the price of a single rifle was a death sentence. My God! But she recalls the event and laughs, "We had hidden the rifles in the boat and the boat was put to sea." Then she sighs, "After that God guided your father and he looked after the farming and stayed in town. But your uncle was one day in town and ten days traveling, a day in Haifa and a day in

Sidon and a day in Beirut. Poor Halima, he had no useful work, not even a whiff."

Did I love my uncle because he spoiled me? He would announce that I was dearer to his heart than the four boys, his two and his brother's two. He would repeat, "Our Lord has been gracious to us and given us this girl, praise to the one who fashioned her." He insisted that I go to school, and he surprised my father by wanting me to go to the teacher's college in Jerusalem after I completed the sixth grade, the last one in the town school. At the time there was a quarrel between him and my father, but the earthquake was deferred; it did not occur until that night when my uncle announced that he was leaving.

"Shame on you, you're leaving when the village is threatened and the young men are guarding it and preparing their weapons."

"It's no use!"

"If I didn't know you as I know myself, I would say that you've given in to fear, like a woman."

My uncle exploded. His voice seemed loud, but as he continued speaking it rose more and more until it reached the houses of the village and the beach beyond, and perhaps even the islands and the sea behind them.

"Haifa fell in two days, it went in *two days*, Abu Sadiq! I was there, and you know it. The city was besieged from all four sides, surrounded by ten settlements. And inside the city they lived on the mountain and we were on the plain, they had cannons and we had to be magicians to obtain weapons. Two hundred fifty rifles arrived from Syria and Rashid al-Hajj Ibrahim only got eighty-nine, because the rest were old and useless. He refused to accept them. And despite that we did all that we could, all that we could—for five months. Attack and retreat, bravery, martyrdom. And Haifa fell in two days! The villages are as scattered as beads from a rosary. Surur Burhum said to al-Hunayti that we would spend the night in Acre and make the road to Haifa safe for the weapons so as not to fall into an ambush. Al-Hunayti wanted to arrive quickly and talked on the telephone, and said, 'We're coming with the weapons.'"

My uncle shouted, "Does anyone in his right mind say on the telephone, 'We're coming with the weapons'? My God! They died and the weapons were lost. No arms and no leaders. Hajj Amin says 'right' and the National Committee says 'left.' Seven hundred soldiers from the Jordanian army were near the city observing events and could not intervene. Do you expect them to intervene when their commander is British? The whole thing is as clear as day. They have weapons and the British are with them and they are trained and they have cohesive leadership, and we. . . ."

"We have God with us because we are in the right."

"We are in the right, yes. We have God with us, I doubt it."

My father's voice rose: "I take refuge with God Almighty from all mighty sins! Blasphemy, on top of everything else!"

"Haifa fell in two days!"

"I know that it fell in two days, but the guerrilla fighters are still resisting on the plains and in the mountains, from Galilee to Gaza, and not a day passes when they don't score victories. The Arab armies will get involved, they will definitely get involved."

"Brother, you can judge a book by its cover. They will not come in, and if they did they would be defeated."

"And the solution is for us to flee?"

"The solution is for us to get ready, a year, or two, or three, even if it takes ten years. Use your brain, Abu Sadiq. They'll enter the village and destroy it and kill the inhabitants and take it over. The solution is to save lives and see what we can do after that."

My father struck one hand with the other in despair. His face was flushed, with a blue tone hidden under the red. My aunt was crying. My mother got up to look for incense, since she was certain that someone had struck them with the evil eye. She was the only one talking, talking in an audible voice as she came and went looking here and there. We didn't know if she was talking to us or to herself, and then she suddenly shouted, "Where has the incense gone?"

That was when the second match fell on the fire: "I'm going to take Zeinab and Halima and Ruqayya and Ezz."

"Are you crazy?!"

"Perfectly sane, Abu Sadiq. I'm taking the dependents."

"You're not taking anyone!"

"The battle is lost, so why should we risk death for them? I'll take them to Sidon and leave them safe with my friends and come back."

"Shame on you, brother! You're saying surrender before the young men do? By God it's shameful!"

"They took over Haifa in two days. Our village will fall in one night."

"Haifa is half Jews, they were barricaded on Carmel, they were on the mountain and we were on the plain. Our situation is different. The young men will protect the town proper and guards are stationed to the north, the south, and the east. And the mountain villages are Arab and not Jewish. The people of Ain Ghazal and Jabaa and Ijzim repelled the attack and we aren't less than they were. Besides, we're not alone; all the surrounding villages are ready to help save us."

My uncle slapped his cheeks in grief. He slapped his cheeks like a woman. The sobbing of my mother and aunt got louder. My father shouted, giving up, "God help you. You go, with your wife and son. But as for my family, I am free."

"Have we become two families, Abu Sadiq?"

"Yes, we have become two families!"

My uncle sprang up, and said to my aunt, "Get up, Halima. We're leaving tomorrow morning."

My aunt got up and my mother followed her. They were both weeping. Ezz and I followed in their wake, not knowing what to do in this situation that was unlike anything that had happened to us as long as we could remember. My mother could not imagine her little sister moving to live in Sidon, farther than Haifa or Acre or maybe even Jerusalem. And my aunt was terrified of leaving her sister, who had been with her every day of her life. They kept crying until my uncle came into the room and scolded them. Then he addressed Halima and told her that she and Ezz might stay in Sidon for several months, and she should take that into account. The sisters' sobbing grew louder. He said, "I only need one change. I'll come back in two days. Come on, you two, get going, enough women's dawdling!"

On the morning of the following day we bade them farewell on the beach. My father did not go to say goodbye to them. He stayed angry with his brother, and all through the following days he kept repeating, bitterly, "You've left my back exposed, God forgive you."

The family crisis did not end. My uncle appeared four days later, alone, coming from the sea. He said that he had come to take the women and children. My father refused, threatening my uncle with a weapon. My uncle left in the boat he had brought from Sidon, taking the townspeople who wanted to leave, women and children and a few men. I was a witness to the event, both halves of it, but my uncle would tell me the story later as if I had not witnessed it. He would tell it with all the details, calmly sometimes and at other times in agitation; and two days before his death he called me and told it to me again in detail, as if he had not told it to me before, dozens of times.

6

Saturday, May 15th

FRIDAYS ARE ALL ALIKE IN being different from the rest of the
week. We heat the water three times, for my father bathes
first and then my brothers. They put on their long garments
and go to the mosque for prayer. When they return my
mother will have finished preparing a midday dinner different from the usual midday meal, "Because it's Friday,"
and because the boys, "Poor dears are far from home in
Haifa, they're bachelors who don't eat enough to nourish
them all week." Even after Haifa fell and Sadiq and Hasan
returned to live with us, my mother continued with what she
was used to. Friday she would cook and huff and puff and
pick up and put down and "Ruqayya, give me this and do
that," "Peel these garlic cloves for me," "Chop these onions
for me," "Take this plate to the wife of my uncle Abu Jamil,
she likes rice pudding," "Take this dish to this neighbor, for
the Prophet said we should care even for distant neighbors."
I get fed up. I say that Friday is my holiday and I work more
on it than I do on school days. When I finished sixth grade
and could no longer use that excuse I would hide. I would
go to the sea. I thought, "She won't see me in front of her so
she'll manage."

It was Friday. It was different from the rest of the days
of the week and from other, similar Fridays. My father did
not bathe. He left the house early. Sadiq and Hasan were
sleeping; when they woke up they did not bathe but rather

asked about my father and left the house in a hurry. None of them returned at mealtime; the food stayed as it was, we did not dish it out or eat. In the village there was a strange silence that made the call to prayer seem nearer and clearer, when it rose at the time for prayer. It was interrupted only by the whispering of the sea, the neighing of a horse or the bleating of a lamb.

In the evening the news was confirmed. It was no longer a matter of apprehensions or expectations but a written statement signed by the leaders of the Jews and announced by Ben-Gurion at exactly four o'clock in the afternoon, amid a gathering in Tel Aviv that was recorded by photographers and broadcast by Hagana Radio and greeted by the settlers with dancing in the street. It was said that the statement would be in force beginning with the first minute after midnight, when the British Mandate ended and they would take its place in governing Palestine. The country would become a state for the Jews and its name would become Israel.

All I remember from that evening is the silence.

But at noon the next day we heard gunshots and uproar, voices cutting across each other. Wisal and I ran to hear the news. All the people of the town were telling each other what the radio had broadcast, repeating the broadcast as if every one of them, young or old, had turned into a moving radio, connected by a wire to the radio playing in the headman's house, and to the ears of the men gathered around it. Everyone was saying it, everyone was repeating it and adding to it. Even the young men in the guard posts suddenly appeared to hear the details. As for the ones who shot off their rifles in the air, they had been forced to stop after the older men reprimanded them for wasting ammunition; they were still standing there, not knowing what to do with themselves. I saw one of them running in a back street, then he jumped and yelled at the top of his voice "Wiiiiii," spinning around like a crazy man. Another was turning somersaults in the air, his head down and his feet up, and a second later he would be standing on his feet again like the rest of God's creatures.

We returned to the house. Our mothers already knew about it. We repeated to them some of what we had heard: "At dawn today the Arab armies entered Palestine. Egypt crossed at Rafah and al-Awja. Syria came in from south of Lake Tiberias, the Sea of Galilee. The Lebanese were at Ras al-Naqura. The army of Jordan crossed over the Sheikh Hussein Bridge and the Damia Bridge. The Iraqi army had arrived at the Majami Bridge, and. . . ."

Wisal cut me off: "And the Egyptian planes shelled Tel Aviv. Twice."

My mother suddenly shouted, "God protect them. God give them victory. God keep them from harm. God bless them and their families, God raise their banner in victory and bring them back safe and sound."

Then she looked at Wisal's mother, who was crying, "Pray with me, you are a good woman and are raising orphans, and your prayers will be answered."

It looked as if the sudden, intense prayer was going to interrupt the news that we wanted to broadcast in its entirety. I cut in: "Listen to all the news first and pray later!"

Wisal laughed, and said, "The Syrian forces are shelling Samakh and two settlements nearby, one of them a big settlement."

Her mother asked, "Where is this Samakh? And Majami Bridge and the other bridges you mentioned?"

Wisal said that she didn't know, and I said I would ask my brothers. Wisal went back to finishing the newscast: "The Iraqi forces entered the Rutenberg power station and occupied it, and took prisoner forty Jews who were working on the project."

My mother asked, "You mean, when they first entered they went right to the power station? By God, good for them! How could they, didn't the Jews land a blow as they were getting near the station?"

"The station is on the other side of the border. In Jordan. The Iraqi forces occupied the station and then they crossed the border."

"In Jordan?" She didn't believe it. She said that we had misunderstood, because if the station was in Jordan the Jordanian army would have closed it and done what was necessary before entering the war. "It doesn't stand to reason that they would leave the enemy behind them and move forward. I'll check with Abu Sadiq and figure out what happened from him."

Suddenly she said, "Turn on the radio, Ruqayya."

Wisal's mother added, her face still flushed from crying, "Maybe there will be news of Qisarya."

I turned on the radio, and we stood listening to what the announcer said. Moments passed. I signaled to Wisal and we left the house, running. I don't remember whom we met or who said what or when we came home or when we were able to sit with Sadiq and Hasan so they could explain the details we had not understood. But I remember the lanes of the village, that they were noisy. I remember bits and fragments of what people said, people who it seemed had suddenly become generals planning the movements of the forces. One said, "The Egyptians will advance on the coast road and enter Tel Aviv." Another thought it was likely that they would head for Hebron and from there to Jerusalem to lay siege to it from the south, while the Jordanian forces would besiege it from the east and the Syrians or the Iraqis from the north. They would catch them in a pincer movement. A third said, "I don't have confidence in King Abdallah, they say he has reached an agreement with the Jews, and even if he didn't . . . how can we rest easy with the army when its leader is an Englishman? God protect us." A fourth asserted that the Syrian forces would head for Haifa and liberate it. A fifth squatted on the ground, grasped a stick from a tree, and drew a map of Palestine on the sand, going on to explain his conception of the movement of the armies: "They'll cut them off here, separating the south of Palestine from the north." He moved the stick again, cutting the map lengthwise and saying, "And from here they will isolate the Zionist gangs in the west from the ones in the east." His companion took the stick and drew a larger map in the sand, designating the cities and towns and movement of the forces. The names multiplied and the directions and movements and who would do what all mixed together. I whispered in Wisal's ear, "I don't know the map of Palestine except for the location of Haifa and Jaffa and Gaza and Jerusalem." I did not tell her that I suddenly regretted my lack of interest in studying geography, which had seemed boring and meaningless to me.

That night I waited up for my father's return. He came in and I made supper for him. I asked him about Samakh as he was eating. He said, "It's in the Jordan Valley, south of Lake Tiberias. It's a few kilometers south of the Syrian border, but because of the train station there Samakh has become the border crossing between the two countries. The traveler stops and they stamp his papers, and customs agents inspect his things."

He finished his supper and said, "A cup of tea, God bless you, Ruqayya."

It was not his custom to drink tea at that late hour. I fixed the tea for him and took it to him. He said, "God bless your hands. Sit down, Ruqayya, sit down."

He took off his head cloth and headband and put them aside. He took off his sandals and sat cross-legged. He moved a little to support his back against the wall. I was glancing at him furtively as he sipped the tea. His mood was different from that of the young men whom I had seen in the afternoon. I recall how he sat, the features of his face, and I ask myself, was he happy? Was he sad, or perturbed and waiting?

How did he move from talking about Samakh to talking about the Haifa–Daraa and the Daraa–Damascus lines, and how did it bring him to talk about his father's hajj journey on the same line, the Hijazi railway line? I was listening to him, fascinated by what he said. Fascinated by that rare moment when we sat together, something that had never happened before and that would not be given to me again. He was speaking only to me. Everyone was asleep except for us two, and he was confiding in me as if he weren't my father, who ordered and forbade and to whom my brothers and I didn't dare lift up our eyes, for fear of meeting his eyes. We would stand like soldiers at attention in his presence, not moving or making a sound. But here I was sitting near him, not glancing at him furtively but looking at him directly, noticing, as he spoke, that his face was handsome, sweet, and good, and that his eyes were an ambiguous color between green and blue, more blue than green, and that in his very black hair there were three white strands.

My father spoke to me, saying, "When we would go to Damascus, your uncle and I, we would take the train from the Haifa East station and arrive in Samakh in a little over two hours. There would be many tourists in the train with us; they would get off at Samakh because they wanted to see the lake where our Lord Jesus walked on the water. There was a walkway connecting the station to the lake, so they would take it to ride in little boats on the lake and look at the city of Tiberias, and then they would take the train back to Haifa. As for us, we would continue on to Damascus.

"At the end of the First World War fierce battles took place between the Turks and the English. Some of them took place in the station buildings, when the fighting was house to house. Samakh is important because it's the key to the road from Tiberias to Damascus. At the time of the revolt in '36, '37, and '38, your uncle Abu Amin and I would go to Samakh a lot, but we would avoid riding the train because the English had created a team of Jewish wardens to guard the railway from the rebels, a team the English trained along with the Hagana. They would inspect the trains and bridges and surrounding areas for fear of rebel strikes. There were a lot of colonies in the area.

"The Hijaz line connected Haifa to Daraa and Daraa to Damascus and Amman, arriving in Medina The Blessed in Arabia. People called it the Hamidiyeh Railway because Sultan Abd al-Hamid was the one who was enthusiastic about the project and ordered it started, and he was the first who contributed to creating it. In the Hijaz they called it 'the sultan's donkey.'"

I laughed, and repeated after him, "The sultan's donkey!" He laughed, and continued, "The line was created from the contributions of the Muslims, Arabs, and Turks and Iranians and Indians, and it was considered an inalienable Islamic trust. The intention was for it to extend from Medina to Mecca and from there to Yemen. When the Turks left and the English came, the project stopped. The existing railroad in Palestine came under the control of the English occupying power, and they named it 'Palestine Railways.' It ended in Samakh, and after that the line was under the control of the French occupying power in Syria. The train stopped at al-Himma, and when it arrived in Daraa the line branched into a railway for trains headed to Damascus and a railway headed for Amman.

"Two years before the beginning of the First World War your grandfather traveled to the hajj pilgrimage by train. My mother bade him farewell at the door of the house, and my uncles, God have mercy on them all, accompanied him to Haifa. Your uncle Abu Amin was four, and he clung to my father and started to cry. My uncles took pity on him and decided to take him with them. I looked up at them. I didn't cry, I didn't say a thing, I just looked up. They said, 'Come with us, boy.'

"We took a horse-drawn carriage to Haifa. We bade my father farewell at the Haifa East station, the station for the Hijaz line. I began to look everywhere, dazzled by what I

45

saw—the station building, the gate, the monument that was higher than anything I had ever seen before, the train. It was colored; I remember that one of the cars in it was painted green . . . and another part was painted red, and even its black was shiny as if it were a color too. And whenever the train whistle sounded I started as if I were frightened, and then I would find myself laughing. I laughed aloud.

"My father bought us lukoum before he boarded the train. When he boarded I saw him through the window and we began to wave at him with our hands. Then the train started to move and I was moving my eyes between my father's face behind the glass and the wheels that were turning slowly, then faster. That day was the most joyful day of my life. It's etched into my memory in its smallest detail, even the pliable feel of the lukoum between my fingers and the taste of the almonds and the powdered sugar in my mouth, I remember it. On the way back your uncle slept, he was deeply asleep, sitting next to two of my uncles in the back seat of the carriage, but my uncle who was driving the carriage let me sit next to him in the front, so I saw the whole horse and I could almost touch his tail, if I leaned forward a little. But my uncle had his arm around my waist so I wouldn't be hurt by any sudden movement of the carriage or the horse. It was the end of autumn; the sky was a little cloudy, maybe it had rained during the previous days. The trees were dense and colorful, green and red and brown, and the earth was also colored, red sometimes and sometimes black, and sometimes the color of coffee before it's roasted. The hills extended on our left, cloudy and milky, in waves as if they weren't hills. The clouds above them were amazing, at times looking like white lambs with thick wool and at times like a sea of shells. I even liked the sting of the cold that day. I was sitting next to my uncle, turning my eyes from the sky to the earth, from the horse to the hills, from the tree that we were passing to the tree we were approaching. The road seemed calm like a dream, disrupted only by the neighing of the horse or the sound of his hooves on the road."

He suddenly stopped. He said, "Good night, Ruqayya. Tomorrow is another day."

It seems I didn't sleep long as I awoke before my mother and found my father sitting next to the radio. I said good morning. He looked up at me and said, "Your uncle is an ass, Ruqayya!" The expression surprised me, threw me into confusion even. I didn't understand until two or three days later, when it seemed clear that there was good news from the battles raging in many places. I took my father's words as a comment on my uncle's decision to leave, which now seemed uncalled for. The Syrians had taken possession of Samakh and the Jews had pulled out after suffering heavy losses. The two neighboring colonies had fallen. It was said that the Egyptian army was moving toward Tel Aviv, and that the Iraqi forces were launching fierce attacks on a large colony named Gesher, with armored cars and airplanes. The Atarot colony on the Jerusalem–Ramallah road fell, and the guerrilla fighters succeeded in turning back the attempted invasion of the old city of Jerusalem.

On the night of Wednesday to Thursday I dreamed that I was visiting Medina The Blessed. When I told the dream to my mother, as she was absorbed in her usual Thursday bread baking, her face lit up and she assured me that it was a vision and not a dream. "The bastards will be defeated and the whole country will become like blessed Medina!"

7

When They Occupied the Village

I DIDN'T HEAR THE NOISES; I was sleeping. When my mother woke me up, I heard them and asked her about them. She said, "Wake up Wisal and Abed. Put out fodder for the livestock that will last two or three weeks, and a lot of water. Scatter seed for the chickens, a lot. And the horse, don't forget the horse. Lift the oil cans off the ground so the moisture doesn't get to them, and put a cushion between the wall and each can. Dress in three layers, and Wisal also, and the boy." I asked, "Where are my father and brothers?" She did not answer the question. She was absorbed in gathering things in a hurry. Wisal's mother was doing the same. Then we found ourselves standing in front of the house, and I asked again. She said that they were on guard duty and would catch up with us when things became clear. I asked her what she meant by "when things became clear," but she didn't answer. It was strange—my mother who wailed in anxiety over her boys in Haifa seemed like another woman, giving orders, managing the affairs of her small flock with resolution and speed, even though I didn't understand the logic of this management. She gave me a four-liter measure of white cheese to carry and took a can of oil, and Wisal's mother took a can of olives. I did not understand, so I asked, "All this cheese and all this oil and olives, what will we do with them?" She did not answer.

We left the house. My mother closed the gate and locked it with the large key. It was strange for me, as I had never seen the door of our house locked ever, nor had I seen the key; it was of iron, large, and my mother turned it in the lock seven times. She put it in her bosom. Suddenly my mother noticed that I was carrying the little goat kid whose mother had died, and she asked, "Why are you carrying that goat?" I said, "I'll take her with me." She did not comment. She announced, "We'll go to the house of my uncle, Abu Jamil." We walked toward his house, my mother and Wisal's ahead of us, each carrying a can in one hand and a bundle in the other, with me, Wisal, and Abed behind them. Wisal was holding her brother's hand in one of hers and in the other carried a square iron box with the papers they had brought with them from Qisarya; I was carrying the goat in one hand and the cheese container in the other. We arrived at Abu Jamil's house. The sound of explosions and the rattle of bullets came to us from the east in the direction of the school, from the direction of the tower in the north, and from the direction of the jail in the south. Umm Jamil insisted that we eat breakfast; she repeated that it would be a long day and that we didn't know what would happen. She gave each of us a flat round loaf and said "Eat!" None of us said that we weren't hungry or that it was the middle of the night and not time for breakfast or lunch; rather we ate, complying with her order, which was firm and decisive. The shelling increased. Abu Jamil said that it was coming from the west. "It seems that they are striking from the sea also." He made his ablutions and began to pray. We heard the cocks crowing, then the dawn chirping of the birds; then we heard footsteps and three armed men burst into the house and drove us to the headman's house. They were threatening us with their rifle butts and firing over our heads. On the way we saw the blind Hasan Abd al-Al and his wife Azza al-Hajj al-Hindi lying near their house surrounded by a pool of blood, then we saw the body of another person I didn't know. Abed began to cry aloud. I let go of the goat and picked him up; he wrapped his legs around my waist and put his arms around my neck. I couldn't see his face to know if he was still crying. The goat kept walking behind me.

They drove us to the beach and divided us into two groups, the men on one side and the women and children and some old men on the other. It was the first time I saw female soldiers: women wearing a military uniform and bearing arms. They spoke to us in Arabic and began to search us, one after the other, taking any money or jewelry they found on us and putting it in a helmet. Every time the helmet was filled they emptied it onto a large blanket stretched out on the sand. The woman soldier didn't notice the goat but she noticed the rings in my ears as she was searching me. She yanked them out, and blood flowed from my ears. I wiped them with the edge of my dress. The soldier moved on to search my mother and Wisal and Abed and his mother. They took the cans of oil and olives and the half measure of cheese. My mother was stripped of her ring and her earrings and the chain she wore around her neck. We were standing close together. I looked at my mother's face and saw her lips moving slightly, continuously, and I didn't know if she was mumbling prayers or repeating verses from the Quran or trembling. I whispered in Wisal's ear, "Was this the way they took over your town?" She said, "No, they didn't stand us by the sea. They took us out of our houses to the bus, but they took the women's jewelry and any money they found on them."

I was standing at the edge of the group nearest the men. My eyes couldn't stop looking, hoping for the sight of my father or either of my brothers. I did not see them; I surmised that they had taken off for the mountains or had disappeared into one of the caves. I saw the "burlap bag": a man standing next to the Jewish soldiers with his head covered by a burlap bag that had two holes in it so he could see. The officer was examining a paper in his hand and would call the men's names, and the man would answer or not. If he didn't answer the "burlap bag" would step forward and point him out;

sometimes he would point without any call. No sooner did the "burlap bag" point to someone than they brought him out. They would take a group of men, five or six or seven, and disappear. Were they taking them to the prison in Zikhron Yaakov? We heard the rattle of bullets fired—was the guard resisting? I took Wisal's hand and she looked at me, as if asking why I was squeezing her hand; she did not ask. The goat came close to me and began touching my feet, but I did not pick her up. Abed said he was thirsty, and his mother told him to put up with it. I said to the soldier, "The boy's thirsty," and she answered me with a foul word, pushing my shoulder with the butt of her rifle. The weather was hot and the sun burning, and I wondered why my mother had asked me to put on three dresses, and why I obeyed her. I was dripping with sweat; I wanted to ask her, but I did not. The soldiers shouted loudly, "Yalla, let's go!"

The procession of women began to move. They led us toward the cemetery. On the way I saw three corpses and then two more, none of which I recognized.

As they were leading us toward the cemetery I noticed that the village had a strange odor, mixed with the scent of the white lilies that grew on the islands and along their beaches at that time of year. I couldn't distinguish the odor even though it remained in my nose after we left the village. Afterward it would sometimes appear suddenly, days or weeks later, without my knowing where it had come from or why the village had had that odor on that particular day.

At the cemetery two trucks were waiting. Threatening us with their weapons, they told us to get in. One of the soldiers took the goat from me as I was carrying it. We were several hundred women, children and old men, maybe five or six hundred. They crammed us into the trucks, and they began to move. Suddenly I shouted and pulled my mother's arm, pointing with my hand to a pile of corpses. She looked where I was pointing and shouted, "Jamil, my cousin Jamil!" But I pulled her arm again with my left hand and pointed with the right to where my father and brothers were: their corpses were next to Jamil's, piled one next to the other at a distance of a few meters from us. I was pointing and my mother was still keening in mourning for Jamil with his mother. The women were wailing and the children were crying, terrified of their mothers' weeping, while the old men stayed stiff as statues.

The trucks left us at al-Furaydis, at a distance of four kilometers from our village, where we were handed over to the headman, our number was written on the papers, and then we were distributed among the people's houses. I did not say to Wisal that we had become refugees like them. I didn't say anything during the entire time we stayed in al-Furaydis. My mother was sure that I had lost the power of speech. She kept saying, "Her father and her brothers will be worried sick when they find out that she has lost the ability to speak."

In al-Furaydis and on the road to the Triangle, and in Tulkarm and Hebron and on the road to Sidon, and during all the years she lived in Sidon, my mother would repeat ceaselessly, never tiring, that her boys had fled to Egypt and that Abu Sadiq had been arrested with the men of the town, that we didn't know if he had been released without knowing where we were or if he was still among the prisoners. One of the women whispered that Umm Sadiq had lost her mind. Another answered, "It's really strange, she's completely rational outside of the subject of her husband and her boys." The first replied, "By the Lord of the throne, I didn't believe my own eyes, I said that a mother's heart knows best and maybe we were mistaken. But one of the young men they took to dig the mass grave saw that Abu Sadiq and his boys were among the corpses they buried."

My mother would say, "Thank God that Sadiq and Hasan fled to Egypt. When things calm down they will come back safely." In Sidon a year after we left she implored my uncle to travel to Egypt to let them know that we were living in Sidon.

"Poor things, they must be heartsick with worry about us, and here we are, living safe and sound."

After we arrived in al-Furaydis some of the boys began to work in Zikhron Yaakov for a few piasters, bringing them back to their mothers at the end of the day so they could buy bread. Sometimes the Jewish boys from the settlement would harass them, beating them and taking the money, and they would come back without it the same way they left. They took other boys and some of the young men of al-Furaydis to our town to harvest the crops. A woman in al-Furaydis shouted, "Good God, we're hungry and the stalks on our land are two feet high!" She said to her sister, "Come with me," and she went to the town to harvest some of the wheat. In the evening her sister returned with her dress ripped and clear marks from blows on her face. She asked some of the young men of al-Furaydis to help her bring back her sister's body; she had been caught unawares by a military vehicle. She said, "They ran her over on purpose, and when I tried to get close to see what had happened to her the car came back toward me and I jumped away. The car ran over her a second time."

We stayed four weeks in al-Furaydis, hosted by the people of the town. They put down beds and divided their provisions, but it was meager; some of the old died. As for the nursing infants, they fell incomprehensibly—every day an infant would die, and sometimes two. We buried twenty-five children in al-Furaydis or maybe thirty, as well as the woman who was run over by the military car and the old people who died. Then the Red Cross took charge of us, and they took us east to a leveled wasteland in the Triangle area, where Jordanian officers took charge, counting us and signing for the delivery. Then they took us to Tulkarm in buses. They deposited us in a school near the Hijaz railway line. In Tulkarm we were shelled by Israeli planes, and the son and daughter of Yahya al-Ashmawi were martyred. Two weeks later other buses came and took us to Deir al-Maskubiya in Hebron.

Every Friday the people of Hebron would butcher lambs, grill them, and bring them to us with rice, bringing enough for everybody. Many children died, perhaps not so much from hunger as from cold, or perhaps because of their mothers' grief. Wisal and I went back to wearing our three dresses, one on top of the other. Wisal talked a lot and I would listen to what she said, but I did not talk. Now I don't know if I had lost the ability to speak or if I didn't want to talk. My mother says that from the time we left the town until we arrived in Sidon, I did not utter a single word. Abed stayed with me like my shadow, and he would not sleep anywhere but beside me. I would warm his hands and feet and keep patting his head until he slept. But I didn't sing to him the way I used to when we were back home, for I didn't have a voice.

In al-Maskubiya, news of the prisoners reached us. They announced over a loudspeaker that letters had arrived from the Red Cross. My mother stood waiting in the line; they did not call her name. The women and children dispersed after everyone had received the letter that had come for him. My mother spoke to the official, and he told her that he had passed out all the letters he had.

We spent six months in Hebron, and then the people of our town started to sort themselves out: there were some who wanted to join relatives they had in Tulkarm or Nablus or Jenin, and some who slipped back into Galilee, and some who went to Syria. My mother said we would go to Sidon, to my uncle. "How will you go to Sidon?" asked Wisal's mother. My mother brought out seven gold guineas and said she had succeeded in hiding them during the search. Wisal's mother said that she had relatives in Jenin, and my mother gave her three of the seven guineas. We bade farewell to the townspeople and to Wisal, her mother, and Abed. We crossed the Jordan River in the company of two families from the town who were going to Irbid; we were a little caravan of sixteen people, most of them children, as well as an old man who knew the road. The weather was very cold, and it was desert road with bare, rocky mountains; I couldn't see the sea, or smell it. In Irbid we stayed as guests with a family related by blood to the two families we had accompanied; we stayed with them for a week, and then my mother decided to continue our trip to Sidon. The head of the family who hosted us said, "The shared taxi will take you to Daraa, in Syria. You will get off there and look for the bus that goes to Damascus. In Damascus you will ask for taxis heading for Sidon; either you'll go straight to Sidon or else you'll take any taxi heading for Rashaya or Marjayoun or Nabatiyeh. When you get to any of them you will be a half hour's distance from Sidon." He repeated the names to her again and emphasized that she should not forget them. Then he said, "God be with you." He wanted to give her money but she said, "God blesses and provides, brother. I have money, thank God."

The next day in the morning the man took us to the taxi stop and we rode with others going to Daraa. He commended us to the driver and to the other passengers. We crossed the border, and after a few hours we and other passengers were settled in our seats in another taxi that was heading from Daraa to Damascus. We arrived at night, and spent the night in a mosque. "The idea was," my mother would say to her sister, "that we would set out early in the morning and reach Sidon on the same day. We slept peacefully, and in the morning I found Ruqayya's face red. I put my hand on her forehead and it was like fire. I said, 'Ruqayya, pull yourself together, it's nothing, today we'll arrive at your uncle's.' But the girl didn't hear me or see me, stretched out on the carpet of the mosque as if she were dead but breathing." I don't remember any of the details of my illness, but my mother says that I had the fever for two weeks, and that she was crying day and night because she was sure I would die. "And what would I say to her father and brothers when they come back safely, she died on me on the road? When she had had the fever for two days and I didn't have any sage or mint, and I couldn't boil a chicken for her so she could drink the broth, I asked the good people about a doctor. I went to him and he came with me to the mosque. He asked for a lira—yes by God, a Palestinian guinea in gold! I gave it to him before he would agree to go to the mosque with me. He examined her and wrote a prescription for me and I bought it. By the time Ruqayya got well, out of the four liras I only had ten piasters left." My aunt marveled, "Ten piasters? Didn't you say that you had four liras in gold?" My mother counted the expenditures on her fingers: "Didn't we cross the Jordan River, and pay for it? Didn't we take the taxis? And food and drink while we were in the mosque, and the doctor, may God not forgive him. And I bought two wool sweaters, one for me and the other for Ruqayya, when we were in Irbid, because the cold cut to the bone." She returned to counting on her fingers. "And I bought the medicine. The sheikh of the mosque, God protect him and bless his children, brought me bread and something to eat with it and sage from his house, and a woolen blanket for us to wrap up in." My aunt returned to the question of the ten piasters: "So how did you get to Sidon?" My mother waved her hand and sighed, saying, "There are many good people." She did not tell her sister, from whom she hid nothing, that she had stood at the door of the mosque and told her story to anyone she thought might help her, among those who passed.

We arrived in Sidon at the beginning of February of the following year. When we met my aunt and uncle I was wearing the three dresses, one on top of the other, and on top of them the wool sweater that my mother had bought for me in Irbid. The first words I spoke since we had left home were what I said in a whisper to my uncle: "My father and my two brothers were killed. I saw them with my own eyes on the pile. They were with a hundred or maybe two hundred people who were killed, but they were on the edge of the pile, I saw them. My mother will tell you that Sadiq and Hasan went to Egypt and that my father is a prisoner. I saw them covered with blood, on the pile."

8

A Boy and a Girl

WHEN EZZ SAID TO ME, "Ruqayya, I want to talk to you," I thought the way he said it was strange. I nearly made fun of him, I nearly said, "Do you want permission to talk to me, or an appointment?" But I didn't. I waited for him to speak, and he said, "I'll take you to the sea."

I walked beside him. When he left the village with his father and mother eight months earlier I was taller than he was, but he had become taller than I was. I remarked on it, and he laughed and said, "I have springs in my knees. Every couple of days I hear them creak, and then I find myself a few inches taller." The smell of the sea was clear in the city. Even though it was mixed with other smells, in the old city it became more dominant as we got closer to the shore, until the only smell was the sea. We took off our sandals and plunged into the sand. Then we sat down next to each other, cross-legged, and Ezz said, "The sea in Sidon is like the sea at home." I looked up and said, "The sea in the village is better. Here there aren't any islands or sugar springs or grottoes. The smell there is different, and the sounds too." He remained silent and I did also, feeling the sea air spread over my hair and face and clothes, staring at the movement of the waves rising and breaking and rising again. I followed the flight of the sea foam. Strange how two images can come together and be superimposed, one over the other! You're in Sidon, girl, and the other sea is there, bound by the dark, rocky islands, the scent of the lilies and the houses that seem like shells or moss, which sprang from the sea originally and then stayed close to it when the waves washed them ashore. I see them as two seas, as if one eye saw one and the other looked at a different sea.

Ezz said, "Ruqayya, I want to talk to you."

"What's the matter, Ezz? Just say it, what's holding you back?"

"I want to ask you . . . are you sure that you saw my uncle Abu Sadiq and Sadiq and Hasan with the corpses on the pile?"

"I saw them."

"Why does my aunt say . . . ."

I interrupted him, "I pointed with my hands. I pulled on her hand and pointed. They were in front of her eyes. She didn't see them, as if she lost her sight for a moment and then got it back. I don't know how or why."

"Did you see them alone or did you see others too?"

"I saw them with the others. The young men they took from al-Furaydis to bury those who were killed told us that they buried them with the others. They said that they buried 120, two or three days afterward. They said that the others had been buried before that, the day they took over the village."

"Do you remember the day we left in the boat?"

"I remember."

"While we were on the way I saw corpses. I saw someone floating in the water. I yelled and ran to my father, pointing with my arm. But my father put his hand on my shoulder and said, 'He died days ago.' I shuddered violently, and my father noticed. He said, 'You're a man now, Ezz, aren't you a man?' I didn't cry. I didn't cry even when I saw the bodies of others floating on the surface of the water. I asked the captain of the ship and he told me that many boats sank on the way because they were small and were carrying more than their capacity, or because the captain of the boat was not skilled enough. I used to like to ride in boats and go sailing in them but I don't like them any more, not boats and not the sea and not traveling."

"Do you like your new school?"

"Something else happened in the boat."

"What happened?"

"A woman began to scream. Then her screaming got louder, and I heard someone say that she was having a baby. Then my mother came and said, 'Give me your knife.' The red knife that Amin gave me, do you remember it?"

"The penknife?"

"Yes. I didn't understand why my mother was asking for it. I asked her and she said, 'We need it for the birth.' I thought they were going to use it to cut open the woman's belly, so I started shivering. I crouched down and fought back tears so my father wouldn't scold me."

"And then?"

"I didn't see anything because the women were surrounding the woman who was screaming and screening her with their bodies. After a while we heard the sound of the baby crying. The women said, 'Thank God she came through safely.' I saw the baby wrapped in my mother's shawl. When she returned the knife to me I hesitated to take it. She was surprised, and then laughed and said, 'We cut the umbilical cord with it.' I put it in my pocket but since we got to Sidon I've kept it hidden, and I don't use it any more. I don't want to."

I said, "Let's walk along the sea."

I put my arm around his shoulders and we walked. The silence lengthened, and then I asked him again about the school.

"I like it because it has a soccer field."

"You used to like school because you were the best."

"I'm not the best any more, because the teacher calls on me suddenly and I don't know what he's been talking about or what the question is. If he repeats it I answer, and if not I stand tongue-tied in front of him, and he scolds me and the boys laugh at me. At first they laughed, but now they've become my friends. They whisper to remind me of what he was saying or to help me answer and I try to catch what they're whispering but I can't make it out if I'm upset. But when we play soccer the game takes over and I don't think about anything but the ball as it moves from one side to the other. I watch it between the feet of the players or I take off toward it when it flies and I fly too, to catch up with it. Soccer has introduced me to all the boys in the school and we've become friends."

"I don't have girlfriends any more. My uncle says that most of the people of the village went to Syria, and we don't yet know where they live. I don't know if I'll ever see them again."

"No problem."

"Why?"

He said, "You'll make new friends, and your old friends will still be your friends when we go back home. My friends here didn't know anything about the village so I told them. When we go back they'll come to visit me. I've gotten to know Sidon and they've gotten to know Tantoura, and when they visit it they'll get to know it better."

"But when I make friends here I'll leave them when we go back."

"When things go back to the way they were, you'll take the train or a taxi and go to them, and they will also visit you there. And who knows, Yahya might work in Jerusalem or in Lid so you'll live there, and you'll have friends in Jerusalem and in Tantoura and in Sidon and maybe in Haifa and Beirut when we go to visit Amin, or in Cairo if Yahya takes you there. The world will open up, and you'll have family and friends and acquaintances everywhere."

I wasn't comfortable with what he said about Yahya. I hadn't brought his image to mind or thought of him since we left the town.

Now I look back from afar: A boy and a girl crouching on the sand. Only God knows what's waiting for them, what secrets the unknown future holds. Two youngsters on a rugged shore with the sea before them, its waves continuously rising and retreating, rising again and breaking. A strong sun tanning their bodies as it hangs suspended above, like destiny. They sit next to each other by the Sidon sea, talking in low voices as if they were adults. I look from afar: two youngsters by the sea of Tantoura, as if they were puppies. The girl runs and the boy runs after her, she jumps and he jumps. The wave lifts them and covers them; they swim like fish. They race and jump and quarrel. Their voices rise, spreading their words and their ringing laughter. They get a little bigger and then bigger still, and they can't swim together—he swims with the boys and she swims with the girls. They meet at home, their heads together looking at the same book, then one of them suddenly jumps up as if stung by a scorpion. They've disagreed. The shouting begins and rises and is only silenced because they have become enemies, each one swearing not to speak to the other as long as he lives. That's a short time, an hour or two or half a day, if it's really long. Afterward they make up because one of them has forgotten that they quarreled, or because one of them wants something from the other that makes him ignore the dispute.

She looks from afar. She sees him under the June sun along the sea of Sidon after the Israelis have taken it over. What he did not live through with her on the sea of Tantoura forty years before he now lives through on the sea of Sidon. It's as if history is repeating itself, although the scene is larger. The people are more, many more. The soldiers are more. The weapons and the armored cars. The burlap bag is reincarnated, one here and another there and a third and a fourth, each looking through the two holes in the bag that covers his head and pointing. Whenever he points the same shudder passes through the ranks, since everyone knows and has known for a long time that the ones pointed out by the burlap bags will now go in a long line to execution or to the prison camp. Not in Zirchon Yaacov or in Ijlil or Sarafand but to someplace here in the heart of Sidon, or in the heights overlooking it.

Ezz will sneak into Beirut. For a moment she won't recognize him, because of the sudden whiteness of his hair or for some other reason. He will sit beside her so he can hear more about his brother, so she can hear from him what happened in Sidon. He will carry the girl, asleep on Ruqayya's knees, to her bed, and they will stay up talking until dawn breaks. A widow and an old man, whose hair has turned completely white in four months and four days. A boy and a girl . . . she looks from afar.

9

The Children's Indictment

THE CHILDREN SAY THAT I was a stern mother, they say their father was more affectionate with them. I repeat disapprovingly, "More affectionate?" They recall the events, and confirm what they say, "You got involved in every detail. You would insist that we be angels!"

They laugh in chorus, and then Sadiq takes the floor, "Yes, the rank of angel was the minimum acceptable! One of us would bring you his report card and with good grades, or even with excellent grades, and your comment would be 'But you're not the best in the class, why aren't you number one? What do you lack for you to be at the top?'"

Hasan adds, "The day we stole the oranges from the big garden, when we were still in Sidon, God! It was a world-class catastrophe!"

Abed laughed, "Do you want the unvarnished truth? When we were little we hated the camp and we hated Palestine, and we hated that you were our mother. It was all a ruler you used to measure our conduct from morning till night, and if it didn't measure up then the ruler was ready to strike!"

I cut off their talk and say, "You're slandering me. I'm going to make myself a cup of coffee and drink it alone to punish you since you're like cats who eat and are ungrateful." They follow me into the kitchen, encircling me. One of them gets the tray ready and another holds the pot and measures the water into it with a cup. Abed, the laziest in household matters and the most impertinent, imitates my way of speaking, "'The boys from the camp apply themselves in school in the morning and work in the evening to earn their daily bread, and they excel in school even though they lack everything! What do you lack?' It's possible, guys, that when we were little she saw signs of mental retardation, or saw some indication that we were from Mars! Or maybe Papa examined us and got scared, and whispered in her ear 'It's strange, Ruqayya, the three boys have a birth defect I haven't come across before. In place of the heart they have a small, smooth stone the size of a large egg, hard and smooth. No blood or flesh or nerves. It's a terrifying miracle, God keep us all!'"

He guffawed, and shouted, "Mama, we haven't come from Mars. And we didn't come to Lebanon as tourists."

He went on, "The camp, whether you live inside or outside, it's your story and there's no getting away from it. Your classmate suddenly turns against you and you don't know what's angered him, only to discover a day or two later that he's found out you're Palestinian and that your existence, the very fact that you exist and that you are you and no other, is a provocation that arouses anger or indignation or, at the very least, disgust. It's as if you were an insect that unfortunately fell in a bowl of soup. And you've known, for a long time before that, the meaning of the 'Phalange' and the meaning of 'the Forces' and what's waiting for you at their hands, and that you are a son of the camp even if you are lucky and don't live in it!"

Sadiq intervenes, "Mama provided for us faithfully. Her sternness was necessary to bring us up properly, and the results are obvious."

Then another mocking phrase: "Umm Sadiq is strong enough to put a dent in iron!"

I'm astonished by my image in their eyes when they were children, for I was just trying to do my job as a wife and mother, whose tasks were not limited to a clean house and wholesome food for three boys with good appetites—good eaters, as they say, thank God. Their bodies were growing miraculously, their legs carrying them higher almost daily— the pants that needed shortening when they were bought now need the hem undone so they can be lengthened, then they're passed to the younger one and then they're unfit for any of them, and are passed on to someone else. Life moves as quickly as an express train, from infants demanding breast feeding and diaper changing and having their wet bottoms wiped, to children forming meaningful sentences, saying yes and saying no more than yes, because they are discovering their will, discovering themselves. Then here they are, in the blink of an eye, boys devoted to the mirror, hurrying the fuzz on their faces and wanting mustaches, preoccupied with their appearance because a girl is nearby. I concentrate on them, I concentrate on every great or small thing and everything in between, because I want . . . what did I want?

I was with the boys on the train and yet I wasn't, because ever since that day when they loaded us into the truck and I saw my father and brothers on the pile, I have remained there, unmoving, even if it didn't seem like it. Maybe my concern for them was exaggerated because I knew, in some obscure fashion that wasn't fully conscious, that I was outside the train. Or maybe this explanation is deceptive, and the reason is different. They say, "You were stern with us," they say, "My father was more affectionate with us," and I find it strange. I wonder, what does a woman do who feels that she has remained alive by chance, by the purest chance? How does she act in the world if her existence, all the years and months and days and moments, bitter and sweet, that she has lived, is a byproduct of some random movement of a strange fate? How does she act in the world? She's aware, at least tacitly, that she's naked, stripped of all logic, because of the impossibility of finding any relationship between cause and effect—or more precisely, the impossibility of understanding the causes when effects fall on her head, effects for which she can't identify the causes. She doesn't do anything and she's not yet aware of anything, not just because she's young but because the collapse of the roof on her head was the starting point, why did the roof collapse at the beginning and not the end? What should she do? How can she deal with the world? I say, there are only two choices: either she is swept away by an overwhelming sense of the absurd, that nothing makes any difference; she lives the moment just as it is, come what may, since meaning is absent, logic is non-existent, and necessity is a figment contrived by the imagination. Or else, since the earthquake has spared her, she becomes—and this is the other choice—like the last man on this earth, as if they had all left and left her their story, so she can populate the earth in their name and in the name of their story. Or perhaps it's as if she's striving in the world with them before her eyes, so they will be pleased with her and pleased with the small garden they may have dreamed of planting. She comes down with a strange kind of fever, planting fever, a strange planting outside of the earth, since the earth was stolen from her and it's impossible for her to plant anywhere but within the confines of the household.

Was I aware of all these things as I was coming out from under the ruins?

When I came out from under the ruins there was a numbness in my mind, like the numbness that comes over the body. A small frightened animal, only. Later, a little while later, like all the creatures of this earth I began to do what would keep me alive. I'm sure that I was aware of these two choices if only dimly, and even if I couldn't have formulated them in words as I do now that I'm approaching seventy, now that I can see the hill of life from above. Then two steps to the right or left or to the rear and I can study the surface on the other side, the lands stretched out near and far. I know that I chose. I chose in spite of being frightened, frightened even of a hand that wanted to caress me tenderly and take me safely to land.

My uncle deliberately asked for my hand for his son Amin in my presence. He said to my mother, "We'll take Ruqayya for Amin, what do you think?"

"And the man from Ain Ghazal?"

"The world has changed; we don't know where he is or where his father is. If he had wanted Ruqayya he would have looked for her. More than a year has passed since the town fell. We've waited for him and there hasn't been any sight or sound of him."

"It's up to you, Abu Amin. Ruqayya is your daughter, anyone who wants her should ask you for her."

My uncle turned to me and said, "What do you say, Ruqayya?"

I didn't utter a word. During the night I cried. It wasn't because I wanted Yahya. He seemed distant; the days had folded him away with other things, and even his image as he emerged from the sea no longer came to me. I cried without knowing the reason for my crying. Then Amin came from Beirut and the contract was written, with my uncle as my witness. He announced in front of everyone: "Amin, I am giving you my daughter Ruqayya. She will be your wife and the mother of your children, but before that and after it she is my brother's daughter, and not one but three martyrs watch over her. So let her be the delight of your eye as she is the delight of my eye and of theirs." Amin wiped his eyes and signed the contract.

Ezz broke in and said to the sheikh, "How can we draw up the marriage contract when Amin hasn't asked me for Ruqayya. Ask me for her now, Amin, or else . . ." He laughed, and so did the others who were there.

Did Amin want me or did his father compel him to marry me because I was the daughter of both his uncle and his aunt, and an orphan with no father or brothers? As a young doctor, what did he want with a girl who hadn't completed her high school education? What did he want with a refugee who was a guest in her uncle's house, when he in turn was living as a guest with the family of a friend of his from Sidon?

I would ride the train without fuss, and remain outside of it also. I would give Amin what was expected of a good wife, affection and little ones, a bite to eat and a clean house, and I would give him myself in an intimate moment and become more confused, because after every intimacy I would wonder what happened. It seemed to me that this was the nature of things. A man would turn to his wife and then take her and she would give herself to him. Perhaps she would be surprised by some unexpected pleasure, not knowing where it came from, and it would add to her confusion.

After he graduated from the university Amin worked as a doctor in UNRWA, the United Nations relief agency. He didn't try to travel to the Gulf as others did when they didn't find work in Lebanon. He would always say that he was lucky, because he had found the work he wanted in the city he wanted. I had my three children in Sidon, then we moved to Beirut because Amin started to work with the Palestinian Red Crescent. We lived near the Tariq al-Jadida neighborhood, no more than ten minutes' walking distance from the Sabra market. When Acre Hospital was established on the south edge of the Shatila Camp, Amin went to work in it. He was absorbed in his work, and he would be gone a lot from the house. It was like a holiday when he was with the children. His work freed him from orders, prohibitions, and controlling the conduct of three boys who could slip from the devilment of kids to become devils. Amin was calm by nature, patient, and spoke little. I never saw him scold one of the boys, even when he made a mistake. He would say, "His own good breeding will correct him, don't worry." Was Amin like me, both outside of the train and inside it, or did his work as a doctor provide him with a private train that belonged to him and tamed the wildness of his spirit? I don't know. In fact I sometimes wonder if I really knew Amin. I search my memory for him when we were in the village; his name was present more than his person. He was seven years older than I was, and he was only there during the summer vacation. No sooner had he finished studying in the village school than my uncle sent him to the high school in Acre, and after that he moved to Beirut to study medicine. Even during the vacation I would see him only when the family gathered for dinner or supper. Where's Amin? His mother would answer, complaining, "He doesn't lift his eyes from the books. I tell him, 'You'll ruin your eyes from so much reading.'" Sometimes he would go swimming with the young men of the village. I had no relationship with him. He was near and far, unlike his brother Ezzedin, who was a year younger than I was. My mother would say, "It's as if those two were brothers born one right after the other." We would fight regularly, every day, Ezz and I, hitting each other, but neither of us could do without the other. We would play together, compete in swimming and diving and picking almonds and peeling Indian figs. Mostly he would win and I would go crazy because I was older. In school he could solve arithmetic problems that were hard for me. He would fill the house with, "Ruqayya's an ass, she's a year older than me and can't solve the arithmetic problem!" I would interrupt, "Liar, it's only nine months, not a year!" I would hate him and decide not to ask for his help in anything. Two days later I would return to him and ask. I know Ezzedin; I wonder, do I really know Amin? I live with him, I take care of his needs. In the faces of our three children some of his features mix with some of mine. Maybe we look alike because we are paternal cousins and my mother is also his mother's sister; maybe, as it usually happens to married couples after living together a long time, the face of each one and the movements of his body have come to mirror the other's. Amin is a doctor; he has never once been unkind to me, he simply speaks calmly, and if he does rebuke it's with an allusion. There is no violence in his treatment of me, and no quarreling. Was it my uncle's admonition to him on the day we were married that dictated this conduct to him, or was he compassionate toward the cousin who had become the mother of his children, an orphan with no brother to turn to if her husband tyrannized her or humiliated her in word or deed? When he would say, "I love you," in an intimate moment, or when he would say proudly "Ruqayya is a great lady and a wonderful mother," and kiss my hand suddenly, I would be suddenly troubled, because even though I knew everything about Amin I did not know Amin, and maybe I didn't know myself. I don't know what Ruqayya wants from this life.

I've completely lost my bearings.

10

The Leap . . . Does It Make a Tale?

AM I REALLY TELLING THE story of my life or am I leaping away? Can a person tell the story of his life, can he summon up all its details? It might be more like descending into a mine in the belly of the earth, a mine that must be dug first before anyone can go down into it. Is any individual, however strong or energetic, capable of digging a mine with their own two hands? It's an arduous task requiring many hands and minds, many hoists, bulldozers, and pickaxes, lumber, and iron and elevators descending to the depths beneath and bringing those they took down back to the surface of the earth. A wonderfully strange mine into which you have to descend alone, because it does not belong to anyone else, even if you find things belonging to someone else in it. Then it might suddenly collapse on your head, cracking it open and burying you completely under the debris.

Perhaps it's more like a bundle than a mine; but can a person tie up his story in a kerchief and then hold it out to others in his hand, saying, "This is my story, my lot in life"? And then, how can you transport a bundle the size of a hand, or a large bundle like those women carry on their heads as they flee east over the bridge, the story of a whole life, a life that's naturally intertwined with the lives of others?

I haven't spoken about my uncle Abu Amin. I haven't told the story of my mother in Sidon, nor the story of Ezzedin. I haven't talked about my own state. When Hasan spoke to me about his new book project I said to him, "If your grand-father Abu Amin were still among the living he would have told you enough to fill volumes. He was with the rebels from '36 on and moved around throughout the towns and villages. He was with the resistance in '47 and '48, and after they took us out of the town he sneaked back. I don't remember all the details but I remember a lot of what he said, and I can repeat it to you." He said, "I'm interested in hearing what my grand-father told you, but now I want your testimony about leaving the village."

Hasan was collecting the statements of the residents of the villages along the Palestinian coast about their forced emigration in 1948.

Hasan didn't record my testimony on that visit, maybe because he noticed the next day and the following one that my face was pale. I didn't tell him that I was suffering from severe pain in my stomach; I took a sedative and forced myself to bear up until he left. I said goodbye and wished him Godspeed and then I went to bed for a week. Had the mine collapsed on my head during that night, as I was recalling some of the details in preparation for giving my testimony?

My uncle was different. He did not become ill when he recalled what happened; he would talk a lot, and in great detail. He would talk about Haifa's garrison, its national com-mittee, the good and the bad in their leadership, the quarrels that arose among them throughout five months, and then what happened in two days and two nights when the city fell and its residents left it. He would not omit any of the actors: the residents, the jihad volunteers, the British army, the Zion-ist gangs, Hajj Amin, the Arab Liberation Army and its field commander al-Qawuqji, and the Arab kings and presidents. He would talk about the day and the hour and the neighbor-hood and the street and the blind alley and the corner, as if he were spreading out all of Haifa in front of his listeners so they could see with their own eyes its sea, its Carmel, its oil refinery, and its rail lines: the narrow gauge and the standard, the Hijaz line that connected Haifa to Damascus via Daraa, the Jaffa and Lid line that took travelers to al-Qantara and from there to Cairo, and the Beirut and Tripoli line that went to Ras al-Naqura through a long tunnel. The Acre line also, which Amin would take every morning to go from Haifa to his school in Acre. He would identify the stations and stop at the Hijaz line station, Haifa East, the largest and oldest. He would describe the station building, its iron gate, and the color of the trains. He would say that they had been brown in the thirties, then they were painted light red in the forties, bearing the English letters *PR* for Palestine Railway. He would specify the names of the neighborhoods and streets, drawing their borders with his words; even the names of the bus companies would find a place in his narrative.

Sidon came into the story not because he was living there now and used to come to it often, but because it was the essential station in the arms smuggling in which he was engaged. The arms would come from Libya; Hajj Amin would buy them from what the British and German armies had left behind and send them by boat to Sidon. The boat would anchor at the Maqasid Islamiya School, and Maarouf Saad would receive them. My uncle would say, "God keep Maarouf and protect him. He worked in the school as the resident head for the boarding students. He would receive the arms at night and bring someone to clean them and grease them and then deliver them to us, and we would take them in boats back to Palestine. Sometimes the arms and ammunition would come from Egypt, from Hilmiyat al-Zaytoun, the headquarters of Hajj Ibrahim, or from Egyptian army storehouses or from Marsa Matruh or Salloum. They would be carried to Port Said and then boats would take them to the shore at Sidon, and they would be unloaded at al-Maqasid."

The Arab armies, kings, presidents, and leaders also had a share in the story. He would recount, categorize, accuse, and corroborate with facts, insulting and cursing and always ending with the same expression: "God have mercy on the martyrs, soldiers, officers, and volunteers." He would amaze us every time with some new detail. He would talk about the Yugoslav volunteers who were martyred in Jaffa three days after the fall of Haifa. "They were twenty, led by a man named Ibrahim Bek, who was from Turkestan. The Jews besieged them in the train station in al-Manshiya. They exterminated them." He would talk about the son of the mufti of Anatolia, who volunteered "with us in Haifa" and was martyred six weeks before the city fell. "We buried him when the almonds were just starting, the blossoms just opening on the branches." He would talk about the volunteer for jihad who had come from India, "Yes, by God, from India. His name was Muhammad Abd al-Rasul. He came from India and was martyred with us in Palestine."

My uncle Abu Amin was not there when they occupied the village, but he was the first of the family to go back to it. He would say, "I went back to Tantoura." Here the story would start and here it would also end. My uncle didn't tell us anything about what he saw in our village when he sneaked back two months later. Did he go back to it once without having the strength to go back again, or was that the beginning of later visits, more like a regular pilgrimage, even if it was an odd pilgrimage that was made by stealth and remained sealed in secrecy?

Only once did my uncle Abu Amin talk about his visit. He said, "There is a three-sided monument of white marble that was erected near Rachel's Tomb, at the fork of the road to Jerusalem and Bethlehem and Hebron. On the monument were carved the names of the martyrs who participated in the battles that occurred south of Jerusalem. Palestinians, Egyptians, Syrians, Libyans, Sudanese, and Yemenis, who are buried there. I visited them, and recited the Fatiha for their souls." Ezz was surprised, and said, "But the two cemeteries

are in the West Bank, how did you go to Jordan from occupied Palestine?" My uncle Abu Amin smiled broadly, and
answered, "God forgive you, Ezz, they divided the country
into three pieces. They divided it but I did not, nor did I
accept the division!"

For many years my uncle Abu Amin did not comprehend
the fact that he was a refugee, perhaps because he did not
come to Sidon as a stranger but instead had been familiar
with it for long years before his permanent residence there.
He would live in it for weeks and sometimes for months; he
had friends and acquaintances not only in Sidon but also in
Tyre and Nabatiyeh and Bint Jbeil. They were colleagues and
friends, and his relationship with them had not started when
the village was lost; rather they were his peers who would
come to visit him in Haifa or Tantoura, just as he would visit
them in their towns. A visit to them might be extended with
no awkwardness, because he had not come to them as a refugee, asking for their generosity, and because he was certain
that in the future he would go back and then host those who
had hosted him, returning the favor and more.

When we came to Sidon we were the guests of one of these
friends. The friend did not consider us guests nor did my
uncle consider himself a guest, for they were lifelong friends
sharing in two types of work. They had shared in jihad since
1936 along with other friends, acquiring experience in buying and smuggling weapons far from the eyes of the British
and French authorities and the Zionist gangs who followed
them. They were also partners in the ownership of a number
of fishing boats, whose proceeds allowed them to pay for the
necessities of life, and to use any surplus in their work for the
armed struggle.

After waiting a year, my uncle decided to rent an apartment in old Sidon, so we moved to it. We did not live in the
camp. For years it was possible for my uncle to avert his gaze
from the meaning of the move, seeing the apartment only as

a way station—a passing trial, hard to bear to be sure, but however long it lasted, it would not go on much longer. When Umm Amin brought up the necessity of registering with the refugee relief agency he exploded at her angrily: "Do you need aid, woman, are you in need of a bag of flour? Shame on you!" My aunt remained silent, and perhaps she thought the idea over and decided that her husband was right. But Ezzedin brought up the subject again, saying that it wasn't a matter of a bag of flour and a can of sardines, but rather it was about maintaining our rights, about the right to go to school and to university and to be employed. He said we must register. My uncle insulted Ezzedin and announced, his face flaming with rage, "I am not a refugee and I will not ask for aid from anyone!"

He was standing in the station waiting to get on the train, returning to where he had come from, so how absurd it was to ask him to register his stop and to get an identity card for waiting. Ezz took his father's papers and those of the family and registered the household on his own at the agency. Until his death, after twenty-seven years of residence in Sidon, my uncle did not know that he was registered as a refugee, and that Ezzedin would accept aid regularly, sometimes taking it to his mother and aunt or, usually, distributing it to the needy.

Perhaps the image of waiting at the station isn't accurate: even though my uncle resisted the idea of accepting his position, absorbed as he was in limited operations across the newly established borders, nonetheless day after day he stood before an alternate reality, which he neither acknowledged nor recognized even as he crept into it by stealth. The camps were taking their current form, making their presence hard to ignore or deny. Some of his acquaintances would tell him about the restraints and pressures to which the camp residents were subjected by the Second Bureau and the Lebanese authorities. He would suddenly shout in a loud voice, "Good God, they need permission from the authorities to leave the camp? Is it a prison?" I was pregnant with my second son when the authorities carried out the forced evacuation of the refugees from the border villages, relocating them to the camps, as a decree had been issued forbidding Palestinians from living in the southern villages adjacent to their lands. My uncle had friends who lived in Bint Jbeil, like him living as guests with their business partners. In accordance with the decree they were forced to move to the Ain al-Helwa camp. I remember my uncle as he struck one hand with the other in despair. He was angry, but he was more troubled than angry, repeating that he did not understand. The Arab kings and presidents had no mercy and left no way open for God's mercy! Why were they moving people far from their land, when, sooner or later, they would move back to it?

My uncle lived in anticipation, like my mother, but her anticipation was different. The concern about returning home hid behind her anticipation of the return of her sons and her husband. She kept saying, "The boys haven't sent any news from Egypt, nor has Abu Sadiq sent a letter from prison." Whenever she heard that a man from our village or from another had arrived in Sidon and had been among the prisoners, she would seek him out and go to visit him. She would congratulate him first, and then ask, "Did you meet Abu Sadiq?" She would return to the house to tell us what the freed prisoner had said, and every time she would repeat the same words: "It's been a long time for Abu Sadiq. One of the spies must have told them that he was in the revolt in '36 so that instead of one charge it was two, and they decided to imprison him longer than the others. How long it's been!" One day my aunt tried gently to prepare the way for her sister to accept what happened. She said, "Zeinab, Sister, they say that some of the men died in prison, maybe Abu Sadiq was one of them." My mother started as if she had been stung by a scorpion and exclaimed, "God forbid! I take refuge with God from you and your thoughts!" For the next three weeks

79

in a row my mother's face was pale, and it became paler if she was forced to speak with her sister or be present with her in the same room.

The wait was not long for my mother. She waited until I married Amin. She sang, she trilled for joy, she joined the women's rhythmic clapping the day the contract was written and the day of the wedding, and on the morning of the following day she and my aunt visited me in my new house in Sidon. They came carrying the usual provisions for a newly married couple. One week later my aunt found her dead in her bed. My aunt said, "Last night she said to me 'Halima, Sister, thank God I've married Ruqayya and she has moved safely and soundly to live in her husband's house. Now it's possible for me to travel to Egypt to look for Sadiq and Hasan.' When I said to her that Egypt is large and that we don't know where they are in it, she said, 'Tell Abu Amin, and if he agrees we'll go together, and if he doesn't agree I'll go alone. I won't come back without them.' Then she went to sleep." My aunt wiped away her tears and got up. She went into my mother's room and returned, extending her hand to me with a large iron key. She said, "The key to your house, Ruqayya."

"Strange. I haven't seen it since we left the house. Where was she hiding it?"

"She hung it around her neck. She didn't take it off even when she slept or bathed. I would say to her, 'Zeinab, Sister, the cord will wear out. Take it off when you bathe and then put it on again.' She wouldn't accept it. The cord came apart as I expected and she got a new cord to hang it on, and continued her habit of sleeping with it and bathing with it."

I took the key. After the three days of mourning I returned to my house. I thought I would give the key to Amin to keep with the papers, his birth certificate, his diploma, and his work permit. I became aware that I had no papers other than the identity card issued by Lebanese security, and I changed my mind. I thought, I'll return it to my uncle Abu

Amin because it's the key to his house also, since it's the same house. He'll put it in the deep pocket of his long-sleeved qumbaz and will finger it from time to time and feel . . . and feel what? I put it on the palm of my left hand and contemplated it. An old iron key, dark in color and polished. It filled the hand; it had heft. I felt it with the fingers of my right hand, acquainting myself with it by touch after getting to know it by sight. Suddenly I smiled and decided that I was stupid, looking far and wide when the clear and simple thing was right in front of my eyes. I grasped the thin cord with both of my hands, raised it, and put my head into it. The key was now hanging on my neck. I held it and began to look at it again, then I put it under my dress, feeling the touch of the iron on the flesh of my breast. As with my mother, the key would remain suspended on my neck, in waking and sleeping. I do not take it off, even in the bathroom, and whenever the cord wears out I replace it with a new one.

Years later when we moved to Beirut and I participated in the campaign for literacy among women in Shatila, and I had to visit the women of the camp to convince them of the importance of literacy, I discovered that what I had inherited from my mother was common. I found it strange—how could the women all do the same thing, without any prior agreement? I remember my first visit. Since it was my first time I was shy and confused, not knowing if the visit would seem intrusive or if it would be welcome. I was met by Umm Ibrahim, an elderly woman in her sixties who lived with her son, her daughter-in-law, and her grandchildren. She introduced herself to me, and I said that I was from Tantoura, and that I was the wife of Dr. Amin in the Palestinian Red Crescent. She said, "We're from Saasaa, do you know it?" She spared my embarrassment by not waiting for me to answer. She continued, telling me about it and about the two massacres that occurred there. She said, "I lost a daughter in the first massacre, in February. She was five years old. We buried her there, in the village. In

October, five months after the Jews had declared their state, they attacked us again. It was another massacre. They took over the village and threw us out."

Umm Ibrahim put her hand to her breast and showed me the key suspended on a cord around her neck. She said, "The key to our house."

Later on I would learn that most of the women of the camp carried the keys to their houses, just as my mother did. Some would show them to me as they told me about the villages they came from, and sometimes I would glimpse the end of the cord around their necks, even if I didn't see the key. Sometimes I would not see it and the lady would not refer to it, but I would know that it was there, under her dress.

My uncle Abu Amin laughed and said, "Congratulations to you both, for . . . *Sadiq*."

The infant was beside me on the bed. I looked up at my uncle and it seemed to me that I was going to say something. I did not speak. I was weak after a long night that seemed like forever. Sounds had escaped from me, driven by that axe that was hitting me mercilessly in my lower back. It shook the body. No, it did not shake it, it convulsed it. It split apart and seemed about to scatter in splinters, or else to collapse and cave in, turning into ruins. Then the pain subsided a bit, as if it was dissipating, almost. Two minutes and then the axe began striking again—is this what a tree feels like when the woodman's axe strikes it? There was no axe and no tree, it was my body, convulsed in labor. My aunt held my hand and said, "The first birth is like this. You and the baby will be fine, God willing, and it will be easier the next time." If she would only stop speaking. I couldn't stand the sound, I couldn't stand the axe. I clung to her hand and squeezed, maybe the pressure would stop the blow that cut my body in two. I shouted, calling for my father. I shouted his name aloud until it seemed as if all Sidon would hear the name and bring him to me, and he would stop the axe and carry me to safety. Suddenly it stopped. It seemed the baby had slipped out. I closed my eyes, or perhaps my eyes and ears closed of themselves. It was as if I had gone to sleep, or fallen into a coma. I didn't hear the baby's cry. I didn't see him when the midwife held him by his feet and lifted him, smiling, announcing that it was a boy, thank God, and then began to cut the umbilical cord and to wipe off the amniotic fluid that remained in his hair and on his body. She must have put him beside me as I was unconscious. I was aware only of my body, tense under the pressure of a pain that was no longer completely there, as if it had slipped from waking to sleep. They all saw the boy before I did. In later years when I had Hasan and then when Abd al-Rahman came, I was conscious, I saw and heard, and I stretched out my hand to hold the new boy. But as for Sadiq, I found him wrapped in white diapers on the bed beside me, when I was roused by my uncle's voice saying, "Thank God for the safe delivery! Congratulations to you both, for . . . *Sadiq*." I opened my eyes and saw Amin's face, pale and exhausted as if he had spent the night in labor. He gave me a bashful smile, and kissed my head. He didn't say anything.

For a moment I wanted to turn my face to the wall, because I was tired and wanted to sleep, or to go far away, alone. I found myself looking at the boy, enjoying him: his hair was black and smooth, his locks covering the top of his forehead. He had a small face and features, a long face, and his eyes were shut. His hands appeared from the swaddling, looking like two rounded, soft pieces of dough; it looked as if some hand had pressed on each of them several times, forming dimples from which grew slender fingers, how long it was hard to tell, since they were closed and contracted like that. I couldn't stop looking at the baby. My aunt brought him to me, here he was in my arms. I felt a tickle in my breast, which had not happened to me before. At the time I didn't identify it as the rush of the milk.

My mother was not present for the birth of any of her three grandchildren. Would the name have made her joyful or sad, would she have blessed it or suggested another name instead? That night, thinking stopped at this question which flitted through my mind, landing in a corner and returning later, after a week or two or three, then disappearing completely, not to return.

My uncle Abu Amin was the one who named Sadiq and Hasan. He named them after I had them, for he did not give names before the birth; first he made sure of the health of the mother and the child, and then he gave the name. When I conceived the third boy I announced when I was still pregnant, in my fifth month, "If it is a girl I will name her Wisal, and if it is a boy he will be Abd al-Rahman."

11

A Young Man's Laughter

EZZEDIN ANNOUNCED, LAUGHING, "SOME PEOPLE have all the
luck! Mulukhiya soup and a job and a scholarship, all on the
same day! Of course the mulukhiya is the most important.
We've eaten the mulukhiya, and now I have to choose: the job
or studying in the university? In fact, I have chosen."

Ezz loves mulukhiya and he loves it more when I make it
for him. He turns the table into a carnival of laughter. He
announces loudly, "Ruqayya's mulukhiya can't be beaten,
she makes it better than my mother and my aunt and all the
women of Sidon." I signal to him with my eyes because I know
that my aunt is annoyed by this talk, but he ignores my signal
and expands on his love for his favorite dish, on the condition
that it comes from my hands, because it strengthens the heart,
hardens the bones, extends life and assures that no one will
defeat the Arabs, despite all appearances to the contrary—and
in all certainty, it will return Palestine to us! We laugh.

I don't know what the house would have been like, or how
it would have been with my uncle and aunt, if Ezz had not
been living with them. With his spontaneity he drew them
into a bubbling cauldron of life, with his comings and goings,
his comments and his stories and his endless wit. There was
also the political news he would bring to his father; Abu Amin
would listen with interest, and it would be followed by a long
discussion about the possible and the impossible. Sometimes
it seemed to me that Ezz could make friends with a passing

breeze. He would introduce everyone to everyone, and his friends would become friends with each other, and his associates' friends would become his friends. He would open the house to them, introduce them to his mother and father and then introduce the family to his family, and they would visit each other and form friendships. The house was never without guests: "This is my friend from Amqa, these guys are from al-Zeeb and they live in Ain al-Helwa, this family is from al-Tira and I invited them to lunch with us." "Mother, what do you think about their daughter, isn't she beautiful?" "Her eyes are small, Ezz . . . the girl who came with her brother two days ago, the girl from Safsaf, is prettier, her eyes are a beautiful black and her figure is like a gazelle's!" My aunt is bothered by all the guests, but she busies herself with greeting and hosting them, and they take her, unawares, into their stories and anecdotes, into what happened and how it all ended. When they have gone and she's overcome with exhaustion she sleeps deeply and peacefully, in spite of everything. Abu Amin, also, has earned standing among many young men: they greet him in the streets of Sidon, they come up to him happily when they see him in the coffee shop, and they come often to the house to ask about him, to consult him, and to listen to his stories.

I said to Ezz, "As long as you're going to go and live in Beirut, I'll ask my aunt and uncle to move in with us."

"Who told you I was going to move to Beirut?"

"Didn't you say that you got a scholarship?"

"I'm not going to accept it!"

Amin joined in, "What do you mean? A scholarship from the agency for study at the American University, what crazy person would refuse that?"

"I graduated from school and that's enough. I have an offer of work as a teacher in the agency. My mind tells me, take the job, boy, stay with the old ones and with your friends and do work you love."

"We're here with the old ones. Your friends won't fly away, and anyway Beirut isn't America, you can come back every weekend."

I left them talking and got up to make the coffee.

I returned with the coffee and found them downcast. I surmised that they had disagreed, and I tried to dissipate the tension by telling them about a new sentence Sadiq had come up with that I thought was witty, but it didn't interest them. Ezz drank his coffee, said goodbye, and went out.

I asked Amin, "Did you quarrel?"

"We differed. I said that he was stupid. He'll regret his decision when he finds that the guys he surpassed in school have become engineers and doctors and men of law, that some of them have gotten their doctorates and become university professors, and he's marking time, a high school teacher for the aid agency. He didn't like what I said. He was annoyed."

"I think he doesn't want to leave his parents."

"That's foolish. I left my parents to study before I was thirteen years old."

"It's different. He feels he's responsible for them."

"I'm responsible, I'm the oldest. I won't fail them. I'll ask them to move in with us."

"I believe that Ezz wants to marry."

"Did he tell you that?"

"He didn't tell me but I know that he loves a girl in the camp. He wants to marry her."

"Has he introduced her to us?"

I laughed. "She's the only one he hasn't brought to visit us or to visit my uncle's house."

"How did you find out?"

"He told me."

"He didn't tell me!"

"She's from Saffurya."

"Have you seen her?"

"I've seen her."

Amin moved his left hand, spreading out his fingers like a fan. "How?"

I told Amin about the girl. I described her and told him what I knew of her family.

There was no doubt about Ezz's wish to marry this girl. I think it was one reason for his inclination not to accept the scholarship, and he may have wanted the job for the salary. He worked in the summers and sometimes during the school year, claiming that he did so because he loved the work, or because So-and-So embarrassed him and he could not refuse his request; but I knew that the financial situation in the family was not the best. My uncle had been forced to sell two of his boats and only one remained; and the house was always open and my uncle was generous as always, never refusing a request from someone in need. Neither Ezz nor my uncle Abu Amin spoke about it, but I deduced it from what my aunt said and alerted Amin. He was embarrassed to speak with his father, but he offered to give Ezz part of his salary regularly, every month. Ezz refused, saying, "You have a wife and son, and Ruqayya is pregnant. Our Lord has been gracious and blessed us, and we lack for nothing." He said that and assured us it was true. But now, as he asserted that he preferred to work, I thought to myself that certainly all this was one reason, and maybe the primary reason and not the secondary one, for his refusal to continue his study.

Ezz began his new work in the aid agency on the first of October, and on the 29th Israeli forces occupied Gaza and the Tripartite Aggression against Egypt began. Sidon blazed with demonstrations; I was following the news and reactions in Lebanon from my bed, as I had given birth to Hasan. I remember that I was carrying an infant of less than three months in my arms when my uncle announced that he was going to Egypt.

My aunt asked in amazement, "Why Egypt?"

He looked at her, disliking the question: "Because it's Egypt!"

My aunt said, raising difficulties, "If my sister Zeinab were with us, she would say, 'Take me with you so we can look for the boys.'" She sighed. "God have mercy on her and compensate her for her patience. For sure she's living with them in Paradise now."

The words escaped me: "Wouldn't it have been better for him to have mercy on her during her life, and leave her at least one of the three!"

"Better, Ruqayya? He has his wisdom that his servants cannot fathom. Say rather, 'Thank God, the only one we thank in adversity.'"

I said nothing.

My uncle went by sea to Port Said, and returned after three weeks, receiving the people who flocked to him as if he were returning from the Hajj. He presided over the room and told his story: "I visited Port Said and Port Fouad and Port Tawfiq and Ismailiya and Suez, and of course, Cairo." He said, "I saw the Canal and swam in its waters." He said, "I took the train to Cairo and attended a concert by Umm Kulthum. I went to the movies and before the show I saw a film called *The Talking Newspaper*, where I saw Abd al-Nasser as if he were standing before me in person, when he was speaking from the pulpit of al-Azhar Mosque and people were shouting for him, and then when they were carrying him in his car. And I saw the planes when they were bombing Port Said." He would say, "I asked about the neighborhood where Abd al-Nasser lived, and I walked in it." One of the young men asked him, "Why didn't you ask to meet him?" My uncle said, his face a little red, "Cairo is big, I didn't know who to contact to take me to him. And anyway he's busy, and those who love him are many—imagine if everyone who loves him asked to visit him, would he attend to the visitors or concentrate his efforts on running the country?"

Two months after my uncle's return, Ezz confided in me that his father had sold half the boat to cover the cost of his trip to Egypt. "He didn't tell me. If I had known I would have managed it for him. I can borrow the money and then return it, since I'm employed and have an income. But he didn't tell me." Ezz laughed, long and loud, and said, "Well done, Abu Amin! Always acting like a king!" I laughed too.

12

Enter the Girl from Saffurya

MY UNCLE LOOKED AT HIMSELF in the mirror one last time. He raised his hand to the cords of his headdress as if he were going to adjust it a little on his head, and then lowered his hand without touching it. Ezz laughed and commented on his father's concern for his appearance, "They'll think you are the groom, Abu Amin!"

His father answered, smiling, "They should. I've never seen a groom like you going to propose like that, with no kufiyeh or cords, not even a jacket—a shirt and pants, as if you were one of the railway workers in Haifa."

"It's hot out."

"But you're the groom. Wear a suit and they'll respect you."

"Let's leave the respect to the army and the Second Bureau."

Sadiq clung to his father and insisted on going out with him. I refused and he cried. His grandfather said, "Let's go, Sadiq." He took his hand and headed for the door, followed by Amin and Ezz. I stayed at home with my aunt and Hasan. My aunt began to ask me about the bride for the tenth or twentieth time, her hair, her height and weight, where she was from, all the details.

"Are her eyelashes long?"

"She's pretty, Aunt, her eyelashes are long and her eyes are deep black. She's light-hearted and charming."

"Is her voice loud enough and does she speak distinctly, or is she like the neighbors' daughter, who speaks fast in a low voice? I can't understand her."

"She speaks clearly, Aunt."

"How many sisters did you say she has?"

"Six sisters."

"All their children are girls, God save us. What will Ezz do with a wife with six sisters? God help him!"

She was silent for a few minutes, withdrawn, as if she were thinking over the description of the daughter-in-law she had yet to see. Then she returned to her questions, "How far is Saffurya from our town?"

"I don't know."

"Is it in the Haifa region?"

"No, near Nazareth."

"When they took over the town, did they take them out?"

"They besieged the town and then they struck from the air."

"They fled?"

"They left on foot for Lebanon. They got to Rumaysh and lived with people they knew. Some months later they went back."

"They went back to their town? What forced them out to Lebanon a second time?"

"They caught them before they got to Saffurya and considered them infiltrators. They put them in prison in Nazareth and then loaded them into trucks and threw them over the border."

"And they came to Sidon?"

"The Lebanese put them with others in an army barracks for a year or more, in an area named Qaroun, then they moved them to Ain al-Helwa."

"It's the first time anyone from the village has taken a woman from Saffurya."

She went back to her questions, "Is her hair soft or rough, like the neighbors' daughter's?"

I laughed. "I haven't touched it, Aunt, I don't know. It looks soft. She braids it. Will you have coffee with me?"

She sighed. "Yes, I'll have some."

I gave her Hasan and got up to go to the kitchen and boil the coffee. I was suppressing my laughter. It seemed more like a judicial inquiry—why didn't she wait two days and see her son's bride for herself? She couldn't wait. My poor aunt dreaded having a strange girl move in with her, sharing her house and her kitchen and her son. She kept saying, "If we were in the village Ezz would have married one of the girls there, or he would have taken one of the girls from Ain Ghazal or Ijzim or Jabaa, our maternal relatives. We've married among them before and their customs are like ours. Saffurya? I've never heard of that town and I don't know a thing about it. God protect us!" She was openly worried. As for my uncle, I did not understand the reason for his distress on the way to Ain al-Helwa to ask for the girl. What was upsetting him? Asking for a bride for his son from strangers he had never met, or missing his brother and relatives from the village, the customary large group that accompanies the groom when he goes to ask for the bride? Or did he dread going to the camp?

Perhaps he was not distressed, but rather something else had settled in him, like coffee after it's boiled, when the dregs are dark and concentrated and bitter, separate from the drink and the flavor we enjoy. My uncle was merry and cheerful over the marriage of his younger son, and the thought of the bride who would live with him in his house. But when he went to ask for her on the evening of that spring day of 1957 he had to go into the camp, which he had not entered before.

After they recited the Fatiha, my uncle wanted to expedite writing the contract and celebrating the marriage, but his in-laws told him that they needed some time to send the news to their relatives in the other camps. The girl's father leaned over to my uncle, "We have to do what we must, Abu Amin. The invitation must reach everyone from the town. If they can attend then that's good, and a blessing; if they can't get the permits, then that's God in his wisdom."

"What permits?"

"Slowly, slowly, Abu Amin. We have to get a permit from the Second Bureau to allow our guests to enter the camp, a hand-written permit. We'll submit the request tomorrow morning. Our guests also have to submit requests to get permits to leave their camps, and praise God, the people of Saffu-rya are many, scattered from Ain al-Helwa to Mieh Mieh to al-Burj al-Shamali near Tyre, to Wavel in the Beqaa and Nahr al-Bared in the Tripoli region. We have to contact them to find out what their situation is and when they can get the permits."

I was not present for this part of the talk since I was in an inner room, changing Hasan's diaper. But Ezz accompanied Amin and me on our way home in the evening, telling his mother and father that he wanted to stretch his legs a bit. When we arrived he said, "I want a cup of coffee from Ruqa-yya's hands," and he went up with us. He was burning to talk. He repeated the bride's father's words to me, and looked at Amin, "You noticed how discouraged everyone became."

"I noticed, and I didn't entirely understand what happened. I tried to distract them by talking about the agency's projects for better health care for families, and how I hope to organize training sessions to prepare young people to administer first aid, something that could possibly turn into a nursing school later on. They were interested, in fact, but Mother was still upset."

"Father was discouraged when Abu Karima talked about the permits, not because he hadn't heard about them before but because every time he heard about them, he decided to drop the matter and forget about it, as if he had never heard of it. Suddenly he finds that his son's wedding and the prepa-rations for it depend on permits from the Lebanese military intelligence. He'll be forced to live with the details, so how can he let it drop?"

"And what's bothering Mother?"

I joined in, "Aunt is worried that the bride's family will be larger than the groom's, as if we had no extended family around us. I heard her saying to my uncle, "Why don't you send for the people from Tantoura in Syria? Maybe some of them would be able to make the trip."

Ezz laughed, and said, "Mother whispered in my ear, 'Who will cook for all these people? What if a hundred people came—we're not at home and I only have Ruqayya and our neighbor, who's ill, and her daughter, and I can't understand her.' So I whispered, 'Don't worry, we'll arrange things later. We shouldn't whisper something that might reach the ears of our guests.' She whispered back, 'They have relatives that are coming from the Beqaa and from Baalbek. What if they turned out to be a thousand, what would I do?' So I got up and sat in another place!"

Ezz burst out laughing, and got up.

"I'll go home and reassure them before they go to sleep. I really needed to talk about that sudden anxiety; I couldn't sleep without talking about it. I've gotten it off my chest and now I'm relaxed. Good night."

Some of the people got their permits and some didn't. Most of those who were invited from Tripoli and the Beqaa weren't able to participate in the wedding, so my aunt wasn't obliged to cook for a thousand people. Despite her constant worry she was singing and humming and welcoming the guests. They bridged the distance from the bride's house and the surrounding houses, where her family and relatives lived in the camp, to my uncle's house in old Sidon. The young men set up the dabka circles in the camp and in Sidon, where the people of the neighborhood shared in the dabka and the call and response of the ataba, miijaanaa, and ooof songs. Even the wedding procession was held according to custom. My uncle brought a horse from one of his friends; they decorated it and Ezz rode it, after his friends had taken him to the public bath and sung the customary songs to him: "The handsome young man comes from the bath, God and his names protect him," and "O you with the kufiyeh and cords, where did you hunt this gazelle?" I sang with my aunt and the bride's mother and sisters:

> Say to his mother, rejoice and be glad,
> Perfume the pillows and bring henna for our hands.
> The wedding is here and the couple is smiling,
> The home is my home and the houses are mine—
> We are engaged, let my enemy die!

Little Sadiq was clapping his hands and joining in the singing.

My aunt outdid herself when she sang *Ya Zareef al-Tuul*—O Tall One. She added some lines to the familiar song which I had not heard before:

> O tall one, O handsome, stop and let me say,
> You're going abroad, when your country would be best.
> I'm afraid, O tall one, that you'll settle there,
> You'll live with another, and let my memory go.

> O tall one, O handsome, you with the laughing smile,
> Tenderly raised by your mother and father,
> O tall one, the day they took you far away
> My hair went white and my back bent low.

> O tall one, O handsome, you're far from your own.
> Don't travel far away and leave us the blame!
> If God wills you'll return, we'll return to the vines,
> We'll harvest the wheat, and gather what we grow.

> O tall one, O handsome, you who've been spoiled,
> If you go to the well, think how to climb out.
> We're scattered, it's for God to bring us back;
> Our Lord scatters and he gathers, that we know.

The girl from Saffurya came into the house, lived in it, and spread out. My poor aunt found herself cramped in a space that was ever smaller, as "the stranger" (as she called her in her absence) shared in ordering the house, and what will we cook today and how will we cook it, and "this couch is better here," and "having this window closed makes the house stuffy, it's better if we keep it open," and "never mind, Aunt, I'll cook." My aunt complains to me in whispers, looking around her. "She has your uncle and your cousin completely fooled. Even the kids are fooled. She's strong, the girl from Saffurya!" Or again, "Thank God they live in the camp. If Ezz had married her when we were in the village he would have lived in their village, and we would only have seen him on holidays."

Since most of the residents of Saffurya were refugees in Lebanon, the whole village and not just the bride came into Abu Amin's house. It was a dense presence that made my aunt feel as if she didn't have any extended family around her, and that my uncle welcomed joyfully. His daughter-in-law brought him her family who became a family for him; in fact she brought Saffurya itself with her, to become part of his story. He would recount what happened in it, and it came to seem as if he had been there when the people were forced to leave it for Rumaysh. In fact, one morning he decided, "We have a duty that we cannot neglect," so he went to Rumaysh to meet the family that had hosted his in-laws the day they left their village, taking with him a "worthy" gift of fish. He thanked them and invited them to visit him in Sidon, and held a banquet for them as if they were his in-laws and not a family who had hosted the family of a girl who would become his daughter-in-law, nine years later.

But he did not go often to the camp. He only went there if he had to.

13

An Essay on Waiting

"HE WAS STANDING IN THE station waiting to get on the train, returning to where he had come from, so how absurd it was to ask him to register his stop and to get an identity card for waiting." I said that before, describing my uncle Abu Amin. I re-examine it. It's not absurd for us to get an identity card to wait. And anyway, an identity card is always condensed, a summary of a long, complicated story, stretched out over time and not susceptible to a summary. It's an insufficient shorthand, but it's an indication.

Waiting.

All of us know waiting.

To wait an hour, a day or two, a month, or a year or perhaps years. You say it's been a long time, but you wait. How long can we wait? Maryam told me about a woman who waited for her husband for twenty years. I said, "Tell me more." She said, "It's a well-known story in ancient literature. The man went to war, and the war lasted ten years. On his way home he got lost." "Who got lost?" I asked. She said the man's name, a strange name that's hard to remember. She said, "He was lost for ten more years, and the wife was still waiting. Men were hovering around her, desiring her and asking her to marry them, and she was weaving on her loom, saying, 'When I finish weaving I will accept one of you.' She would weave on her loom during the day and at night she would undo the weaving." I was drawn to the story, but I said to myself that it fell short, that waiting is not like that, it's inseparable from life and not a substitute for it. You wait at the train station, and at the same time trains take you east and west and north and south. You have children and you raise them, you study and move on to a job, you love and you bury your dead, you rebuild the house that collapsed on your head, you erect a new house. A thousand details take your attention, that's the wonder, as you are waiting in the station. What are you waiting for? What is Ruqayya, in particular, waiting for?

Thinking exhausts her. Putting it all into words exhausts her, but she knows that while she was waiting, she had three children. At the station. Amin planted the sperm, and under the umbrella of waiting she bore a child she named Sadiq, then followed him with a second child she named Hasan, and after them came Abd al-Rahman.

Like a newborn puppy whose eyes are still closed, the boy looks for the nipple of the breast, knowing his way by feel or scent, and learns how to nurse. He grows a little and his small, soft hand closes over her finger, gripping it with his fist. He crawls. He coos like the birds. He walks. He forms meaningful sentences, then takes off talking. He runs. To school. To the university. To women. To a home of his own, and children. The scene shifts as if in a film that sums up whole lives in two hours. Ruqayya at less than fourteen, following her mother on the way to Sidon, without speaking. Ruqayya at less than fifteen being married to Amin. Ruqayya at twenty-four with three children, the youngest a nursing baby. With Amin in Beirut. The children in schools. The children in universities. In the demonstrations. Behind a barricade, threatened by another barricade in front of them. The children in airplanes. Ruqayya sitting on the stairs during the shelling of Beirut, bent double until her head nearly touches her knees, holding Maryam who had fallen to her as if from the sky. We begin again. Maryam crawls. Maryam walks. She forms meaningful sentences. She runs to school. To the university.

A story that can't be summarized.

And then, what is the place of fear in the way station?

Fear is hidden away like inner waters, present in waking and in sleep. Open fear when the city suddenly shakes. A few moments and then she notices that the building that has turned into a heap from which smoke and flames are rising, by some incomprehensible accident, is the neighbors' building and not the one she lives in.

A story that can't be summarized.

Waiting had an independent existence, true, more like the earth we stand on. But that other thing also had always been there, piling up intentions that announced themselves suddenly. How else could I explain my uncle Abu Amin's behavior and what happened after 1967, and that sudden change in the camps? (Was it really sudden, or was it a natural move, the result of what had gone before?) The change was clear in the faces of the girls and the young men, in the look in the eyes, in the stance, the walk, the gesture, and the sense of the place. Would that Maryam were here so I could ask her to give me more details of the story of the woman who waited twenty years. Penelope. She said that her name was Penelope. No one undoes their weaving even if it looks that way. No one is frozen in the act of waiting.

My uncle continued his trips infiltrating the country. I can't report the details because I don't know them, and because Abu Amin, so enamored of talking and telling stories, kept silent about his trips. He would absent himself from the house, a week or two or sometimes a month; it would seem as if he had gone to sea with the fishermen. Then my aunt's fears and later the fears of us all as we waited for his return would confirm that we knew what he had not told us, and that he had gone there. To do what? Did he go alone or with others? Did he plan and set a goal that called for the risk, or did he go only because he wanted to? He did not say, and we could only imagine.

When Abd al-Nasser's voice rang out from the pulpit of al-Azhar one Friday in the fall of 1956, Sidon and Tyre and

Nabatiyeh and Bint Jbeil and other villages and towns listened exactly as they listened in the camps. The little ones, with that wondrous spring in their knees, suddenly leapt from childhood to youth. And it seems that the spring wasn't limited to the knees, that spring that stretched them not by one hand span but by two. Did the camp also have knees and a spring, to take it from one state to another insensibly and with no notice? Did it demand of the camp also, like them, that it sit once again before the photographer so he could take a picture that reflected its new shape?

Then came 1967.

What did it do to us? The girl from Saffurya said that her father and uncles on both sides and everyone she knew from Saffurya, and maybe the people she knew and those she didn't from other villages in the camp, brought out the keys to their houses and prepared their identity papers and the deeds that established their ownership of their lands and houses. She said that her mother wanted to know, "Will we go back the way we came, on foot, or will a car take us there?" When her father said, "Only God knows," she became tense and said, "I want to know what to keep and what to get rid of." She had spread out around her all the clothes and household items they had. This she folded with care because she would take it with her and that she put in a pile to one side because she didn't need it and would leave it by the door for whoever found it. Then she stopped, suddenly at a loss as she held the sweater she had knit by hand for the youngest girl; it was too small for her now, and she didn't know whether to get rid of it because no one else would use it, or to keep it because she remembered her joy when she finished it and her daughter's joy when she wore it for the first time, on Eid al-Fitr after Ramadan. Suddenly she said to one of the girls, or to herself, "We have a stove there in the house that's larger and better, there's no need to take the stove. And our bed there is new. No, not new, time has passed; we'll take the bed. The kerosene heater will be useful in the winter, we'll take it with us—can we rent a truck to carry the things?" Then she looked suddenly at her husband and asked, "Should we keep the identification from the aid agency? I think we should tear it up, what do you think?" He answered, "We'll tear it up as soon as we enter Palestine."

My aunt did not act like her son's mother-in-law. She did not sort the clothes or household items. In the afternoon of June 5 my aunt announced, "We will not act as if we had no upbringing and are ungrateful for favors, and leave without a word." She began a crowded schedule of visits, that included the neighbors and the neighbors' neighbors, in al-Sabil and Abu Nakhla and the surrounding neighborhoods. Every day she made two or three visits, saying goodbye, expressing her thanks and gratitude, inviting them to visit the village and asserting: "Our house is large, and everyone is welcome. I beg you not to put it off, we'll be waiting for you."

When things happened as they did, and Abd al-Nasser announced that he was stepping down from his post and that his decision was final, it seemed to me that we were going to undo the weaving like the lady in the old story.

I was stupid. Just a mother of small children, who had as yet learned only a little. I didn't notice that the outpouring of millions of people to demand that Abd al-Nasser continue on his path was significant.

I didn't notice until I was surprised one day to find that the camp had left its place. It up and moved from the edge of town to the center, and settled there. Every time the army besieged it or fired on it, it became more prominent in the story and consolidated its position.

My uncle Abu Amin began to drink his coffee hurriedly in the morning. Then he would put on his qumbaz and jacket and affix his kufiyeh and its cords; he would grasp his walking stick and say loudly to my aunt, "Don't wait for me for lunch, Halima, I'll spend the day in the camp. I have a lot of work to do." He would raise his staff and then strike the floor with it, and go out. Sometimes he would be there until late in the evening, so he would ask one of the young men from the organizations who had a telephone to call the Abu Nakhla Bakery or the coffee shop near the house; a boy would come and knock on the door, Ezz would open it for him and the boy would deliver his message: "Uncle Abu Amin called to say not to wait for him because he will spend the night in the camp, the young men there need him." Ezzedin would laugh, and his mother and wife would come to hear the news. Ezz would say, laughing still, "Father's spending the night in the camp. Watch out, Umm Amin, it looks as if the old man thinks he's twenty, maybe he has his eye on a girl there!"

Since Amin and Ezz were working in the camp they told us how popular their father was among the residents and the young fedayeen. His activity branched out in several directions: he would tell them what he had learned from experience about the roads and pathways on the other side of the border, he would help with training in identifying weapons and using them, and perhaps most importantly he would tell his story, giving them details of his memories of Sheikh al-Qassam, of the Arab Revolt of 1936, of the battles of 1947 and 1948, of what happened on a given day in a given village, and the lessons learned. His audience was no longer restricted to his household and a few friends he would meet in the coffee shop in the old town, rather it was the youth of the camp and others among the people of Sidon and the young men who came from far and near.

My uncle would take Sadiq with him and enroll him in the 'Lion Cubs' team, carrying thick white paper for Hasan. He would spread it out in front of him and say, "Draw the map, boy, make it large and use colors." Hasan would spread out the white paper on the ground and bend down as if he were praying on it, drawing the outline with pencil and using the eraser to adjust the line and make the curves precise. Then he would open the box of crayons and begin with the sea, coloring it blue, moving on to the Negev Desert which he would color yellow, and absorb himself in identifying the cities and the villages. After half a day of concentration he would call his grandfather and say, "What do you think, Grandpa?" Abu Amin would bend down over the map, trying to bend his knees and kneel to study the details; but his knees would not cooperate so he would sit cross-legged in front of the map, staring at it. He would laugh and show his gold tooth that a young doctor had made for him. (He still remembered him gratefully, and would say, "God help him and protect him wherever he is. He studied at the University of Cairo and opened a dental clinic in Haifa.") Hasan would have distinguished Tantoura by writing its name in larger letters than he used for the names of Haifa or Jaffa or Jerusalem, marking its place with a large circle that he colored in red, as if Tantoura were the district capital and not Haifa. Abu Amin would scrutinize the details more closely, then scoot over and sit on the map, reaching out and taking the pencil from Hasan and adding towns and villages neither I nor Amin had ever heard of. He would say, "Here, you forgot these villages of Jabal Amil; they are Lebanese villages that the Jews captured after the truce in '48: Metulla, Ibil al-Qamh, al-Zuq al-Fawqa and al-Zuq al-Tahta, and al-Mansura." He would specify the site of each village with a little red circle, and then his hand would slide a little lower, "Here are Hunin, al-Khalisa, al-'Abasiya, al-Naima, al-Salihiya, and Zawiya, near each other, no farther from each other than half an hour's walk on foot." Then his hand would slip farther, "Below them and a little to the east are Qadas and al-Malkiya. Your uncle Maarouf Saad defended them when he was fighting in Palestine. The young men would come from Tripoli, Baalbek, Bint Jbeil, and elsewhere and train here in Sidon, in Bab al-Sarail Square; afterward they would head for northern Palestine. Al-Malkiya is important, boy." He would put a big red circle around it. Then his hand would move to the left part of the page and stop before it reached the blue sea: "And here are Kafr Bir'im, al-Nabi Rubin, and Tarbikha." He stares at

the map again and says, "Where's al-Shajara? I don't see it."
He marks the site with red. "Here, a little east of Saffurya,
do you see Hittin? Go down a little and a little to the west.
You know your uncle Naji, boy? Naji al-Ali, the cartoonist
from Ain al-Helwa? He's from al-Shajara, and the poet Abd
al-Rahim Mahmoud was martyred there. Do you remember
what he said, boy?" Hasan falters; it's hard for him to understand poetry or memorize it. Sadiq intervenes, reciting:

> I will carry my soul in the palm of my hand, and cast
> it into the chasm of death,
> To live, and gladden the heart of a friend, or to die,
> and bring to the enemy wrath.

"Perfect, perfect! Memorize it, Hasan. And don't forget
al-Shajara again, Uncle Naji might get mad at you if you
forget it."

Then he suddenly noticed that little Abed was sitting next
to him on the map, asking for attention, so he said to him,
"What have you memorized, Abed? Go on, tell us."

Abed sang the anthem "My Homeland," *Mawtani*:

> My homeland, my homeland,
> Splendor and beauty, majesty and magnificence
> Are in your hills, in your hills.
> Life and deliverance, pleasure and hope
> Are in your air, in your air.
> Will I see you, will I see you
> Safe and sound, blessed in honor?
> Will I see you, so sublime
> Reaching the sky, reaching the sky,
> My homeland, O my homeland?

Sadiq broke in, "'Reaching the stars,' not 'the sky.' 'The sky'
is a mistake!"

"Hold on, Sadiq, go a little easy on Abed. Good for you, Abed, excellent!"

Abu Amin reached into his pocket and gave Abed three sugar-coated almonds. He had begun to make sure to buy them and keep them in his pocket when he had become a grandfather with young grandchildren.

14

Abed of Qisarya

HE DIDN'T GIVE ME A chance to look at him. He didn't allow me to stop and connect the little boy to whom I had bid farewell twenty-five years before in Deir al-Maskubiya in Hebron with the man who stood before me. He opened his arms wide and embraced me, to the surprise of the children and confusion of their father. He held me away a little to look at me. He said, laughing aloud, warmly, "Your eyes haven't changed, and of course not the tattoo. I looked everywhere for you, I went to Sidon and to Ain al-Helwa, and when they said, 'They went to Beirut,' I asked in Sabra and Shatila and Burj al-Barajneh. If I had known your husband's name it would have been easier for me. I went back to Sidon again and they said, 'Are you sure that they are from Tantoura? The people from Tantoura live in Syria.' I was there a whole week until I found an elderly man who said that he knew Abu Amin and who took me to him. He gave me your address in Beirut."

Then came telegraphic sentences about Wisal, about his mother, about himself. He asked me about my mother. I said, "She's passed, God keep you safe." A moment of silence, then the talk flowed again, naturally. It seemed natural. Then I left him with Amin and the children and went to make dinner. Abed had become taller than I am, how? I carried him to the sea when he was shivering and saying, "I don't want to go," and I kept saying, "We'll swim together, you'll love the sea, believe me." The wave came and he held tighter to my neck, and then he began to cry. How could I connect the fearful little boy with this lean, handsome young man who came up unaffectedly and hugged me as if he were one of my brothers, come back from the dead? Had I forgotten him? I had not forgotten him but I had resigned myself to his absence. Or had I? He said, "I knew we would meet. The day I graduated from school, the day I graduated from the university I said to Wisal, 'How will I send news to Ruqayya that I've graduated? I wonder if Ruqayya has married, and how many children she has?' Wisal has married and she has five boys and one girl, what do you think, Sadiq, shall we ask for her for you?" Sadiq laughed, "If she's pretty, I agree!" He said, "I'm working in Beirut. God help you, Abu Sadiq, I'm going to keep bothering you with my visits. Consider me Ruqayya's brother or her firstborn son or an unwelcome guest, stickier than the best bandage. There's no help for it."

Abed descended on the food ravenously. He said, "It's the most delicious food I've eaten in my life." After he left, little Abed said, "He ate like he was famished, he didn't leave us anything for tomorrow." His father scolded him, and I laughed. I was in a good mood, as if I were happy, but I couldn't sleep that night. Abed had brought the whole village with him as if he were bringing it to me, then he left it, secretly, and went away. What kind of present was that? Why hadn't my mother thought about taking a little iron box with her, like Wisal's mother, with our papers in it? There had been a picture of my father and brothers that had been taken of them in Haifa. I remember my father had on a kufiyeh and was wearing a qumbaz, with a jacket that showed the leather belt around his waist. On his right Sadiq was wearing what was appropriate for a young employee in the Arab Bank: a suit and a fez, and on his left Hasan was in shirtsleeves and pants. Why had Abed brought them to me, as if they were his family and not mine? I didn't look at them a lot; I knew they were there, carefully locked away in some corner of my heart, but Abed had let them loose on me like mad dogs. What kind of image was that? How could I compare my father and brothers to mad dogs? The memory perhaps, the memory of the loss was like mad dogs that gnashed mercilessly if they were let off the leash. How could I pluck the serene picture and the clear smile before the photographer's lens from the three bodies there on the pile?

Did my father inspire respect because he was my father? Because he was strongly built and broad shouldered? Because he rode a horse that had a long neck, long legs, and a long tail, and a beautiful face? Or did the kufiyeh and the cords—he was rarely seen without them—inspire respect? (When he washed or made his ablutions or went to sleep he would take them off, and with his black hair loose he would look younger.) I look up at him, slender, his head high, seated on the back of his horse, holding the reins and guiding the horse, who sways with him because he's nearing the house. I look up as he's leaving, and I see his back and his shoulders and the kufiyeh from behind. The horse walks with him, gently and softly; then he runs, then he lengthens his stride and gradually settles into the run. I watch until my father and his horse become like a single, spectral body, going farther and farther away, until it becomes an indistinct point in space. Was my father forty? Forty-two? My mother would say that they were married when he was eighteen. Sadiq was the oldest, and he was twenty-two when they took over the village. He did not resemble my father; he was more like my mother, small in stature and less massive than his brother, who was younger in years. Despite his fez and his suit he seemed like a pupil in high school. As for Hasan, who was in high school, his knees had suddenly lifted him up, and he kept growing taller until he surpassed his father. Like him he was broad shouldered and strongly built. The faces are clear; when I summon them they come to me easily, and along with them the picture of them on the pile. Isn't it possible to separate the two pictures?

My relationship with heaven became complicated, complicated to the point of being completely ruined since that moment when I saw them on the pile. There was no acceptable or reasonable answer for "why?" however much it rose up, loud and insistent. I did not ask "why." I mean I didn't speak the word, and perhaps I was not conscious that it was there, echoing in my breast morning and evening and throughout the day and night. I didn't say a thing; I fortified myself in silence. And now this handsome young man arrives, laughing and eating too much, to say purely and simply, "Abed from Qisarya," and open the gates of hell on me that I had shut long before. To let loose on me the dogs of memory. Why don't you keep your distance from me, boy? Why don't you leave me in peace? I had tried to forget until it seemed that I had forgotten. And then there were Sadiq and Hasan and Abed, others to stare at and busy myself with, as if they were the origin, as if I had forgotten the origin. What do you want from me, boy?

Amin said, "What's the matter, Ruqayya? You're tossing and turning, shall I give you a sedative?"

I did not answer. I left the bed and stayed on the balcony until the first streaks of daybreak appeared. I made myself a cup of coffee and went down to the sea.

I said to Abed on the next visit, "Tell me about Wisal."

He said, "She's still pretty, but she seems older than you. Maybe it's the difference between life in the camp in Jenin and your life in Beirut." I looked into his eyes—was it a criticism? His expression seemed normal. He said, "She married a farmer from Marj ibn Amir, a refugee like us living in the camp. The first years were hard, and then my mother bought a sewing machine on installments and began to sew for the neighbors. After that Wisal got married and I got a scholarship to the University of Jordan. Things were okay. I would study in Amman and go back to Jenin for the summer vacation, and if I could manage I would go every two or three months. When the West Bank was occupied I sneaked back to Jenin twice."

He bound up a quarter century of life events in a kerchief and said, "This is what happened."

Abed would visit us regularly, once a week at least, and I would invite him to lunch with us. Sometimes he would call and ask that we meet to have coffee in one of the coffee shops scattered along the shore of the sea. Amin said that he was a respectable young man, even though he seemed a little worried by a familiarity that he wasn't used to between me and anyone else, man or woman. But he did not comment, leaving that to little Abed, who on any and all occasions made known his irritation with this guest who "popped up like a jack-in-the-box." He would ferret out the negatives: he talked a lot, he laughed in a loud voice, he forgot he was a guest and that a guest should not stay too long or eat too much, "Didn't you teach us that? So why don't you say that he's ill-mannered?" I scolded him, trying to camouflage the laugh that nearly escaped me when I noticed that little Abed was simply jealous of him, and annoyed that I had named him after him. Sadiq was not there, he was preoccupied with his adolescence and his studies and questions about being a Palestinian in Lebanon. As for Hasan, he became attached to him. Was it because he liked him purely and simply (for affection is God-given), or because the kind of work Abed did was interesting for a boy of fourteen who had questions and was looking for a field in which he could pursue them? I don't know even now after all these years whether Abed influenced Hasan, so that he chose his field of work and his lifelong project, or whether it's the opposite, and the young man became attached to the older because he found in his thinking and his concerns something that suited his own need.

It's strange. The man bestows a drop of sperm and then a second and a third, he implants each of them in the same womb to grow unfettered in its closed confines. Then it emerges into the world, each resembling only itself in form and spirit. Strange! My older brother did not resemble his brother; perhaps a stranger might notice some similarity in the face, but they were different, this one small and lean and that one tall and broad. I remember them laughing, I remember their eyes clearly, and their voices as well. There was a similarity in the voice but Sadiq's eyes were a beautiful black, and his little brother's eyes were like his father's—an indeterminate color between blue and green. I remember Sadiq carrying me on his shoulders and running to the sea. I remember him keeping my mother from beating me because I had disobeyed her. I remember their love of Indian figs, how their faces contorted when the thorns would stick their fingers, how they would freeze like soldiers in ranks when they heard my father in the house, and then their uproar after my father left us and they were alone with us. I bring them to mind easily, walking next to each other as they left on their way to Haifa or as they were coming to the house on their return. I asked the older Abed, "Do you remember Sadiq and Hasan?"

He said, "I don't remember their facial features, but I remember that the older one, Hasan . . . ."

I interrupted, "Hasan is the younger."

"He was taller and bigger so I remember him as the older. Hasan picked me up from the ground once and spun around with me, and then said, 'I have a better game.' I don't know how he put me on his shoulders; he took my hands and flipped me over, and put me down on my feet. In less than a minute I was standing on his shoulders, then here was my head near my feet, then here were my feet standing on the ground and my head was once again on top. I asked him to do it again and he did, several times. Every time fear would mix with pleasure and anticipation and shouts from us both. He was shouting to make the game more exciting and I was shouting because I was afraid, and maybe because I was imitating him. He left and I waited the whole week to play the same game.

Every day I would ask Mother, 'How many days are left until Thursday?' I would count the days on my fingers, and then count them again, several times every day! The night before Thursday I would look proudly at the one finger remaining until Thursday, as if by dint of waiting I had gotten to the day I wanted. As if I were fasting, for example, and had borne it until I had reached the time for the iftar meal."

He laughed loudly, until his eyes filled with tears.

"And I remember that the younger . . ." He corrected himself, "I mean the older, Sadiq, gave me five piasters and told me to buy chocolate with them from the shop. I gave the five piasters to Wisal and she bought five little pieces of chocolate which she passed out to us, to me and you and Ezz and Umm Sadiq and my mother. I divided the piece she gave me between us because she didn't take anything for herself. When I ate the chocolate I found out that it was very delicious, so I went back to Wisal and asked her for the half that I had given her. She had eaten it. I cried so you gave me the chocolate that Wisal had given you."

"Strange, I don't remember."

"I remember it clearly. I also remember that you would give me everything. You would carry me and I would put my arms around your neck. I would only go to sleep next to you."

My face reddened in embarrassment. I changed the subject: "Do you remember how afraid you were of the sea, and how you would yell and cry when I was trying to teach you to swim?"

15

Wisal

ABD AL-RAHMAN HELD OUT HIS hand with the telephone receiver and said, "Talk!"

I grasped the receiver and put it to my ear. I heard her voice and I knew it, even though I asked in confusion, "Wisal?" Then my voice was cut off. No, the telephone line wasn't what was cut but rather my voice, as if I had returned to al-Furaydis and lost the power of speech. She filled the silence with words of welcome and with questions.

Abd al-Rahman took the receiver from me and said to Wisal, "Ruqayya is crying. I didn't know she loved you so much. I wanted to surprise her—she didn't know you were on the line, she didn't expect it. Okay, better next time. I'll call you tomorrow."

Where had all these tears been? My tears flowed for an hour or two. I would dry them, and dry them again. I would blow my nose and then dry my tears. Those who passed by in the Center didn't notice that a woman was crying in their colleague's office, or that the crying inside her, even though it was bound by silence, could have been raised to fill the ears of those passing in the street. I didn't notice that Abed had left the office until he came back carrying a box of tissues and a glass of water and a sheet of some pills. He gave me a pill and the glass of water and I took them from him.

He sat facing me in silence. Then I noticed my silence, and his, and my tears, and was filled with embarrassment. I wiped my face and got up. I said, "I'm sorry, Abed, I'm so sorry." I headed for the elevator. He followed me, and we got in together. As soon as the door shut he opened his arms wide and hugged me, hugged me strongly and kissed me. He wanted to take me home but I refused. What happened? I walked in the streets of Beirut, not knowing if I was headed for home or not. Was I walking or scurrying or running? I look back from afar: a woman of thirty-five walking as if she were running, or running strangely and sporadically, not going anywhere. Why? Does she want to flee from her story? From scenes that loomed unexpectedly from their place when Abed appeared days ago and when Wisal's voice followed him, so that the door that had been closed for years and chained with a large lock opened wide? How had an old, heavy door opened like that, without a sound or a squeak? It opened, and it all followed. Then the boy hugs her in the elevator, hugs her strongly, and she goes to him as if she had been waiting for years. What happened? She kissed him as he kissed her, why did he kiss her and why did she kiss him? She runs from the question, from herself, from Abed who had suddenly appeared to her in the form of a man, as if he were one of her brothers come back from the dead. And does a brother kiss his sister like this, on the lips? She was shaking like someone with a fever. She stopped suddenly on the street, and sat on the sidewalk. She sat for a few minutes or maybe an hour or two. When she calmed down a little she went toward the house.

The children were waiting, expecting their mother to be whole and complete. Here she is standing in the kitchen preparing lunch as if nothing had happened. Here she sits with them at the lunch table. They ask her why she's not eating. "My head hurts. I'll sleep." She sleeps, and at night she says to Amin, "Wisal called me from Jordan." The rest of it was on the tip of her tongue: "And Abd al-Rahman kissed me in the elevator," but she did not say it. Her tongue was tied, as if it had decided in her place not to say it.

What will I do about this kiss? Where will I go with it? I'll forget the whole thing completely, as if it never happened. I'll lose it intentionally, and it will be lost. I went to Wisal, I took refuge with her, just as she and her mother and little brother had taken refuge with us one faraway day. I barricaded myself behind her, concentrating on her voice. The voice seemed strong and painfully near. Who said that the telephone can connect us? It does not; it asserts the distance while forcing you to visualize what you know, and you visualize it now on your skin like a knife blade that touches a nerve, that cuts deeply into your living flesh. Her voice came to me close and clear and I was on the other side, like two women divided by a glass barrier, as if it were the barrier separating the prisoner from his visitor, or more precisely, separating one prisoner from another. So be it, I'll prepare and talk to her as she talked to me. I'll subdue the lump in my throat and control the tremor and my tears. Tomorrow.

But the following day I did not go to the Center where Abd al-Rahman works, and not on the day after that. I did not go and he did not come. When two weeks had passed without his appearing, Hasan began to ask about him. He took his telephone number and called him. He said, "Mama, I invited him to dinner tomorrow." I did not comment. I woke up at dawn as if I had set an alarm. The thought of him and his image and perhaps my fear of meeting him woke me. Can things go back to the way they were? How will we bring them back? He came promptly. I busied myself with preparing dinner, and he busied himself, or was busy with talking to Amin and the boys. I didn't speak to him directly or look at him, nor did he look at me. The evening passed safely. He no longer came to visit us unless Amin or one of the boys invited him. He no longer knocked on the door unannounced, laughing when it opened and saying, "The unwelcome guest has arrived."

One morning there was a knock on the door. I was cleaning the house, still wearing my nightgown. I opened the door, and Abed was standing there. He said, "I know Amin and the boys aren't at home. I wanted to tell you good morning, and to have a quick word with you." He remained standing at the door, and for a moment or two I stood staring at him, not knowing what the next step was. I laughed suddenly, and said, "Welcome, come in." I said, "One moment." I changed my clothes quickly and went to him. I said, "I'll make you a cup of coffee." The coffee boiled over, so I filled another small pot with water and added three spoons of ground coffee. I stood watching it. Why had Abed come? It boiled over again—had I ever made coffee before? He called from the living room, "Ruqayya, I won't stay long, I'll have a quick word with you and leave. The coffee boiled over, didn't it?" In a voice that surprised me by how loud it was I said, "It didn't boil over, I'll be with you in a minute." The third time. I fixed my eyes on the coffee pot and moved it a little away from the center of the flame. The coffee boiled up, and I poured two cups. I offered him one and then brought in my cup and sat on the facing seat. A sip, then with the second sip the cup spilled on me. I laughed to hide my embarrassment, and said, "I don't know what's come over me today." He laughed, and I laughed. Then we laughed more, and I got up to change my clothes again. When I returned he was standing, preparing to leave; he said, "I have to go to work." He leaned down a little and kissed my head, and went down the stairs with rapid steps. He did not look back.

16

Beirut (I)

My aunt says that two-thirds of a boy comes from his maternal uncle, repeating the popular saying when she suddenly notices a gesture or a look or a tone of voice in one of the boys that reminds her of her sister's two sons. She was right, Sadiq resembled Hasan, tall and broad like him. And Hasan resembled his uncle Sadiq, in the shape of his small body, the color of his eyes, his sweetness and calm. He seemed quiet and shy, compared to his big brother—traits he took from his uncle and from his father, since Amin was also like that. As for little Abed, he differed not because of his devilment, for which scolding and punishments were useless, but rather because of his shrewdness, his charm, and the ready answers always on his tongue. His answers would pull him out of any scrape as clean as a whistle, stir up laughter and let him preside over any discussion, even though he was the youngest. He was rambunctious and talkative and always on the move, tirelessly demanding attention. His grandmother would say, "He's a bastard, that one, he's a black sheep." Her attachment to the two oldest boys was obvious, Sadiq because he was the first grandchild to rejoice her, and Hasan because he was "steady and kind and affectionate." And Abed? She waved him away, scowling: "Devil take him, you're no better off with him than without him." He was also her declared foe: he would not answer her when she called him, then he would say, "I answered, by God I answered, what can I do, she's hard of hearing!" She would ask him to buy something from the market, and he would go and return. "Where, Abed . . . ?" "Ah . . . I forgot!" What had begun as little tricks and a childish retaliation for her preference for his two older brothers went on to set the tone of the relationship between them until she passed away.

When we moved from Sidon to Beirut in the fall of 1970, Sadiq had enrolled in the first year of his university studies, and Hasan was a student at the end of middle school. Two young men, one didn't need to fear for them. They read the papers and followed the news. We moved in September, when the battles between the fedayeen and King Hussein were in progress. The two boys would follow what was happening day by day, joining us in discussing and analyzing it and in our apprehensions and concern. As for little Abed, he was in elementary school and the news didn't hold much interest for him since he was busy with soccer, or with the slightly higher grade his rival in class had received. Did I say that Sadiq and Hasan were alert and that one didn't need to fear for them? I reconsider the second part of the expression. In the next year and the year that followed I became more worried about them. Sadiq would return to the house and I would know from his appearance that he had been in a demonstration. He did not say it but I knew, and sometimes from his pale face I thought it was likely that one young man or maybe more had been hit by army bullets. Or Hasan would return looking wan and quieter than usual, his stomach hurting. I would boil him some sage or mint but the pain would still be there. When his father returned he examined him and found nothing worrisome, but days later Sadiq told me what happened: "It was a physical reaction to something that happened. One of his classmates at school insulted the Palestinians and Abu Ammar, and said that his armed gangs deserve to be burned up. I told him that his stomach hurt him because he didn't hit the kid, 'If you had hit him he wouldn't have dared to repeat talk like that. Your answer stayed stuffed in your stomach, so it started hurting.' I told him, 'If anyone hits you, hit him, and if anyone humiliates you, wipe up the floor with him.'" I don't agree with Sadiq, for in the end school is not the place for hitting and fighting. I'm afraid of the army's bullets, of the militias and the Phalange and their evil intentions toward us. I'm afraid of a clash at school that would result in the boy coming home with his blood flowing. I'm afraid of Beirut. When I confide my fears to Amin he says, "We live far from their neighborhoods. And Abu Ammar is an ally of the national forces, and they are getting stronger every day. Not even the army will be able to keep up all this violence, the national forces have militias and we have the fedayeen. Don't be afraid."

Maybe because of this fear Amin suggested that I continue my education, or maybe he noticed that I was becoming more withdrawn and introverted. I didn't go out or meet any of the neighbors, and even Abed the elder no longer came to the house often; he came only rarely, and on special occasions.

At first I made light of the suggestion, perhaps because I was embarrassed at the thought of going back to school when I had had three children, the oldest of whom was in the university. What if I failed, what would the children say? Amin urged me, and then Sadiq and Hasan took his side. "Why not?" they said, "Try, you have nothing to lose, and besides, you can quit if you find it's hard."

I returned to books and notebooks. Instead of one teacher I had two, with Sadiq and Hasan helping me. Little Abed didn't like being excluded from the game, so he observed, "It would be better if Mama studied by herself, you aren't teachers, and a poor prof makes for a poor student!" Or the gleam in his eyes would say that he was enjoying the role reversal, and the transfer of the power of right and wrong from here to there. He laughed, and Sadiq asked him, in a tone tinged with rebuke, "Why are you laughing?"

Abed answered, "A funny thought occurred to me. Is it forbidden to laugh?"

I would wake at five in the morning, as usual, and plunge into housework until Amin and the boys woke up. We would have breakfast, and everyone would go on his way. I would spend the day studying until they came back. In the evening I would ask the "two teachers" about what was hard for me to understand.

Amin said that I was making astonishing progress, and that I would be able to take the baccalaureate examination in 1973. But I did not take it.

I had not known the writer Ghassan Kanafani personally, and I didn't follow what he wrote in the newspapers and magazines. I had never met Dr. Anis Sayegh, the historian and activist, no one had spoken to me about the three Fatah leaders in Verdun Street, nor had I heard any of their names—and if I had heard them I had forgotten them, because I didn't know the role of any of them or what his position was.

I had read one short story by Ghassan Kanafani that had fallen into my hands by chance, when we were in Sidon. I remember its title: "The Land of Sad Oranges." I didn't remember anything of the story other than one line, which read, "When we arrived in Sidon, in the evening, we became refugees." Who said that, and in what context? I don't remember. The expression kept ringing in my ears for days and nights, as if it were a line of poetry. I spoke to Ezzedin about the story and a week later he brought me a novel and said that it was the best of Ghassan's books. I read it in one night: a novel about three Palestinians, a boy, a young man, and an older man, trying to get to Kuwait smuggled in an empty water tanker. The border guard delays the truck and the three die of suffocation inside the tank. The driver delivered them to their death, even though he wanted to help them. The borders killed them. I didn't read anything else of Ghassan's, neither books nor articles, and I didn't follow the magazine where he was the editor in chief; but Ezz knew him personally and talked about him with great admiration. He said, "Do you believe it, Ruqayya, we were born in the same year, and he's a journalist who publishes his articles in any number of papers and magazines, he writes stories and novels, he draws, and he's active in political work, among the leaders of the organization!"

I remember the day clearly. It was a day in July. Beirut was like fire, and the humidity was suffocating. The boys went to Shatila to participate in a summer program. I said goodbye to them in the morning, repeating to them, "It's very hot today. Walk in the shade, and drink water whenever you can. Otherwise you'll get sunstroke."

After an hour or less young Abed rang the doorbell like a crazy person. He rang it continuously, as if he couldn't wait. When I opened it he burst inside the house, saying, "They've assassinated Kanafani. He left his house and got into his car, he turned the key and the car blew up with him and his niece inside."

He circled through the house like a hyena, twice, then I heard the door slam, shaking the house, and I ran after him, calling. He must have heard me since I could hear his steps rapidly going down the stairs, but he didn't answer. I shut the door and sat motionless on a chair.

Eleven days later I heard the news of the attempted assassination of Anis Sayegh. I had seen him only in my imagination, for the older Abed would describe him to me when he talked about his work at the Center. I knew he was a great scholar, stern in his work, precise, demanding excellence from all the researchers who worked with him. He was a man of small build, short and rounded, bald, with penetrating eyes in which kindness mixed with intelligence. That's how Abed described him to me.

When I heard the news of the explosion in the Research Center I found myself running in the street. I stopped a taxi and said, "Sadat Street." The movement of the car seemed slow to me, because of the traffic, and I asked the driver to stop. I got out and started running. I was afflicted with temporary insanity, because as I was running I was talking to my brothers, saying "Leave him. Why do you want him with you? Go away, now, I beg you." At first I said it calmly, then like someone bereaved, and then I was shouting at them in a loud voice. When I got to the Center I was told that the young men had taken Dr. Anis to the emergency room in the American University Hospital. I asked, "And the others?" They assured me that no one else had been hit. I repeated the question, and they confirmed the answer. I ran down to the street. Another taxi. In the hospital I found Abed, his face blue and the look in his eyes distraught. He said, "He's still alive. The doctors are operating on him. He was hit in the face, in his eyes and ears and left hand. Go home, I'll call later to reassure you." I remained sitting.

In the evening one of the three doctors announced that he had been forced to amputate three of the fingers on the left hand. The two others said that they had done everything they could for the eyes and the ears. "We might be able to preserve some of his sight and hearing." They asked the young men to leave. His father the priest remained, an old man who never stopped praying in whispers, along with two of his siblings, his sister and brother.

"Let's go, Ruqayya," said Abed. We left the hospital. He took me to the door of the house and went on.

I didn't run into the streets the day of the Israeli operation in Verdun Street, nor did my brothers appear for me to argue with, chasing them away like flies, because when the news was announced the next day, the town was boiling over. It was as if hundreds of thousands of people had been transformed overnight into a single body, the body of a fantastic animal, great and awe-inspiring, proceeding deliberately with steps that shook the earth. I saw that with my own eyes in the funeral of Ghassan Kanafani in July. Then later, nine months afterward, in the funeral of Kamal Nasser and Abu Yusuf al-Najjar and Kamal Udwan, the Fatah leaders killed in their homes by Israeli commandos, I saw it again and understood what I had not completely understood the first time.

I look from afar. A woman went out with her husband, her three children, her uncle, her cousin and his wife, the brother who wasn't born of her mother, the spirits of her mother and father and her brothers who stayed there in the unmarked mass grave, all the friends and neighbors she knows here and countless people she doesn't know, the march stretching out over several miles. They bid farewell to a young man who fell to an assassin before his time. They walk to the Martyrs' Cemetery. They notice, or not, his wife and two children: a boy and a girl, the oldest a boy of ten lifted on someone's shoulders. He shouts and his voice is drowned in the voices of hundreds of thousands. The woman looks behind her, seeing the wave surge and heave. She looks ahead, and she sees it. She looks to her right and left, staring into the faces of her children. She sees them clearly, perfectly, as if memory had not enfolded them and the moment had not passed long before. She looks closely: Sadiq narrows his eyes as if he wanted to protect them from the sun; his voice roars in a shout that he emphasizes with a movement of his arm and fist. Hasan is silent like her, his features working as if his face had become a mirror, reflecting the wave on its surface. As for Abed, she barely recognizes his face—why has it lengthened like that, the eyes rounding and the mouth open in the picture of a scream, without any sound? She wonders if it's possible to read the future in the faces of boys walking in a funeral.

I look from afar. A woman goes out with her husband, her three children, her uncle, her cousin and his wife, the brother who wasn't born of her mother, the spirits of her mother and father and her brothers who stayed there in the unmarked mass grave, all the friends and neighbors she knows here and countless people she doesn't know, the march stretching out over several miles. They bid farewell to four martyrs, three men and a woman who were killed in their bedrooms in Verdun Street. They walk to the Martyrs' Cemetery. The woman looks behind her, seeing the wave surge and heave. She looks ahead, and she sees it. She looks to her right and left. The funeral is not a funeral and the mourning is not mourning.

I look from afar, contemplating the woman. She's thirty-seven. She was slow to learn the lesson, slow. It's astonishing, and strange; it brings a smile to her lips, a little sad but holding a great deal of gratitude. The site of the lesson, the funeral; the topic of the lesson, life. She accepts the funeral, and she gives herself to life.

17

The Trees of Shatila

THE BEE IS A GOOD image. Yes, I became a bee. I would do the cooking and prepare breakfast. Amin and the boys would wake up, and I would feed them. They would go about their business. I would wash the dishes, straighten the house, and leave for Shatila, not returning until late afternoon. Every day had its schedule. There were literacy lessons for the adults, tutoring sessions for the elementary children. Statements to copy on the typewriter, when the young men brought them to me. And visits, no weekly schedule and sometimes no daily one was without them. Women whose homes I entered for the first time or whom I had met previously, whom it was necessary to visit for condolences or congratulations or perhaps to solve a family problem about which they had approached me. I came to know the lanes and neighborhoods of the camp by the houses piled one on top of the other; mostly they belonged to families from villages in Upper Galilee, who had come as a group to south Lebanon and then later had moved to Shatila. They came from Majd al-Kurum and Safsaf and al-Birwa and Deir al-Qasi and Saasaa and al-Khalisa and elsewhere. I didn't meet anyone from Tantoura in Shatila. I asked once or twice and then no more, held back by shyness. The women of the camp became pregnant seven times, or ten, or sometimes more; whoever perished, perished, and one or two boys would remain, and if they were lucky, three. Why had my mother had only two boys? They perished, and she had no one left.

This kind of question hadn't crossed my mind before I started going to Shatila. In Sidon I had been busy with childbearing and tending the little ones. I hadn't gone to Ain al-Helwa, except for limited visits to Karima's family, when congratulations or condolences were called for. By the time Ezz moved to live in Ain al-Helwa we were already living in Beirut.

I did not take the baccalaureate exam as Amin and the boys wanted, nor did I enroll in the university. I learned in the camp.

There I acquired a new extended family—children, girls, women of my own age, elderly women, each of them with the key of her house hung on a cord around her neck, like my mother. In Shatila I learned that the world of women is more compassionate than the world of men. The men were formed into factions, each with its office and territory and armed young men. They differed and quarreled like cocks. Oh my God, cocks with weapons! And cocks at home, too; they came back to their women and issued orders and prohibitions. The woman is plunged into her daily chores: She picks through the lentils and the rice. She makes mujaddara lentils for seven or ten or fifteen people. She rolls grape leaves and stuffs squash. She bakes the bread on the baking sheet. She makes labneh from milk. She puts up olives. She puts her shawl back on and goes to congratulate or share condolences. She puts the shawl back on and takes one of the grandchildren to the medical center or the hospital, because his mother is in bed, only three days have passed since she gave birth. She hurries back to serve the lunch she's cooked. She washes piles of clothes, clothes without end. She complains about her stubborn youngest daughter, who insists on continuing her studies and on working with the fedayeen.

"What's wrong with her being with the fedayeen, Auntie?"

"Am I against the fedayeen? I support them with all my heart, as God is my witness. The day the Second Bureau left and the fedayeen entered the camp, I danced and clapped

with the others and sang and trilled. The whole camp was
celebrating, the sound of the bullets in the air made it seem
like a hundred weddings, not just one. God comfort them and
protect them and bless them, the fedayeen, God guide them
and calm their spirits, so they don't draw their weapons on
each other every time a jug knocks against a jar! I'd do anything for the fedayeen. But that girl leaves in the morning and
doesn't come back until evening, saying she's getting weapons
training. For God's sake, use your head, girl!"

She leaned toward me and began to talk in whispers.

"Just between you and me, Sitt Ruqayya, don't tell anyone
else. Our neighbor saw her twice standing with the same boy.
I asked her, 'What's going on?' and she said, 'He's my comrade in the organization.' I said, 'Comrade or not, don't keep
standing with him, it's not right. If he's hanging around you,
let him propose, and we'll ask about him. What's his family?'
She laughed and said that she wasn't thinking about getting
married, and he wasn't thinking about it either. I said, 'Then
don't spend a lot of time with him, so people start talking
about how you're behaving.'"

She looked at me and raised her voice a little, "Anything
but honor, Sitt Ruqayya!"

Then she went back to whispering: "She stands with the boy
and people put two and two together, someone says something
and the next day there's talk. The girl's nineteen and says she's
not thinking about getting married! At her age I already had a
boy and a girl and I was pregnant with the third."

"Times change, Auntie."

It was a different time. Was that good? At the time it seemed
so, to me. I would look and see a certain confidence or hope or
perhaps strength in the faces, in the posture of the young men
and the girls, in their walk and way of sitting, in the way their
hands moved in spontaneous gestures, in the tilt of the head
when they nodded. It was in their laughter, in the tone of their
voices when they discussed events, in their looks. I would speak

with them, but I would make an effort to meet the elderly women of the camp. I love to listen to their stories, even if they're sad at first, because the stories always began with "there," with what happened when "they took over the village and threw us out and we fled to Lebanon." The story moves on, but sometimes not completely, because as it advances in time it goes back, and remembers. The stories resemble each other but also differ, like the faces that tell them.

The face of Umm Nabil lights up as she talks about the pomegranate tree "that you'll find on your right when you're heading for the door of the house." She describes its height, the shape of its branches and the green of its leaves at first, and then later, when it's covered by them and when it flowers. When Umm Nabil comes to the fruit she doesn't talk about it, she simply stretches out her hand and picks it and opens it, spreading the seeds before your eyes so that you see their crimson red, which somehow moves from her hands to your tongue, so you taste its tangy sweetness.

It's strange, every woman is a tree. I mean, every woman has a tree, there. The lemon tree of Umm Samir; the orange tree of Umm Ilyas; the carob of Umm Haniya; the almond of Umm Abed; the palm of Umm al-Nahid; the blackberry of Umm Muhammad; the fig of Umm Sabah, "the figs were the green kind, their sweetness would entice the birds, and they would perch on it and peck the fruit before dawn." Her face lights up and then darkens, because the story is coming to the part that's hard to tell, or the harder part that can't be told. Then her face lights up again, because, "Our Lord consoled me and the kids' father found work," or "We bought a cow and began to sell the milk and nourish the little ones," or "The girl graduated and began working," or "The boy went to the Gulf and began to send home part of his salary on the first of the month," or because "At the worst of the trials and the tribulations, with barely a bite to eat, we turned the corner, yes, by God, we turned the corner."

Umm Ilyas tells us: "The bastards, four months before they threw us out they occupied the village farmland, which was to the west of us. They set up ditches and military centers, and the village was separated from its lands. We were on one side and our fields were on the other. Then the harvest season came; we said, "The crops will spoil, what should we do?""

"First the young men scouted them, so we knew the position of their lines, where they were and when their patrols passed. At night they passed the farms but on the paved road, going in cars. We knew that, and put our trust in God. Every night we would wait for sunset and then sneak across the valley, going in a roundabout way that took us to our fields. We would go in groups of ten, men and women and boys and girls. We would go through the valley like ghosts, without any light or noise or even a breath, until we got to our land and gathered what we could of the tobacco crop; and at daybreak or a little later we would cross the valley coming back. Sometimes the young men keeping watch on the hill for our security would sense danger, and distract their soldiers by firing on them; they would answer the fire and not notice us as we passed beneath them in the valley, hearing the bullets whistling over our heads."

Umm al-Nahid told a similar story, though the planting was wheat rather than tobacco: "When they took over the village we fled to the neighboring villages, in the hope that the Arab Liberation Army, which was camped a few kilometers away, would help us. When May was over and June came, we said that the crops would die on their stalks; we didn't have much left and our children were hungry. We said, 'We'll face them, come what may.' The news spread to the neighboring villages and the young men came to help us. They set out; some carried a rifle and those who didn't have them armed themselves with sticks or knives. '*Allahu akbar, Allahu akbar*,' and they attacked. The Jews were frightened and fled." Umm al-Nahid laughed. "The wheat was harvested and in sacks. They saw the young men attacking and heard the voices, so they left the bags and fled. They left three machine guns on the land, set up on stands and aimed at us. And seven reapers, big machines they used to reap our wheat. When our men entered the village, before they inspected the houses they wanted to make sure that none of them were still there, so they headed for the houses of Abed Darwish and Ahmad Ismail Saad, which they had turned into their headquarters. They didn't find any of them; they found the tea still hot and poured into cups, and they found quantities of coffee and sugar and canned goods, and cardboard boxes, the whole courtyard was boxes. They opened them, and what did they find? The bastards had collected what they could carry from the town and packed it into boxes—our clothes and our men's clothes and our kids' clothes, and excuse me, Sitt Ruqayya, even the underwear! And the blankets and towels and sheets and pillows. The men began slapping one hand with the other and saying, 'Good God, it's not enough to steal the land and the crops, they even want the clothes we're wearing and the blankets we wrap up in!' Believe me, Sitt Ruqayya, they didn't even leave a sieve—there was one box with the sieves they had gathered from the houses. Were they going to sell them? To give them to the people of the 'company'? To give them to the Jewish Agency? God only knows. Anyway, the men decided to leave the boxes as they were temporarily. Every one took a bag of wheat to the village where his family was. They gave us the wheat to grind so we could feed the little ones, and went back to the village because they decided to secure it before they came back to us. Two days, and on the third about a hundred soldiers from the Arab Liberation Army arrived. They said that they would take over protecting the village and asked us to evacuate it, because they expected heavy shelling. The men left the village and came back to us. Two days later the battle began, the Jews shelling from their positions on the west and the Liberation Army answering them from the village and the surrounding area. Then the Liberation Army withdrew and the village fell. The Jews attacked the neighboring villages and we fled to Lebanon. Afterward Abul Nahid and three others went back to find out what happened to our houses. Abul Nahid had hidden twenty liras under the palm tree. They arrested them and put them in prison; when they let them go they loaded them into a truck with twenty other prisoners from other villages. They blindfolded them and set them down at the border crossing to Lebanon. They said, 'Run there, anyone who looks back will be killed.' They took off running with the Jews firing on them. God have mercy on them all. Abul Nahid and two others who went with him were martyred. The third is the one who told me."

When I listen I'm no longer outside of the train. I don't jump inside it, because the train I used to express our situation has disappeared. The earth becomes rounded like an embrace, an irony I do not understand and which confuses me, because the elderly women were telling the stories of the theft of the land and of those they lost among their families and children. They also talk about the camp in the beginning: the tents they weighted with stones so they would not fly away, the zinc roofs, standing in lines for water, the fist of the Second Bureau and its agents, and "It's prohibited for you to visit each other in the evening, it's prohibited to sit in front of your houses, it's prohibited, it's prohibited . . . ." They recall their fears the day they heard that the government intended to drive the people out of Shatila and destroy the camp; the day when talk circulated about building a high wall around the camp, because it didn't look right in Beirut or for the tourists, who wanted to enjoy the city's beauty; the day when the army encircled the camp and began to fire on it for no known reason. The story reassures me, in some strange and wondrous way I can't understand.

Umm Muhammad laughs as she tells the story of enrolling her second son in the camp school the year following their arrival. She says, "He was four years old, and he looked younger than his age. He was very articulate, no one better. He got up in the morning and asked, 'Where's Muhammad?' 'He went to school.' 'Why didn't you wake me to go with him? Where's the school?' I didn't tell him; he was angry and he left the house. He kept asking until he found the school. It was one room, originally a bath, and the teacher was a patient young man. He saw a barefoot boy about as high as a hand span and a half coming in, and he asked him, 'Where are you going?' He pointed to his brother and said, 'To Muhammad. I'm his brother. My name is Said, I was born on Laylat al-Qadr so they named me Said, 'Fortunate,' but my grandma calls me Mabrouk, "Blessed."'" The teacher laughed and said, 'Go home, Said, and come back tomorrow with your father and your papers, and we'll register you in the school.' He said to him, 'My father leaves the house at dawn because he's a baker and doesn't come back before night, when I'm fast asleep. What should I do? Friday, before prayers, I'll bring him with me.' 'School is closed on Friday.' 'Why is it closed? Open it so my father can come. Anyway what do you want with my father? Is he the one who wants to go to school or me?' 'He has to bring your birth certificate and sign the application for you to go to school.' 'Can I sign?' 'Do you know how to write your name?' 'Not even my father can sign his name. He stamps his finger. Give me the blue ink and I'll stamp for you!' The teacher laughed, and said to him, 'Instead of your father, bring your mother and the papers, and we'll register you in school. And put on shoes or sandals; boys in the school must . . .' Said interrupted, 'But Muhammad is wearing the shoes!' 'Okay. Go home, and tomorrow we'll have a chair for you to sit on. How can you learn when you're standing?' Said said, 'There's room.' In the back of the class there was a sink without any water in it and without a faucet. Said went straight over to it and jumped up and sat in it, cross-legged. He said to the teacher, 'I'm comfortable here. Please go on with school, however you like.'"

Umm Muhammad laughed, and her pleasant face became rosier and her full breasts shook. She raised the edge of her sleeve and wiped a tear that had escaped her eye. She said, "See how it was fate, Sitt Ruqayya. He went further in school than Muhammad, the older one. He completed elementary school and middle school and high school, going to school in the morning and working in the evening. He went to the university and graduated and got a job, thank God."

18

Family Concerns

MY AUNT DID NOT FORGIVE the woman from Saffurya for two things. The first, as she said, was that "The girl from Saffurya wasn't satisfied until she dragged your cousin to the camp, to her family." She did not believe Ezz, who told her time and again that the move to Ain al-Helwa was his idea and that his wife had not suggested it, because the school where he taught was there, and because he had to stay in the camp until late at night because of his work with the young men, telling her that "Living in Ain al-Helwa is more convenient for me." But Umm Amin did not believe him; and that was connected to the second reason, which my aunt would hint at, with sneers and innuendoes. Finally she stated it frankly, and Ezz said to her, "We went to the doctor, Mother. I have a problem. I'm thankful that she's going to stay with me, even though I can't give her any children."

When my aunt heard that, her distress and anxiety grew. She said, "That's unbelievable, unreasonable. It has never happened to any of the men of the family."

"We've gone to the doctor, Mother, and he confirmed that it's my problem."

"Go to a different doctor. For sure the doctor you consulted was from her community, and they agreed with him that he would say that."

Then she changed her mind, "But why go? I'll look for a bride for you and in a month or two you'll know you're fine. Your wife will get pregnant and in nine months you'll have a son."

Ezz laughed, and said, "What do you say we go together to the doctor of your choice, so you can hear from him in person that your son can't have children?"

At that point my aunt decided there was no use talking, even if she didn't say that to her son, because the girl had bewitched him. She had tied him to her, and he wouldn't leave her and would end up "with no family of his own." She turned it over to God, although that didn't prevent her from calling on him to witness what the girl from Saffurya had done to her and her son.

We would go to Sidon on the weekend, Amin driving us in his Renault. The boys loved Sidon. Hasan was the one who was most attached to the city, saying that he loved its smell, the narrow lanes of the old city and its architecture, the gardens stretching around it, and the sea. He would say, "In Beirut we barely notice the smell of the sea. Here the smell of the sea is clear and sharp, it mixes with the scent of the orange blossoms." Hasan loved the scent of orange blossoms. When they were in season he couldn't wait for the weekend, he would come home from school and say, "I miss my grandfather, I'm going to Sidon." "And your homework?" "I'll do it when I get back." I know he wasn't lying and that he really did miss his grandfather, but why did he miss him more during the season of the orange blossoms? An hour going and an hour coming, then an hour or two there, and when he came back he would have to stay up late to finish his homework, not finishing sometimes until morning.

When the family went to Sidon to spend the weekend or to stay with my aunt and uncle during the summer vacation, Hasan would go out for an hour or two and then come back to be with his grandfather. He never tired of listening to his stories. Sadiq and Abed were different, no sooner did they arrive in Sidon than each was off looking for his friends, and we would barely see them before bedtime. When we went back to Beirut and my aunt and uncle would say goodbye, my aunt would say what she always did at the end of every visit, "What's your rush, Amin, why do you need to work in Beirut? Come back and work in Sidon. We'll all be together, and you might be able to convince Ezz to come home, instead of living there among strangers, in the camp."

On the way home, Hasan repeats his grandmother's words. He doesn't understand the reason for leaving Sidon, and he pesters his father to reconsider our living in Beirut. I glimpse sly smiles in Sadiq's and Abed's eyes; years later, only years later, would I understand why they were smiling.

While we're in Sidon Ezz complains about my uncle Abu Amin's behavior; the matter of his participating in demonstrations has become a source of tension in the house. "Because you're no longer young, Papa. In one of these demonstrations you'll be killed by the army's bullets. You can't run when they fire on us. Consider me your representative, all the young men represent you." It's no use talking. My uncle doesn't confine himself to participating in demonstrations starting from Bab al-Sarail Square in old Sidon or from Ain al-Helwa, rather he travels from town to town, "Because it's a duty."

The army decided to close down the Fatah office in al-Khiyam. My uncle declared, "I'm going to al-Khiyam."

"The army has set up checkpoints and barriers all along the way, how will you go?"

"How can I not go? The people of al-Khiyam are demonstrating for our sake, should we just watch? Besides, I know roundabout ways that will avoid the checkpoints; I'll show them to the driver."

The scene would be repeated in later years, Ezz's words and my uncle's answer. Ezz would speak and my uncle would stubbornly take a taxi and set off for the demonstration in Tyre, or al-Khiyam, or Nabatiyeh, or Bint Jbeil, or al-Rashidiya. Even when Imam Musa al-Sadr organized a demonstration a year before my uncle died, in which nearly 100,000 people participated to demand political reform and arming the residents of the border villages, my uncle could not be convinced that the demonstration was for the Shii residents of the southern villages. He answered Ezz, "For shame! They did not fail us, how can we fail them?"

Demonstrations became part of my uncle's weekly schedule, and worry became a fixture on Ezz's schedule. He complained, "He'll die by an army bullet in one of these demonstrations. He has constant pain in his knees. He won't be able to run and avoid the bullets. God, my heart nearly stopped the day of the protest demonstration against the siege of the fedayeen in Kfar Kila. The bullets from the army were like rain, the demonstrators were falling by the dozen, killed and wounded, and I was worried about Abu Amin, and Abu Amin was completely oblivious, he was at the head of the demonstration shouting as if he were twenty. It came out okay. But he was five years younger, now he's over seventy and I don't know how to keep him from going."

Ezz laughed bitterly. "They'll kill him. What can I do, imprison him in the house? Tie him to the foot of the bed?"

My uncle did not die by an army bullet in a demonstration. He was not hit, unlike dozens of young men who were better able to run and maneuver. Ezz was not obliged to imprison him in the house or tie him to the bed; illness forced him to stay in bed. He would ask my aunt to call me on the telephone in Beirut three or sometimes four times a day. He would say, "How are you, Ruqayya? I wanted to hear your voice."

I would speak to him for two or three minutes and then he would give the receiver to my aunt.

I decided to go to live with him for a while.

I sat down with Sadiq and Hasan and Abed, and told them that I would stay in Sidon a week or two or three, or maybe more, until my uncle got better. Abed protested, "He has my grandmother and my uncle Ezz and his wife. We need you too!"

Sadiq commented, mocking him, "Abed needs to nurse every three hours, how can you, he won't be able to bear it!"

Abed hit him on the shoulder and said, without smiling, "Ha, ha, ha, you're really funny!"

I scolded them both.

Hasan said, "Don't worry, we'll manage."

I said, "Hasan knows how to prepare a quick meal for you. If you could, Hasan, or you could buy them something to eat. Sadiq is responsible for straightening the house and Abed will wash the dishes."

"Every day?"

"Yes, every day! Because Sadiq will straighten the house every day and Hasan will take care of the food every day!"

Abed said, "And the wash?"

"Bring it on the weekend and I'll do the washing and ironing."

"Why aren't you giving Papa any job? That's discrimination."

"You should be ashamed of yourself. Your father works in the hospital from daybreak until night."

Abed went back to his grumbling. "We'll die of hunger. We'll live for two weeks on macaroni and rice and eggs and fried tomatoes? Hasan doesn't know anything else."

"Enough, Abed, you're fifteen years old. You are to cease all this childish nagging and listen to Sadiq and Hasan."

"On top of everything!"

"And if I hear that you quarreled with either of them I'll stop speaking to you!"

"As if I were Israel!"

"I'm not joking."

"Okay, but I have a condition. . . ," he corrected himself, "Two conditions: When we come to Sidon on the weekend you'll make me maqlouba once and musakhan once and kubbeh bi-laban once."

"Agreed. And the other condition?"

"You'll make us thyme tarts and spinach tarts and kubbeh to bring back with us when we return to Beirut."

"Agreed."

"Every week."

I laughed, and so did Sadiq and Hasan. Abed looked at his brothers and said, smiling proudly, "Learn the art of negotiation. I've secured tarts and kubbeh for you that will help us on the days of famine and culinary catastrophe produced by Chef Hasan!"

19

1975

AMIN AND THE BOYS WERE not able to come to Sidon the next weekend nor the following one. The roads were blocked between Beirut and Sidon. Automobile traffic stopped, and strikes, demonstrations, and fires spread through the streets of Beirut, Tripoli, Tyre, and other cities. In Sidon dozens fell in clashes between the civilians and the army. The battles continued for five days and stopped only after the withdrawal of the army from the city—a short truce that allowed the civilians to bury their martyrs, count their wounded, inspect the damage to their houses, and gather the information coming from the hospital in Beirut.

The previous Wednesday had seemed like an ordinary day, cloudy and laden with rain. In Sidon there was a demonstration; nothing new. The people of Sidon often demonstrated to express their opinions.

The populist political leader Maarouf Saad was at the head of the demonstration, as usual, with Dr. Nazih Bizri, Sidon's representative in Parliament. It was a demonstration for needy fishermen against the government, which had granted a monopoly on fishing for ninety days at the height of the fishing season to a private company belonging to powerful men and headed by Camille Chamoun, the previous president of the republic. Rain was pouring down, and the demonstrators were few. Then a single bullet flew, seeking Saad. He was hit. They took him to the hospital of Dr. Labib Abu Zahr, and in the afternoon transferred him to Beirut. It was said he had suffered bleeding and a sharp drop in blood pressure.

Sidon ignited, Lebanon blazed.

My aunt stayed long at her prayers because she was beseeching God to heal Maarouf and return him to his home and family safe and sound. "O Omnipotent, O Generous, O Kind, O Merciful, O Compassionate." I was overcome by silence, silence steeped in clear, heavy fear; and my talkative uncle was suddenly silent, like me. He stayed in bed and kept his eyes shut, so we didn't know if he was awake or asleep. My aunt would call to him, "Are you awake, Abu Amin?" and he would answer her with a sigh, without opening his eyes.

On Thursday, March 6, nine days after being struck, Maarouf became a martyr.

The news spread before it was broadcast officially. It was said that the government was waiting for his body to be taken to Sidon before announcing the news, but it reached people in the south and they marched toward Beirut. They met the body halfway and continued on behind it, returning to Sidon, where the funeral was held the next day in the Great Mosque of Umar.

I went to the funeral. I hadn't advanced a single step into the house on my return or even closed the door behind me when I heard my uncle calling me: "Come here, Ruqayya."

"I'm coming, Uncle."

"How was the funeral?"

"All of Sidon was there. The leaders of the National Movement came from Beirut, and thousands of civilians and delegations from the south and the Beqaa and Jebel al-Shouf and Beirut and Tripoli. They carried his bier in a fishing boat; the fishermen carried a boat draped in black and filled with flowers. The young men carried pictures of him and signs saying "Hero of the Battle of al-Malikiya" and "Martyred for the Poor" and slogans of the Lebanese National Forces, of the Palestinian resistance groups, and of the delegations that came from the Arab states. The men were crying and shouting, and the women were crying and trilling and scattering rose petals and basil leaves and orange blossom water."

My uncle suddenly sighed, and said, "Our hope lies in the youth. I'm going to sleep."

I called Beirut, and found only Hasan at home. He said that the funeral in Beirut was very large. They carried a symbolic bier from the Mosque of Umar to the Martyrs' Cemetery, and there were processions and parades and symbolic funerals in many various places.

"Was there gunfire?"

"Gunfire and anthems and loudspeakers broadcasting stirring words and speeches."

"When your father and Sadiq and Abed get back call me, even if it's late. I won't be asleep."

From that Friday to the next my uncle Abu Amin kept silent. My aunt said that maybe he had lost the ability to speak. She would sit next to him on the bed, talking to him and asking him questions, and he would not answer. When she insisted he would reply by a terse expression, and then close his eyes and turn his back to her as if he was going to sleep. But when Amin and the boys came on the next Friday night he greeted them and told them that he wanted to talk to them. He said, "Tomorrow, if we live."

In the morning my uncle asked me to help him change his clothes. I took him a basin of warm water, soap, a small jug, and a towel, and I helped him wash and change his clothes. He had breakfast and then asked that I make him a cup of coffee. He drank it and said, "Call the boys."

They sat around him, and he said, "I want to tell you something."

I glimpsed a smile starting on Abed's face, and for a moment it seemed to me that the boy would be silly enough to say that there was no need, because we know it. I scolded him with a look; he received the message and kept silent.

My uncle began to speak about Maarouf Saad. He said, "I met him for the first time in '35 when he was teaching in Madrasat al-Burj in Haifa. For two years he was teaching and participating with us in the armed resistance. He would go back to Lebanon on Thursdays and Fridays and during the summer vacation to share in implementing the boycott decisions, and to work with the youth here in the south to prevent the export of fruits and vegetables over the Palestinian–Lebanese borders, to the settlers and the occupying British authorities. They would wait for the trucks coming from Beirut at the Awali River or in Tyre or Nabatiyeh or Marjayoun, blocking the roads. They would make the driver get out and would throw out the cartons of fruits and vegetables."

Strange, by God it was strange. My uncle talked two or three hours, or maybe four. He gathered the beads of his words from here and there, stringing them before our eyes like a rosary. He specified the place and the time, moving from one time to another and from place to place, from a well-known date to personal events he had witnessed and in which he played a part. He would mention the leaders and commanders, "May God not forgive them," and his companions, "God have mercy on the martyrs." He would visualize their images and leave them hanging on the wall in the background of his words. He continued speaking.

I said to myself, my uncle will live a thousand years. He'll recover from his illness and be just fine.

Suddenly Hasan said, "Rest a little, Grandfather. Rest now and in the evening you'll finish the story for us."

He said, "The time for rest has passed, Hasan. Listen, boy, listen. Maybe you'll tell the story one day to your children."

I imagined I saw tears in Hasan's eyes. I looked, and then averted my eyes, and listened like the others.

In our country they call it "sweetness of the spirit," the last outpouring of energy. I had heard the expression often, thinking that I understood it; but I did not understand it before that day.

After Amin and the boys returned to Beirut, my uncle spoke to me only of Tantoura and his father and mother and brother. He told me long stories of his childhood, with abundant details. He ended only by recalling the day he differed with his brother about leaving, the day he returned from Sidon to take the women and children and his brother drew a weapon on him. He said, "You were with us, Ruqayya, you saw it. Have you forgotten?" I said, "I have not forgotten, Uncle." But he repeated for me everything that happened, as if I had told him that I had forgotten. He would always end his words with the same expression, "My brother didn't understand me. He was angry with me and left before I bade him farewell. Whenever I sneaked back into the village, I visited my mother's and father's grave, but I didn't know where his grave was, to propitiate him and make peace with him."

My uncle cried, so I moved from my seat to sit near him on the bed. I rubbed his shoulder and calmed him.

Then he passed.

Years later Ezz would say to me, "It seems to me sometimes that Abu Amin knew by intuition or inspiration that he could not bear the terror of the coming days. Would he have been able to bear it, Ruqayya, 'Free Lebanon' dependent on the Israelis? Would he have been able to bear the siege of Tall al-Zaatar and the alliance of Syria and the Phalange? Did he realize that Arafat's group and Amal would fight each other in the south, or that Amal would lay siege to the camps? It's as if he knew intuitively, and said to himself: 'Your time has ended, so go with your friends and your contemporaries.'"

20

The Spring

I KNOW MY AUNT MAYBE better than I know myself. As soon as she moved in with us in Beirut, I told her that I was exhausted from the housework. I suggested she take over the kitchen. She refused at first, and then accepted. I was sure that this was the first step to make her feel that she was in her home, and not a guest.

Abed protested, "I don't like Grandma's cooking."

I chided him. He said, "Everyone has certain likes or dislikes, it comes from God."

Sadiq laughed loudly, "Abed has become a philosopher!"

The boy went on, "Mother, you love the scent of wild lilies, right? And Hasan loves the scent of orange blossoms, no one can deny it! Uncle Ezz loves mulukhiya, so you make him mulukhiya. I don't like Grandma's cooking! Should I die of hunger or force myself to accept what I hate?"

I said firmly, "You'll get used to her cooking, and when you get used to it, you'll like it! If you don't want to eat her food, you're free not to. Die of hunger. You have olive oil and thyme, or let salt be your supper. Do what you like! The discussion is over."

The battles in the house intensified, and blazed up all the more because we were forced to put the three boys in one room, to empty a room for my aunt. Since the room could not take three beds, in addition to the two desks where Sadiq and Hasan studied, we commissioned a carpenter to make a bunk bed. When the new bed arrived, Abed decided he wanted the top bunk; he liked the idea of climbing the wooden ladder to his bed, and the possibility of looking down on his brother from above, as if he were the older. A week later he said that his knees hurt him from climbing up and down, and that he preferred the lower bunk; since Hasan shared the bed with him, he gave up his place to him calmly. After a few days Abed began complaining about the bed again.

"I get nightmares when I'm asleep, the whole time I feel as if Hasan is going to fall on my head and I'll die. Besides, he farts in his sleep. The smell hits my nose directly, as if it were aimed at me intentionally. Anyway, how can you expect me to get A's when I don't have a desk? The desk is in Grandma's room, and she goes to bed with the birds after the evening prayer, so I sit at the dining table, or in the kitchen. If I fail, it's your fault."

The problems of the bed and the desk, which came up whenever the question of "my room, which Grandma is occupying" arose, did not go beyond our circle to reach my aunt. But the enmity in dozens of other instances was open and acknowledged, and like a vicious circle. Abed would behave badly with his grandmother and I would chide him and punish him, so he would attribute the punishment to his grandma and mutter that she was "an ill-omened old woman who brought us nothing but upset stomachs and bad moods." I would pretend that I hadn't heard him, because acknowledging that I had meant another round of scolding, calling to account, and punishment.

Sadiq said laughing, commenting on the situation, "Abed isn't satisfied with the civil war we're living with in the streets, he's decided that we should live with it at home." He used English for emphasis: "A 'super' war outside and a 'mini' war at home!"

Abed was annoyed by his words. "I am not starting wars. Your grandmother is old and it's hard to get along with her, and besides, she's occupying my room!"

"You're like the Phalange, you create a disaster and then you're the first one to cry 'They attacked me!'"

What happened? Abed seized his brother by the collar and screamed at him like a crazy man. "Don't compare me to the Phalange! How can you compare me to the Phalange? By God, by God, if you weren't my brother I'd kill you!" Sadiq pushed him away and knocked him down; Hasan separated them, shouting. I entered the room to find Sadiq kneeling above his brother. I quarreled with Sadiq and Abed for a full week. Sadiq would walk behind me in the house, saying "Why are you angry with me? I'm the elder and he attacked me." I would say, "Because you are the elder you ought to have behaved better." He tried to appease me; as for Abed, he decided that everyone in the house was allied against him, even Hasan: "He told the story wrong, he claims to be neutral and there's no such thing as neutrality!"

Were there other sides to Abed, or was the difference between him and his brothers that he was at the height of adolescence, and he was unable to hide the turmoil that we all hid? I did not understand him, I didn't understand his foolish little wars nor his need to create problems. I look back from afar and feel that tickling that I first felt the day that Sadiq was born. Because he's far away? Because he has become a handsome man, despite the torment he's endured? Because I've understood, if only recently, that the boy didn't know what to do with himself, with the wrath inside him? His manhood was in its tender, green beginnings, asking him if being a man required him to bear arms and kill.

Sadiq commented, "You can't confuse the younger and the older. The proper positions must be maintained, just like sizes!"

Hasan answered, "With the exception of shoe sizes!"

Sadiq said, looking slyly at Abed, "If the measure were shoes sizes, then Abed . . . ."

Abed broke in, interrupting him, "And if the measure were intelligence then the ranks would be reversed. The smaller would be greater, and the greater, smaller. The middle would stay in the middle!"

They were laughing as they continued their usual verbal fencing. They were certainly unaware of the action of the spring inside, and its surprises. It was released in the knees, and here was Abed, in just two years, moving from a short, thin boy who seemed the smallest among his classmates at school, to a young man taller than his brothers and his father. Was the action of the spring restricted to the height and breadth of the body? I don't know if Abed desisted from his childish foolishness because of the action of the spring that enlarged him from one day to the next, or if he stopped because he found another outlet for his energy. He suddenly became busy: a student part of the time, bearing arms to guard the spot assigned to him part of the time, and a cadre in the camp with responsibilities part of the time. He would come home late, eat what was available and sleep a few hours, waking to the sound of the alarm. "I have a test tomorrow and I haven't studied enough." Amin said to me, "I nearly advised him to focus on his schoolwork, at least until he finished the baccalaureate, and then I was ashamed of myself. It's as if we were saying that our children are for the future and the children of the camp are to defend us, unto death if necessary." Amin's words rang in my ears. I said to myself that he was right, but my heart didn't listen to the words. There were barricades in the streets, movable barricades and permanent ones. People were killed and kidnapped on both sides, because of what was written on their identity cards. I would be in the house, as if I were safe, and then I would hear the rattle of gunfire in this or that direction, or the sudden, heavy sound of an explosion. One of the boys would be away from home or else they would all be I knew not where, or Amin would be in the hospital, or have just left, or the time would have gotten late and he might be on his way home. I would panic, and my imagination would run wild.

I would wait for them all, but I would wait for Abed more than the others. I wouldn't sleep at night until I heard the key turn in the lock; I would stir at his steps and say "Abed?" I would hear his voice and then give myself over to sleep. His grandmother barely saw him; it did not seem as if she missed him. When he happened to be home during the day he would bend over her playfully, seeking a kiss, or say, laughing, "Will you marry me, Grandma?" She would cling to the old relationship, muttering as she waved her hand dismissively, "Good-for-nothing!" He would laugh and say "By your leave," and go out.

21

Amin's Gift

I SAID THAT I WAS beset by panic, and that my imagination was running wild. No, it wasn't my imagination but the earth that had gone wild, making everything wild and savage familiar. Was Ruqayya completely sane in those days? Before the boys wake, before "good morning" or boiling the coffee, she goes down to the street to buy the newspapers. She takes them home and reads the large headlines and the small ones and the details, the commentaries and the articles, the first page and the last and everything in between. Before "good morning," she buys the newspapers and takes them home; she leaves them folded just as they were, not glancing even at the headlines. She does not buy the newspapers; Amin or the boys bring them. In the evening one of the boys asks, "Where are today's papers, Mother?" "I don't know." She helps him look and then remembers, "I used them to clean the window glass." "I put them at the bottom of the wastebasket." "I gave them to the garbage collector." "Didn't you notice they were today's papers?" She doesn't comment; she doesn't say, of course I noticed. Then she goes back to going out early to buy the papers. . . .

She says to Hasan, "Show me a sketch of Beirut's neighborhoods and the suburbs." She knows where East and West Beirut are; she knows the museum and Martyrs' Square and the hotel area and the site of the markets. She knows where Khalda is and al-Naima and al-Damour. She does not know exactly where Ain al-Rummana is, or the Ghwarna neighborhood, or Sabnay. Where is al-Nabaa, where are al-Maslakh and al-Karantina, where is Ashrafiyeh, and where is Furn al-Shubbak? She comes back and asks Hasan to draw her another map. "I drew you a map, Mother, where's the map I drew you?" She looks at him questioningly, as if she were the one waiting for the answer from him. Then she notices, and says, "I tore it up."

Amin spends his day at the hospital and comes back exhausted, not given to talking. If he does say something he does not allude to the war or the number of killed or wounded who were brought to him. Hasan is preparing for the baccalaureate examination; she doesn't know how he can keep the noise of the rockets away from what he's studying in the book. Sadiq is going to the university, to get his certificates and graduation papers. She knows that he and other students chafe against the administration and the Phalange youth, holding sit-ins and demonstrations, but the area of the American University is relatively safe; no rockets fall on it and the war in it is curbed and kept within limits.

Ruqayya returned to her old silence. She had not lost the power of speech; she would speak to her aunt to reassure her, or exchange brief words with Hasan or Sadiq or Abed or Amin, but if that wasn't necessary, speech would retreat into silence. She lived barricaded in it.

She can't wait for Sadiq's trip to the Gulf, to work there; she can't wait for Hasan's trip to Egypt to enroll in the university. "Can't we send Abed to Egypt with Hasan, to study in a high school there?" Unlike every other mother, she wants them to leave her and go away, to travel to any place far away. Any place.

The two boys departed, and all that was left was waiting. Waiting for Amin to come back from the hospital at a late hour of the night. Waiting for Abed, who would come back one night and stay away for two or three. She took care of her aunt. I look from afar: I know that the old woman's needs and requests and her talk, however disordered at times, were all a mercy that relieved the pressure of waiting.

Then Amin brought Maryam.

He came carrying her one night and put her before me, saying, "She will be our daughter. Tomorrow I'll begin the official adoption process."

Sometimes a man commits a stupidity, or his eyes dim and he loses all power of sight. I said, "The time for raising children is over, so why are you bringing me a nursing baby and telling me to start over? Besides, my aunt has become like a child, needing care morning and night—should I occupy myself with her and take care of her, or watch over this little one who needs everything, from nursing to cleaning her bottom to teaching her to walk and talk?"

I was angry and I didn't understand why Amin had chosen to adopt a nursing baby, put her in my hands, and just simply go off to the hospital, as if he had not left her behind him. He was calm, as usual. He looked at me and said, "Look at her, Ruqayya. When they brought her to me to examine her I looked into her face and she captured my heart. I said, 'A daughter has come to us, a gift from heaven.' A rocket destroyed the house and everyone died, the mother and the father and maybe the brothers and the neighbors; only this child was destined to live. The ambulance brought her to me from beneath the ruins. There wasn't a wound or bruise showing but they thought she must have internal bleeding or a wound that didn't show. I examined her, and she was fine. Look into her face, Ruqayya, how beautiful her face is!"

I did not look.

I look now from afar: I'm carrying Maryam, perhaps out of pity, because she's an infant without a mother, poor thing. I do what's needed, as if she were the daughter of a neighbor and I must look after her until her mother returns and reclaims her from me. Then one night when the shelling was intense I carried her and took my aunt's hand and we moved to sit on the stairs, and I hugged the girl. I looked into her face and felt that tickling in my breast, as if my breasts were about to produce milk. Maybe there was a lump in my throat, and a film of tears in my eyes. Until now I don't know if I was protecting her, in that moment when I encircled her completely with my arms and shielded her small head from a likely rocket, or if I was seeking protection in her.

She became a daughter to me. The most beautiful and dearest of all that Amin left me.

I say that her face was like an angel. Then I reconsider: none of us has seen an angel, and here she was before my eyes, more beautiful than the angels we imagine.

Yes, it was falling in love, purely and simply. Perhaps it surpassed motherly love, which nothing can surpass—because that love comes cumulatively and following preparation, the nine months of pregnancy and the birth, and then you find the boy before you and he's yours, flesh of your flesh, from his father's seed. But Maryam just came to us, she just came, without any preparation. I denied my feelings as a lover does, for a day or two, a week or possibly two, then I accepted that I had fallen in love. It was love in the time of war, of killing for one's identity, of rattling bullets and explosions and rockets and dynamite and car bombs and chasing people out of their houses and neighborhoods for no fault of theirs other than being Muslim or Christian; in the time of chaos and stealing and confusion between a noble effort and the greed of petty thieves. Maryam was here before me gurgling like a bird, assuring me with every morning that in spite of everything, this life held something worth living for.

Abed rejoiced in the girl, playing with her when he passed through the house to reassure us or to eat or sleep. Amin would delight in her face in the morning, and contemplate her sleeping when he returned from the hospital late at night. Only my aunt did not understand why this infant had appeared without preamble and took all this attention. One day she said, "Ruqayya, I haven't wanted to cause you any distress, but I must make you understand: I think that Amin has taken another wife and that this girl is his daughter with the other woman."

"But Aunt, why would he bring me the other woman's child, why wouldn't he leave her with her mother?"

"God only knows!" Maybe he didn't get married and she's his bastard."

I laughed. I was used to my aunt's quirks and her constant doubts of others.

"She's an orphan, Aunt, and the ambulance brought her to him from beneath the ruins. They didn't know of any family of hers, not even any distant relatives."

"You're free to do as you like, I've alerted you and done what I should. There are a lot of orphans in a country at war, and they have a refuge to shelter them. Why did he bring this girl and not the rest of the orphans?"

"Oh, Aunt, everything is written and ordained."

22

1982

WAR TEACHES YOU MANY THINGS. The first is to strain your ears and be alert, so you can judge where the firing is coming from, as if your body had become one large ear with a compass to show the specific source of the threat among the four directions, or rather the five, since death can also rain down from the sky. The second is to resign yourself a little and to have only a certain amount of fear, the necessary amount only. If your fear exceeds the amount by a tiny bit, you will leave your house needlessly, when the shelling is on the other side of the city. Your fear will turn into a malignant disease that will eat away your body every day until it destroys you; the rocket will spare you and your fear will kill you. And if your fear is a tiny bit less, you won't hurry down the stairs to the shelter or to sit on the stairs far from the windows and the balconies, and the rocket will kill you just like that in the blink of an eye, because the shelling is aimed at the street where you live and perhaps at the building in which you live. The third thing that war teaches you is to be careful when you must leave the house to take the most important things first. For example, a bottle of water or the old lady, who might get lost as you are checking on your little girl or the limbs of your body. It's certain that there are fourth and fifth and sixth things that war teaches you, but it always teaches you to endure, whether at the beginning or the end. To wait and endure, because the alternative is to become unbalanced, in short to go mad.

The war handed us over to war, and war to war . . . What? Here the sentences stumble and the words are confused, because I don't know how it's possible to summarize what we lived through in those years. I don't know how to communicate the meaning, and I wonder about how useful it is to go into the details—the details that are not details. Every discrete detail is a story affecting hundreds of people, perhaps thousands. Take for example Black Saturday at the end of 1975. The Phalange kidnapped three hundred Muslims and killed seventy others, and the National Movement answered by taking over the hotel area; afterward chaos and organized plunder broke out in the heart of Beirut. A big story or a detail among hundreds? Before that, sixty-three Syrian workers were killed and thousands of them were forced to flee. Oh my God, it's only one thread in the fabric, or one spark in the flames of the fire. After that was the siege of Tall al-Zaatar and Jisr al-Basha and Dbayeh and the shantytowns in al-Maslakh and al-Karantina and al-Nabaa—details? And then Israeli invasion in 1978 and the hundreds of thousands from the south who thronged to West Beirut. Then the larger invasion in 1982.

We were in the siege, at the height of the summer, and of the siege. There was a knock on the door. I opened it, and I nearly screamed, not because I recognized Hasan but because the boy standing in front of me at the door was a shadow of Hasan. I thought, my mind has wandered and imagination has taken over. I thought, shadows are taller. I thought, but this is his shadow, the exact image of him, but smaller, as if it were Hasan in the first year of high school, and sick. He said, "Mama." I put my arms around him and held on. He began to slip away; I didn't realize he was suppressing tears. I let him slip away and began to stare at him, touching his face and his neck and his shoulders.

"You've been sick?"

He laughed. "Illness is easier."

"Tell me what happened to you."

"Who's going to go first?"

"Your father and Abed are fine. Your uncle Ezz . . . we don't know . . . ."

"I found out from my father."

"When did you see him? Did you go to the hospital first?"

Did he sense a note of blame in the words? He smiled; it wasn't his shadow, it was Hasan, with his lively smile and his sweet eyes.

"I was afraid to come straight home." He faltered. "I said I would go first to the hospital. In the hospital I would find my father and ask him about you, and if I didn't find him I would find someone to give me the news. Where's Grandma?"

He went in to greet his grandma.

"How did you get here, Grandson?"

"From Cairo. I took a plane to Damascus and from there by land to Beirut."

"Thank God you got here safely, Grandson. Were there fedayeen or Israelis on the way?"

"There were fedayeen in some places and Israelis in others."

"And Ain al-Helwa?"

"What about it?"

"Didn't you go by it to set your mind at rest about your uncle Ezz and his wife?"

"No, Grandma, the road from Damascus is in one direction and Sidon is in the other."

"Thank God you got here safely, Grandson, we've missed you."

Hasan would remain with us throughout the period of the siege. He worked in civil defense, distributing water and bread and newspapers to the civilians. He was often at the *Safir* newspaper, helping with some of the volunteer work there.

On the day of the departure Beirut came out by the thousands and hundreds of thousands, scattering rice and rose petals over the young men piled into the trucks that would take them by land to Syria or to the wharf where the ships were preparing for their departure from Lebanon. Maryam was walking ahead of Amin and me, holding Abed's hand on one side and Hasan's on the other. She was wearing a summer dress, open at the neck and baring her arms. Her hair was as I had combed it for her, gathered into a ponytail. She would speak to her brothers and then turn around to me and her father and laugh.

Abed embraced her, then he climbed into the truck.

We waved to him, and here was Maryam asking a woman carrying a bucket of rice for a handful of it. Hasan lifted her off the ground and she moved her arm with all her determination, and opened her fist suddenly, so the rice she had intended for her brother scattered over her head. She laughed, and called at the top of her voice, "Come back soon, Abed!" Her voice was lost in the crowd and in the roar of the trucks as they pulled away, amid thousands of hands waving and extending a bridge of voices, shouting and singing and scattering rice and rose petals and crying. The August sun beat down, unchecked. "God be with you, God be with you." "Take care of yourselves." "Goodbye." "We'll meet again soon, God willing."

Suddenly Maryam said, "Mama, can you buy me an ice cream?" I looked at her, and I looked at Hasan and Amin; for a moment my spirit slipped away, as if I were suddenly dying. Then I took a deep breath and looked at Maryam: "Let's go buy you an ice cream."

In the evening I heard the key in the lock. I wondered, which one has come back early, Hasan or Amin? But here was Abed standing at the door. He said in a strange voice, before he stepped into the house: "Before the truck entered the port I decided to stay in Beirut." He quickly went into his room and closed the door.

In the morning he said to Maryam, "You told me to come back quickly, and I did what you told me." She put her arms around him and laughed. He slipped away from her and left the room; I heard his muffled sobbing.

23

Flies

HOW DID I BEAR IT? How did we endure and live, how did a drink of water slip down our throats without choking and suffocating us? What's the use of recalling what we endured and bringing it back in words? When someone we love dies, we place him in a shroud, wrapping him tenderly and digging deep in the earth. We weep; we know that we must bury him to go on with our lives. What sane person unearths the tombs of his loved ones? What logic is there in my running after the memory that has escaped, trying to flee from itself? Do I want to kill it so that I can live, or am I trying to revive it even if I die because . . . because why? I suddenly scream: Damn memory, damn its mother and father, damn the sky over it and the day it was and the day it will be. Damn the flies!

I saw the flies with my own eyes.

In a deep pit, that was yet big enough.

Ambulance crews with gloves and protective masks

Were scattering white powder,

Bringing the bodies on stretchers,

Placing one body next to the other.

They were stretching a sheet over them all, a covering

Of the plastic

From which garbage bags are made.

They would take their stretchers back to the narrow lanes, to bring other bodies.

They came and went.

From daybreak until sunset.
A smell
And clouds
Of flies.
Let it escape, let it go. May it never return.

Stretch out a sheet as you saw them doing, to cover what you saw throughout years, and the day of the smell and the flies.

Leave the page blank, Ruqayya.

24

The Girl from Nablus Enters the Family

I'VE MADE A LEAP THAT cut five years from the story. I'll go back and pick up the thread: we're still at the end of 1977.

Sadiq called from Abu Dhabi, saying that he had met a girl he liked from the West Bank, and that he wanted to propose to her. His father said, "How will we propose to her for you when we can't enter the West Bank?" He said, "I'll arrange things. We can all meet in Amman."

Sadiq sent the bride's picture and a long letter describing her, telling the story of his meeting her and what he knew about her family.

I told my aunt, "Sadiq wants to get engaged."

"To someone from Tantoura?"

"No, from Nablus."

"Your uncle, Abu Amin, God rest him, visited Nablus many times. He said that there was nothing like the kunafa dessert they make in Nablus, but that they served it before lunch!" She added, "But the girls from Nablus are stubborn, and God made them all fat."

I laughed, and showed her the picture. She looked at it and then waved her hand dismissively: "She's weak and wasting away, thin as a reed."

"Didn't you say that the women of Nablus are fat, and here she is like a willow branch!"

"Soon she'll get fat from eating kunafa."

"The main thing is that he likes her, and her family are good people."

My aunt waved her hand and said, capitulating, "Okay. God willing you'll have better luck than I did, and she won't take him to live in Nablus so that we never see him."

"What's the matter with you, Aunt—Nablus is occupied, so Sadiq can't visit it."

"Isn't Sadat saying that he's going there to ask them to end the occupation?"

"And you believe him?"

"No, I don't."

"We'll meet her family in Amman, and ask them for her, and hold the marriage there."

"They won't agree!"

"They will agree, Aunt, because we can't enter the West Bank; we don't have any control over it, and neither do they."

"If they agree, they want to marry their daughter and be done. How many sisters does she have?"

"Three."

"Thank God, some trials are easier than others. The Saffuriya has done us in, with her six sisters. God forbid."

Abed observed, talking about his brother's plan, "We've gotten over Barrier Number One, may the same be true for Barrier Number Two. After that the road will be open for me."

I laughed, "Do you have a plan?"

"Plans: a fair one and a dark one and a tall one and a short one, and the fifth is indescribable—she carries a rifle and talks politics and is our ally because she's from Kamal Jumblatt's group, and she's beautiful as a moon and light-hearted to boot."

"Then the fifth is precisely what you want."

"There's no call to anger all the others!"

I didn't know where the line was between joking and seriousness, or if he had many girlfriends or was alone, his heart still filled only with fantasies of girls.

Hasan returned to Egypt to study, and I didn't know if he was happy or miserable. He said that Cairo was large and the Nile was fascinating but he missed the sea and Sidon and the scent of orange blossoms. I would send him pictures of Maryam and talk to him at length about her in my letters. He would say, "I'm happy to have Maryam's news but I've read the letter twice, thinking I had skipped a paragraph, and when I read it again I became certain that in a five-page letter you didn't say a single word about yourself. How are you doing, Mother?"

I asked Hasan to call Wisal in Jenin and tell her that we were going to Amman for Sadiq's engagement, and to ask if it was possible for me to meet her there.

Amin insisted that Ezz come with us to Amman. I said, "Who will take care of my aunt?"

"We'll leave her with Ezz's wife, she can come with him from Sidon and stay with her until we get back."

"But my aunt can't stand her."

"God help Karima, she can put up with my mother for three days."

Ezz and his wife came from Sidon. He suggested that we leave Maryam with his wife, because "She's little, and the trip to Jordan by land will exhaust her, and she'll exhaust you." I did not agree.

On the morning of the following day a taxi carried us to Damascus by way of the al-Masna crossing, and from there we crossed the border at al-Ramtha on our way to Amman. I carried Maryam on my lap and sat in the back seat with Ezz and Abed; Amin sat in the front seat next to the driver. We had barely set out when Amin turned around, looked at Maryam and smiled broadly, and said, "God bless our trip. It was exactly the right thing to do, Ruqayya, to bring Maryam."

We met at the hotel, where we found Sadiq and Hasan waiting for us near the desk. Neither of them had seen Maryam before. Sadiq planted a quick kiss on her head and then turned his attention to his father and uncle, and I was busy examining Hasan. He was thinner and seemed smaller in size, as if he were a middle-school pupil. He lifted Maryam in his hands, saying again and again, "Now I understand why you write three quarters of your letters about her! She's amazing, where did she get all this beauty?"

Sadiq sat with his father and uncle to discuss the details of the engagement, and Abed joined them. I went up to the room carrying Maryam, with Hasan trailing after me. In the evening we went to the bride's uncle's house.

The bride seemed kind and affectionate, younger than I had imagined even though Sadiq assured me before and afterward that she was only two years younger than he was. The formal living room was very large, with big chairs whose wooden frames were painted in gold. In the middle was a large rectangular table, covered with a piece of glass; on it were large crystal ashtrays and a number of rosaries that seemed to be valuable, because they were displayed as if they were fine pieces. I was intrigued by three large pictures hung on the wall, each in a gold frame: the middle was of a porter or a water-carrier who was carrying a picture of the Aqsa Mosque on his back; the pictures on each side were of a sluggish sea, and of a table holding a platter with fruits in dull colors.

The room was crowded with men and women, and I learned only shortly before we left which of the women was the bride's mother and which was her aunt and which her uncle's wife, and who was more closely and more distantly related. The men turned aside to talk over the arrangements for the marriage. Afterward we moved to the dining room, where the table and the rest of the furniture also was huge, crowding the space with chairs and china cabinets.

When we came back to the hotel Amin asked me, in front of Ezz and Sadiq and the other boys, "What do you think of the bride, Ruqayya?"

"She's very nice, congratulations."

Sadiq said, "Mother, I don't understand what made you suddenly say, for no reason at all, 'We are refugees, our family lives in the Ain al-Helwa camp and we have relatives in the Jenin camp.'"

I found his comment strange, and I said, "Isn't it the truth?"

He said, "I don't object, but the words came as a surprise, for no reason. Anyway, who of our family lives in the camp in Jenin?"

"Wisal and her mother."

"They are people we know, not relatives."

"They're my family. I have no one left but Ezz and Karima in Ain al-Helwa, and Wisal and her mother in Jenin, and Abed too—even if he lives in Beirut he's from the camp in Jenin."

Ezz broke in to end the tension that had begun to form around us without our having noticed: "I attest that the mulukhiya was respectable, one more degree and it would reach the level of the mulukhiya you make, Ruqayya. If it were two degrees better it would surpass it. Watch out, if the girl cooks like her family it will slip away from you, and I'll go to Sadiq's house for the mulukhiya."

Sadiq laughed, and said, "Then we have to start now to try to get you a visa to come to the Emirates."

"Yes. And I'll write that the reason for the trip is mulukhiya."

They laughed. I joined in with a smile, but I was down-hearted. I said, "I'll put Maryam to bed."

"Then you'll join us?"

"I won't leave her alone in the room. She might wake up and be frightened to find herself in a strange place."

Sadiq said, "It would have been better for you to leave her in Beirut with my uncle's wife."

Ezz said, "That's what I suggested."

I did not comment. I lifted Maryam and went up to the room, followed by Hasan. I put the girl to bed and sat with

175

him. We talked a long time about Egypt and his studies and the situation in Beirut; but neither of us mentioned the visit or the bride or her family's house. We didn't notice that we had passed midnight until Amin came in. He planted a kiss on Maryam's head, as she was fast asleep, and said to Hasan, "Ezz and your brothers are waiting for you in the coffee shop; I'm going to sleep. Good night."

25

Wisal (II)

I DON'T USUALLY PAY THAT much attention to the clothes I wear, but when I was getting ready to visit Wisal, I changed my clothes three times. I put on one of my dresses, looked in the mirror and then decided to put on another one. I went back over my directions to Amin about Maryam, if she gets hungry do this, if she wets herself you'll do that. He laughed and said, "Come on, don't worry," and then, "Go ahead, Hasan," as he had decided to go with me.

A taxi took us to al-Baqaa Camp; we looked for the house for some time, and at last arrived at the address. The door was open, and Hasan clapped his hands. A woman came, and I was embarrassed to see her as I did not know if it was Wisal or someone else. She was my age. She extended her hand and greeted us as she welcomed us repeatedly, so I realized that she was not Wisal.

In later years I would recall the moment we met, in that small house in al-Baqaa Camp on the heights above Amman, at the beginning of 1978, because when Wisal came into the room she did not extend her hand in greeting but rather opened her arms wide and embraced me, and also because as I embraced her, I was certain that the scent filing my nose was not from my imagination. It was my friend, the girl of Qisarya who had come to me now from Jenin, bearing with her the scent of the sea. I tell myself that a wish can create an illusion and sustain it; but then I say no, the scent did not come from my mind but rather from her body and her long dress and her hair, reaching to my nose and from there penetrating my head and breast and bowels—how could that be the effect of an illusion?

Wisal brought me a traditional Palestinian dress and told me that she had begun embroidering it after that telephone call that Abed had made from Beirut. She said that she had finished it three years earlier, waiting for us to meet. I fought back tears as I contemplated her handwork on the dress she had brought to me over the bridge from Jenin. It was not cut and sewn, as she left it for me to sew, to fit me. It was three pieces of fabric: the first was large, for the body of the thawb, from the collar to the hem, which she had embroidered over the breast and around the hem, and two smaller pieces for the sleeves, with the same motif embroidered at the border of each. She had not chosen the usual black fabric for me but rather an indeterminate light color, almost off-white, which she had embroidered with thread of every hue and shade of blue, from light sky blue to the deepest color of the sea. I looked at the dress and could find nothing to say; my tongue was tied, and I felt that my gifts were not appropriate. I left the wristwatch and the heart suspended on a golden chain and the bottle of perfume in my bag, repeating to myself, they do not suit the occasion. I heard Hasan's voice saying, "I must go. Do you know how to find the way back, or shall I come back to pick you up in a couple of hours?" Then with a haste I did not understand, he said to Wisal, "Goodbye, Aunt," and kissed her hand and left rapidly.

Wisal was the one who began to talk. She pulled me in, and I entered first with timid steps; then my tongue came untied and began to listen to her and to exchange stories with her. Then she asked, "When are you going back to Beirut?"

"Tomorrow."

"God forgive you, Ruqayya, stay one more day. One day, and then go in peace. I want to meet Dr. Amin and Sadiq and little Abed, and I want to get to know that handsome young man who perched like a little dove for a moment and then flew off. Tomorrow we'll have lunch together, God willing."

"As you say, Wisal."

In the hotel, after Maryam and Amin had gone to sleep, I looked into the mirror for a long time. I saw myself with Wisal right next to me, in her embroidered country dress and her full, fertile figure. Why had she seemed older than I, years older? She had become tall and plump, her country dress and its belt emphasizing her plumpness; I had remained as I always was, thin, my thinness emphasized by the dress that was tight on my body, falling narrowly from the waist to end just below the knee. Perhaps my hair, drawn back and held in a narrow black ribbon, made me look like a schoolgirl when I had passed forty? She covered her hair with a white shawl, showing a lock of hair in which white was mixed with the black.

I moved my eyes between the two images, wondering. It wasn't only the thinness here or the plumpness there, but rather the clothes, maybe, or the posture or the difference in the hands, the face and the forehead. Was it by chance or for some other reason? Was it the difference between Beirut and Jenin, or because she was the wife of a peasant, a son of the camp, while my husband had studied at the American University of Beirut, becoming a doctor, and we moved easily from place to place? Was my way of speaking different? How did I used to speak? How did I speak now?

I stared at the two images, finding it all strange, confused by questions that weren't completely clear and to which I could not easily find an answer. One thing that was clear and about which I harbored no doubt was that Wisal, whom I had known as a girl back in Tantoura, and who now lived far away in Jenin, whom I had met once after thirty years of separation, had opened her arms wide and embraced me, and it had seemed as if nothing had happened. I felt that I wanted to cling to her coattails and follow her wherever she went, and wherever she was.

I changed my clothes and lay down in bed, with the caution I had grown used to so as not to awaken Maryam or Amin. Then sleep came over me, and I dreamed I was in Tantoura, repeating that the gift must be a bouquet of the lilies from the village. I smelled their scent and followed it, hoping it would lead me to them, but I did not find them. I went back to my mother, crying, "Who picked the lilies? They were here and here and here and there, does it make any sense that someone picked them all? And can the scent stay even after they've gone?" My mother made light of it, saying, "There are a lot of flowers. You have red anemones and lilies of the valley and daisies and knotweed and lavender, so make your gift a bouquet of them." But I wanted lilies. I looked for them far and wide in the town, from the tower north of it to the police station south of it, from the beach to the school east of the railroad, but there was no trace of the lilies, even though their scent was penetrating and filled the space around me.

On the next day we all went to see Wisal, except for Sadiq who preferred to spend the day with his bride and her family. When we said goodbye at the door, she brought a can of olive oil and two bottles of olives, two large, plastic soda bottles into which she had pressed all the olives she could. She said, "The oil is from our olive trees in Jenin, and the olives too. I put them up myself and sealed the bottles well, so you won't have any trouble taking them to Beirut."

From the beginning of the year until the end, we ate from Wisal's olives and olive oil. As it was the custom, we always had a supply of olives and olive oil in the house, but Wisal's oil and olives were only for special occasions, holidays, Hasan's return from Cairo for the summer vacation, when Ezz and his wife came from Ain al-Helwa, or when the elder Abed came for one of his visits, which now were rare. I would spoon out some of it and place it on the table with the rest of the food, and Amin would laugh and say, "This is something Ruqayya does not grant us except on very special occasions." On the holidays I would also visit the tomb of my mother and my uncle in Sidon; and whenever Wisal visited Amman she would call me on the telephone, and that day would be like a holiday. She would tell me her news and her family's news, and I would sum up our news for her. I would say, "Maryam is growing up day by day," and she would say, laughing, "My youngest son is only nine years older, he'll wait for her." I would laugh, and she would laugh. "Take care of yourself, Ruqayya," "Take care of yourself, Wisal." I would replace the receiver not knowing if I felt sadness or satisfaction, or something suspended between the two.

26

Where Are We, Maryam?

HASAN WAS THE ONE WHO suggested that I write my story. I said, "I'm not a writer!"

He said, "Tell the story, write what you have seen and lived and heard, and what you think about. If it's hard to write, then tell it orally and record what you say, and afterward we'll put it on paper. This is important, Mother, more important than you imagine."

I repeated, "I'm not a writer. Every craft has its craftsmen. I have never excelled in composition, even when I was a pupil in school. I was amazed by the ability of some of my classmates to write well, whatever topic the teacher assigned us."

He said, "Mother, what I'm asking for isn't a composition but testimony. Do you remember that day when I asked you to record your testimony about what happened in our village, and I told you to gather the details and get ready? You became ill and it wasn't possible for us, because I left after that. What I want from you is testimony like that, even if it's long and detailed, concerning the large events and the small ones, too. Write whatever comes to mind, and tell it however you like."

I said, "I wish I knew how. Besides, it's hard to tell, it's not something to tell. It branches out, and it's heavy. How many wars can a single story bear? How many massacres? Anyway, how can I tie the small things, important as they are, to the terrors that we've all lived through? Tell it yourself if you like, you have a lot of the details, and whatever you lack I can make up, I mean, if I have anything to add. You are gathering people's testimony, you read countless books, you research and you record and you compose. You write it, and if I have anything to add, I will."

He said, "If I weren't confident in your ability I wouldn't burden you by asking."

I said decisively, "I don't know how."

I refused, but I couldn't get the thought out of my head. It stayed with me like a disagreeable guest who doesn't want to leave. I said to myself, I can't and I don't want to. I threw it out and locked the door. Years later Hasan once again began to insist. Then one evening he surprised me with a large notebook, on the cover of which he had written "al-Tantouriya." The woman from Tantoura.

He said, "Write anything. Write about the village, about the sea, about the weddings . . . . Repeat some of what you used to tell us when we were little. As for the catastrophes, write what you can stand to, an allusion, even an allusion might be enough for the purpose." He smiled suddenly and reminded me of the homework he used to demand of me when I was preparing for the baccalaureate examination. "Consider it part of that homework, as if it were a school requirement. The difference is that I'm not demanding it for next week. Begin to write, and then we'll see what happens."

I changed the subject. "You taught me Arabic and English and history and geography and social science, and Sadiq took charge of math and sciences for me. You were a better teacher than he was."

He said, "Maybe you were more inclined to the subjects I helped you with, and so you imagined that I was better than Sadiq in explaining the lessons?" He laughed. "And Abed would look at us resentfully because he was out of the game and didn't know how to share in it."

I laughed.

Hasan snared me. The notebook was waiting. The title was seductive, and the blank pages whispered suggestively, aren't you the Tantouriya? Temptation. I would avert my face and tell them, go away, I don't want you. At night when I lay down in bed I would find them waiting for me.

One morning I picked up the pen and here I was writing about the young man the sea cast ashore for me. A passing adventure under the heading of love, awakening the senses, preparing them.

It was pleasurable and interesting to summon on paper my mother and my father, the village sea, and a wedding from long ago.

It was pleasurable and problematic to describe the almond tree in the spring. (I wrote it once, twice, three times. I said to myself, it's no use. It was a queen in its land, I can't transfer it to paper.)

It was delightful to set down a song, the colorings of the voice and its rhythms ringing in my ears—and then I would stop, wondering how a song can be imprisoned on paper, bare of its melody, except for someone who knows it and has heard it or sung it before.

Then I advanced farther along the rough trails of memory and of words. I said, Hasan has snared me. Here I am after writing two notebooks and dozens of pages, incapable of continuing. How can I tell the next four months? How have I told the first four months? I've told the little part I lived, a part entwined with thousands of others, lived by other people during the same months; how can the story be completed without all of these parts?

Four months there at home, and another four in Lebanon, our second home, where we are now classed as aliens. Four and four—pure coincidence, or the workings of destiny? An arbitrary destiny, a butcher, not satisfied with a few slaughtered carcasses to hang in its shop window and to cut according to the buyer's wishes, but slaughtering out of greed. The perfect setting for the most horrendous nightmares. But in sleep nightmares are usually restricted to a few silent images, the fear when you're chased or a feeling of strangulation— nightmares are meek and gentle, and they have their limits. Here, insanity overflows: shelling from airplanes, battleships, heavy artillery, bombs, charges that explode cars which just minutes before had seemed tame as sleeping cats, fires. The water is cut off, and the electricity. There's no bread. You go to look for it and the earth explodes beneath your feet. God's heaven is your enemy all day long, a siege from all six directions. Senseless bombs bring down buildings, which collapse on their residents and leave a deep ditch, before which all we can imagine of hell and its deepest pit seems small. Cluster bombs continue exploding, as if forever. Maryam is crying from the pressure of the noise in her ears; I block her ears for her with earplugs, and surround her completely with my arms. Can they hear the noise in Jenin? If only it were Jenin. Maryam says, "Tell me a story." I remove the plug from one of her ears, bring my lips close and begin to speak; she listens for a bit and then cries again, from the intensity of the noise.

In this hell on earth my relationship with Beirut became solid. Strange; how did it happen? Its tame, everyday sea was no longer its sea, its land was no longer its land, its sky was no longer sky. Your house, and the one next to it and the one next to that and the rest of the buildings in the street where you live and in the next street, and at a distance of ten minutes' walk in the direction of the Sabra market, or a little father in the lanes of Shatila or in the other direction toward the Cola Bridge and the Fakahani, all of them surprise you with something you're not used to. Shells have hit them here and here and here and there. Glass has turned in an instant from stable panes in the windows, reflecting the sunlight playfully, to scattered fragments on the ground; cars and the feet of pedestrians pass over them, grinding them, and they emit a sound like a moan. Balconies, wooden shutters, ceilings have flown without wings, and fallen as debris on the street. Even the walls have lost their expected civility, under the shelling, and revealed what had been concealed inside the homes. I lift my head and look, and I see a bed, clothes, a chair, half a table, food dishes, suspended in the open. Or a lucky family, not killed by the shelling, may be reunited in a room from which the fourth wall has fallen, leaving someone passing to lift his head and say "Good evening," or to avert his gaze and pass as if he saw nothing. I walk toward the Fakahani neighborhood, the Arab University of Beirut, Afif al-Taybi Street—what has happened to the street? The Abu Iyad Building, the PLO Planning Center and Unified Information, the Writers' and Journalists' Union, all were destroyed. Just one street in Beirut—where did the street go?

Amin would return to the house whenever he could, when the firing stopped. He no longer kept regular hours in Acre Hospital because he was occupied with preparing medical centers and emergency units in this or that neighborhood in West Beirut. Abed the younger was with the resistance and I hadn't seen him for weeks; I didn't know in what position he was or behind what barricade, in the heart of Beirut or on its heights? Near the airport confronting the Israeli soldiers, or near the museum confronting the Phalange, or on the beach confronting the battleships? Where was Abed now? Hasan was with the civil defense, distributing bread or water or newspapers, on duty whenever he could be in the *Safir* newspaper. Where was Hasan, at this moment? Where was Amin, where were Ezz and his wife? My imagination wandered after them, hovering over the streets, looking for them. I let it wander as I hurried to accompany Maryam and my aunt to the shelter in the building. At the end of the raid I would go out to the street to inspect it, to inspect Beirut, or Ruqayya; I would return and take Maryam in my arms and try to sleep.

At the entrance to the apartment I kept a small overnight case and two shopping bags which could be picked up quickly when the shelling intensified. Maryam would run for the stairs to the shelter carrying the smaller bag, as I had taught her, the bag with the candles and the Lux battery and lighter. In her other hand was a small transistor radio. I would follow her with slower steps, in my hand the overnight case with a towel, some clothes, a first-aid kit, and another bag with a bottle of water, some loaves of bread and a plastic container of cheese or labneh or olives. With my other hand I held my aunt's hand, guiding her slowly down the stairs toward the shelter.

I had not told my aunt about what had happened in Sidon and Ain al-Helwa; I had not spoken with her about the destruction of the camp or the arrests or the mass killing. I had not told her that we had had no news of Ezz or his wife for four weeks. But she had learned of the invasion. She said, "So, are we going back to Tantoura?"

I did not answer. She said, "What's the matter, Ruqayya? Have you become hard of hearing? I asked you, are we going back home?"

I said, "I heard you, Aunt, I heard the question. How would we go back? I told you that the Israelis have entered Lebanon; they've occupied the whole south and gotten close to Beirut."

"I understand. But it's possible the fedayeen will defeat them—is it possible, or not?"

"It's possible."

"And when they defeat them they'll follow them to Palestine and we'll go back to the village. What does Ezz say?"

"The lines to Sidon are down. He hasn't told us the news from where he is."

"Is he all right?"

"He's all right, Aunt."

"And the resistance?"

"What about it?"

"Is it all right?"

188

For a moment it seemed to me that I would slap my face in despair and yell at her, "How should I know whether it's all right or not?" It was certain that the Israelis had occupied the whole south and the Shouf and had arrived at the heights above Beirut, and they had destroyed Ain al-Helwa and taken half its men to prison or to their death.

I patted her shoulder, and said, "God be thanked, Aunt, the resistance is fine."

She sat up on her bed and said, "Give me one of Amin's cigarettes."

I did not comment, but handed her a cigarette. She said, "Why are you just standing there? Where's the lighter?"

I brought the lighter and lit the cigarette for her, and she began to smoke it calmly. She didn't cough nor did any twitch appear in her face to indicate that this was something new for her. I stood watching my aunt's hand as she brought the cigarette to her mouth, inhaled the smoke and then lowered her hand as she exhaled from her nostrils, as if she had been smoking for countless years. After my surprise, which was closer to astonishment, I found myself laughing and saying to my aunt, "What do you think, should I buy you a pack of cigarettes?"

During two months of intense daily shelling, going down to the shelter and leaving it and going down again, my aunt did not ask again about the news of the war and the fedayeen; she contented herself with asking about Ezz. I would tell her that he had managed to find a way to contact Amin. Every two or three days he would call him and say remember me to Mother and don't worry about me. I would fabricate the words, finding them strange as they emerged from my mouth, loud and complete, clear and stiff, to hide the lie, or to overcome the lump in my throat. I did not know the fate of Ezz or his wife, after the planes had destroyed Ain al-Helwa and artillery had shelled it for ten days, leaving no stone atop another; they had even destroyed the hospital on top of everyone in it. I would repeat, Ezz is fine, Aunt. She would nod her head, as if agreeing with what I said. I don't know if she believed it or if she had decided that her share in the battle was to overcome her fears, not to express them, and to endure. When the building would shake and the glass in the window would fly in shards that could kill us in a moment she would not comment, saying nothing. But in the shelter she would talk and talk about one subject, never deviating from it: Tantoura. She would talk about it continuously and in detail, attracting the attention of those who heard her. She always ended with the same words: "When we go back home, I beg you to come and visit us. The village is beautiful, it's worthy of you, and you are worthy of it." Umm Ali would assure her that she would visit her, if God willed.

Umm Ali was like a dovecote, everyone was at ease with her, whoever they were. At the height of the shelling, if she was not absorbed in one of her numerous long prayers, she would joke and soothe and set minds at rest. How could she keep her calm amid the minefield in the shelter, under almost ceaseless shelling? Yes, it was a minefield, because when our nerves were shot someone would explode at the others or at himself, with or without a reason. I hit Maryam. My hand got away from me and I slapped her face. I yelled at her, or I just yelled at no one, and then I cried. I would bathe her in the least water possible; she would stand in the basin (I remember it clearly: a basin of green colored plastic). I would soap her head and scrub her body and then pour out a little water, just a little. I would not throw away the water left over from the weekly bath but use it to clean the house, keeping a little of it to water the plants that by some strange accident had managed to remain alive: stalks of basil and sage and green thyme. The plants were smart and judged the situation, and like us they came to make do with the least little bit of water. Maryam suddenly urinated in the basin, and my hand got away from me: I slapped her,

190

and then I slapped my own forehead. Then I cried, and Maryam also cried—was it from the slap, or from my sudden tears?

Where did Umm Ali get all these bonbons? Who had the wit to think of bonbons and the neighbors' children when the bombs were as continuous as Judgment Day, beyond the imagination of the ancients? She would put her hand into her deep pocket and bring it out, opening her palm, and the children would see the candies, their shiny, transparent wrappers showing their colors: red and green and purple and yellow and white. The little ones would rush to take one or two for each of them. Years later I asked Maryam about her memories of the shelter, and she said, "Three things: The noise. The intensity didn't only hurt my ears, but made me feel as if the missile had entered my ears and come to rest in them, continuing to explode."

"And Umm Ali's bonbons?"

"I don't know where she bought them, because no matter how I tried to find some like them later on, I couldn't. They had a different taste—I can still remember it."

"Don't you remember the day I slapped you when I was giving you a bath?"

She hesitated, and then said, "I remember. At the time it seemed to me like the worst thing a person could do in her life. Afterward I would wake up from sleep and run to the bathroom terrified, whenever I really needed to pee. Once I woke up horrified because I had wet the bed. I took off my panties and the sheet and washed out the dirty part with a little water. I spread it out on the balcony, and stayed awake until it dried, then I put it back on the bed."

The conversation stopped. Perhaps Maryam noticed, for she began speaking again, "The second thing I remember is the day I went with three kids from the camp to Mustafa Umda's shop."

"Who's Mustafa Umda?"

"He had a shop in Shatila, a little shop that sold candy and hardware. I bought a chocolate and the other two girls bought sugar-coated almonds. There was a boy with us who asked for marbles. The shop owner brought out a cardboard box, and when he raised the cover I saw those little, transparent crystal balls, with touches of color: blue and green and orange. Some were small and others larger. I was dazzled, and even more so when we left the shop and the boy stopped and crouched down and began to roll them on the ground. He was a little older than we were, maybe he was eight; he seemed old and handsome and amazing, as he rolled one and then aimed the second one at it. Then he changed his position and crouched down again and tried to hit the two with the third marble. I said I would return the chocolate and buy marbles. The boy was very nice—he said, don't return the chocolate. He gave me one of the three marbles that he had bought. I offered to divide the chocolate bar with him; he smiled and said, "Thank you, I don't want it." Strange. I still remember his smile."

"And the third thing?"

"The day one of the neighbor women screamed at you and said, 'You're the reason, you all are the reason. If it weren't for the Palestinians, Israel would not have destroyed our country.' She was screaming at you and your face was a strange yellow color. I expected you to answer her, to slap her face, but you dragged me by the hand and went to the farthest corner of the shelter. You asked for a cigarette from a neighbor and left. I followed you, and you yelled at me: 'Return to the shelter, I'm going to smoke this cigarette and then come back.' But I stayed clinging to you. I sat next to you on the stairs and saw you smoking for the first time."

Umm Ali was amazing. She didn't speak to me about the matter the whole time we were in the shelter; afterward she came to visit me at home and asked that I make her a cup of coffee. She sipped it with me, and then said, "In war people act different from the way God created them. They go crazy, and become unbalanced; at that point it's not just their hair or their clothes that are disheveled, but their hearts also. I know she hurt you, but you are kind. Say: God forgive her, and forgive her yourself."

I did not comment.

Umm Ali said, "I'll bring her to visit you in the evening and she will apologize to you and we'll drink coffee together."

I don't know what Umm Ali said to the neighbor who insulted me. She didn't bring her to visit me, because a few hours later we all found ourselves in the shelter. I did not approach the neighbor nor did she approach me, but her son was playing with Maryam near me. Then at a moment when the shelling shook the earth I opened my arms wide and enfolded the two little ones, each one in an arm; I hugged them to my chest and my shoulders curved, my head leaning over them to protect their heads. The woman came and said, "Forgive me." She cried. I did not say anything.

My aunt also loved Umm Ali, and she liked to talk to her. They might have been the same age but my aunt was small in size and had been affected somewhat by senility; as for Umm Ali, she was tall and plump, in good health and skilled in conversation. She had given birth twelve times, "Ten boys and two girls, no more, and anyone who saw me here in Beirut with only Abbas would think I'm without any family. May God not forgive Israel." Umm Ali had come to visit her son when Israel occupied the south in 1978. She stayed with her son, Dr. Abbas, and the rest of the children and grandchildren and their families remained in Bint Jbeil. She was also waiting.

At the end of the third month the resistance left Beirut. It seemed that the war had ended; it ended in our defeat, in the occupation of Lebanon and in the departure of the fedayeen, but it had ended. Those who had been forced out returned to their homes in Sabra and Shatila and began to repair the war damage. Hasan went to Cairo, and Amin went back to regular hours in Acre Hospital. He and his colleagues also began to repair the floors that had been damaged in the hospital, because the war was over. That was what we believed.

On Tuesday afternoon news was broadcast of the explosion of the Phalange headquarters in Ashrafiyeh. I was terrified, as if the ones killed had been our own. It's strange, that instinct, like dogs that scent danger from afar. I knocked on Umm Ali's door, and told her; she said, "God may grant a reprieve, but he does not forget." I said, "If Bashir is among the killed, Lebanon will burn." She said, "It has burned, that's already happened." At night the radio broadcast classical music, funereal as it seemed; I assumed that Bashir Gemayel had been killed. A little later the news was confirmed.

On Wednesday we were awakened by intense shelling; it wasn't yet six in the morning. I carried Maryam, who was half asleep, and woke my aunt and took them down to the shelter. Then I went up another time and brought down the overnight bag and the two shopping bags. The shelling was continuous, as if we were still at the height of the war. By means of the transistor radio we were able to follow the description of Bashir Gemayel's funeral in Bikfaya; from other stations we learned that the Israeli forces were advancing to occupy West Beirut and that they had encircled the Sabra and Shatila camps, and the adjacent neighborhoods. In the evening Amin returned. He said that the Israeli forces had set up barricades near the Kuwaiti Embassy traffic circle, in front of the hospital. "A number of their soldiers entered the hospital and asked about the "saboteurs"; we told them that there was no one there but patients, doctors, nurses, and workers. They said, 'Look, pal, if you don't kharm us we won't kharm you. We're coming to protecht you!' They ate in the hospital cafeteria without permission, and then, to add to the humiliation, they passed out candy to some of the kids. One of the nurses told me that she saw them giving cookies and bonbons and chocolate to the kids near the checkpoints, and allowed them to play near them." I asked him, "How do you explain it?" He said, "Remember that long meeting that Abu Ammar held in the Gaza hospital. He said, and I quote: 'Don't be afraid, I'll ask for international forces for you at the entrance to the camps, to protect you.' There are no arms or fighters in the camps now; the weapons depots were confiscated by the Lebanese army, and the fighters have left. The international forces have left, I don't understand why, maybe to leave the way open for Israel to consolidate its control over Beirut. But I believe that now that the Israelis have occupied the town they don't need any more violence. They've shelled, invaded, and killed enough, and accomplished what they wanted. Abu Ammar and the fedayeen have left and the Israeli army has entered West Beirut, so they've reached their goals completely. Now it's the other face, chocolates and bonbons and chlorophyll smiles and 'We've come to protect you.'"

Amin went to sleep, but I was between sleep and waking all night long. I felt him leave the bed, so I got up. I looked at my watch and it was near to six. He ate a hurried breakfast, and kissed Maryam's forehead and his mother's, as they were both deeply asleep. He said as he was taking leave of me at the door, "I don't think that there will be any more shelling. I'll be home in the evening."

An hour after he left I went down to buy bread, but there was none; the street was nearly deserted. I hurried home, and then I remembered the newsman who had moved his counter from the street to the entry of the neighboring building. I passed the house and went to him. I found him, and bought the paper and carried it home.

Strange; I didn't wait to climb to the apartment. I stood at the bottom of the stairs. The headlines on the first page had nothing new: the attack on Beirut on five axes; the funeral of Bashir Gemayel in Bikfaya; the national forces were preparing for the attack. I had heard the same news the night before on the radio. I moved to the interior pages: pictures of Israeli tanks and military equipment in Bir Hasan; on the Sports City Road; in Ramla al-Bayda; at the lighthouse and the Military Bath. I stopped at the ninth page, at the details of the first item. A declaration from the White House, which I didn't read. Then: "Subsequently yesterday a spokesman for the Israeli army announced that the Israeli forces are continuing to establish control over vital areas and crossroads in Beirut. He said that the Israeli armed forces are advancing without meeting resistance except in a few areas, where there has been an exchange of gunfire from light weapons between our forces and the saboteurs. The Israeli Defense Forces are taking these steps to prevent the 'fedayeen' and the leftist militias from reforming in the Lebanese capital . . . Israeli Army Radio said that the army had invaded the Fakahani neighborhood . . . and the Kuwaiti Embassy Square, which was among the most important strongholds where the saboteurs sought shelter."

Where was Abed?

I sat on a step in the stairway, continuing to read the details as if the question and possible answer were ordinary or reasonable. A marine landing at the Military Bath, and debarkation on land at the airport. The advance of the forces along five axes: the airport road, leading to the Shatila traffic circle; the Kuwaiti Embassy traffic circle, Sports City, the Cola traffic circle, the Fakahani; the road from the sea to Ouzai; the museum; Barbir.

Where was Abed? They wouldn't give him bonbons or chocolate.

Maybe he was in the house of one of his friends, sleeping, not knowing that the Israeli tank was below the house in which he was sleeping.

I took the newspaper and climbed the stairs. I put the key in the lock, and realized that I had forgotten Naji's cartoon; I hadn't seen the last page.

I saw it. I no longer remember what I did.

Did I strike my face in despair? Perhaps. Did I open the door and remain standing? I went into the house, turned around in it twice, like a hyena, and then left. Did I lock it and go down the stairs only to discover that I had to go up again? I don't remember. I only remember that after that I was in Umm Ali's apartment. Good morning, good morning to you. The Israeli tanks are in the Fakahani. I couldn't find any bread. The Israelis are giving kids bonbons and chocolate at the barricades. I said it, and didn't hear what she said. Then the apartment of the next neighbor, then the third neighbor. I repeated the same words like a tape recorder. Then the shelling began to intensify and become continuous, so I carried Maryam and my aunt to the shelter. Where was Umm Ali? I left Maryam with her grandmother and went up to Umm Ali; she was baking bread. I yelled at her, is this any time to bake bread?! She said, I found some flour and said, I'll make bread. Anyway I've almost finished. She insisted on continuing: "Our lives are in God's hand, Ruqayya." My voice rose as I tried to convince her; perhaps I scolded her, perhaps I spoke insolently to her. Did I say something harsh, did I quarrel with her? I don't remember, but she did not come down. After mid-afternoon, as the shelling was becoming insane, Umm Ali came down, carrying the fruits of her labor. She distributed the loaves and gave each of the nine children present in the shelter a pastry the size of a fist, sprinkled with sugar.

A little before sunset the shelling stopped, so we left the shelter. After that the firing of illuminating flares began; they lit the sky in the area suddenly, lighting it brightly, as if we were in broad daylight. What was happening? None of us needed to draw near to the balcony or the window to see the sky; the room we were sitting in, which had been almost black because of the lack of electricity and the shadows cast by two small candles, suddenly lit up as if we were in the middle of the day. I went to the window; these illuminating flares were being fired from the south, toward al-Horsh and Bir Hasan, maybe over Shatila. Was it a new weapon? I didn't see any thick smoke or fires, as was usual after the shelling. Umm Ali was muttering prayers and my aunt suddenly began to say that maybe it was Judgment Day. The day of accounting is in our favor, our Lord will punish them now for everything they did to us. Maryam seemed excited by the possibility of lights illuminating the night like this, saying, "Mama, the electricity is cut off, maybe this is a new way they're using to light the houses." I didn't understand what was happening. I tried my best to push far away a feeling that a new disaster was on the way. The feeling was overwhelming, like certainty. What kind of disaster was it, what was its nature? I didn't know, and that disturbed me even more.

I suddenly asked Maryam, "Where are we, Maryam?" My aunt shouted, raising her hand with all five fingers extended, "Do you see my fingers?" I laughed aloud, hysterically. She said, "I thought you had suddenly lost your sight. That happened before, to a woman back home, long ago. I didn't realize that you were joking." I didn't tell her that I had not been joking, nor that my eyes were completely open and that I could see clearly, but that for a moment I had lost all direction. I didn't know where we were, in our apartment or in the shelter or in a third place, so I had asked Maryam.

That night I heard a knock on the door. I thought, Amin, or Abed. I didn't think that each of them carried a key and would not need to knock. I jumped up and opened the door.

27

The Abu Yasir Shelter

IN THAT FIRST MOMENT I didn't recognize her. Then I knew her, even though I still stood stiffly, as if I first had to understand why she looked like that and what had brought her at this late hour of the night. She spoke first:

"I'm Haniya."

More seconds while my mind ran in all directions. Had she been hit by shrapnel? Where? Why did she look like that? Had the Israelis raped her? Had her house been destroyed on top of her? Suddenly I wrapped my arms around her shoulders, and said, more loudly than usual or than was necessary, "Come in, come in, welcome, Haniya, please come in."

She was carrying her infant son in her hands; her daughter she was carrying like a pack on her back, tied on by fabric she had likely torn from the hem of her long dress and the sleeves. I undid the knots and took the girl, who was deeply asleep; I put her on my bed. Then I said, "Wash your face, Haniya, then we'll sit and you can tell me what happened. Can I get you some supper?"

"I'm not hungry."

"Tea?"

"A drink of water." She gave me the infant and went to wash her face; then she returned and took him from me. I handed her a glass of water, and she drank it at one gulp.

Haniya had come to our house daily for two weeks; she was a nurse who gave my aunt a shot that she refused categorically to let Amin give her. Why not, Aunt? Amin is your son. Even if he's my son it's not right for me to bare myself to him. So a nurse came whom my aunt did not accept, saying that her hand was as heavy as a sledge hammer and that she would kill her. She took the first shot and refused to take the second. The next day Amin told her that he would send Haniya to her, and that no one had as light a hand as she did—the patient would think that she was about to plunge in the needle to give him the shot, and she would have inserted the needle, emptied the serum and withdrawn it without his feeling it. He said, "Anyway, Haniya's family are from our neighbors." My aunt's face lit up suddenly, "From Tantoura? From what family?" Amin stuttered, and then said, "She was born twelve years after we left. Her father is from Jabaa and worked at the oil refinery in Haifa, and was living in Hawasa near Balad al-Sheikh." My aunt said, "The people of Jabaa are our maternal uncles." My aunt was happy with Haniya even before she saw her, and she was even happier when she came. She was friendly and good-natured and humored my aunt; she would insist that Haniya stay and have supper with us, and Haniya would say to her, "Umm Amin, I've been in the hospital all day and I have to go home, because my daughter is with my mother, and my husband is waiting." Haniya had not yet given birth to the baby she brought with his sister when she knocked on our door.

Was it that night that Haniya told me the details of what had happened Thursday evening in the Abu Yasir shelter, or did she tell me some of it and did I hear the details from her and others later on? I don't know, I don't remember. All I remember is that she said: "When the shelling got intense we went to the Abu Yasir shelter, a hundred yards away from our house. My mother and father refused to go with us to the shelter and stayed in the house. I went with my husband and the little ones and my sister and her husband and her kids. An hour later some armed Lebanese came in and began to shout at us, 'Where are the saboteurs?' A Lebanese neighbor shouted, 'For God's sake don't kill us, we're Lebanese!' But they began to fire in the shelter; some fell, and there were loud screams. Then they ordered us to leave the shelter. They stood the men in a line against the wall opposite the shelter; as for the women and children, they stood them in another line and said they would take us to Acre Hospital. They were shouting at us, using obscene words. We began to move, and then we heard shots, a lot of them close together, so we knew they were killing the men they had lined up against the wall. How did I pick up my daughter and lift her off the ground? How did I carry the two kids together and get out of the line and run away? I don't know. It's as if my legs were the ones that decided to save me and the little ones. I found myself running away, an odd kind of running because I was jumping high and zigzagging to avoid the shots they were firing at me. They were shouting insults and telling me to stop and firing at me. Even when I escaped and couldn't hear their voices any more, my legs kept running from lane to lane, passing the corpses thrown down in front of the houses. My legs didn't stop to investigate that strange, penetrating smell that surrounded the place. They didn't stop for a puddle my feet waded into; the water flew onto my face and my dress and my hands and I only noticed later on that it wasn't a puddle of water. Then I stopped, a moment or maybe two, because the baby had started to cry. I was afraid the noise would alert them. I tore off a piece from the hem of my dress and I tied it over his mouth."

"How did I get to the Gaza hospital? I don't know. As soon as I went in I began to yell at the top of my voice, 'They're killing people. I saw them with my own eyes.' They didn't believe me, so I began to repeat that they were firing on us in the shelter. That they lined the men up against the wall and killed them. A nurse gave me a sedative pill and then began to give me first aid—I hadn't noticed that there was anything on my body that needed it. The director of nursing at the hospital came and wrapped her arms around me and said, 'I know that these are hard days, dear. The entry of the Israelis into Beirut isn't easy for any of us.' I pushed her away and said, 'The men who were killing were speaking Arabic. They are from the Phalange. The killed all the men who were in the Abu Yasir shelter in al-Horsh. I saw other corpses in front of the houses, piles of corpses.' She spoke to me firmly and said, 'Don't scare people, we don't need any rumors!' I left her and went out to the courtyard where there were hundreds of people who had come to the hospital, and I said: 'Run away, they'll come here and kill you.' Then I asked a lady my mother's age to help me load my daughter onto my back; I told her, tie her on my back, and she tied her and I carried the boy and came running to you. What should I do now, Sitt Ruqayya?"

Haniya arrived at one in the morning; it was three before she responded to my insistence that she lie down on the bed for a while, until morning came and we could go together to the camp to find out what happened. I was stretched out on the couch in the living room, between sleep and waking, beset by nightmares; I would doze off a little and then become alert again, horrified by the question: what if they invaded the hospitals? What would they do to Amin? And Abed, where could Abed be? The office of the Popular Front was very close to Acre Hospital; it was still open and Abed went there sometimes. Was he there now? Maybe he was with his friends, dispelling their boredom by playing cards or arguing about what Abu Ammar did: this one curses Abu Ammar and holds him responsible, and that one thinks that the man did as much as he could to protect the Palestinian people. A daily battle that ended in shouting or that came to blows between the supporter of Abu Ammar and his decision and the one who was angry with the leadership and its policies. Abed was like a bull in a pen. He had spent three days after the resistance left without leaving his bed, then he began to stay away from home, saying, "I'll stay with my friends." Or he would come back late with the smell of whiskey on him, and I would reproach him for being drunk. Once I scolded him and he answered me, "Leave me alone. If I had hashish I would smoke it and if I had opium I would sniff it." I wonder where Abed was now? Why did the director of the Gaza hospital say what she did to Haniya? Had Haniya lost her mind with the long shelling and the terror? What if what she said was true? What would we do?

I found her standing in front of me, "Sitt Ruqayya, if I may, I'll leave the two little ones with you so I can go see what happened to my husband and my mother and father and my sister and her children."

I looked at my watch. It was five in the morning.

"I'll go with you."

I gave her one of my dresses and asked her to change into it. I knocked on Umm Ali's door; I knew that she woke up early for the dawn prayer. I decided not to tell her anything, only to ask her to take care of Haniya's children until we came back, and to tell my aunt and Maryam when they woke up that I had gone out and would not be late. No sooner did Umm Ali open the door, before good morning and good morning to you, she asked, "Have the Israelis gone into the camps?"

I said, "It seems that they have gone in with the Lebanese Forces."

"Lord have mercy! But where are you going?"

Haniya said, "We're going back to Horsh Tabet to reassure my family, then we'll go to Acre Hospital, and God willing everyone will be fine. I'll come back and pick up the kids and take them to my mother, and then go to the hospital. It's not right for me to be away from my work; there must be a lot of wounded."

We did not succeed in getting close to the camp nor to Acre Hospital; the place was tightly encircled. Haniya suggested that we go to the Israeli barricade, talk to the soldiers and ask them to allow us to pass. I tried to talk her out of it, unsuccessfully. She insisted. She said, "That's all we can do. I'll go. Come with me, Sitt Ruqayya." I was not afraid of them; I would go up to them, and maybe they would smile. What would I do? I had no weapon. All I could do was spit on them. How absurd! Spitting on one side of the scale, and on the other three months of shelling and killing and destruction. No, that's not correct; on the other side were all the years of my life. My father and my brothers. I was nailed to the ground.

"Haniya, they won't help us. Let's go back to the house."

"I must find my husband and my sister and my mother and father."

I saw her go, almost hurrying toward the Israeli barricade. What would I do now if they fired on her? Would I leave her wounded or maybe a stiffening corpse, and run away . . . or would I go up and carry her away and add a new victim to their tally? They did not fire. I saw her stopping at the barricade, speaking with them. They allowed her to pass. What generosity, what kindness. Haniya entered the camp at seven in the morning on September 17, and I stood waiting for her an hour or two, and then returned to the house to care for her little ones, and to wait.

28

A Letter to Hasan

DEAR HASAN,

Why have you entangled me in this writing? What sense does it make for me to live through the details of the disaster twice? I stopped last week at the morning of Friday, September 17. The day was before me: I had to face it again, to retrieve it from a memory that struggles with me as I struggle with it, as if we were wrestling in a ring. The simile is not exact, Hasan, for it's not a game and in the end there is no victor or vanquished, no audience applauding in admiration for the victory. It's not a game. And if it is, then it's a strange game, dangerous and lethal.

What do you want from me? To transmit my feelings then, or my feelings now, or what was recorded by people who know more than I do and are more capable, in articles and testimonies and books? Twenty years ago Sitt Bayan Nuwayhid, the wife of Shafiq al-Hout who was the director of the Lebanese chapter of the PLO, contacted me. She told me that she was gathering the testimony of those who escaped from the massacre, the people of Shatila and Sabra and the adjacent neighborhoods. She wanted me to bring her together with those I knew among them, and I did so. Sitt Bayan listened to Haniya here in my house, she listened to Abed and to other men and women whom I arranged for her to meet. Twenty years later Sitt Bayan called me and said that she had finished the book and it had come out. She took my address in Alexandria and sent it to me. The book arrived, and I opened the envelope. It was a hardback book, with a jacket that had a colored picture of three of those killed: a young man whose mustache had barely appeared, sprawled on the ground fully dressed, his head resting on the shoulder of another victim; on his left thigh were the feet of a third victim, of whom we could see only his running shoes and his legs in their jeans. (Running shoes exactly like the shoes your brother Abed used to wear in those days. Maybe if I had seen the picture at the time, before I saw Abed, I would have screamed that my son was gone.) On the upper left there was another, smaller picture, of two blackened corpses; it was hard to make out anything of their features. I could not bear the book jacket. I tore it off and hid it in one of the bedroom drawers. The huge book remained, with its sturdy, blue cover; that was bearable. I said I would read it. Two years have passed with the book on the small table next to the bed; I have not placed it upright among the rows of books in the bookshelf, nor have I opened it. Sitt Bayan must have spoken at length about what happened in Acre Hospital. She must have mentioned Intisar, whom I found charming, and whom they raped until she died. She must have mentioned her other coworker, whose name doesn't come to me but whose face and tone of voice I remember, I mean the other nurse they took turns raping until they killed her.

Dearest Hasan, your mother can't bear to read a book that recalls what happened and examines the details, so how can you ask me to write about the subject?

I often think about my mother as I am writing. She could not bear the thought of the death of her sons, so she sent them to Egypt. She lived under the protection of an illusion she had created in order to live. Maybe I'm like her. Haven't I lived for years with the illusion that your father was among those kidnapped? I wait for his knock on the door, to open it and find him in front of me. Perhaps he is thinner, or there is more gray than black in his hair; he's exhausted from years of absence, broken because he was forced to tear up his identity card and deny that he was Palestinian in order to live. I open the door and see him in front of me, whole. I enfold his shoulder with my arms and lead him into his house. I seat him, and sit down. I sum up for him the story of his family, what they have seen and gone through during the years of his absence. It's strange, I sum it up without any voice or words. I am at peace with him and he is also at peace, having returned to his wife and his home. He leans over a little and rests his head on my shoulder, and sleeps.

I promised you, Hasan, that I would finish this book, but when I got to this part of the story I knew I could not do it. Forgive me, my dear. But this is all I can do.

Love,

Ruqayya

It was as if I was afraid of retreating and tearing up the letter. I put it in the envelope and hurried to the post office, and mailed it.

Five days later Hasan called me.

He asked me about how I was. He talked about Maryam and Abed and Sadiq. He talked about his wife and his two children. He talked about his work. He took his time with the preliminaries. Then: "I got your letter. You say, what sense is there and what's the use? I say that I wanted others to hear your voice, the voice of Ruqayya the woman from Tantoura. Your four children, we know that voice because we were raised with it. We know you and we know that you have a lot to tell people. It's not only the story I'm interested in, I'm after the voice, because I know its value and I want others to have the chance to hear it."

I nearly said, mockingly, "I'm not Umm Kulthum or Fairuz, and what I lived through can't be sung!" I didn't say that or anything else. His voice came to me over the telephone, "Mama . . . are you there? Hello, Mama?"

"I hear you, Hasan. I hear you."

"I know from my studies and from my experience in life that conveying our voice is hard, it's demanding. Even peoples, even groups work long and hard to make their voices present and heard, so what about an individual person? Leave the writing for a few weeks, and then take it up again and continue. Promise me that."

"Give my best to your wife and the little ones."

"Don't run away from the promise."

"I'll try, Hasan. But what if I die? The writing will kill me."

"It won't kill you, you're stronger than you think. Memory does not kill. It inflicts unbearable pain, perhaps; but we bear it, and memory changes from a whirlpool that pulls us to the bottom, to a sea we can swim in. We cover distances, we control it, and we dictate to it."

I was no longer listening to what he said. Then, once more, "Mama, are you with me? Hello, Mama."

"I'll try. I'll try. Goodbye, Hasan."

I hung up. The words had provoked me, and I was angry. I don't understand educated people. I don't understand this strange talk about the voice. What voice? I didn't like his talk about the sea, either. Didn't like? That's not precise; I was upset by what he said, as if the words were choking me. Afterward I felt angry. I wanted to scream at him, why are you torturing me, Hasan? Leave me alone, God forgive you, go away! Your mother is seventy. She's tired. She raised you all, that's enough. Her battle with fate is unending. I did not scream at him. Hasan is the most gentle of my sons, the sweetest, the most mild-tempered, ever since he was a child. But he's determined; he asks for something and works toward it as if the revolution of the earth on its axis depended on his effort. He's always like that when he begins new research or a book project. He learned to become a researcher and a writer; he was trained in it and research has become his profession. Why is he driving me into an area I have nothing to do with? Besides, he's demanding that I drill into my living body. I'm not an oilfield, and these excavations that pierce through layers of earth are being made in my spirit. What does Hasan mean by the voice? Have I not learned enough to understand his words, or are his words complicated and incomprehensible? I won't write. I'll tear up the two notebooks. I'll tear them up and throw them in the wastebasket so the garbage man will take them away. I'll block all roads leading back, as if I were emigrating from one country to another, because the airplane is hovering over me, threatening a shelling that will bring down the roof over my head and kill me.

I did not tear up what I had written. I hid it, like the jacket of Bayan Nuwayhid's book, in one of the bedroom drawers.

Each of my sons calls me on the telephone once a week, and sometimes twice. Sadiq and his family call on Thursday evening, and Abed on Friday evening. As for Hasan, he calls on Sunday evening, which is morning in his time zone. Then Monday and Tuesday and Wednesday pass, waiting for the three following days. When Abed called from Paris on Friday evening I found myself asking him spontaneously, with no forethought, "Abed, do you remember when Sitt Bayan interviewed you for her book, on one of your visits years ago?"

"I remember."

"Didn't you record it?"

"I recorded the interview, and so did she."

"Do you still have the tape?"

"Didn't you bring the tape recordings we had in Beirut with you to Alexandria?"

"Yes, they're all here with me."

"Then you'll find the tape among them. The other tapes have labels of what's recorded on them, all except for that tape. I remember that we were afraid of putting a label on it."

I found the tape easily. I put it in the tape recorder, and began to listen.

29

Abed's Testimony

ABED SPOKE, SAYING:

"When the agreement was reached for the withdrawal of the resistance from Lebanon, they left the choice up to the young men who carried Lebanese travel documents, because they were from families who had arrived as refugees in 1948. They said, 'You can stay if you like or go with the resistance fighters.' I was angry over the agreements that Abu Ammar had accepted, and I was not alone. We felt that they were agreements that stripped us bare and accepted a defeat for which we weren't responsible. His leaders fled from the south. The thugs fled, it was natural, because they were thugs. Our young men, even the 'cubs' who were not over fourteen or fifteen, faced the attack with astonishing courage, beyond what you could imagine. By 'our young men' I don't mean just the men of the Popular Front, of course not, I have to be honest. The men of Fatah and the Popular Front and the Democratic Front and all the other Lebanese and Palestinian organizations, the Communist Party and the Labor Organization and the Progressive Socialist Party and the Syrian Nationalist Party and the Murabitun and Amal. The men of all the organizations, Lebanese and Palestinians, we all confronted them and defied them in Beirut for eight weeks, and then here was the leadership deciding to evacuate the resistance. It was important that the fighters leave in good order. My ass. I'm sorry for the expression, Sitt Bayan, but was that a military parade? It was not. It was a matter of life and death—they left, and death came to us. They left with their military uniforms and the arms on their shoulders, with Abu Ammar standing smiling and raising his fingers in the victory sign.

"I was born in 1960, Sitt Bayan; I did not witness the situation in the camps before the resistance came, but the old men in the organization told me about it. Before the resistance the Second Bureau tyrannized us. Once a microphone was stolen in Wavell Camp in Baalbek; they gathered up the young men and took them to the headquarters of the Second Branch in Beirut and beat them with whips for three hours. After that it seemed easy to them; every week they would gather up a group of young men and take them to Beirut to be beaten, and return them. It was a weekly trip: you go on an outing to the secret police, get beaten, and go back. Moving from one camp to another or having a visitor from outside the camp required a visa and a q and a session. Hammering a nail, building a roof, adding a room, all of that was forbidden, because the camp had to stay a temporary camp, to confirm that we were refugees. To preserve our right to return. Thank you very much! My direct commander in the organization told me that up to the sixties, most of the houses in Shatila were roofed with sheets of zinc covered with fabric and held down with stones, because it was absolutely forbidden to build a roof. And if the wind was strong, people would sit on the roof to keep the zinc sheet from flying away, but sometimes they did fly away, and you would see the owners running after them to catch up with them. They might not get to them before they crashed into people and injured them. When the resistance started the situation changed, and when the leadership came to Lebanon and Abu Ammar came the situation in the camps changed. It was just a flash in the pan, it seems. They came and they went. I asked myself, would the situation return to what it was? I was scared and apprehensive and expected disasters, but what happened exceeded anything I could have imagined. I don't just mean the massacre, but also what happened in Sidon and here in Beirut and in the camps when the Phalange took over the government. There was kidnapping and killing and making examples of corpses and imprisonment and torture, during the fall of 1982 and throughout the following year. During the invasion half the residents of the camps in the south became homeless. The shelling destroyed Beirut. That happened in June; for four months, Sitt Bayan, Israel refused to send bulldozers to remove the debris or permit any building materials to come in, to raise houses in place of the ones that were destroyed or even to repair what could be repaired. Only in October did UNRWA announce that it had been allowed to import tents, to shelter 48,000 in the Sidon region and 15,000 in the area of Tyre. We were asked to live in tents. So utter devastation, and utter humiliation. Before we could catch our breath the struggle between Abu Ammar and Syria intensified, so Amal besieged the camps, and the camps paid the price. Not only during the months of the attack and the siege, but also during years of terror and continuous calamity.

"Yes, you're right, Sitt Bayan. The siege of the camps by Amal is another subject. You want me to talk to you about our response to the evacuation decision. Some of my comrades among the young men from the 1948 families decided to leave with the resistance, and some of them decided to stay. There were some who decided to go and said goodbye to their families and settled their business, and then turned around and came back before reaching the port. And there were other cases when the opposite happened; someone would say 'I'm not leaving,' and then as he was saying goodbye to his comrades who were leaving he became frightened and overwhelmed by the separation, so he jumped into the truck and it took him with them to the ship. I was wretched—each of my brothers was in another country far away, should I leave my father and mother and Maryam and my grandmother? Why should I choose a new refuge? We were refugees, yes, but I was born in Lebanon and had lived there all my life, so why would I leave it and become a refugee all over again? Why would I go farther away from Palestine? I sneaked into Sidon—it was a dangerous adventure, in the presence of such a number of occupying troops—but I managed to get to Ain al-Helwa. The bastards had destroyed it beyond all imagination. I got lost in the streets, because the destroyed houses had changed the look of the place. I went to say goodbye to my uncle Ezz; I wasn't about to leave without telling him goodbye. Then I came back to Beirut and decided to go; then I changed my mind at the last instant. They left and I stayed. My morale was at its lowest, I don't know how my mother put up with me. I was overcome by a feeling of absurdity, as if I had never been one of the fedayeen and carried a weapon. My mother doesn't know that I was thinking of suicide. The truth is that I had decided; the only thing that held me back was a discussion with one of my comrades. I told him it was natural for us to commit suicide, and here was my comrade, who was two years younger than I was, scolding me as if he were a teacher and I were a small boy. He said, 'You want to kill yourself? Kill yourself, no one needs you. Because when you think about suicide you're fleeing from the battle and abandoning your family, who had confidence in you. It's disgusting, how easily you say, "Confront it alone, as for me I'm going to die and to rest." Damn your god, brother, you're stupid, an animal.' He insulted me and left the place, and I cried like a kid. Usually I grab the throat of anyone who insults me and make him pay the price twice over; but he insulted me and I cried. On the next day I went to him and kissed his head.

"On the morning of Wednesday, the fifteenth of September, the Israeli tanks entered West Beirut. I had spent the night with comrades of mine who live in the Fakahani. Wednesday morning we had seen the tanks advancing. There was no one in charge to turn to; we decided to act on our own

214

authority. They were centered on the College of Engineering, and there were clashes between us and them. We were different groups, some of them very young, cubs. The battle continued all day. Then the Israelis pulled back behind the College of Engineering.

"The next day we decided to investigate the situation and go to our office opposite Acre Hospital, to see if we could get more weapons. I repeat, Sitt Bayan, there was no local leadership; the leaders who had gone had not left us any instructions, nor was there any committee responsible for the security of the camps. They left us cut off, as if we were foundlings or orphans. With the situation like that it was natural for the residents to feel that the presence of any armed man or any weapons in the camp was a threat to the camp and to everyone in it. Many people got rid of their individual weapons; sometimes they got rid of them by wrapping them in newspaper and throwing them in a garbage can, or in any heap or pile.

"I headed for the office of the Popular Front with a number of my comrades, and a group of young men and two girls joined us there. I remember that one of the girls was from Fatah. We decided to skirmish with the Israeli soldiers, using hit and run tactics. One of us would fire a magazine or half of one and rush off to another place. Notice, Sitt Bayan, that up to that moment we did not know about the presence of the Lebanese Forces; we thought that we were confronting Israeli soldiers only. We were able to hit an Israeli officer and two soldiers, or maybe three. They were standing near the Kuwaiti Embassy, on a hill, looking toward the camp with binoculars. We fired a B7 rocket-propelled grenade and bullets at them.

"There was another group from the Arab Front. Their office was in the Farahat neighborhood, southeast of the camp. When the Israeli shelling concentrated on them they decided to blow up the arms depot they had, to make the Israelis think they were facing stiff opposition. The depot contained Grad and Katyusha rockets and artillery missiles;

imagine, a weapons depot that we were blowing up with our own hands, since what good were the weapons after the evacuation of the trained cadres and leaders who could tell us when and where to use them?

"There was a cub named Hani who was known in the camp. A cub from Fatah. Somebody shouted to him, 'The Israelis are underneath you, Hani.' Hani threw a grenade on an Israeli truck carrying soldiers (at the time we thought they were Israeli soldiers, they might have been Israelis, or maybe they were from the Lebanese Forces). He hit them, then he came back and hit a half tank. He was one individual, acting alone. There was also a girl named Fatima from Fatah, who caught up to us and joined in with us. That evening we lost Comrade Butrus, that was his name in the movement, he was from the Popular Front fighters.

"When it got dark, we decided to withdraw and meet again the next day. Some of us decided to spend the day in the house of friends in the camp; a comrade of mine and I decided to leave the camp. We hadn't heard about what was happening. We didn't know that the Lebanese Forces were killing the residents with bullets and axes and knives. We were naturally walking cautiously, scouting the place and then moving on our way, noiselessly. On our way back we met a Fatah fighter who told us that he had seen the Lebanese Forces invade the Abu Yasir shelter in the Horsh Tabet neighborhood. It was the first time that we heard that the Lebanese Forces had entered the camp. He said, 'We have to get the people out of the shelters and lead them calmly out of the camp.' He assigned each of us a shelter and told us how to behave, and the way out. We carried out his instructions, and we were able to get hundreds of residents safely out of the shelters and to lead them out of the camp. But despite what this fighter told us, none of us realized what was happening. I mean, when we put our heads on our pillows on the night of Thursday to Friday we knew that the camp was under siege, and that Israel was lighting up the sky of the area with illuminating flares to make it easier for the Lebanese Forces to go in, and that the Forces were carrying out the task of inflicting harm on the residents for Israel, killing some of them and capturing others. But none of us imagined at all that we were facing a massacre of that magnitude, or that the Phalange and the men of Saad Haddad were going into the houses and killing the people with axes and knives and raping the girls, and destroying the houses with bulldozers, bringing them down on top of the people who lived in them. We had never known anything of that magnitude before, we hadn't heard of anything like it, so we didn't conceive of it. It wasn't possible for us to conceive of it.

"On the morning of the next day the area was completely surrounded. We failed to get in, despite repeated attempts. I did not witness what happened in Acre Hospital nor in Gaza Hospital. You said that you want my statement as an eyewitness; what I saw ends with the night of Thursday to Friday.

"Afterward many people told me what they saw during the three days. I was asking and listening, determined to know what happened in Acre Hospital moment by moment because my father was in the hospital. We don't know what happened to him; he was considered to be among the kidnapped. I examined all the details in order to learn my father's fate. It was also because I wanted to give the details to my brothers, because they were working outside of Lebanon and I was the only one still living through the situation. I felt that I was responsible for learning what happened and telling them. If you like, I'll tell you, and if you like I'll give you a copy of the report I sent to my brothers, to Hasan in Cairo and to Sadiq in Abu Dhabi."

At the time I did not look at this report. But when I wanted to put the tape of the interview back in its plastic box, I found in the box three sheets of foolscap folded several times.

30

The Report

ABED WROTE:

Dear Sadiq and Hasan,

This is the picture I have been able to put together, piece by piece, of what happened in Acre Hospital on Friday, the seventeenth of September.

Beginning at five in the morning on Friday, calls were heard over loudspeakers, coming from the Israelis that were surrounding the camps: "Surrender and you'll be safe. Everyone must return to their houses and put any weapons they have in front of the houses. Surrender and you'll be safe." The calls caused turmoil among the residents, and hundreds of them had sought refuge in the hospital for protection the previous night. Some thought that leaving the place was the only guarantee of safety, and others that staying in the hospital was safer. There were those who calmed the others and reassured them, denying the talk that was circulating about a massacre and considering it a rumor, despite the arrival of a woman shouting and crying and confirming that there was a massacre, and that the killers were on their way to the hospital to kill the people. In short the witnesses all agree that between five and seven in the morning a state of terror, turmoil, and chaos reigned. Then the residents began to leave the hospital, gradually.

Between eight and nine in the morning a meeting was held for the employees of the hospital—doctors and nurses and administrative workers. Here, also, opinion was divided between those who said it was necessary to go and those who advocated staying, because moving the sick would not be easy, and because there was a greater possibility of their being hunted down outside the hospital. They decided to stay. At the same meeting they discussed evacuating the children but the director of the hospital said he opposed the idea.

After the meeting the two nurses from the night shift went away to sleep; two nurses remained in the emergency ward, two European nurses stayed to take care of the children and the crippled, there were two nurses on the ground floor, and one or two on the upper floor.

Two things happened right after the meeting: a woman who worked in the hospital went out to buy a pack of cigarettes for one of the doctors and was hit by a sniper's bullet, and died. And Urabi, a young Egyptian who worked in radiology, went out to bring in one of the hospital cars so it wouldn't be hit by a missile. He crossed to the gas station in front of the hospital. (Maybe Urabi went out for another reason. Someone suggested the possibility that he was maybe trying to flee, but I think that's unlikely, because his wife was a nurse in the hospital and she was there that day.) Then the nurses looking out the window saw someone stretched out on the ground and suspected it could be Urabi. A lady arrived at the hospital driving a Renault car, and they got her permission to use her car to cross to the other side of the street to the gas station, to save the person lying there if he was still alive. (There was sniping and gunfire.) An Egyptian woman who worked in the kitchen drove the car and two European nurses went with her, Ann the Norwegian and Erica the Frenchwoman, crouched in the back seat so that their heads would not appear in the window. The Egyptian worker drove the car fast, protecting it with the buildings, right and then left and then left, until she got to the gas station. It was Urabi stretched out on the ground, lifeless. The three woman together carried him to the car and returned to the hospital with him. He had been hit by bullets and a missile had torn off part of his face. (Hasan, you are in Cairo and maybe the authorities in Egypt have attempted to learn more about the subject. Was anything published about Urabi in the Egyptian papers? There were also two other martyrs, a worker at the fuel station and a hospital cook, who were Egyptians, was anything published about them?) No sooner had my father finished putting Urabi in a shroud than the first of the Lebanese Forces soldiers appeared, followed by the rest. It was eleven o'clock.

After they encircled the area, the Israelis had entered the hospital a number of times. They asked about the "saboteurs," and were told that there were only patients and workers in the hospital. They walked around in the hospital and ate in the cafeteria and left.

The Israelis were not the ones who burst into the hospital on Friday; there were also Lebanese Forces, the Phalange, and Saad Haddad's men. That's what some of them said, without mincing words.

One of the nurses told me that she said to my father, before they burst in, "We must flee, they will kill us." He reassured her and said to her, "Your family is in Tyre. The Israelis occupied it but they did not just kill civilians arbitrarily. They shell us with airplanes and artillery, but when they occupy the place they don't interfere with the women and children. We're in a hospital. At worst they will imprison us, the men." She said to him, "But they are the Phalange and they won't have any mercy if we fall into their hands." He laughed and said to her,

"I thought you were braver than that." The nurse told me, "Minutes after that they invaded the hospital. They came in the emergency entrance and I went out another door, three nurses and I and a little boy we took with us. We spent the night far from the area."

When they entered the hospital they were speaking roughly, in Arabic and English, shouting and hurling insults and speaking obscenely. Then they took out the doctors and the hospital workers. They stood the foreigners in a line and the Arabs in another line. They examined the foreigners and then spread out a blanket for them and allowed them to sit on it. They gave them cigarettes and gum. They were relatively nice to them, but when they allowed them to go and saw them returning to the hospital to go on with their work they began to insult them and treat them differently.

My father was seen standing in the other line along the wall, with about ten or fifteen men. Then he was seen an hour or two later, as he was walking among the hundreds they were leading to the Sports City. It was obvious that he had been beaten and tortured.

Two doctors and two employees managed to flee from the hospital by way of the Yacoubian Building, adjacent to the hospital. They went in the gate and came out from the gate on the other side of the building.

As the foreigners and the doctors were standing outside the hospital, some of the Phalange men remained inside. They were laughing and joking sometimes, and asking the girls for tea and coffee. One Lebanese girl who had accompanied her father and brother, injured during the carnage the previous night, told me that they treated them like servants. Then they began to talk obscenely, so she was afraid, and fled. The girl's instinct was right because at about the same time they took two nurses, one of them Palestinian and the other Lebanese.

They pulled Intisar the Lebanese by her hair and took her down to the shelter of the hospital and took turns raping her, then they shot her. Then they returned for her coworker and raped her until she died.

I don't know if my father tried to flee and they killed him, or if they tortured him and then killed him, or if they drove him to the Sports City and he was carried away by those trucks that took people to unknown places from which they didn't return. There are two other doctors besides my father of whom no trace has been found, Dr. Sami al-Khatib and Dr. Muhammad Uthman. Someone saw four bodies floating in the pool of the Sports City, wearing white coats; but we don't know if my father and the two other doctors were among them, because there were three ambulance workers from the Red Crescent who were shelled and killed when they were in an International Red Cross car. They were also wearing white uniforms. I didn't see the corpses floating in the pool, but others told me the story. If I had seen them I would have been able to recognize my father whatever his state.

When the International Red Cross arrived—they came twice, at two in the afternoon (when the Forces were still in the hospital), and again at four-thirty in the afternoon (when they had left)—they transferred some of the patients to the Najjar hospital, and some of the children, with a foreign nurse, to the Amal Center. They also took four bodies: two women and a doctor and an Egyptian worker (the hospital cook or the worker in the gas station across the street? I don't know). Was my father the doctor? The witnesses assert that my father was not among them.

A nurse from Shatila told me that she went to the hospital on Saturday after the Forces had left the area. The hospital was in a miserable state: the glass was broken and the curtains were burned and the cafeteria was demolished, including the refrigerator; all the supplies were strewn on the floor and the picture of Abu Ammar was torn, its frame broken and the glass smashed. They had trodden it underfoot. The children's section was empty, and the nurseries also. The next day this nurse found a child killed and thrown into the hospital garden. She added that when she went back to Sabra she found there children who had been in the hospital and whom she knew, aged a year or two years or three, killed, including a paralyzed child who had been killed with an axe. She thinks that they threw them there so it would not be said that they killed children in the hospital. A number of people testified that in a closed shelter southwest of the camp, in the Irsal neighborhood, they found bodies piled on top of each other, and among them were the bodies of nursing infants and children not fully formed (I think that they were the newborns that they took from the nursery).

Going back to Father, there are three possibilities: that Father was killed or taken or escaped. Each of the three poses questions we have no answers for:

If Father was killed, then how, and when? Did they torture him, and what did he say or do? Where is his body? Did it stay under the rubble? Was he buried in one of the mass graves that they dug during the massacre, and that the government has refused to dig up? Was he taken by one of the three bulldozers that were seen leaving Sabra on Saturday, piled with victims? Or did they throw him in the sea, as they did with others, near al-Naima and al-Damour, after putting him in a sack and weighting it down with stones? Or did Father have the good fortune to be buried with religious rites, performed by Sheikh Salman al-Khalil or his brother Sheikh Jaafar al-Khalil on the following Monday, when they buried the martyrs in groups of ten or twelve, until they had buried eight hundred in one day in a single mass grave?

If Father was driven with hundreds of others to the Sports City, there is the possibility that they shot him just like that, for no reason, which is what they did to many. There is the possibility that they sent him down into one of the death pits where they buried people alive. Perhaps he was able to flee, because when they were driving the people a man shot an RPG missile at them and there was chaos and confusion among the guards, so dozens fled, as eyewitnesses asserted. Did Father flee then? And if he escaped then why has he not contacted us up until now, when three months have passed since the massacre? Is he imprisoned? I have tried to learn if the Phalange have any prisoners, but I have not obtained any information.

Legally, Father is among the missing. The Lebanese government has not issued an official report up to now, even though it's known that there is a report prepared by the military prosecutor, Asaad Germanos. He completed it less than two weeks after the massacre. This report was not published, even though the *Safir* newspaper recently ran a summary of it. Perhaps it was not published because the number of victims it advances is ridiculous, since it estimates the number at 470 killed. The International Red Cross estimated the number of victims at 2,750, and the sources of the Lebanese Red Cross estimated it at 3,000, not including those who remained under the rubble, nor those who were bulldozed, nor those who were kidnapped or lost. Agence France Presse estimated the number taken away in trucks and never seen again at 3,000 persons. Other estimates say that they were 1,300. These numbers alone translate into insanity, when the difference between one estimate and another is 1,000 or 1,500 people.

My dear Sadiq and Hasan,

I have tried my utmost to investigate what happened at Acre Hospital on Friday morning, September 17; that's what I promised you. I've only written four pages, but it took me months to get the details. I have many papers and clippings from the newspapers and reports and statements, as well as observations and testimony and a roster of the names of the witnesses whom I listened to and to whom we can return if we need to. I have tried as much as I was able to concentrate the information I had, and to present it clearly. As for the writing, it's hard, really hard. We owe it to our father to find out what happened to him, and this report is only a small step at the beginning of the path. If he was martyred then we must be certain of that and learn the circumstances of his martyrdom, and the grave where he lies. If he was captured we must search for him and turn the world upside down to get to him. If we don't, we do not deserve his name or his efforts to raise us and teach us or a single hour of the love he gave us. And I know we agree that he gave us an incalculable number of those hours.

Your brother, Abed

Beirut, December 17, 1982

31

To Cut a Path

ABED DID NOT SHOW ME this letter when he wrote it, nor when he gave a copy of it to Sitt Bayan. I read it, and was brought up short by the date. Nearly twenty years later I understood Abed's strange behavior on the day his grandmother died.

She died on December 16, 1982 and we buried her the next day, the same date as the one Abed had placed on his letter to Sadiq and Hasan.

I found her motionless in her bed. I ran to Abed. For two days he had not left his room, sitting at his desk with his beard growing and his hair as disheveled as the papers and newspaper clippings that he surrounded himself with.

I said, "Abed . . . your grandmother . . . ."

He got up from his seat and followed me to her room. He confirmed that she had died. He said, "I'll go look for a doctor and do what's necessary." But when he was putting on his clothes he was swearing and cursing as if his grandmother had played a trick on him with the timing of her death and had died purposely to make him miserable. The next day he suddenly asked me, "We buried her and it's over, and people came to pay their condolences today. Will they come tomorrow?"

I said, "Usually condolences last three days."

"I don't want any visitors here tomorrow, I'll throw them out if they come. She lived her full life and died in her bed, and we buried her fittingly. It's over."

He shouted again, "It's over!"

Abed was twenty-eight years old, could I slap him? I nearly did. I don't remember what I said, or how I reacted to his insolence. All I remember is that he was shouting at the top of his lungs like a deranged person, and that Ezz put his arm around his shoulders and led him gently into his room and closed the door; it stayed closed for an hour or more. Maryam was sitting beside me, then she put her head in my lap and went to sleep; I stayed still as a stone, without moving or thinking, until I heard the door open and saw Ezz coming out of the room. It seemed to me that I had not seen him for years. The dark blue circles under his eyes had become fuller; when had he gotten so old? Why hadn't I noticed it before? He noticed Maryam and said in a whisper, "She'll get cold." He took her and placed her in her bed, and came and sat next to me. He extended his hand with a pack of cigarettes, giving me one and taking another. We sat smoking in silence.

Two or three days later, Abed surprised me: "I'm going to leave the College of Engineering."

"You'll graduate next year."

"It doesn't matter."

"You chose to specialize in architecture, no one imposed it on you."

"I'll transfer to studying law."

"You'll start over?"

"I'll start over."

"Can you explain the reason to me?"

"I have reasons, but it takes a long time to explain them."

"I'm listening. Explain, even if it takes days."

He left me and went out of the house.

We would peck at each other daily, like roosters. He couldn't stand me and I couldn't stand him. I told myself again and again that I had to be patient. You are his mother, Ruqayya, and he's a boy, a young man laboring under a burden. I would try; then he would explode in my face like a mine, and I would explode. The house seemed like a war zone; no sooner did we put out one fire than another sprang up. Even Maryam would run all over to put out the fires. The thought makes me smile: a girl not yet seven, in second grade, wearing a helmet and jumping up the ladder to face the burning fire with a water hose many times longer than she was tall. She said to me, "Mama . . . don't you love Abed like you love me?"

I smiled.

"And doesn't he love you like I love you?"

"I don't know, Maryam."

"He loves you and you love him, so why do you fight every day?"

"We aren't fighting."

We were fighting, and we kept fighting, as if we were a married couple on a boat that was about to break up, after which each one would go off on one piece of wood. I complained to Sadiq, and he said, "Abed is devastated. If you don't put up with him, who will?" It seems as if he called Abed and spoke to him about the subject, because Abed came to me like a crazy person and said, "Sadiq called me to tell me to take care of you. He said, 'Your mother is tired, be more considerate of her.' God damn Sadiq, he talks as if you were my stepmother, and as if he were responsible. Of course he's responsible as long as he sends a few dollars every month. Do you know what your responsible son said? He said that he's arranging to take you and Maryam to live with him in Abu Dhabi. He said that next July he'll take his wife and children to Europe, for a change of scene. He said, 'Two weeks only, then Mama will come here and we'll register Maryam in the school here.' Did he tell you that? Do you want to live with him? Have you decided to leave Lebanon? God damn him!"

I hadn't had the slightest idea of Sadiq's intentions, even though my surprise was lost in the sharpness with which Abed threw it out. It was as if he were a prosecutor about to send me to prison after he got the confession.

I wouldn't leave my home, I wouldn't leave Beirut. Stubbornness? Maybe. It seemed as if it was a decision I had made and could not reexamine. Why? Why wouldn't I take my son and daughter and escape with them, far from this place that had come to say implicitly to us, 'Get out of the country, you're aliens.' Did I say implicitly? That's a mistake, they said it frankly every day. I saw it with my own eyes written on the walls. In the newspapers there were leaks about plans to reduce the number of Palestinians in Lebanon from half a million to fifty thousand. Did they want to throw us into the sea? They threw leaflets into the camp, menacing and threatening us. And it wasn't just empty words: the army tyrannized the camps, and the Forces did what they pleased. Daily arrests, killing at the barricades, kidnapping, destruction of any wall built in the camp—how can people live in houses without walls? And strangulation: there was no work, there were no work permits. The men of the camp were killed or imprisoned or had left with the evacuation, and the few remaining were unemployed. Once again women took care of themselves and their dependents as if they had just emerged from the summer of 1948. No, it wasn't only the Palestinians who were undesirables; the Lebanese who had immigrated from the south and al-Metn, who lived in Ouzai and the southern suburbs, were exposed like us. The army clashed with them and martyrs fell among them. They wanted to destroy their houses, or more precisely to remove them, as the houses had been destroyed since the invasion and the battles that had occurred in the area with the Israeli army. The government did not allow the residents to rebuild or repair their houses, to bring back water and electricity to them, to remove the debris or the waste. All that was forbidden; they were required to leave. But where to?

In the future I would think a long time about it, asking myself why I didn't leave. Had I inherited from my uncle Abu Amin the sense that I was not a stranger, or had I come to imagine, gradually and over time, growing up in the place,

230

that my estrangement was that of the people there, or of some of the people, those who were like us? Perhaps I didn't want to go farther away, as if the shore of Beirut would lead me to the shore of our village, as if Shatila were one end of a street that I could follow, walking in a straight line, to arrive in Tantoura. Just a long street, one line like the line between Tantoura and Haifa or Tantoura and Qisarya, Wisal's town. Maybe it was simpler than that: I hated to leave my life and go, as the young men had gone. They were forced to leave; the leaders ordered them and they left. No one had ordered me, so why would I leave?

Ezz told me at length what happened in Sidon: the kidnapping and the killing, the disfigured bodies that they found near Ain al-Helwa and al-Mieh Mieh, in the heart of Sidon. They would find leaflets signed by "the Cedar Rebels" demanding that the residents throw out the foreign terrorists who were oppressing Lebanon and causing its devastation. "We will not permit the Palestinians to live on Lebanese land." In the leaflets they called us killers and germs and garbage. They said that the Israelis had come to save them and that Lebanon and Israel would become stronger by working together. They said that the two civilizations would be combined. The Phalange didn't spare anyone and the Israelis were forming militias of local workers, claiming to keep the peace in the villages. They didn't limit themselves to the militias of the Phalange and Saad Haddad and the Cedar Guards, but also created other militias. They forced the chief of every village to designate ten people from the village to work with what they called "the Civil Guard," and they forced them to come up with the money for their expenses. Everyone complained, even the traders. Israeli fruits and vegetables came to be everywhere. They brought their products to sell in the south. So it was death and humiliation and utter devastation, and of course, fear. It was a fear I hadn't seen in the camp before, even during the time of the Second Bureau, in the fifties.

Ezz told me, "Sadiq is right, we no longer have any life in Lebanon. Go to Abu Dhabi." He had decided to go to Tunisia; Karima didn't want to go, but she couldn't convince him to change his mind. He took her and went; I remained. Why? Had I begun to think that slowly and gradually, another stream would cut a path in the earth? Yes, I was following the news of the resistance in the south, searching for the details every day on page five of the paper. Demonstrations, sit-ins, armed operations. Confronting the occupation face to face, confrontations between armored soldiers carrying weapons and the housewives of a village, or its men or its mosque or its pupils.

At the end of February in 1984 I went to Jabsheet to offer condolences to the family of Sheikh Raghib Harb. A year later I went to Sidon to visit my mother's tomb and that of my uncle Abu Amin.

The Israelis had gathered their equipment and withdrawn.

32

The Center (1)

I SAID TO THE ELDER Abed, "Your wife visited me yesterday."

He said, "She came to complain to you about me, didn't she, to tell you that I hit her?"

"She didn't say that."

He looked me in the eyes, disbelieving. I had not lied. His wife had talked to me a long time about his state and complained to me, but she had not said that he had hit her.

He said, "I can't stand myself. I can't even stand our little boy. I don't know what to do. I leave the house in the morning as if I'm going to the Center, I walk in the streets or sit in a café, avoiding the usual ones since I don't want to see anyone I know or to talk with anyone. When exhaustion and hunger become too much, I go home. I want to sleep but I can't sleep, I'm hungry but I'm not interested in eating, I turn to my wife suddenly as if in desire and then I discover that I'm incapable of intimacy with her. I don't read or write, my ability to concentrate is zero."

"Don't you go to the Center?"

"They closed it, the government closed it. They summoned the Center director and the next day army trucks came and loaded the furniture and the equipment and what remained of the archives."

"I'll make you a cup of coffee."

"No thanks, I'm leaving." Then, "I'll come by tomorrow or the next day with my wife and the boy, to say goodbye to you and Abed and Maryam. I'm going back to Amman."

He said it quickly, as he was rising from his seat. He did not shake hands, or stand at the door, as usual, to finish saying something he had begun or to say something he had wanted to say during the visit and had forgotten. He said, "By your leave," and then I heard his steps on the stairs.

The humidity is suffocating, my face is dripping with sweat. I wipe it with a tissue, and notice that my shirt is soaked with sweat. I wash my face and change my shirt. I boil a pot of coffee and take it and the cup to the kitchen table, and sit down. I pour the coffee and light a cigarette.

When the Israelis entered Beirut nine months earlier, they stormed into the Center and stole half of its library and archives. Abed told me, "Thank God Dr. Anis was no longer director of the Center. The mine that exploded in his face ten years ago didn't kill him, but I'm sure that the sight of Israeli soldiers in the Center would have killed him. Neighbors in the building across from us saw the soldiers removing cartons loaded with books and putting them in trucks, for three days. They saw some of them throwing books and papers in the street from the windows and balconies. We found some of them and put them back in their place—that was on the fourth day, when we were able to go back to the Center. They weren't satisfied with plundering, they also destroyed the furniture and the equipment they hadn't taken, and wrote obscenities on the walls. We thought, so be it. We brought paint and wiped out all trace of the obscenities, and reorganized the work."

For nine months, Abed never visited me, either alone or with his wife and child, without referring to the Center. He would talk about any subject and then suddenly bring up the Center, obstructing the flow of talk for half a minute or so; then he would retreat and allow the talk to flow again.

Six months after the plunder of the Center a car bomb exploded, burning the building and martyring a number of those who worked in it. I did not run in the streets like someone touched in the head as I had done eleven years before, the day of the first explosion, which had hit Dr. Anis in the face. I didn't know about it until Abed himself told me the next day. I ask myself now, if I had known at the time, would I have run through the streets, shooing away death as if it were a fly, or had my senses been dulled by all the mines that had exploded? If I ran at the news of every mine that exploded in any place where I had friends or acquaintances, I would have spent my whole day running in opposite directions, running toward Shatila, or toward al-Rausha, or toward the Fakahani, or toward the sea. Who blew up the Center? Abed said, "The Lebanese security forces. Their head is Zawi Bustani, a Phalangist. They say he is a spy for Israel, on their payroll."

The building was no longer safe, but Abed and his colleagues insisted on continuing in it, going to work every day. The security forces and the army did their duty. After three months the Lebanese Army surrounded the Center and broke into it. Abed said, "They stood us against the wall as if they were going to execute us. They inspected the place and left. We met afterward, and agreed that we would not close the Center. We will not leave."

Now he's leaving. I looked at my watch, and jumped, leaving the house. How could I forget when Maryam's school was dismissed? I looked at my watch, hastening my steps, nearly running. When I glimpsed the door of the school at the end of the street I looked at my watch again.

I found her inside the school near the door, with a girl and a boy, schoolmates. She was not crying, and bore none of the signs of fear I had expected. I kissed her, and she said, smiling, "Mama, you're late!"

"I'm sorry, Maryam, I'm sorry. Were you afraid?"

"I wasn't afraid. My friend Farah was afraid and cried. She said that two weeks ago a car bomb exploded near their house, and that one of their neighbors died in the explosion. She said that the same thing might have happened to her mother, and began to cry. Samir and I kept her occupied by talking to her, and it worked."

I looked at the little girl. She was younger than Maryam, thin and delicate. She was laughing now, talking with the boy. I said, "When we're a little late, assume that it's because of the traffic, or because a guest has appeared suddenly and made us late, or that the clock is broken."

I kept the children occupied until the boy's mother and the girl's sister arrived, and everyone left safely.

Maryam asked, "Mama, why were you late?"

"Uncle Abed visited me. He's going to Amman. They closed the Research Center."

"Who closed it?"

"The army."

"Why?"

"Because it's a Palestinian Center."

"Mama, why does the army hate us?"

I changed the subject: "I'm going to buy you some chocolate because you didn't cry when I was late, and because you helped your friend when she was afraid and cried."

Maryam said, clinging to my hand and skipping, "Buy me chocolate because I like it. I'm not so little that I cry when you're late—I have a mind that tells me, 'Maryam, don't be afraid now. Wait, and if Mama doesn't come before night, then there's a problem, because it can't get dark before Mama comes.' And it was only natural to take care of Farah, because the older one helps the younger—the teacher told us that. I'm two years older than she is, because I'm seven and she's five."

She emphasized the age by spreading out the fingers of her left hand and the thumb and forefinger of her right, and then folding the two fingers and leaving the five.

"But you didn't answer me—why does the army hate us so much?"

"Because all their leaders are from the Phalange, and the president is also from them."

"Why do the Phalange hate us?"

"That's a long story, I'll explain it to you later. Are you hungry? Today I made you . . ."

"You said that Uncle Abed is going to Amman. Is he going to live there?"

"Yes."

"And my brother Abed, is he going too?"

"I don't know. He hasn't said."

"If he goes we won't have any relatives in Beirut. Will we go too?"

"If we went, who would you miss most in Beirut?"

"First, Umm Ali. Second, my teacher and my friends at school. Third, the thyme-flavored snacks that Umm Nabil makes, in the camp. And Umm Nabil and her children. Fourth, Dr. Hana in the Maqasid Hospital—maybe I'll be a doctor like her when I grow up, and like Papa, of course. Papa's been away a long time, Mama. I mean, they kidnapped him, where? When we play in the camp we find the boy who's hiding, we always find him. Maybe we need to look more."

I changed the subject again. "Sadiq says to come and visit him in Abu Dhabi. What do you think?"

"Vacation is coming in a week and we can visit him. But we'll come back before the beginning of school."

"What if he said, 'Stay here with me'?"

"It's better to visit him for a month or two and then come back to our house. Would Abed come with us?"

"No."

"Why?"

"He has his studies and his own concerns."

"I would rather he come with us, or that we stay with him."

I go back and forth to the camp. I encourage someone's mother, or one of her neighbors, because her son has disappeared or because the army has arrested her husband. I read the *Safir* newspaper to the elderly ladies who can't read. I help to prepare the list of those kidnapped, I take part in small parades of women (the time of large demonstrations has passed), organized by the Women's Union for the Families of the Kidnapped. I take part in helping someone's mother and her eight children, when she has no one to support her and no work and her house has been destroyed. I look for some connection or I arrange the necessary sum to free one of the young men. I contribute to reopening the nursery schools that have been destroyed, to help the women who go to work because they have been widowed in the war or the massacre or because their husband left with the fighters. I take care of the children of one of my acquaintances who has gone to Ain al-Helwa to check on her family, or to take a message, or to bring her sisters' embroidery to sell in Beirut, so she can send them the money to help them through financial difficulties. I take Maryam to school and then I go to the camp; I stay there until her school day ends and I go back to take her home. Sometimes if I need to go to the camp in the afternoon, I leave Maryam with Umm Ali, or I take her with me, and she plays with her friends there.

33

Abed's Detention

ABED DIDN'T COME HOME FOR three nights. I was somewhat concerned; I thought he's with his colleagues here or there. A momentary anxiety assails me: what if he's infiltrated the south? He has infiltrated before, and I didn't know about it until after he returned. I chase away the anxiety; there's nothing new in his being away from home for a night or two. On the fifth day the anxiety grips me; it's no longer anxiety but certainty, something bad has happened to him. Has he been kidnapped? Have they killed him at one of the barriers? I jump out of bed and look at my watch: the hands show two in the morning. I have to wait until daybreak, and then make arrangements. How will I do that, where will I start? By visiting those I know among his friends in Beirut? By going to the Popular Committee in the camp? To an official of the organization? Where will I find an official in the organization? Why haven't I done that before? For sure you've become feeble-minded, Ruqayya—"Delusions," you say, what delusions, when kidnapping happens every day and killing young men is routine? Where did you get this foolish calm, from apathy or stupidity? I get up to boil a pot of coffee; it boils over. I wipe up what has spilled on the stove and wash the pot, filling it with water and adding the coffee gradually. I watch the pot carefully, waiting for the coffee to boil, concentrating my attention on it so it won't boil over. I lift the pot from the fire with care—and my hand suddenly shakes, spilling the pot and everything in it on the floor and on my clothes. God help me! I throw the pot in the sink and bring a rag to clean the floor. I change my nightgown, wash the pot and fill it with water. I sit in the living room sipping the coffee and smoking. Abed might be with a group of his friends, dividing his time as usual between his studies and his political work, distracted from us, forgetting to come home. That has happened before. I calm myself by recalling this day and that, when he stayed away and then returned, until my imagination concludes that he is safe, and that my concern is only unfounded anxiety. Then it jumps in the opposite direction— have they taken him? Kidnapped him? Beaten him? Maybe they've killed him, what would I do then?

After the dawn prayer I knocked on Umm Ali's door. She did not open, so I knew that she was still praying. I waited at the door and knocked again after a few minutes, and heard her heavy steps coming to the door. She asked who it was, and I said "Ruqayya." She opened the door and said, "Good morning." I said, "Abed hasn't come home for five days, maybe they've kidnapped him." She asked me to sit down and then made me a cup of coffee. She suggested that I visit the houses of his friends first, saying, "I'll take Maryam to school and you go to them right away, before they leave for work. If you don't find him with any of them, we'll begin looking for him."

My son was lucky and I was too, because many of the young men who were kidnapped disappeared or were killed; their families didn't know that they had been killed, and when they were sure they didn't know where they were buried. The Phalange were no longer the only ones who detained Palestinians, nor were the Christian militias. Amal had suddenly appeared on the scene—my God, how? Why? A friend in the camp, a very old man, said to me, "Sitt Ruqayya, have you forgotten Tall al-Zaatar? Alliances change between the leaders and our young men pay the price. The camp pays the price. Now Syria and Abu Ammar are enemies and Amal is allied with Syria, so it aims its canons at Shatila, and we call the men of Amal enemies. In the very recent past we faced the Israelis together, in Khalda, in the Shouf and in the south. God help us!"

How can I free Abed? I don't know.

We followed many trails. Sadiq asked for the help of a businessman among his associates in the Gulf who had a business relationship with an influential figure in Amal. Umm Ali spared no relative, near or distant, nor anyone among her acquaintances or the acquaintances of her acquaintances, visiting them all and asking for help. "We want to know the boy's fate," she said. "I raised him with my own hands, can you take my son and beat him? If he's with you, free him, I'll vouch for him." In the evening Umm Ali put before me the day's yield: whom she had visited, whom she had spoken with, who had taken her and put her in touch with whom. I looked at her in amazement at her ability, at this age, to go to five places in one day. I followed her heavy steps as she carried the coffee or the thyme snacks she had baked, and I realized that the legs and feet struggled to carry her heavy body.

In my daily search I met a person who assured me that he knew the way to Abed. He said that the kidnappers had asked for a sum of money, which he named. I sold all my jewelry and gave it to him.

Did Umm Ali's visits bear fruit, or the money I paid, or did the men who had detained Abed just decide to free him, without any reason, just as they had decided to take him without any reason? Were they young men from Amal or were they from the Phalange or from an independent group, brigands profiting from the chaos all around to make some quick money by getting information and selling it to this side or the other? To this day I don't know.

After he was freed, Abed told me his story: "I was leaving Shatila, and here came three guys calling me. They were young men in civilian clothes. I thought they wanted to ask me the time, or that they were not from the area and wanted me to guide them to a street or a place. When I got near, one of them asked me if I were Lebanese or Palestinian. I had a bad feeling, but I answered, 'Palestinian, why do you ask?' And here was one of them pointing his weapon at my head. I don't know where he had been hiding the weapon. He raised it at me and the other two grabbed me and dragged me roughly into a building. We went into an apartment on the first floor, and they began to interrogate me, asking about the organization I belonged to, about the head of the organization, about the camp, the names of the leaders in it and the quantity of the weapons and the tunnels that connected the buildings. I said I didn't know, and they began to beat me. I repeated that I didn't belong to any organization and that I'm a law student in the Lebanese University, and that I don't live in the camp, and I don't have any information or the answers to their questions. The beating got worse. Then they blindfolded me and took me to another place and took off my clothes, and beat me again, until the blood flowed from my face and chest and back. They said, 'We'll kill you if you don't talk.' They shoved a revolver at my head. I said, 'I don't have anything to say.' They tied my hands and feet with a rope and threw me in with three other guys. Every day they came to us and said, 'We're going to kill you,' and then they left. After three days they took me in the trunk of a car, tied up and blindfolded. We came to a place at Bir Hasan. They took off the blindfold and untied me, and put me in a cell by myself."

"After ten days, they opened the door of the cell and blindfolded me again. Then they sat me in a car. After less than ten minutes the car stopped and they pushed me out. I lifted the blindfold and found myself in the vacant land between Ard Jalloul and Gaza Hospital. I walked to the hospital, and they cleaned my wounds and bandaged them and gave me medicine. Then I came home."

Yes, Abed was lucky, and I was even luckier. I said, "You should leave." He said, "I'm going to stay."

Sadiq called his brother, every day sometimes, insisting, "Please, Brother, give up, get out of Lebanon now!" but he dug in his heels. Then they took him again; it lasted only three days. After that he decided to leave and he procured a travel document, but to his surprise it was stamped, "No return permitted." He became like a hyena in a cage, turning around himself in the house and pouncing on anyone who came near him. Then he left.

Sadiq insists that we move in with him and his family in Abu Dhabi. I say, "We have to stay here to carry on with your father's case and find out what happened to him." I'm lying to him; I had accepted that Amin had gone with the thousands who were killed during the three most terrifying days out of the three months of war that paved the way for the fourth month, the month of the massacre. He insists again: "Why stay alone, you and Maryam, in Beirut? The city's not safe, it's a war of the militias—a car bomb here and a mine there and fights in a third place and kidnapping in a fourth and fifth. Have mercy on me, Mother, I can barely sleep for worry over you two!"

34

To the Gulf

SUDDENLY, I ACCEPTED. AS IF I had not spent four years in evasions, alleging real or fabricated reasons for staying.

The airline tickets and passports are in my purse, and the suitcases are in the back of the taxi taking Maryam and me to the airport. I know the airport, the arrival and departure halls, and the walls, but I don't know what's behind them; I have never taken a plane before in my life. I have never extended my hand holding a passport to the officer, as the actors do in films, so that he will stamp it and they can get on the plane. Was I waiting for the Israelis to withdraw from Sidon, so the way would be open for me to visit the graves of my mother and my uncle, Abu Amin? I went to Sidon and said goodbye to them; then I returned to Beirut and visited my aunt's grave.

And Amin? He is the one who came to say goodbye to me, on the eve of our departure, in a dream. Perhaps it was not a dream, as I was not sleeping. He kissed my head and asked me to take care of Maryam. I cried, and kissed his hands.

Maryam is excited by the thought of traveling, the airplane, meeting her brother and his family, and the new school. She chatters ceaselessly. The seatbelt is fastened securely; the plane circles above the clouds. I follow the progress of the trip as if I were in another place, following from afar, hearing Maryam's chatter and not listening to what she's saying. The plane lands. When I emerge from its door I'm surprised to find that there is no air, where did the air go? It seems that Beirut on its most humid days is more merciful. But there's no time to gasp for breath, we must stand in line, present our travel documents, pick up our suitcases. Then comes the meeting, a tumultuous meeting with Sadiq, Randa, and the little ones. Noha is now seven; her knees have raised her up and she looks as if she's Maryam's age. Huda, who was stumbling with her words and her steps the last time we saw her, has become a schoolgirl with a backpack who goes to nursery school every morning. Little Amin, whom I have not seen before, has begun to walk and to say a few words.

We arrive at Sadiq's house. Coffee, a full table, and more coffee. Conversation. Good night, good night. Maryam and I are in the area set aside for us, which Sadiq calls a suite. Maryam goes to sleep; I open the balcony to smoke a cigarette. There is no air; I put it out and close the balcony. The noise of the air conditioner is like a hidden train. There are no tears, where have the tears gone? I go back to open the balcony and smoke a cigarette, then I get in bed. I wonder what Sadiq would say if I asked him tomorrow to return to Beirut.

I think the banquet during the week following our arrival settled the matter. It settled it early on, even though it took me years to make the decision and follow through with it.

Sadiq's wife wanted to honor me; she meant well. She announced two days after my arrival that she was having a dinner in my honor. She invited her relatives and friends and acquaintances, to introduce them to me and me to them. For three days she was issuing orders and directions and giving instructions, as well as taking part in the preparations. There were two servants in the house. Sadiq explained, "One is an educated Filipina, whom we entrust with the childcare. Her salary is double that of the Sri Lankan; her English is excellent. The Sri Lankan comes from the country, but we have trained and taught her. Her job is to clean the house and cook. When she came she didn't know anything, just barely how to cook the food of her country; then Randa taught her, and she has become excellent."

I wanted to help but there was no place for me in the kitchen. I remembered my aunt and Ezz's wife, and smiled, nearly laughing, although the situation was different. During the two days preceding the banquet Sumana and Evelyn prepared what was asked of them, under Randa's supervision. On the day of the banquet two other girls arrived, whom I later learned were the servants of Randa's sister and cousin, a Sri Lankan and a dark-skinned African. Randa later told me that she was from Somalia: "My cousin is very religious and will accept only Muslim servants."

I nearly asked what being religious had to do with the matter, but I didn't. I asked about her name.

"Muslima."

"Her name is just 'Muslim'?"

"She has another name but my cousin decided to call her Muslima. In fact she always names her servants Muslima; she used the same name with the previous one and the one before that also. It's simpler!" Randa laughed.

I don't remember many details of that banquet. Perhaps the details of other banquets floating in my mind have become mixed with them, so that I don't know if they were part of that day or of other days in which the house was packed with guests. Sadiq is generous and his wife is too; they have banquets once every two or three weeks, to which they invite their relatives and friends and the friends of their relatives and friends. The four servants stood in the corners, at our disposal. It seemed they wore special clothes for the occasion, dresses of the same color and cut, with a starched white apron tied at the waist. They passed around cups of juice, placed the plates and cleared them, took away ashtrays filled with cigarette butts and replaced them with shining clean ashtrays. The dining table was spread with varieties of food, and on a side table were rows of plates, small and large. Each guest took his plate and helped himself to what he liked, then moved to small square or round tables, each of which was covered by an embroidered white tablecloth, carefully starched and ironed, on which were forks, knives, spoons, and cups. Each one took his plate and sat at a designated place at this table or that. They repeated the process when the servants took the plates and they moved to serve themselves sweets and fruit. At that first banquet the whole scene was new to me, in all its details. Before, during, and after the dinner, as the girls passed coffee, tea, and "white coffee" made from orange blossoms, I did not open my mouth to say a single word, as if I had been struck with the old muteness. After the guests left, Sadiq said to me, reproachfully, "They came to meet you—you should have favored them by speaking to them. They wanted to hear about what's happening in Lebanon."

It seemed as if I was not going to answer; then I was surprised to find myself saying, "The news of Lebanon is in the daily papers, and if they are illiterate they can follow it on the radio and television. Are there any illiterates among them?"

His face paled, and he did not comment. After a while I broke silence, "Thank you, Sadiq, thank you, Randa. Good night."

I withdrew to the "suite." I was angry. Was it because I had wounded Sadiq when he had wanted to honor me? Angry over the scene itself? Angry with Sadiq because he didn't understand? He didn't understand. Why, when he's smart and perceptive, why did he want me to make polite conversation with his guests, why? Didn't he want his guests to enjoy the delicacies his wife had spent three days preparing? He was angry when I told his wife's family, the day we went to them to propose in Amman, that we were children of the camps. There were three wars and a massacre between the two banquets.

There was a sea there, a closed gulf to which we went in an air-conditioned car, which carried us from here to there.

The car is always air conditioned, twenty-four hours a day. Between sleeping and waking, I thought to myself that my legs were going to lose the ability to walk. And my hands?

I'll put them to work. I look from afar: Ruqayya works non-stop, there in Sadiq's house, knitting. Next to her is a nylon bag with balls of wool, one or two or three, and in her hands are two metal needles she moves mechanically, the index finger and thumb of her right hand joining in when she loops the thread over the needle, rapidly and repeatedly. Sadiq comments, laughing, "It's beautiful, Mother. But knitting wool in a country where no one wears wool, that's comical!"

I say, "I'm making sweaters for my friends' children in Lebanon."

I finished seven wool jackets which I sent to Lebanon. Then I made a sweater for Hasan in Canada, and another for Abed in Paris. In the future when I looked at the pictures of one of the children in Shatila or one of my children or grandchildren wearing the sweaters I had made them, I would stop and let my thoughts wander. Not just because I was happy that they were wearing what I had made for them, but also because I knew that knitting, during those years, was more like a refuge in which I sought shelter from shelling. I correct myself, how can I say that? Under shelling one is terrified and knows that death is watching. The simile doesn't suit the purpose, it's mistaken. But perhaps the image of shelling isn't far from the truth, for shelling is frightening and earth-shaking, and so was my memory of Beirut during the last year I lived there. The siege and the Israeli planes, even the massacre seemed understandable, reasonable even in their unreason. The enemies were known and specific. You realize they want to get rid of you, to wipe you out if possible, so you rally, because the people who are confronted defend themselves. But the war of the camps crushed me. At first it seemed as if it was a stupid, passing conflict, ridiculous, like the ones that spring up suddenly between the young men of two different Palestinian factions. It starts with a difference or a quarrel, then each draws his weapon on the other, and instead of fighting with words one shoots the other, and the foolish lawlessness turns into a conflict. Oh my God, a conflict! I thought, it's the first of Ramadan, nerves are out of control, with the accumulated tension and pressure of the last three years. They will calm down and things will go back to normal. But they didn't calm down; the siege continued, and the army and Amal were shelling Shatila, shelling the camp mosque. The young men in the camp shelled Amal positions. Oh my God, as if the sons of Amal had become Israelis, as if the sons of the camp had become the enemies of the Shia, as if the young men here and there had not fought together, as if their blood had not mingled behind the same barricade. Who was responsible? The leaders of Amal, the policies of Abu Ammar, Syria? I would go to Umm Ali and she would come to me, trying to understand. I left Beirut and I still didn't understand; I left defeated, with a lump in my throat that would not go away. It was stuck near the uvula, neither strangling me so that I could be done with the whole story nor dissolving, so that I could breathe like other people, and live.

I ruminate on what happened in the camps. I knit, in a feverish, mechanical movement that does not stop, that might take my mind off questions that drive me mad. I've come from Beirut with a heavy heart. Why did I come?

But Maryam is happy. She says that the new school is bigger and more beautiful. She enjoys her life with Sadiq and his family, keeping the girls company and spoiling the little boy. Sometimes she practices mothering them, and sometimes she asserts herself as their leader. As for the pool I was surprised to find in the garden of the house, that is what makes her happiest. She always loved swimming, and she swims every day. She eats with an appetite, and grows, not exempt from the law of the springs in the knees. I think, so be it; Maryam is happy, so be it.

35

Sumana

HOW DID MY FRIENDSHIP WITH Sumana begin? And why did I befriend her, while I remained distant from Evelyn? Was it because Evelyn often used the word "Madam," which embarrassed me? Or was it because she spoke English well and fluently, while I stumbled over my words, aware of my broken English? She reminded me of an Asian doctor who worked in Gaza Hospital, whom Amin invited to dinner one night with the other foreign doctors. That night also I spoke in the briefest possible terms. What would I say to these doctors? I confined myself to a welcoming smile, to "Welcome to our home," and to "You honor us."

I understood from Sumana that Evelyn had a bachelor's degree in science, that she had graduated from the university in her country, and that she wanted to make it clear that she was the children's governess who taught them English, and not a servant. She maintained her position, correct and distant. Was I annoyed, without being aware of it, that her full responsibility for the children stood as a barrier between me and my grandchildren? Was I jealous of her, or is it that some spirits are in harmony while others clash, for reasons no one knows?

My relationship with Sumana was different. We communicated in shattered English on both sides, flavored at times with a few sentences in Arabic, fortified by gestures when necessary. I repeated, "There's no call for this 'Madam,'" so she began to call me "Mama." She would ask me to teach her a new way to cook, and I would do it, or she would squat beside me to see how I was shaping the shoulder of a wool sweater I was making. When Randa was out of the house on her morning visits to her friends, Sumana seemed more able to communicate with me. She would make me coffee without my asking, and sometimes I would sit with her in the kitchen while she prepared the food.

I was sitting with her in the kitchen when she went to her room and returned with a large envelope. She opened it and brought out a pile of pictures, and began to show them to me.

A colored picture of two boys of ten: "Arawinda and Saminda, at twelve."

"Twins?"

"Twins, but Saminda is a little taller than his brother. Look, Mama . . . ."

They looked alike, two thin, dark boys, each with a lock of smooth black hair covering his forehead. They were wearing identical shirts and shorts. I looked closely at the picture; one of them was a little taller than the other and thinner, and he had his arm around his brother's shoulders. They were laughing in the picture.

"As beautiful as the moon, may God keep them for you!"

A single picture of a girl of five or six: "The smallest, Amanti."

The girl was not smiling, perhaps apprehensive about the idea of the picture. She was staring with wide, anxious eyes, her hair tied with a white ribbon; she was wearing a beautiful white dress.

"As if she's a princess!"

Sumana laughed happily. "A mother doesn't love one child more than another, but sometimes I feel as if I love Amanti more. I miss her more."

I said, "Because she's the youngest."

She said, "I wanted a girl, and I had to wait. The twins came first, and then a third boy, and at last Amanti. I haven't seen her for a year and nine months."

Then another picture, of a very handsome boy. She said, "This is the third boy. My mother gasped when she saw him, he was so beautiful. We decided to name him Padman; in Hindi, it means 'lotus flower.'"

Then a picture of Sumana carrying her daughter when she was an infant. She muttered, as if apologizing, "This is an old picture."

She looked like a young girl in it, and she was very thin. It was as if it had been taken twenty years earlier.

"This is a picture of the whole family: my mother and father, and this young man is my husband, and the children."

I wanted to affirm the closeness. "This is Arawinda and that one is Sawaminda and . . . ."

She laughed. "Saminda."

She began to repeat the names slowly, as if she wanted to carve them on my head so I would not make a mistake in them: "Arawinda. Saminda. Padman. Amanti."

I repeated after her: "Arawinda. Saminda. Padman. Aminta."

"Aa-maan-tii."

I got up to the stove and filled the coffee pot with water. Sumana caught up to me, and said in confusion, "I'm sorry."

"Why are you sorry?"

"I should have realized that you wanted a cup of coffee. I'll make it for you."

"I want to make it."

The coffee boiled, and I poured two cups. I offered her one and she murmured "Thank you," but I noticed that she did not drink it. She said, "My husband goes out with other women, and that hurts me a lot. I say it's not right. He denies it, and says, 'Don't believe your mother.' But he takes care of the children and is very affectionate with them. He spends what I send him on them. My mother says that he also spends on his girlfriends. I don't know who to believe."

"What does your husband do?"

"He repairs bicycles. In our area we use bicycles a lot. But he is suggesting that he buy a motorcycle, so he can do another job too and make a lot of money, taking fish to market, or vegetables."

"There's a sea in your country, isn't there?"

"Our village is on the sea. Our house is a few steps from it."

When I went back to my room I decided to write down the names of Sumana's four children so I wouldn't make another mistake in them. I forgot the name of the third boy; I wrote "Lotus." When Maryam came back from school I told her, "Ask Sumana about the names of her children, and when she tells you the name of the third boy, remember it well. Don't say that I asked you to ask her." Maryam laughed, and asked me, "Have you decided to give Sadiq's next son a Sri Lankan name?" She was joking, but I was not comfortable with the comment.

Later I asked Sumana about the sea in their country. She understood some of what I said, but she didn't understand all of it. I wanted to hear from her about the scent of the sea there, and about the flowers. She said, "Fa-low-erz?" not understanding. I said, "Are there flowers in your country, like these?" I took her to the large vase where there was a bouquet of artificial roses. She said the names, and I did not recognize any of them. But she did not forget the question, because weeks later she brought me a Sri Lankan magazine and showed me pictures of flowers. She said, "This one is found in our village; this one, no." Then on another page: "This one and that one too grow near the sea, and these birds."

Sumana writes regularly to her family. Once a week she holds out her hand to Sadiq with two sealed envelopes, and he takes them from her. She waits for his return so he can reassure her that he has put the envelopes in the mail; and as long as he is going to the post office, he might find letters from her family in the box. Generally he brings her a letter, but sometimes he says, "I'm sorry, Sumana, nothing came for you." She thanks him and gives him a courteous smile.

One day traces of weeping appeared in her eyes. I asked her and she said, "It's nothing." I asked Randa, and she said, "I scolded her because she broke a plate and burned the kubbeh she was frying. She's been holding a wake since yesterday night because her mother sent her a letter saying that her husband is living with another woman. Evelyn told me. Men are like that, you can't rely on them. As long as she was worried about her husband, she should have stayed with him! In any case I called her in and told her that personal matters have nothing to do with work."

I said to Randa, "And if she got news that her four children had died in a traffic accident, would she be allowed to cry, or would she have to be careful to serve kubbeh that's not burnt?" Randa was surprised by what I said. She picked up her purse and said that she had an appointment with the hairdresser.

I was sharp. I acknowledge that Randa and Sadiq put up with my sharpness. It would surprise me; I didn't speak much, and I would be surprised by what I said as much as Sadiq or Randa would be surprised by it. Sadiq tries. Sometimes he says, "Let's go, Mother." "Where to?" He takes me in his car, usually to an air-conditioned coffee shop. During the two months of winter, when the scorching heat and humidity retreat, he drives his car to a spot on the beach where we can walk in the sand. We take off our sandals and walk beside each other. Sometimes then the knot in my tongue comes untied and I talk to Sadiq, and he also talks to me.

36

A Lesson

I SAID TO MARYAM, "I want to talk to you. Don't go to the club with Sadiq and his children tomorrow morning; we'll sit and talk."

"Is it a punishment?"

"Not a punishment, but a talk that will take time."

"Why on Friday morning? Let's talk now, or Friday evening.

"I want you on Friday morning."

"Mama, the talk won't go away. I wait for Friday all week, so I can go to the club and meet my friends."

I ended the discussion firmly: "No club this week."

She left me, grumbling in protest, but she obeyed.

I was amazed that when Maryam recalled what happened and told her brother about it, she remembered the conversation down to the smallest detail. She was talking to Abed in my presence more than ten years later, flavoring her words with some of the Egyptian expressions she had picked up since we had moved to live in Alexandria.

Maryam told him: "She cornered me in the room and beat the hell out of me. It was a lesson in morals and history and geography and the family tree: 'Your father was . . . your grandfather Abu Sadiq was . . . your maternal uncles . . . your grandfather Abu Amin was . . . ,' and the refrain: 'We're Palestinians. Refugees. Children of the camps.' And me, 'Mama, what did I do?' She said that she had noticed that I was putting myself above the Sri Lankan maid and that I had begun to act like the girls here in the Gulf. 'And if our living here is going to change you into one of them, we'll go back to Lebanon. We'll go back to Sidon and live in Ain al-Helwa, and the camp will cure you, it'll teach you who you are.' It was heavy, Abed, and your sister was completely lost! I didn't understand why Mama was so angry. I was twelve, and I couldn't comprehend the nature of the crime. She hauled me before a court where she was the judge and the prosecutor, and I was seeing stars."

I broke in, "Stop exaggerating. All I did was point out that you were slipping into a style of life that we don't belong to, and that we can't belong to. I don't remember the details, but I remember that I heard you calling Sumana as if you were issuing orders, and I was horrified. I didn't sleep all night."

Abed laughed. "We've all graduated from that institute before, with the same book and the same lessons!"

Maryam said, "You were three, you could get it off your chest with each other. Poor me, who could I complain to?"

"So which actress should play you, Fatin Hamama or Shadya?"

"Fatin, she's an orphan and wasn't treated fairly."

"And Mama?"

"Mimi Shakib, the stepmother. She's fat and mispronounces her R's and wears tighter clothes than she should, to call attention to the size of her breasts and buttocks. She leaves her hair disheveled on purpose and dyes it bright yellow, and she persecutes me!"

They dissolved into laughter. Then Maryam realized that she had gone too far, so she jumped from her seat, put her arms around me and kissed my head. She bent over my ear and said, "Thank you. You were right."

I was afraid, that's for sure, and being away from home made me more worried. I brought up the children as well as I could. I held each one's hand and accompanied him on the path from childhood to youth without any unfortunate accidents, and now each was responsible for himself. That left Maryam; I wanted to bring her up properly. Was I afraid for her only, or was I afraid that she would go over to the other camp and leave me alone and completely isolated? It was absolute isolation, utter and complete, in a two-story house with two servants who had come from the Far East, where a single one of the banquets given cost a sum that would have been enough for a large family in the camp to live on for a year, or maybe two.

I did not spend time alone with Sadiq as I did with Maryam, to raise her. My mission and my role in life, and maybe the meaning of my life now, was Maryam. As for Sadiq, my attitude toward him was ambiguous and strange. I thought about it, and it seemed as if I had entered a maze and become lost. He was an architect and a contractor, successful in his work, his company growing day by day, bringing him money in amounts that were inconceivable to me. He helped his brothers and supported his sister and me. He made contributions to this or that Palestinian foundation. He took responsibility for the education of three young men from Ain al-Helwa, following their progress and guaranteeing them a job on graduation—and then he took on three others. What did I have against him? He had worked hard, and had been helped by his education, his acumen, and by luck. In short, he had strived in an oil-producing country and been rewarded— what was the problem, what was wrong with that? Use your mind to judge, Ruqayya, and reckon calmly: Would you have preferred that he suffocate in the tank truck on the way to oil country? Or that he stay in Ain al-Helwa, looking for work, falling afoul of the law, and not finding anything? Or that he bear arms and end up in one of the offices in Tunis, or as a besieged fighter in the camps in Yemen or Algeria, with no way to see his wife or children? I jumped over the maze, or sneaked outside its walls, but it caught up with me, became larger, and threw up new walls around the area I had run to. Don't they suffer from isolation in Ain al-Helwa, too? I wonder where Haniya is now? Has she found a job in another place, or has she been forced to deny that she's Palestinian to find work in one of the hospitals in Beirut? Where will I go, where will we go?

37

Abu Muhammad

IT WAS CHANCE, PURE CHANCE, that brought us together.

Sadiq took me to a large shopping mall to buy some things for Maryam. He said that he would come to take us home two hours later, and told us about a coffee shop on the second floor where we could sit to rest, or to wait for him if we finished shopping before he came back.

I finished buying what Maryam needed in less than half an hour; we went down to the second floor and headed for the coffee shop. As soon as we went in I noticed him. He was sitting alone, with a kufiyeh on his head. He was wearing a qumbaz with a leather belt around his waist and a jacket over it, like my father and my uncle Abu Amin. We sat at a nearby table; I ordered the ice cream Maryam wanted and a cup of coffee for myself. I thought, he might not be Palestinian, maybe he's Syrian, from the country; but I thought it was likely that he was Palestinian. His face seemed familiar, similar to many of the elderly men in Ain al-Helwa and Sabra and Shatila. He was between sixty and seventy, maybe older but not showing his age. He was tall and thin, his face dark and gaunt, his forehead broad. He had a penetrating look in his lively eyes, despite the prominence of his forehead and his bushy white eyebrows. I turned away my eyes; what would the man say, with me staring at him like that?

"Yes, Maryam."

She protested, "I'm talking to you and you're not listening!"

"Yes I am, I'm listening."

She returned to her chatter, but I only followed a little of what she said. I interrupted her, "Do you see that man sitting at the table to our right?"

She pointed with her hand, "That man?"

I suppressed a laugh. "Maryam, when will you grow up? It's not polite to point to him like that. I wanted to tell you that he reminds me of your grandfather Abu Amin."

Maryam looked at him directly.

"Don't look at him like that, he will realize that we're talking about him!"

He realized. Perhaps he felt awkward and wanted to change the situation, so he greeted us: "Hello."

I said, "Hello, how do you do?"

He said, "I arrived in Abu Dhabi yesterday. One of my acquaintances asked me to take a letter to his son, and I called him on the telephone as soon as I arrived. He said, 'I'll meet you in the shopping mall, in the coffee shop on the second floor.' It's half an hour after the time he gave me, and he has not appeared. Is there another coffee shop on this floor?"

Maryam ran to one of the employees in the shop, and asked. She returned to her seat, and said, "There are many coffee shops in the complex but this is the only one on the second floor."

"No problem, I'll wait."

Maryam asked him, "Do you live in Lebanon?"

"I'm Palestinian, I've never visited Lebanon in my life. I've come from the West Bank to visit my son. I live in Jenin. Originally I'm from Tantoura, do you know where Tantoura is, girl? It's . . ."

Did I scream or shout? Did I laugh? Was I preoccupied by the thought that I would not have looked at him like that if I hadn't known him even though I didn't know him, because blood calls to blood? I invited him to sit at our table, and it was easy to talk.

When the man looking for the letter came and took Abu Muhammad to another table, he seemed to me like an uninvited guest who had no right to spoil our meeting like this. I kept waiting, looking at my watch every few minutes, only to discover that just a few minutes had passed. Why doesn't he take his letter and leave? Why doesn't he leave Abu Muhammad to me, so I can ask him if he knew my father? He's younger than my father, maybe ten years younger; or maybe he was of the same generation, and just doesn't show his years. How had he escaped the massacre? Maybe he was not in the village on the night of Saturday to Sunday; where was he? Had he lost anyone in his family? Why was the recipient of the letter sitting so long with Abu Muhammad? He came an hour and ten minutes ago, and he doesn't seem ready to leave. He got the letter, what does he want now—and what if he took Abu Muhammad with him? Maybe it would be wisest if I got up now and took his telephone number, or a way to reach him. Will he live in Abu Dhabi, or is it just a passing visit? I was becoming more and more tense, and Maryam was complaining that I was not following what she was saying. I said, "I'm listening to you, Maryam, I'm listening." But her words came to my ears as a handful of sounds, which did not translate into any meaning in my head.

At last Sadiq appeared, and I introduced him to Abu Muhammad. They spoke a few minutes, and before we left the coffee shop Sadiq invited him to visit us with his son, exchanging telephone numbers with him.

The next day as we were having lunch, Sadiq said, directing his words to me, "It's a coincidence more amazing than the one yesterday. Muhammad, Abu Muhammad's son, works with us as an accountant in the company, a young man in his thirties. The predicament is that I've never invited any of the employees, and now it will seem like clannishness for me to invite him because he's from our village."

I looked at Sadiq, "Where's the predicament? How can it be clannishness to invite a person from your village whom you want to get to know?"

Sadiq laughed. He seemed split between embarrassment and pride, "Mother, your son is the president of the company!"

"So?"

"I can invite an employee on some occasion, but can't favor a minor employee by inviting him to my house unless he's my brother or my cousin."

I said, "Consider them your uncle and his son!"

"The problem is that his colleagues will feel as if it's favoritism." He laughed suddenly, not without embarrassment, "Should I explain that my mother wants to meet his father because he's from Tantoura?"

I was not comfortable with his words, and I didn't understand what he meant.

After Abu Muhammad and his son visited us, I was careful to return the visit. I took Maryam with me and I met Muhammad's wife and two children, and asked them all to lunch at Sadiq's house. I said that I would cook, and I prepared a feast worthy of people from Tantoura. Sadiq did not seem to welcome my conduct; maybe he considered it rash, unjustified, and incomprehensible. That's what I sensed, though he did not add anything to what he had said previously. But I decided to leave him to his confusion and worry, and to do as I pleased, visiting them and inviting them to the house. The day Abu Muhammad left for Amman, Sadiq took me, unwillingly, to the airport to see him off. He said, "Didn't you say goodbye to him yesterday? I sent the driver as you asked, didn't you go?"

"I did go."

He smiled. "You forgot to give him the wool sweater you made for Wisal?"

"I gave it to him. I asked him to look for her, and to give it to her."

"So?" He was looking at me in surprise. I said, "Sadiq, humor me, I want to see him off at the airport."

"As you wish."

38

The Prisoner's Tale

ABU MUHAMMAD TOLD ME HIS story.

"I was among the forty they stood against the wall. I
no longer remember if I had resigned myself to death
and pronounced the shahada, or if I was still clinging to
God's power over everything, to his ability to change one
state into another, in the blink of an eye. I only remember
that we were standing, raising our hands as we had been
ordered, our faces to the wall, barely seeing what was going
on behind our backs: the rifles leveled at us, the contempt
on their faces and the look of fear and bloodthirstiness. Yes,
Sitt Ruqayya, they were afraid—how else can you explain
all this killing after the battle had ended in their favor, after
they had killed some and occupied the town? They were
talking at the top of their voices, as if they were in the desert
or as if they thought that everyone around them was deaf.
They were shouting insults and curses and pushing this one
with the butt of a rifle and beating that one on the head.
We were standing near the village center, which was suddenly invaded by a strange odor, stronger than the smell of
the sea. Then suddenly they said 'Yalla, yalla, let's go,' and
drove us under the threat of arms into trucks, we forty who
were to be executed at the wall and others from the town.
They stuffed us into the trucks like sheep and took us to the
Zikhron Yaakov colony in Zummarin. We were several hundred, maybe three or four hundred men.

"Why didn't they kill us at the wall? Some say that Yaqub, the headman of Zikhron Yaakov, is the one who saved us. They say that an old man from our town knew him and was standing in another line to be executed, and that he said to Yaqub when he saw him, 'Abu Yusuf, the town has fallen and you've taken the weapons. What more is there after that?' and that Yaqub answered, 'We want to make peace between you and the Hagana so that we can stop the killing.' They say that the headman left the village and came back with a written order to stop the killing. They say that some of the residents of Zikhron Yaakov, who had neighborly relations with some of the townspeople, intervened. Some say that they wanted to stop the killing because they needed us to work in their settlements, and some say that they wanted us alive because Abd Allah al-Tall had captured three hundred of them in the battle of Kfar Atsiyon near Jerusalem, and they wanted to exchange us. God only knows.

"In any case the trucks unloaded us in Zikhron Yaakov, at the building that was the headquarters of the English army. They held us, thirty to a narrow, dank, dark room that was only big enough for us if we stood. We spent three days in those mass graves, without any food but beatings with rifle butts, insults, and abuse.

"I'm sure you understand, Sitt Ruqayya, our morale was very low. The town had fallen, and we had seen piles of bodies with our own eyes. In fact, four of us had been told to move some of the bodies and bury them in a large ditch. Everyone who had seen anything spoke about it. Some said that they saw groups of people from Zikhron Yaakov walking around the town, with the bodies everywhere, singing and clapping their hands, and that others were doing the same thing on the boats in the sea near the beach. They were celebrating. One would say, 'I saw So-and-So's body.' 'So-and-So fell, killed before my eyes.' 'I saw Abu So-and-So and his brother and the three children of his brother killed near the mosque.' Those who were martyred in the battle were few. In fact, more of them died than of us; that was also why they were afraid and lusting to kill. But most of those who were martyred were killed after being stripped of their weapons, after the end of the battle. Then we saw the women and children and old men in trucks, and no one knew where they took them. One person among us saw the Israeli soldiers assaulting a girl before his eyes, and when her father tried to protect her, they killed him. No one talks about rape now because it's a painful subject for the family, and they don't want to go into it, but we learned of it when we were held in Zikhron Yaakov. I was twenty-two and was not married, but I had four sisters; you can imagine my state, and my fears. We were all thinking about the old women. I mean, death and destruction and the greatest possible humiliation. All of these things, Sitt Ruqayya, were lead weights. It was a terrifying despair; I never knew anything like it, before or since, except perhaps in 1967. I was imprisoned twice later on and I did not despair, even though I was older and had a family and children I was worried about. In the seventies I was imprisoned for five years, and in the Intifada I was held for six months. Both times I was part of a group that believed it was powerful. We were part of a resistance organization, and in the prison camp there was a meaning to life; we weren't without hope, or without moments of contentment, satisfaction, even cheer. In 1948 the situation in the camp was completely different. The despair was total, and life was narrow, dark, dank and oppressive, like the room we were crowded into.

"After several days they loaded us up again and took us to Umm Khalid. Do you know where Umm Khalid is? It's a village in the district of Tulkarm, in the middle of the road between Tantoura and Jaffa, on the Natanya line, near the sea. They had occupied it and thrown the people out. They held us behind barbed wire and would take us to forced labor in the quarries, from sunup until sunset. We cut stones and carried them on our backs, taking them to the places they designated. It's strange that we withstood it. I mean, I don't know how our bodies bore it, because they gave us a single potato in the morning and half a dried fish in the evening, and they beat us and abused us.

"Then they moved us again, to a big prison camp in Ijlil, on the road between Umm Khalid and Jaffa. Instead of the work in the quarries they began to drive us to the villages they had occupied and where they had destroyed the houses, to take the stones. We were carrying the stones of the houses of our people, so they could use them in building their settlements. And they used us to build fortifications, military fortifications, and to bury the Arab martyrs. They took us to Qaqun, where there had been a battle between them and the Iraqi army in which they were victorious. We had to bury dozens of the bodies. We counted them: ninety bodies. Human nature is amazing, by God it's amazing. I had not cried since I left our town, but I cried that day when I was burying the young Iraqis. I was sad for the young men and repelled by the odor of their bodies, and the repulsion made me more disturbed. I thought, 'Why? They're martyrs.' I would bury them and cry, sobbing aloud. I remember the ones I buried. I remember all their faces, but one face in particular comes to me sometimes in sleep. He speaks to me, but when I wake up I don't remember anything he said, even though I'm sure it was a long speech.

"In Ijlil a truck arrived carrying hundreds of men. It was obvious that they had not had a drink of water for days. They set them down at a single water faucet. The men rushed for it, and they shot at them, and some died. We later learned that those men were prisoners from Lid and Ramla.

"There were Egyptian prisoners in Ijlil, including a pilot whose plane fell over Tel Aviv on the morning of May 15, so he was the first Egyptian prisoner, bearing the number one. That's why I don't remember his name—we called him

'Prisoner Number One.' There was another pilot named Abd al-Rahman Inan, who was the leader of the flight of five planes that attacked the area near Haifa the following week. The weather was so bad when they took off from al-Arish that they had to turn back. Then an order came to take off again. Inan said that the British were the ones who brought down the five planes, and that he was the only one destined to survive. They treated the Egyptian prisoners harshly, like us. Inan told one of our mates that the Israeli soldier grabbed a small copy of the Quran that he was carrying, threw it on the ground and began trampling it underfoot.

"Twenty-five of the young men from Tantoura were able to flee from Ijlil. They discovered it in the morning and they became very agitated. Beatings and insults and abuse. Afterward they brought us back to Umm Khalid and from there they took us to Sarafand, near Ramla. It was a big camp with nearly 1,500 prisoners. In Sarafand there were other prisoners from the Egyptian army, officers and soldiers. They separated us from them but we found ways to communicate with them. We comforted them and they encouraged us. In captivity prisoners console each other.

"Also in Sarafand representatives of the International Red Cross arrived. They recorded our names and told us that we were prisoners of war, and that the Geneva Conventions applied to us. They informed us of our rights, and permitted us to write messages to our families, messages no longer than twenty-five words. After that we were treated a little better. They put us to work as agricultural workers, picking the fruit from the Arab lands they had occupied. In return for the work they gave each of us a card that allowed us to get some food from the canteen, because the camp food was very meager, not enough to satisfy our hunger.

"I got out of the camp after a year and a half. I was lucky; two months after I got out of the camp I found my family. They were in Damascus; they were in a very rough situation, but they were all alive—my mother and father and four sisters and the two little boys. They were all among those who had been loaded up and taken to al-Furaydis. By chance, by a lucky chance, none of them died, either in the massacre or from hunger and the difficult journey that followed it. We spent a year and a half in Syria, and then we moved to Jenin. My sister moved with her husband, and then her husband sent word to us that he had rented a house in Jenin and that by the grace of God he had enough money, and he asked us to join him there. In Jenin God comforted us. I worked with my sister's husband to support the family. I saw to my sisters' marriages and my brothers' education."

Abu Muhammad smiled, perhaps for the first time since he had begun to speak, and said in an apologetic tone, "That's why I married late. I married only after my sisters were secure and the two boys had graduated from high school. After that I got married, and our Lord blessed me with Muhammad and the rest of the children."

39

Wedding

MY IMAGINATION COULD NEVER HAVE reached Piraeus, however much it circled or took wing, or stumbled and lost its way. How could it ever get there without any prior knowledge of it, or its location, or even its name?

As usual, Sadiq began by objecting. He said, "How can you, Brother? Are you going to spend your whole life in Canada? If you marry her she won't be able to live with you in Lebanon or in the Gulf or in any Arab country, except maybe Egypt. And in Egypt they won't give you residency or a work permit, and every time relations are strained between Abu Ammar and the Egyptian government they won't allow us to enter. God, it's a big problem, Brother."

Sadiq advanced his arguments, piling them up in front of his brother, and he said "Impossible!" It was a long call, followed by a second and a third—give and take, like a tug of war. After two days Sadiq agreed.

Hasan had told me before telling his brother. He didn't mention the subject of marriage; he told me about the girl, and said, "I'll send you a long letter."

I understood and said, "Should I congratulate you?"

He was silent, so I knew. I said, "May God bless it for you."

I heard him stumble over his words: "There's a problem."

"What's the problem?"

It never occurred to me. The possibility that she was older than he flashed through my mind, that she was divorced and had children—or that she was married and had not yet gotten her divorce. She couldn't be foreign, her name was Fatima.

"She's from Lid."

"And so?"

"I mean that her family still live there. We won't be able to go to them to make the proposal, and she won't be able to come with me to meet you."

I didn't grasp it; I said, "Randa's family live in Nablus, and we met them in Amman. Didn't we write your brother's wedding contract in Amman? It's manageable, dear, and God willing, good will come of it. I'm waiting for your long letter. Send me her picture. Whose family is she from, in Lid? How old is she? Is she still in school or has she finished? What's her subject? I've kept you a long time. Don't worry. Congratulations, a thousand congratulations!"

I had plunged into a flood of questions. I didn't understand that there was any problem, even after I replaced the receiver, and I didn't stop to wonder what was worrying Hasan. The news excited me and flooded me with joy, leaving no room to think about the details.

Sadiq is the master of details; he becomes absorbed in them. He begins with no, with an absolute no, then in the end he gives in to what his brothers want. He becomes absorbed in carrying out what they want, enthusiastically, as if the idea had been his and he had never opposed it.

I looked up at Sadiq. He was sitting in the chair opposite, wearing reading glasses and holding a pen and notebook in his hand. He was absorbed in the details. He raised his eyes and said, "Cyprus or Greece—I don't see any other solution." He picked up the telephone and called Hasan. "What do you think about meeting in Greece? In Piraeus. Yes, we'll have the wedding there. A week. No, of course not—I'm the head of the family, and I'll underwrite it. Airline tickets, the stay, the night of the wedding. It's my responsibility. Slow down, Hasan, there's no reason for this talk—I'm the head of the family. It's done, no more discussion of this subject. What matters now is the arrangements—you'll have to call your uncle Ezz in Tunis first, to get his permission and set the date with him. Then call the girl's family and see if the date suits them, and find out which of them will come. Don't limit the number, it's not right—say that everyone is welcome, and stress the invitation to her uncles on both sides. Of course the bride's brothers and sisters and her mother and father. Within a week I want the specific number and a fax with their names, so I can send them the tickets. If you have friends you want to invite, invite them. Wisal and Abed? Of course. Call them, invite them. God keep you."

He replaced the receiver and returned to his notebook. Suddenly he lifted his head, looked up at me and said, "How can I go to the travel agency I work with and buy airline tickets from Tel Aviv to Athens to Tel Aviv?"

I said, in an attempt to ease his mind, "Don't complicate matters, Sadiq. It's obvious from the names that they're Arabs."

Sadiq did not look like his grandfather Abu Amin, but when he looked up I remembered my uncle the day he went to the camp to make the proposal for Ezz, and Abu Karima talked to him about the permits necessary to leave the camp or to receive visitors in it. Suddenly Sadiq called Sumana in an angry voice, as if he was about to scold her for some mistake she had made. "I want a cup of tea with sage." He forgot the "please" with which he always ended his requests. He looked up at me with a frown on his face and began to curse Hasan and himself and Tantoura and Lid and Palestine, that had imposed this separation on us.

Piraeus. How had the name acquired this halo between one day and the next? How had it suddenly been transformed from the name of a place to the name of a time we wish we could jump to, passing above all the intervening days to get to it? It was as if I had become a girl again, counting on her fingers every morning the days left between her and the Eid holiday at the end of Ramadan. I had not seen Hasan for five years; I had not seen Abed since he left Beirut in 1985; I had not seen Ezz since he went to Tunis with his wife; and I had not seen Wisal since I visited her in her sister-in-law's house in al-Baqaa Camp, more than ten years earlier. I'll see them in Piraeus. How strange; we'll hold Hasan's wedding and meet his bride and her family, we'll ask for the girl and marry the two and become family, all in one week. There in Piraeus.

Abed leaned over and said, smiling slyly, "I've had my doubts for years, but today I know for sure."

I looked at him questioningly. He said, suppressing his laughter,

"It's clear to see that you love Hasan more than us. What do you think, Sadiq?"

"There's no think about it, it's a fact, as clear as day."

Maryam caught onto the game and joined in immediately: "I can't compare, because I was little when Sadiq got married. But for sure I haven't seen my mother this happy since I was born! And I haven't seen her this beautiful. What 'Aboud' says is right—admit it, you love Hasan more than us, we have proof!"

Abed joined in, "The matter of beauty is a whole other subject, open to discussion. People get old, and you get younger and prettier, as if you were a girl of twenty. The girls have all gotten complexes, and poor me! Every time I like one, I make comparisons. Then you come and say, 'Why aren't you getting married, Abed?' as if I were responsible! What do you think, Aunt Wisal?"

Wisal laughed, and spread her five fingers in his face. "Five and five again! I'll put a spell on her to protect her from your jealous eyes." She looked at me, "Ruqayya, as soon as we get back to the hotel I'll put a spell on you. Sadiq, where can we get incense? Are there perfumers in this country?"

We laughed. I heard the children, even though I was distracted by Fatima, stealing glances at her. It was as if I wanted to make sure. In fact, she looked like him, calm like him, and petite. There was a sweetness in her green eyes, and like him she had a childlike face that made her seem younger than her years. I looked at her as they were coming toward us in the transit lounge, and it was as if they were a girl and boy of no more than twenty. That wasn't what amazed me; what amazed me was that when Hasan was walking beside her he seemed even more mild-tempered than he always was, and more self-confident. It was as if he was finally able to show his sweetness without embarrassment, or as if he had found a secure place to hitch his reins and he could relax. Where did these ideas come from? My imagination? Later, during the seven days we spent together in Piraeus and during the coming years, I would discover that my intuition had been correct, and that sweet little Fatima was a woman of amazing strength. She was able to love Hasan without any fuss, to keep his feet on the ground and to protect him—as if she were a wolf, or a guard dog, or an angel.

Then came the night of the wedding.

It was a small restaurant on the seashore, and Sadiq wanted to rent it completely so that we would be the only guests. But the owner of the restaurant suggested that he accept other guests, as a full restaurant would add to the liveliness and cheer of the evening; everyone would join in the singing and dancing. Sadiq objected and spent half a day in discussion with the owner of the restaurant, and then he agreed to his suggestion.

He was right. As soon as the musicians began playing their instruments the Greeks began to sing. They inclined their heads and torsos right and left with the singing, and then the chairs couldn't hold them and they began to leave them, individually and in couples, for the dance floor. They danced, and then the circle widened; they formed a big ring, linking their arms, and became absorbed in a collective dance to the rhythm of the music. One of them motioned to Maryam to join the ring; she looked at Sadiq, but before he gave her permission Abed drew her by the hand, and then drew Hasan and Fatima, and they joined the dancers. Abed came back and tried to convince the elderly ladies to join in; Wisal said to him, "Wait a little. We'll dance and sing when the time comes. It's coming, our turn is coming." When it came, Wisal got up from her seat and advanced a few steps, and burst out singing a *mhaha* song:

> *Iiwiihaa* . . . he adorns youth itself, he adorns our home.
> *Iiwiihaa* . . . you cannot contain him when you seek to describe!
> *Iiwiihaa* . . . he's a young prince and worthy to reign.

Then she loosed a long trill that surprised the Greek guests in the restaurant. They had not yet understood why she was standing, or the meaning of what she was doing. Then:

> *Iiwiihaa* . . . I've brought henna from Mecca for your hands, O bride,
> *Iiwiihaa* . . . O bright, full moon, all the jewels are for you,
> *Iiwiihaa* . . . the henna is worthy of your hands alone,
> *Iiwiihaa* . . . O Fatima, most beautiful of brides, to Hasan I bring you!

She trilled again, more loudly than and stronger than the first time, and Maryam, Karima, and Randa joined her. Then:

> *Iiwiihaa* . . . I've been running after the noble ones, to marry among them.
> *Iiwiihaa* . . . The winds of love rose, and threw me at their door.
> *Iiwiihaa* . . . I pray to the Lord in heaven to bring them victory,
> *Iiwiihaa* . . . a dear victory that will make them proud.

The third trill was not limited to the bridal table, rather it rose from all over the restaurant. The other guests, who had been watching the old woman in a long embroidered dress with a cloth belt tied below her stomach, leaving space for her large chest, had understood the game and wanted to share in it. They trilled after their own fashion, and the expert trills mingled with cheerful gargles and laughing shouts that imitated the original. As she returned to her seat, Wisal said, "Where are you, Samir? What are you waiting for?"

Like a conjurer, Fatima's cousin Samir brought out the tabla drum and the reed flute. He gave the flute to his brother and began to beat the drum and sing:

Welcome to you, to your guide and companion,
Welcome to the road that led us to know you.

Were it not for love, we would not have come walking,
Nor ever set our foot in any of your lands.

We are the headmen, the pillars of the town,
We are its firm mountains, when all others are overturned.

Then: "Where are you, men? Where's the dabka line?" Sadiq, Hasan, Abed, Ezz, and the father of the bride got up and made a line near the flute player, who went on playing the flute. Samir accompanied them by beating the tabla and singing:

The horses swept in dancing,
In the plaza of the groom,
God's blessings on Muhammad,
And for Iblis, his doom!

The horses swept in dancing,

In the plaza for the two,
God's blessings on Muhammad,
And for Satan, his due!

"Come on, Maryam—*Dabkat Lubnan*"!

Abed said it from his place in the dabka line, then he jumped to where we sat and pulled Maryam after him. He announced in a loud voice, as if he were introducing a professional singer, that she was going to sing Fairuz's song, *Dabkat Lubnan*. I thought, Abed is rash, and he's embarrassed his sister. She'll be overcome with fright, she won't be able to get her voice out and she'll sing off key.

She did not sing off key. The voice trembled a little at the beginning, and then it became firm and free:

There's Lebanese dancing in the gathering, dabka with lifted arms,
The knights came down to the circle, brandishing their gleaming swords,
The plaza was lit up by its guests, the arena by their swords,
While the gazelles watched to see them, dancing and linking their arms.

They danced to the sound of the flute, and to Maryam's singing. Their arms were linked, their shoulders leaning lightly; their torsos would lean and stand erect, and lean again. The knee would bend, a little or a lot, the feet prominent in the dance, leading it. They step, jump, advance, returning and moving forward and always striking the floor with resolution. Five men, no more, as if they were a clan of jinn. Maryam kept her eyes fixed on them as she sang. Had the dance dissipated her fear so that she forgot that she was afraid, or had the words and the melody of the song captivated her, so that it flew away with her as it did with the dancers?

The girls have come down laughing, they come with hips
swaying,
You might say they're riders, leaning on long lances.
The steps to the house are high, worn down from all the
cook fires,
A poet bearing gifts sang to me, and went to live near you.

My God, she's no longer a child, but a young woman with a
full voice. It's strange, Wisal was thinking the same thing. She
leaned over to me and whispered in my ear, "Has she reached
puberty?" I said, "Yes. She was thirteen two months ago."

The noble steeds came running, they came to the courtyard door,
The towers trembled in their place from their coursing
horses,
They came from afar, they appeared, the door shook and
opened,
O years, your glory is returning your castle to the heights.

"O protect her from the evil eye!" Wisal was saying it in an
audible voice, as if she was talking to herself. Samir was
creating a parallel rhythm with his loud expressions of appre-
ciation for the singers and the dancers. From time to time
"God is great!" would suddenly burst out, or "My beloved!"
"God bless the Prophet!" "The pick of the nobles!" "Welcome, young men, welcome!"

The protectors have returned to the house,
Let it be lifted up with the good news!
Where is the feast, where are the dangerous eyes
That lift up the feast, and spread it in the yard?
The coursing horses have appeared from afar,
Life, long life, for those who protect us,
Welcome, welcome, welcome, God give you health

Hedged with glory
Hedged.

We all repeated, as if we were a chorus or a group singing anthems, or perhaps a crowd or a large audience:

Hedged
And walled with goodness
Walled
And fortified on high
Fortified
And radiant
Welcome, welcome, welcome to your eyes, your eyes.

What did Maryam's voice do to me? I had never danced in my life. I mean, I had not danced since they threw us out of Tantoura. I used to dance there, but then I forgot.

I announced, "I'm going to dance with Fatima."

I danced.

Did complete calm suddenly come over the place, or were my five senses occupied with celebrating the bride, so that I went to her sincerely unaware of the presence of anyone else? Even the sound of the flute, which continued, seemed as if it was coming over a long distance, reaching us from afar, or trying to. I put out my hand to the bride, my fingertips touching the ends of the fingers on the hand she stretches out to me. I turn her around, and I turn, slowly. I bend lightly with her, and she bends. It was as if my body had become a light breeze. She inclines, and I incline. I lead her shyly, and surrender gladly.

Why did I dance, and how? Was I dancing, or doing something else? I don't know. All I remember is that when I returned to my seat at the table Hasan got up and faced me without looking into my eyes, then bent over my hand and kissed it. I noticed a light moisture on the back of my hand.

The next day, Wisal said to me, "Give me a cigarette."

As I handed her the cigarette I said that I didn't know that she smoked.

She said, "A cigarette every few months. Ruqayya, everyone says that Wisal knows how to talk, that she can express herself with ease."

I smiled, and said, "It's true. If only I were like you. I'm the opposite, and you know it."

"I know. But yesterday . . . I wanted to put what I saw into words, but I couldn't. What happened?"

"You mean the party?"

"I mean your dance with Fatima."

"I didn't know that I was able to dance, or that I knew how."

Wisal looked at me and said, "It's strange."

"What's strange?"

"That dance. In your dance you said what words can't express."

40

The Battle of the Dress,

or What Do You Want Me to Say?

WE WERE WALKING ON THE beach, and a man of medium height was following us, looking toward us and smiling. The man went up to Samir and spoke to him, then said goodbye and left. Wisal stopped and asked, "What does he want? He keeps staring at us, and at me in particular."

Samir said, "He spoke to me in English and asked, 'Are you from Israel?' I wondered at the question, and he pointed to your dress, and smiled, and said, 'I knew from the dress.'"

"What did you say?"

"I didn't say anything, I let him go."

"How could you let him go?"

Wisal hurried toward the man and we hurried after her as she was calling, "Sir! Sir! Hey, *Mister*!"

The man looked around and stopped, waiting for the lady whose thawb had caught his eye. He was smiling broadly.

Wisal grasped the collar of her thawb and said, "This *no Izrael*. This is a Palestinian thawb that I embroidered with my own hand. Translate, Maryam."

Maryam translated.

"*Izrael* is a thief, it stole our land and turned us out and slaughtered us, and it even wants the clothes off my back! Translate, Maryam." She pointed to her chest with her finger. "This stitch . . . ."

Maryam interrupted and said in despair, "Aunt Wisal, I don't know how to stay 'stitch' in English."

"It doesn't matter, say 'embroidery,' say 'handwork.' I worked late many nights to embroider this. It's called 'peasant embroidery,' and this is a Palestinian peasant thawb. What does *Izrael* have to do with it?"

She pointed to the man with her finger and asked, "*You Izraeli?*"

The man shook his head and said, "No."

"Then why do you smile when you say *Izrael?* Any respectable man is grieved when he hears the name *Izrael.* I'll tell you what *Izrael* means. Translate, Maryam."

Wisal began to enumerate what Israel does in the West Bank and Gaza, and what it did before the West Bank and Gaza. The words flowed from her in a torrent, as Maryam tried to catch up, saying, "Slowly, Auntie, slowly, translating is hard."

Wisal said, pointing with her finger to herself and then to each of us, "*This*, and *this* and *this*, everyone is Palestinian. Do you know Tel Aviv?"

The man nodded his head. His smile had disappeared and his face had darkened; he was in a hurry to bring this situation to an end.

"Tel Aviv itself is stolen. They stole Jaffa and named it Tel Aviv. Translate, Maryam."

We drew Wisal away so she would let the man go. When he moved on Wisal noticed Samir's presence, and asked him, "Don't you speak English?"

"I speak it."

"For God's sake! Then why didn't you tell him what Israel's worth? Son, don't you know better than anyone else what Israel means?"

The young man blushed, and we decided to go back to the hotel.

But the incident that had made Wisal so tense turned into the subject of jokes. Samir told it to anyone who hadn't been there, and they insisted that Wisal tell them again what happened. Her skill in telling the story astonished me, for it seemed livelier and more detailed when she told it: "The man was no more than three hands high, his forehead was just a dent in his face, his eyes only a hole here and a hole there. And he was opening his big mouth, his face flushed for his dearly beloved! Maybe if his mouth was a little smaller it would have been okay, or if his face was a little bigger it would have only been half a disaster, but his big mouth swallowed up three quarters of his face! That was at first, before he discovered that we weren't his dearly beloved, but their cousins. The more I insulted Israel the more his shoulders sank, so he looked shorter; his eyes became narrower, and his face turned colors—it went red like a fez, then yellow like a lemon, then the color drained and darkened." She stopped suddenly and asked me, "Was he cross-eyed or did I only think so?" She laughed, then ended with a deep sigh, "Oh well, you don't need to tell me that we can't bring Palestine back with words!"

Wisal talked to us at length about the Intifada. When Sadiq asked her, she said, "What do you want me to say? You can follow the news better than I can. In Jenin we only get the Amman station on television, and the Israeli stations. Your television has God knows how many stations from the whole world, and you read what's written in the newspapers and in books." When we asked her, she didn't talk. But she would open up when we were talking about this or that and the subject of the Intifada came up unexpectedly, and the talk turned to what happened. The strange thing was that Wisal always laughed when she told her stories, always choosing comical incidents. Was it because she gained strength from laughter? Or was it that despite the sacrifices, the Intifada was like the resistance when it entered the Lebanese camps after 1967, when it filled the residents with pride and confidence?

She said, "Kids, by God, just little kids. A boy the size of a hand span, with no idea where God had put him, with a cooking pot on his head and in his hand a weapon half again as big as he was. They tell him, 'Go and kill,' and he's scared, scared of killing and scared of being killed. Armed and armored, screened by the door of his armored car. A house mouse, sticking his head a quarter of the way out and aiming his weapon, and the next second hiding behind his door. God bless our kids, they attacked them like lions."

I remembered her words as I followed the events of the Intifada on television in Abu Dhabi. I would follow the little ones as they carried their slingshots and aimed their stones at the soldiers. I would follow the soldiers as they swooped down on the young men and put them in the police vans, or took one aside to smash his head or his arm. I would think a lot about Wisal and her children, and look closely at the pictures whenever a woman appeared in an embroidered peasant dress, raising her hand with determination to throw a stone at one of the army cars, or to quarrel with the soldiers in order to release one of the children they had arrested. She seems to be Wisal. She looks like her, but it's not Wisal. I wonder what she's doing now? I would not meet her again until five years later in Alexandria, although I saw her twice in my dreams. Once we were in Tantoura, walking on the seashore, just two girls walking barefoot on the wet, sandy shore, walking along the edge of the sea. Were they talking? I didn't hear any talk in my dream. I saw them coming, and I saw their backs as they moved away. The other dream was a nightmare. I remembered it when I opened my eyes; maybe it woke me up, as a man will be wakened by a fit of choking or a bad pain in his belly. I calmed down a little and went back to sleep, and I couldn't recapture the dream when I tried to later on.

41

Surprising Maryam

NAJI AL-ALI SAID IN A newspaper interview that he created the character of Hanzala to protect his spirit after he moved from the Ain al-Helwa camp to Kuwait to work in the press there. I read the interview when it was published in the paper on the anniversary of his martyrdom, reading it with interest because I loved Naji al-Ali's drawings and had followed them in the *Safir* newspaper when I was in Beirut, especially during the days of the Israeli invasion. I was also interested because Naji was from Ain al-Helwa and was a friend of Ezz, and my uncle Abu Amin knew him and talked about him with admiration. When he was martyred I became more interested in him; I thought his drawings must have had great importance since they feared them to the point of killing him. Is it true that Abu Ammar had a hand in it? Rumors about that circulated, but I say it was Israel.

In Beirut I began to follow Naji's drawings out of curiosity, since he was near to me, a countryman, someone we knew. Then gradually I began to notice that he expressed things that I wanted to say, even if I was not aware that I wanted to say them until the moment I saw the drawing. It was as if he spoke first, defining what was said before I put it into words or even conceived it in my mind. Or as if he knew me better than I knew myself. I didn't notice that Hanzala resembled me; it never even occurred to me. After all, Hanzala was a boy of ten, his feet bare, his clothes patched and his hair disheveled.

Naji said in his interview that his hair was like the quills of a porcupine, dressed and ready to defend him (before I read the interview, the little lines surrounding Hanzala's head had seemed to me more like the rays of the sun). Naji said in his interview that he created Hanzala to protect his spirit, as if he were an amulet protecting him from error. I wondered at what he said, and then I thought about it and remembered that I had brought five clippings from Beirut, each one a drawing of his that I had cut out when it appeared, and kept. When we were getting ready to move to Abu Dhabi I was afraid I would lose them, so I put them with my identity card in my wallet. I put four of them in the wallet, and then stopped a long time at the fifth, the only one below which I had written something: *al-Safir*, 9/16/1982. I remember the moment I saw the drawing, standing by the door of the house: Hanzala was looking at a mass cemetery, crosses stretching as far as the eye could see, as far as the horizon, where the earth met a black sky. Each of the crosses was like a crucified man, the horizontal wooden bar as if it were two arms stretched out and ending on the left in a hand, pointing, all of them pointing to a small Israeli soldier at the far left of the picture. Strange; Naji saw the massacre a day before it happened, and spoke out.

For the next three days the newspaper did not carry Naji's daily drawing. Because what happened surpassed all words? Or because he mourned for three days? Only on Wednesday, September 22, did the newspaper publish a drawing of Naji's in its usual place, on the last page: the Lebanese flag, with the cedar in the foreground, cut lengthwise by a band on which he had written 'The End' in English, and beneath it in Arabic. Under the flag there was a pile of bloody bodies, with Hanzala looking at them.

Strange; I remember the dates as if years had not passed since then, or as if I had learned them by heart.

I read the interview with Naji in the morning, and at night I took the newspaper to bed and read it again. I thought, when Naji moved to the Gulf he was afraid, like me. He was a young man, and he was afraid for himself. I'm no longer young—I've become a grandmother, and my children are the age he was when he left Ain al-Helwa to work in Kuwait. I slept, and then got up; and before I lifted my head from the pillow, I found myself thinking, I'm not afraid for myself but for Maryam. What amulet does she have?

As she was getting ready to go to school, I talked to her about Naji and Hanzala. She said, "I used to follow his drawings, I really loved them." I found it strange.

In the evening when I was alone with her in our room, I returned to the subject of Naji's drawings. I said, "What do you like about the drawings?"

She said, "The clarity."

I didn't understand, so I asked her to explain what she meant. She said, "Hanzala is clear, from his name that means a bitter fruit, to his shape, and to his stance. He's a little boy who looks on. His enemies are also clear: men who are short and fat and look ugly, who want the world completely at their disposal. They're also clear in the destruction they cause."

Tears nearly sprang from my eyes. I hugged her, and she asked, laughing, "Is this a sentimental Arab film? What happened?"

Maybe I shouldn't be so afraid for Maryam. She surprises me. One day Abed called her "Surprising Maryam," but he hadn't seen her for two years, so even he was surprised by that same spring inside her. It's different from the young men's spring; they call it "the girls' lathe." Abed found his sister a teen, a small woman. She was no taller than he was or than her two other brothers, but she had grown suddenly from a child with two braids into a teenager with all the curves of a young woman. She had been shaped on the girls' lathe. I smiled. But the spring was working on her mind also. It takes me by surprise.

She was sixteen, in the second year of high school, when she came back from school and announced proudly: "I received full marks for my composition! The teacher told us in class: 'I've been working in teaching for twenty years and I've never given a student full marks. But I liked what Maryam wrote so much that I even thought of giving her full marks, plus five marks.' The girls laughed at the idea. When class was over they gathered around me, wanting me to read what I wrote. I said, 'Tomorrow. I'll give it to my mother to read first."

I asked her, "What was the subject the teacher set for you?"

She said, "'The memory of a man you love.' Most of the girls wrote about their grandfather, but I've never seen my grandfather Abu Amin."

Sadiq laughed, and said, "You wrote about your grandmother?"

She said, "No," so I knew she had written about her father. I changed the subject: "Turn on the television, Sadiq, we'll miss the news."

Sadiq smiled, "Mama watches the news seven times a day!"

Maryam laughed. "In Beirut it was the newspapers and the radio, now it's the television!"

"In Beirut you were little and you wanted attention. You were even jealous of the newspaper!"

"Mama, admit it: did you read the newspaper or did you stop at every paragraph and every line and every word, as if you were going to be tested on it the next day? Maybe all you needed was a red pen, to underline the important paragraphs so you could learn them by heart! And the scissors, they were always near you so you could clip a news item here or an article there, along with Naji al-Ali's daily drawings. Abed insisted that you were working secretly for some archive, which we didn't know anything about!"

I laughed and so did Sadiq. He said, "It's strange."

"What's strange?"

"In an earlier time Mama would go out early to buy the papers. She would go out before having her coffee. Then she would throw them in the trash without reading them. 'Where are the papers, Mama?' She would say, 'I don't know,' and then admit that she had gotten rid of them!"

Randa said, "I don't believe it."

Maryam said, giving me a pat and putting her arms around my shoulders, "Believe it. That's Mama. Every time period has its own set system."

I said, "Raise the volume, Sadiq, the news is starting."

The children are right, I've become addicted to the news. Sometimes we turn on the television to watch the news and Sadiq or Maryam or Randa says, changing the channel, "There's nothing new." But I ask them to go back to the same channel; I follow the pictures of the young men throwing stones at the soldiers of the occupation. A woman facing an enlisted man, her hands in his face, shouting. Enlisted men wearing armor firing their rifles or pursuing kids down the side streets. Army cars, ambulances, police raids, arrests, demonstrations, the refrigerators of the autopsy room, the funerals. Yes, I had a desire to watch what I had watched in the previous newscast and maybe the one before it. Why? I don't know.

I watch, and I wait.

42

The Son of al-Shajara

MARYAM WROTE:

On July 22, 1987, someone shot the Palestinian cartoonist Naji al-Ali, using a pistol equipped with a silencer. The shooting occurred in London and resulted in the death of Naji al-Ali five weeks later. The fifth anniversary of the event fell during the vacation this last summer, and some newspapers called attention to it. I did not learn the date of the anniversary from the newspaper, however, because I remembered it, and I don't believe that I could ever forget it in the future.

In July of 1987, which was the first summer after we moved from Lebanon to live in Abu Dhabi, my older brother and guardian took me and my mother and his family to spend some of the vacation in Greece. I was eleven years old, and I loved playing, I loved the sea, I loved the sand, I loved eating fish, and I loved listening to the Greek music that resounded in the restaurants and cafés to which my brother took us. I even loved the line dances they would dance in the restaurants; I would jump up and join in, giving my right hand to the person standing on my right and my left hand to the person on my left, and dancing. These were among the happiest days of my life. When we returned to Abu Dhabi I learned by chance, from some words that passed between my mother and my brother, that Naji had been assassinated in London. I cried out, "Naji of Ain al-Helwa? The cartoonist?" Afterward, for a week or more, I was very distressed. I was sad over the passing of Naji al-Ali, but my distress and my anger with myself were greater than my sadness. My father was a doctor in Acre Hospital and was martyred in the massacres of Sabra and Shatila; would it be possible, for example, for Acre Hospital to be mentioned, or for the anniversary of the massacres to pass, when I was immersed in the pleasure of a beautiful summer resort, and that I would not stop for a moment, if only in my imagination, to mourn and to salute his memory? I had not known of the martyrdom of Naji al-Ali at the time, and I hated myself as if I had committed a crime.

Naji al-Ali was a native of the village of al-Shajara in upper Galilee, in Palestine. His family went to south Lebanon as refugees at the time of the Nakba—Catastrophe—in 1948, when he was a boy of eleven. He lived with his family in the Ain al-Helwa camp, and he remained connected to the camp even after he grew up and moved to the Gulf to work as a cartoonist. He never forgot that his land was stolen from him and that he was unjustly turned out of his country, so that he was forced to live as a refugee in a camp in Lebanon. He did not forget that he was a son of the camp, and that his mother made his underwear from leftover sacks that had contained flour distributed by the aid agency, and that she also used them to make a cloth bag in which he could put his notebooks when he went to school. He did not forget that when he was a boy he worked selling vegetables and picking oranges to contribute to the family income. He did not forget that his family lived in Ain al-Helwa and that Israeli planes shelled the camp regularly, as if killing people were a daily duty assigned to them.

I love Naji al-Ali's cartoons; there are many of them, and they are rich in meaning, teaching us a great deal. I love Hanzala, because he has become familiar due to his reappearance in the drawings, and because he makes me think that I am like him, for some reason I don't understand. This happens even though Hanzala is barefoot and his patched clothes show that he is poor, while I have not just one but several pairs of shoes, and my father was a doctor and my brother works here in Abu Dhabi, where he provides us with an easy, even luxurious life. I love Hanzala's mother Zeinab; even though she wears a peasant dress, she still carries the key to her house in Palestine suspended on a cord around her neck, like my mother. Hanzala's father is a peasant with big feet, barefoot and defeated; he always makes me think of my father and brothers, because I know that they feel defeated. Even the fedayeen fighter whom Naji draws swimming, returning to Beirut after the departure of the fedayeen in 1982, reminds me of my brother Abed, who was a fedayeen fighter and who was about to get on the ship when it was decided that the fedayeen would evacuate Beirut, but who turned around and came back to us in the house. Finally, Naji drew the children of the stones and named them before the Intifada arose and before they were known by this name; he drew the children as they were throwing stones at the occupiers, and from the little stones he formed an oncoming tank. He even drew our Lord Jesus on his cross, lifting his hand to throw a stone at the oppressors.

My mother is from Tantoura, a little village on the Palestinian coast, not one of the villages of Galilee, and I don't believe she ever met Naji personally. But she loves his drawings. All during the war and the Siege of Beirut she followed his drawings, and sometimes she would show me a cartoon in the newspaper. Since I was six years old, she would explain the meaning to me. When we moved to Abu Dhabi, my mother brought five clippings of Naji's drawings with her in her wallet. Among them was the drawing of a girl looking out of an opening made by a missile in the wall of her house. Our house in Beirut was also struck by a missile that made a hole like that one in the wall, but fortunately it struck the other side of the building. In the picture the opening looks like a window, and under it Hanzala is raising his hand with a flower and saying, "Good morning, Beirut." My mother told me that the cartoon appeared in the *Safir* newspaper after a night of shelling so heavy that people thought that day would never dawn; and when the day did dawn and the newspaper came out, they found Hanzala saying good morning to them with a flower.

There is another cartoon among the five in my mother's wallet that I would like to talk about. The father, the peasant with his two bare feet, is squatting on the right side of the picture, holding up a sign on which is written "In memory of Hittin." He's thinking, "If only Saladin were alive." On the left of the picture, Hanzala is looking at short, fat men with big rears, and thinking, as if he heard the thoughts of his father, "They would assassinate him."

Naji al-Ali was not a political or military leader like Saladin. It was not to be expected that he would lead us in a battle in which we would vanquish our enemies and liberate Palestine. But his drawings speak for me, and they make me discover my feelings and the things that weigh on me and hurt me, and the things I want to accomplish.

Naji al-Ali's cartoons make us know ourselves.

When we know ourselves, we are empowered.

Perhaps that is why they assassinated him.

43

Another Time

SADIQ SAID TO ME, "I'VE been cherishing the hope that Maryam would major in architecture and work with me here, in the company. The girl is smart and hard working, and she will be important in her field. I'll send her to study at the American University of Beirut, as soon as she gets her high school diploma."

He called Maryam, and said, "Then you intend to enroll in the College of the Humanities?"

She looked at him in surprise, and said, "'Then' referring to what?"

He laughed, "Referring to the subject of the beautiful composition you wrote."

She said, "First, it's not a composition. Second, I'm going to go the College of Medicine."

Another one of her surprises. She had given no previous indication of that.

Sadiq said, "Seven years of study, and afterward, a specialization. When will you get married?"

Maryam flew to an eloquent defense of her desire to enter medical school, why she wanted to study it, why this profession was right for her, why . . . Sadiq laughed.

"Neither literature not architecture. The best would be for you to become a lawyer—you and your brother Abed could work together to change the system of the whole universe, by words!"

Maryam returned to asserting that she would enroll in the College of Medicine, and Sadiq announced that these were the dreams of a child, that she just thought that this was what she wanted, that she was too young to decide. He settled the discussion by saying, "I will not permit you to enter the College of Medicine."

No sooner had he left the room than she looked at me and said, "And I won't permit Sadiq to impose a major on me!"

Maryam is older than her years. I repeat to myself, why are you so afraid for her? There's nothing to fear for her. But I am afraid. In the future Maryam would say to me, "Your constant anxiety over me is unjustified. It chains me and I'm distracted by your fear, and concerned for you."

I said, "I've lost four men who were the dearest to my heart. It's natural for me to be afraid."

She said, "Think about the other half of the glass—you have four men as beautiful as roses."

I looked at her in surprise. "Four?"

"Sadiq and Hasan and Abed and Maryam!"

I laughed.

"In reality they are six: Sadiq and Hasan and Abed, and Maryam counting for two men. And Maryam's husband."

"And where is this husband of Maryam?"

"Somewhere."

"There's a young man I don't know anything about on his way?"

"When I choose the chosen one, who might be a charming elder or a matchless, cheerful young man, I'll choose to tell you, also." She jumped to the old question: "How many *ch*'s did I use in my sentence?"

"Maryam, stop playing games. I'm asking seriously, is there a young man?"

"Young men, not just one!"

"Tell me about them, and I'll help you choose."

"That would be interference in state sovereignty and the right of peoples to self-determination!"

I laughed, and noticed that she had cleverly moved the direction of the talk far away from my fear and from the four I had lost.

"Since we have become a small family, just a mother and a daughter, what's to prevent your showing me the long line waiting for you?"

"Mama, I'm joking. I'm twenty-one. I have two years ahead of me to finish medical school, and the year of internship, and several years of specialization. Serious decisions will have to wait at least five or six years, possibly seven, and maybe . . ."

I groaned. "I was engaged before thirteen years of age."

She knew the story of the son of Ain Ghazal.

"And I married your father when I was fifteen."

She laughed, "It was another time."

"I know, but twenty-six is a lot. You'll have missed the train."

She chuckled. "The Egyptians say, 'If you miss out on government work, then roll in its dust.'"

"Meaning?"

"The proverb is about the importance of government work and of getting a government job at any price."

"And what relation does that have to do with what we were talking about?"

"If I miss the marriage train I'll run after it and hang onto it. Isn't marriage like a job? A government job, Umm Sadiq. Imagine Maryam running after the train and hanging onto the door, and then falling from it and rolling in its dust. That's if luck is with her, and if not, she'll cling to it under the wheels!"

"God forbid."

"I should sing you a song."

"Yes, please sing."

We were in Alexandria and Maryam was studying in the university there. Why am I getting ahead of events? I haven't finished with the story of Abu Dhabi, we are still there.

44

The Project

ON OUR WAY TO THE airport to meet Abed, Sadiq said, as he was driving, "I bet Abed intends to get married."

I said, "Has he hinted at that?"

He said, "He hasn't hinted, but I haven't seen him for three years. Every time I travel to Europe I get in touch with him so we can meet, and he says he's busy. Last year I urged him to come to spend the vacation with us in Austria, and he said he was busy. I said, at least come to see your mother and your sister, have some consideration for them! Then he contacts me suddenly and says, arrange a visa for me as fast as possible, I have to see you. He must be intending to get married."

Sadiq's criticism of his brother irritated me, but I did not comment. Perhaps Abed actually does intend to get married and has come to tell us about it, or to ask his brother for help with his finances. I know Abed; and Sadiq, I know him too. He acts as if he is the master of the family, he intervenes and criticizes and objects and says, "I don't agree, you are free to do what you like but then it's your responsibility." Then you find that he's standing next to his brother, shoulder to shoulder, carrying the load with him, or he says, "Let me help you, Brother," and lifts the heaviest part of the load.

On the way back from the airport, I asked Maryam to sit in the front seat next to Sadiq, and I sat in the back seat with

Abed. Sadiq remarked, scoffing, "Does it make any sense, Abed, to come from Paris without a suitcase? I thought you were joking when you said that you didn't bring a suitcase. Are you going to spend a week in Abu Dhabi in the same jeans and shirt?"

"I don't carry suitcases when I travel."

"You only carry a backpack!"

"It has everything needed: two shirts and socks and two changes of underwear."

They went on bickering and laughing, and Maryam joined in their talk. I only held Abed's hand and looked surreptitiously at his face. The lock of hair on the side, which covered the right side of his eyebrow, did not hide how his hair receded from his forehead, nor did I fail to notice a few white hairs among the black. Now I could only see his face from the side; in the airport when he came toward us, I saw him fully. He had become thin, and with his height he seemed extremely thin. Doesn't the boy eat, living away from home? What does he eat? He wears jeans and a shirt and a pair of the running shoes that are popular among schoolboys. It's hard to imagine that he has passed thirty, and that he's a lawyer with experience in his field. And that backpack, hanging from his shoulder! I nearly laughed; Sadiq is right. Another stolen glance: his hair is a little longer than usual. Did he forget to go to the barber, or was it a response to the beginnings of baldness? Oh Lord, when will we marry him? I squeeze his hand without noticing.

He looked at me, "What does our dear mother say?"

"I've missed you, Abed!"

He kissed my hand. I felt the blood rush to my head, and I didn't find anything to say.

The topic of Abed's clothes occupied an unreasonable share of the visit. Or was it just a longing on the part of the boys for their old relationship, which was based on bickering? Sadiq said, "How will you meet my friends and acquaintances when you haven't brought a suit? Why didn't you bring a suit, a shirt, and a tie? You're not my size."

"I don't own a suit."

"Then we'll go together tomorrow and buy you two suits and two shirts and . . ."

"God bless you, Sadiq, I can buy a suit but I don't need a suit because I don't wear one."

Sadiq acted as he saw fit and came back the following day with bags and boxes: three suits, six shirts, three ties, and two pairs of shoes. He took them out of the bags and spread them out before us, saying, "This one is navy, for formal occasions. This one is light, you can wear it in the morning and for informal appointments. I liked the third one but I saw it after I had bought the other two, so I thought, it's all to the good. These shirts and ties are for the navy one, and that tie is for the other. These shoes are for the navy one, and those . . ."

Randa added, "And *signé*, too!"

I leaned over to Maryam and whispered, "What does *signé* mean?"

"Literally it means that it has a signature, and what's meant is that it was made by a company famous all over the world— that it's a worldwide, expensive brand."

Abed began to laugh, to laugh aloud. For a moment Sadiq was confused; maybe he had lost his way. It looked as if he didn't understand, and I didn't understand, either. I thought, Abed is laughing out of embarrassment; but when the laughter increased, I became anxious. It had all begun as joking and bickering, but it would turn into trouble—Abed would become angry and refuse the gift, and Sadiq would be hurt and embarrassed by his brother's behavior.

"God forgive you, Brother. How much did you pay for these clothes?"

"Tell me first what's making you laugh?" Sadiq was annoyed.

"It's because you took it on yourself to spend a large sum on clothes I won't wear. Now let's act wisely—come with me to return the clothes to the shop where you bought them and get your money back."

"What's wrong with my giving my little brother some elegant clothes?" His voice had begun to rise and it had an edge.

"Even if I need what they cost?"

"Take the gift and tell me how much you need and I'll give it to you."

"I need a million dollars, and if you could give me more, there's no objection."

"Slow down, Abed, stop joking. This talk is raising my blood pressure."

"Since when do you have high blood pressure? No one told me. Do you take a pill every day?"

"It's not the time for that. How much do you need? Why didn't you tell me that you're going through a financial crisis? Why should I work like a mule here if I can't provide what my family needs?"

"First, I'm sorry to hear about the blood pressure—I hope you get better. Let's talk calmly, and let's not mix the subjects. The gift is one subject; the money I need is another, I came from Paris especially to talk to you about it. The problem is that your gift is expensive and its price could be added to the sum I came to ask you for."

"Have you decided to get married?"

"Absolutely not."

"Are you in debt?"

"No."

"Then what's the matter?"

"It's the project. Listen."

Randa withdrew. She said, "It will be a long night; I'm going to sleep." It seemed to me that Abed might need to talk to his brother alone, so I said, "Let's go, Maryam."

Maryam said, "I want to know what the project is. I might be able to help Abed to convince Sadiq; didn't Sadiq say that I would be a good lawyer?"

Abed said, "Sit with us, Mother, I want to hear your opinion. You stay too, Maryam, you might be able to help me defend the project."

Maryam winked at him and said, "If I am convinced!" She laughed, but Sadiq did not laugh.

We sat until four in the morning. Abed explained his project at length, Sadiq interrupting him to question and to ask for clarifications, or to pose objections or protest, or to shake his head suddenly, as if he had realized that he had to wake up after roaming in the imaginary. At the end of the session Sadiq surprised me, he surprised me even though what he did was completely like him. He said, "I agree. I'll give you a quarter of what I own." He added, laughing, "According to the canonical law: a quarter for me and my family, a quarter for you, a quarter for Hasan, and a quarter for Mother and Maryam."

I wanted to ask, "What do you mean, 'according to the canonical law'?" but I didn't. My energy was taken up with trying to keep from crying. I didn't want to cry and divert their attention, or wake up Maryam, who had put her head on my shoulder and gone to sleep.

Sadiq said, "On one condition—that you take the gift."

Abed said, "According to the canonical law. I'll take a suit and a shirt and a pair of shoes."

"What law?"

"My own law."

"And the two other suits and the shirts? They're not my size."

"We'll take them back to the shop and trade them for one for you and one for Hasan, or you will get your money back. It's agreed."

Perhaps Sadiq was exhausted. He said, "Okay. Good night, all."

Abed leaned over Maryam and said in a loud voice, intending to wake her up: "Maryam, shall I carry you as I used to when you were little?"

She opened her eyes. "What happened about the project?"

45

By the Law

HOW CAN I DESCRIBE THE SCENE? I'm trying to recall it, yet
I know it's hard to describe—not because memory drops
some things and adds others, or highlights some and pushes
others into the background, but because what happened
went beyond the words that were spoken. I write what was
said in order to tell what happened, well aware that what
I am describing is closer to a dream of something than it
is to the thing itself. It's as if it were a well of which we
can see only the small amount that the bucket has scooped
up. Tension? Yes, there was tension in the scene. Alarm?
Perhaps. The relationship between the brothers was like a
ship's rope, thick, showing how firm it is when it's pulled
taut. Roles were reversed in the flash of an eye, and then
were reversed again, and then a third time and a fourth.
Which one was the older, then? Sadiq is fragile in his relationship with those he loves; it's a natural thing, that's how
lovers are. Abed rushes ahead blindly, like an engine without
a driver. Sadiq says, "I'm the eldest!" and he suddenly seems
tyrannical. Then the wave of arrogance breaks when it hits
the beach and becomes calm and tame, like the water in a
stream. And Amin? He was present there, even if he did
not appear, nor was his name mentioned. Was it a stormy
session? Yes, but not sad; for when I was alone that night
I cried, as if I had made peace with the world. As if it had
accorded me what it had begrudged my mother.

Abed introduced his project with a long, expert speech about the back-and-forth contest taking place in Europe over internationally binding regulations. He said, "There is serious legal debate about the creation of an international court to punish individuals responsible for crimes of genocide or any crimes against humanity. There are groups actively pushing for this. Personally, I expect that in the next few years internationally binding regulations will appear, strengthening the Geneva Accords and the treaties concerning torture. This is in addition to the fact that the laws of some European states have clauses allowing that cases be brought against crimes not committed on their soil, in which the accused is not one of their citizens, and allowing the plaintiff to be an individual and not a state. And . . . ."

Sadiq interrupted him, "What does that have to with your project, Abed? What's your project?"

"Have patience with me, Brother. Current regulations may not permit us to file suits, or else we haven't studied these regulations enough to find the opening that would allow us to file suits. We have to prepare. Here's the value of the project: I'll sum it up for you now, in its essential elements."

I nearly intervened. I wanted to say to Abed, what's come over you, boy, do you believe that we can get our land back by bringing a suit before a European judge? But I said nothing. Sadiq said, "You're nuts! You were one of the fedayeen, carrying arms. Why? Answer me, why?" He gave him no time to answer, but answered for him: "Because international law did not give you your rights, from the beginning to the end. No law or international society nor the United Nations guaranteed you the right of return, nor of reclaiming the lands occupied in '67 or any right that had been usurped from you. How many resolutions were adopted by the United Nations? How many massacres occurred afterward? Was Israel punished, even once?"

"Our project rests on three bases: The first is the purely legal basis, which depends on studying the law in the various

European countries, searching for openings we can use to file suits. The second is making a list with a number of potential suits, and providing the necessary evidence for them—documents, testimony, studies, etc. The third basis is the human element: contacting the injured parties in whose names claims might be made or who would accept the role of witnesses, and contacting lawyers. What I mean is the formation of two networks, a network of injured parties and another network of jurists, lawyers, and legal consultants. That's a rough summary, since I don't want to go on and on, or drown you in legal jargon."

"Abed, are you dreaming? Or looking for work for yourself? Damn it, Brother, what you're saying isn't worthy of a young man like you, who knows the history of the Palestinian cause and the role of the international community in our disaster." Sadiq looked at me, mocking, "Your son has been affected by the talk going around about disavowing violence and the possibility of solving our problem peacefully. Have you visited Egypt recently, or have you met Abu Ammar?"

Abed's face reddened, and he raised his voice, "Shame on you, Sadiq. I'm talking seriously. If you're interested, listen to the end, if not, I'll leave tomorrow."

"Neither your mother nor Maryam nor I have any part in this visit! If only out of respect for us say, 'I'll leave the day after tomorrow, and I'll spend the day with you because I miss you!' What's happened to you, have you gone mad? Sometimes I'm tempted to kidnap you and bring you here to work and get married and live like the rest of God's creation. Europe has made you lose your mind—no wife and no suitable work, you dress like a bum and hang a backpack over your shoulder. What's happened to you?"

Abed jumped up. "Do you have anything to drink?"

"Yes."

"Will you have a glass?"

"I will."

Sadiq got up and brought the bottle of whiskey, two glasses, and ice cubes, and poured for himself and for his brother. Abed looked at me.

"Will you join us?"

I laughed. "No, thanks. Enjoy it."

"I'll illustrate it for you by two examples, one easier and apparently simpler, and the other more difficult and more complicated. We can file a suit, not now but in a few years, since I expect new legislation to be promulgated in a year or two. We can file a suit against those responsible for what happened in Sidon, for example: shelling the school and killing everyone in it, the destruction of the hospital with those in it, what they did in Ain al-Helwa. What's needed? First, that we contact the injured parties and we inventory the damages: mass murder, imprisonment, torture, destruction of homes, etc. One or more people will file the suit on their own behalf or on behalf of themselves and others. So the second requirement is to contact those people, to listen to them, to identify those best suited to file the suit and who want to do that, and those best suited to testify as witnesses. We can contact the director of the school and get detailed testimony from him. We can go back to the man responsible for civil defense in the south; he has the reports of foreign reporters published in their newspapers at the time. We have the mass graves, including the one now at the basketball court in the school courtyard, covered by asphalt."

"Who will you file the suit against?"

"Against the Israeli defense minister and the chief of the general staff, and others as well."

"But it was war."

"It was an invasion. But neither war nor invasions allow massacres or shelling the houses of civilians or destroying hospitals on top of their patients or killing children in their schools. The conventions on the treatment of prisoners of war do not permit torturing or killing them. All of that happened in Sidon and Ain al-Helwa. We will have to study what happened, to work on the legal definitions, to research criminal legislation in European states that allow claims of this kind to be made."

"Let's assume you can file the suit. Can the judgment be made in absentia? And does international law allow you to demand that the accused be handed over? What about state sovereignty and the immunity of national leaders?"

"The basic principle of internationally binding legislation gives states the right for their courts to investigate the most flagrant cases, specifically crimes of massacre, torture, war crimes, and crimes against humanity, even if these crimes occurred outside of their territories and if there is no direct link between these states and the criminal, the victim, or the site of the crime. Those who have immunity today, because they are prime ministers or ministers, will lose their immunity after a year or two. Now I'll give you the other, more difficult example: imagine if the legislation that we expect will be promulgated, for which we are already seeing good omens, imagine if it allowed us to bring a case concerning Tantoura. Our mother could bring it: there's the massacre, a war crime, and a crime against humanity. There's the plunder, which requires compensation for the village lands, fields, plantings, and animals that they seized, and for the houses and furnishings."

"Will we give up the right of return?"

"Of course not. That's the right for you to return to your country. They threw us out, and we have the right to return. They plundered our private possessions, so we have the right to go to court to reclaim them."

"Who would you bring the case against, in this instance? Would it fail because of how much time has passed? Most of the leaders of the Israeli army in '48 have died, maybe all of them."

"This point is subject to research, and we need dozens of things to research it: we need capable jurists, researchers, and

historians, and we need to convince the residents of the useful-
ness of making the claim. Filing a suit is expensive, but I'm not
talking about filing suits now, because that comes later and our
project may not take part in it directly. We only want to prepare
the ground, in the sense of a), researching the legal grounds;
b), forming a network of residents whose interests are affected,
on the one hand, and of capable jurists and lawyers who want
to participate in the project, on the other; and c), setting up a
database of documents and studies that will permit us to file
suits in the future. Imagine, Brother, if a person or a group of
people from a Palestinian village that was destroyed, where the
lands and the residents' possessions were plundered, brought
suits—the courts would have 418 cases at the least. If the residents of the villages that experienced massacres brought suits,
we have before us twenty massacres, some bigger than those in
Tantoura and Deir Yasin. These massacres are well known, but
researchers might discover others no one recorded."

Sadiq was now pacing back and forth. He stammered,
"You're dreaming, Brother, by God, you're dreaming. If only
we could get our rights by law—who among us would choose
all this blood?" He sat down suddenly and said, "Why didn't
you mention the case of the massacre in Sabra and Shatila,
and the kidnap victims, when you have a direct interest in it,
you and me and Hasan and Mother and Maryam?"

"There are ten files on the schedule, each of which has a
probable case that needs work, including Sabra and Shatila,
of course. Maybe the whole idea came to me when I was
thinking about what happened in Acre Hospital. In short,
Brother, we need time, we need money, and we need to work
night and day."

"And what will you do if none of these regulations that you
are counting on is issued?"

"They will be issued, all the indications are that they will.
In fact, a law of this kind was issued a few months ago in Belgium, but it's not sufficient."

"What if you file a case and a second and a third, and lose them, or what if contrary regulations were issued, limiting cases of this kind?"

"That could happen. You're as likely as not to lose when you embark on a new project. But then the cases will generate public opinion, informing people of these crimes."

"What people?"

"In Europe."

"They can go to hell, they're complicit. These crimes happen before their very eyes and they don't lift a finger."

"That's an oversimplification, Brother. People in general are not that bad. There are giant corporations with vested interests who are murderers, prepared to go to any length. Then there are people, the mass of people, ordinary people who want to live securely, to raise their kids and to enjoy small pleasures, a soccer match, or two weeks of laziness on a sunny beach. People who are concerned and who feel real pain when they see children killed unjustly. They aren't animals, just people like you and me, and sometimes better, because they haven't experienced the violence that would breed violence in them."

46

The Chain

I BURST OUT LAUGHING, AND I laughed so much I had to hold my sides. I said, "You're incredible, Abed!" We were sipping coffee, about to leave for the airport to see him off.

Sadiq said, "Be sure you have your passport and your plane ticket. Be sure you didn't leave your wallet or any of your cards. Be sure . . ."

Maryam laughed. "Sadiq, why do you insist on treating us as if we were kids?"

Saying goodbye is hard. I think that I've gotten used to it, and then when the time comes, I discover that that's a delusion. Abed looked at his watch. "We're leaving in ten minutes, aren't we? Five minutes and I'll be ready." He went into the room where he slept and came out carrying his small leather bag, hung over his shoulder, with a thick nylon case for the suit his brother had given him in his left hand, and a nylon bag in his right.

Sadiq commented, "What wrong with a suitcase? Wouldn't that be better than having something in each hand, like this?"

Abed put down the bag with the suit next to him and opened the other bag, saying, "This bag is for you, it's gifts."

"What gifts?"

"The gifts I brought for you."

"And you're giving them to us now, when you're leaving?"

"I forgot. I missed you so much that when I saw you, I forgot!"

I laughed, and kept on laughing as I saw Abed give Maryam and Sadiq and his wife and children their gifts. When he extended his hand to me with a very small bag, smaller than half my palm, I was still laughing.

He said, "It's a silver chain."

I spread it on my palm to look at it.

Abed said, as he kissed my head, "I'll tell you the story of it on the way."

He wanted to keep me from becoming emotional over it. He plunged into a long story about his Iraqi friend Mustafa, who designed the chain for him. Mustafa is a Kurd but his teacher Yahya Nasir is a Sabian, do you know who the Sabians are? He talked about the Sabians, and about Yahya Nasir who taught Mustafa silversmithing. He talked about Mustafa's family, living in Kurdistan, in Iraq, and he talked about the Kurds. He said that Mustafa is a visual artist and not a silversmith by trade, but that he designed the pendant. He said, "He's a genius." He talked about his art, about the show he had in Paris, and how dazzled people were. He talked about how he met him, and how he became his friend. He talked about when he left Iraq and why he left it, and how he moved around in a number of countries until he eventually settled in Paris. Abed did not stop talking until we went into the airport and he had only enough time left to kiss us, to say goodbye, and to pass to the other side of the wall.

On the way back Maryam started talking endlessly, like her brother. She talked for half the trip, and then the words stopped. She said, "Shall I sing for you?"

Sadiq said, "No." We made the rest of the trip in silence.

No sooner did I return to the house than I put on the chain. It has stayed on my neck, its pendant hanging two inches below my throat, with the cord around it and hanging lower, to the top of my breasts, with the key to our house in Tantoura. I wake and sleep with the two chains, and like my mother, I do not remove them, even to bathe.

It's strange: I would have asked Abed to stop talking about his Kurdish friend and the friend's Sabian teacher, were it not for the awkwardness. But that boring talk became part of the gift, not only that night, when I opened the latch of the chain to put it around my neck, but also whenever I look in the mirror or touch the pendant with my fingers or feel it on my skin. The silver pendant looks like the cover of a book the size of a finger joint, or a miniature page torn from a miniature notebook. A silver sheet with one word inscribed and enameled, in ornate kufic script: "al-Tantouriya," the woman from Tantoura.

47

The Research Center (II)

SADIQ CALLED SUMANA AND GAVE her the letters he had brought
her from the post office box. Then he opened a brown envelope and took out some journals, saying, "Hasan sent them to
me by mail. He has an article in them. He sent a copy for me
and a copy for you and one for Maryam."

He handed me the journal, after opening it to the beginning of the article. I saw the title with Hasan's name under it.
I paged through it; it was a long article.

It's strange. I read everything Hasan writes, even if I don't
grasp half or two-thirds of it. I read his master's thesis because
it was written in Arabic; the doctoral thesis was in English, and
I was not able to read it. It reached me by mail when we were
in Alexandria, and I asked Maryam to read it and summarize
the contents for me. Maryam laughed, and said, "I would have
to read it and then make sure that I understood it, so I would
have to read it again, and then summarize it, and then Hasan
will come and you'll discover that your daughter is a dunce
who summarized it wrong because she got it all wrong!"

Hasan insists on sending me a copy of any article or book
he publishes. He waits two or three weeks, and then he calls.
"What do you think?"

I laugh. Every time I laugh and I feel the blood rush to
my head. I say, "I never got beyond high school, Hasan!" Or,
"I haven't finished a book since I left school except for your
books, so how can you ask my opinion?"

He always repeats the same expression: "I care about your opinion. Anyway I didn't write a book of physics or math. Did you read the book?"

"I read it twice and I liked it a lot, but . . ."

"But what?"

"I'm biased. Besides, when I read what you write I imagine you as you write, I see your face, how you sit, the movement of your hands, your desk, and I miss you more!"

I said that once, and then I blamed myself for letting myself become emotional. It will bother the boy, it's enough that he's living so far away. I began to tell him what I thought frankly: I liked this, I didn't understand that, I was bothered by this, that part seemed boring, etc. But I would always end by saying that those were just my impressions of what I read, and they hardly qualified as an opinion. He would laugh, laugh contentedly, and every time he would say, "It's an important opinion, which I respect and learn from. You won't believe me, but I'm telling the truth!"

I took the magazine and went to my room. I sat on the comfortable seat opposite the bed and began to read Hasan's article. Under the title, "Testimony," Hasan had written:

A very personal introduction:

I began my relationship with the Palestinian Research Center in Beirut by telling a lie to my father. I told him that I needed a suit because I was invited to the wedding of a friend's brother; I must have a suit, a new white shirt and a tie. I was fifteen.

The visit to the Center was an important occasion I had been anticipating for weeks, a dream that seemed about to be realized. I wanted to be up to the dream, older, and convincing. That's where the idea of the suit and tie came from.

When Abd al-Rahman Ali, a researcher and a family friend, took me there, he did not need to tell me the way, because I had gone to the place more than once. I would go to the end of Hamra Street, then turn up al-Sadat and turn down to the right on Colombani Street, and after a hundred yards I would find the six-floor building. I would stand there, unable to muster the courage to enter. I would remain standing in the hope that I would catch a glimpse of Dr. Anis Sayigh; when I didn't see him, I would move on.

One day in the summer of 1972, the first day of the summer vacation, I took a shower and put on the new shirt and suit and tie, and shined my shoes with such care that it looked as if I had bought them moments before. I met Abd al-Rahman at the corner of Hamra Street and al-Sadat, and together we headed for Colombani Street. We went into the building, and Abd al-Rahman introduced me to the Center and to some of the workers in it, as well as showing me the facilities provided for researchers.

Suddenly I found Dr. Anis in front of me, as if he had just emerged from one of his pictures: the round face, the glasses, and the thick mustache. In a flash I realized that he was younger than I had imagined, and stouter. Abd al-Rahman presented me to him, and Dr. Anis shook my hand and asked me what college I studied in. I said that I had just finished the first year of high school, so he smiled, said goodbye, and moved on; but the sting remained in my ears, and I was conscious of the redness of my ears and face, and wondered if Dr. Anis had noticed it. Abd al-Rahman left me in the library, after he showed me the sections and how to find a book or a map. I requested a book and sat a long time in front of it, reading without taking in anything. I was agitated and angry over the suit, which had produced the opposite of the desired effect. When I returned home, my mother asked, 'Why did you wear the suit before the wedding?' I said, 'I had an important appointment. And the wedding has been cancelled.'

A week after my visit the letter bomb exploded in Dr. Anis's face, and his face, shoulder and left hand were wounded. At the time I was in the camp with the 'Lion Cubs,' and as soon as I heard the news, I flew to the Center to learn the details.

Despite the tumult, this was the beginning of a warm relationship that tied me to the Center. I would go there during the summer vacation, reading, unfolding maps in front of me and looking at them a long time, as if I were going to draw them over again. The workers in the Center came to know and accept me, and Dr. Anis, when he healed and came back to work, came to know me. He would say, "How are you, Hasan?" and smile at me in encouragement. I would return the greeting and smile, but I did not dare to look up at him, though even without looking up I could see his three amputated fingers, and the thick glasses which made up for a little of the vision he had lost.

This is a quick, personal introduction, by a boy inspired by the Center, which nourished his imagination, his mind, and his awareness of who he is, opening wide before him the doors of research, the doors of the future. How many researchers, both young and old, has this Center served with its library, its documents, its maps, its manuscripts, its periodicals, and its other publications?

Let us turn to the heart of the matter:

When the Israelis entered Beirut on September 15, 1982, the Israeli soldiers stormed into the Center. The headline in the *Safir* newspaper on the 18th of September read:

Beirut under Occupation
Wide Campaign of Raids and Arrests
Invasion of Office of the Palestine Liberation

Organization and Research Center
Confiscation of Most of the Documents and Records

The newspaper did not carry the details of the raid, which had occurred the previous day (Friday, September 17), which was the day in which the Israeli forces completed their occupation of Beirut. The newspaper had to cover the sites reached by the Israelis, the battles between the national forces and the invasion forces, the places shelled by Israeli tanks, the fires that broke out, the numbers of killed and wounded, and the arrests and raids, which included homes, hotels, party headquarters, magazines, and news agencies. In short, the newspaper could not dwell on the occupation of the Research Center while the forces of the occupation were penetrating the capital, making fast their grip on the city and the suburbs. The newspaper dedicated a complete page to detailed coverage of the events of Friday (the subject of the headline in the Saturday edition), in which we find the following lines about the Center: "Likewise a number of Israeli officers stormed the Palestinian Research Center in al-Sadat Street. Eyewitnesses reported that the officers stayed about two hours in the Center, after which they emerged, having planted an explosive device in one of the walls. It was ignited electronically from outside, where two tanks and a number of soldiers were in position; then the officers returned to the Center with large sacks. The witnesses reported that they took a large number of documents from the Center." Here ends the part concerning the Center, which comes within the coverage of the raids and the arrests. If we go to the eighth and last column of the same page, we find a few lines that say: "In the southern suburb also numerous Israeli forces raided private homes in Burj el-Barajneh and the Shatila Camp. Reliable sources have said that elements of Saad Haddad's militia have entered the Burj and Shatila and Sabra Camps, and reports speak of the torture of Palestinians by the Haddad militias."

Thus it is clear that the news of the massacre, which had begun on Thursday night and continued throughout the day on Friday, did not reach journalists until Friday night, so they did not learn of the occurrence of "torture" of Palestinians. Only on Sunday, after the end of the massacre, would the news spread and the headline on the first page read:

Massacres in the Camps

After that there were two pictures which had been taken of some of the victims, next to each other, stretching across the entire page, with a smaller headline underneath them:

News of 1, 400 Killed and Wounded in Sabra and Shatila
The Raiders Invaded Houses and Hospitals
and Exterminated Everyone in Them,
Including Wounded, Women, and Children

I apologize for the digression (although it is necessary, at least in my view), and return to the Research Center. The Israeli troops were intent on storming it as soon as they deployed in Beirut. Thus the massacre was simultaneous with the destruction of the Center and the plunder of its contents, the two separated in time only by a few hours, since the massacre began in the evening while the Center was invaded by day (because relative darkness in the first instance was a necessary tool, whereas daylight, in the second instance, was needed to examine the books and documents). They examined, ripped, destroyed, and laid waste, and then they left, having taken what they did. It's said that the contents of the Center library were transported in a caravan of trucks headed for Israel, and that experts joined the officers and the soldiers in examining what they wanted to plunder. They carried away nearly ten thousand books in Arabic, English, French, and Hebrew, not to mention the manuscripts and rare maps and documents, including the documents of the Supreme Arab Authority and the All-Palestine Government, as well as the papers of the Palestinian secret police during the Mandate and a complete set of statistics and documents from the Land Agency in the government of the British Mandate in Palestine, with a documented register of land ownership in Palestine at the time of the Mandate, together with papers and magazines from the time of the Mandate, and files and microfilm tapes and voice recordings.

Then they smashed the Center's furniture and the equipment in the reading room—typewriters, copiers, microfiche readers—and left the place completely destroyed.

Dr. Anis Sayigh, director of the Center from 1966 until 1977, says that out of concern for the contents of the library, the Center had prepared four microfilms of the files of information, keeping two copies and giving one to the Arab League and another to Baghdad University. He says that the Center issued a periodical with lists of the library's acquisitions of new books, which was sent to significant libraries. In addition he put in place a secret plan to preserve the rare books, documents, and maps, which would allow them to be transported rapidly at any sudden danger. He says, "We had a comprehensive secret plan for preserving the contents of the library, known to the Center officials; why did they not carry it out?" Dr. Anis asks the question in his low voice, looking out from behind his thick glasses, and repeats the question calmly, as if the ferment in his breast were a personal matter, something one should not make public or show to others.

Like him, I wonder. I wonder all the more because the researchers in the Research Center and its officials, who returned to work days after the event, did not prepare any lists of the stolen books, documents, and maps with the help of the films deposited with the Arab League or Baghdad University, or with the lists of new books preserved in more than one library.

At the end of 1983 negotiations ended between the PLO and Israel, by means of the International Red Cross, with respect to the exchange of prisoners. The negotiations included the plundered contents of the library, and their return was agreed to. The books arrived in Geneva from Israel in 113 large wooden crates, and were taken by a representative of the International Red Cross to Algeria, in order to deliver them. No one appeared to represent the Center, and the PLO office in Algeria did not have a list of the plundered contents, so it kept deferring the delivery. Then finally it took delivery of them.

After the crates were received they were transported to al-Kharouba Camp, and from there to the Tibissa Camp, which had received the units of the PLO army that had left Beirut with the resistance at the end of August in 1982. Samih Shbeib, a researcher with the Center and the head of its documentation department, says that he went to Algeria at the beginning of March in 1986, in the company of Sabri Jiryis, director of the Center (i.e., two and a half years after the date when they were supposed to be in Algeria), and that they met the Palestinian ambassador there, who informed them that the representative of the Red Cross and the representative of the International Archive had remained in

Algeria two weeks, waiting for the director of the Center or his representative in order to deliver the books and documents to him, and that in the end he had been forced to accept the crates by weight without examining what was in them, because of the absence of any list of the contents.

Samih Shbeib says that he traveled to Tibissa to examine the contents of the library. When he arrived he asked the director of the camp about the library of the Research Center, and says that the man was amazed by the question, as he had no knowledge of the matter. After a thorough investigation it became clear that the library was in the custody of an Algerian officer in a camp bordering on the Palestinian camp in Tibissa. Shbeib adds that the officer accompanied him to a large, locked warehouse, and that he found the corresponding crates covered with tarps. The Algerian officer said to Shbeib, "This is the Palestinian archive, which I have been guarding for more than two years, inspecting it daily, fearing rodents and the like. Thank God it has remained just as it was delivered; it is an important trust. God help you and bring you back to your homes!" The next day Shbeib was able to examine twenty crates, all of which were intact.

Shbeib continues the story saying that he spent forty days in Algeria trying to obtain a permit for shipping the books to Cyprus, where the Research Center had moved. Sometimes implicitly and sometimes openly, he points to some officials of the Algerian government who offered the Palestinian ambassador a building in the Algerian capital where the Center could resume its work, and where the library could be transported. He says that the ambassador was inclined favorably toward that suggestion, and so he did not make any attempt to simplify securing the necessary shipping permits. Likewise Abu

Ammar preferred to delay transporting the library, in the hope that the Egyptian government would agree to open the Center in Cairo. Later Abu Ammar—according to Shbeib—sent Sabri Jiryis, director of the Center, to Cairo to propose giving the library to the al-Ahram Foundation, which has a center for strategic research. The gift was not accepted.

Shbeib concludes his story by saying that the library was later transported to another camp, al-Bayyad Camp, to which the Palestinians were transferred, and that "the library was not given any serious attention. Not even minimal conditions for storage were provided. Ruin began to affect it, in addition to the effects of the rodents, and lastly, of men."

A few months ago I met Dr. Anis in Amman and asked him about the library. He said that the books which had not been stolen were transported to Cyprus in 1983, and then to European capitals; he did not know how or why, or what happened to them. As for the plundered books, the Red Cross had succeeded in moving them to Algeria and it is said that they were lost there, just as it is said that a part of them arrived at the port of Ashdod by sea, and that Israeli harbor authorities notified the PLO without receiving any answer. Then they warned the PLO that they would destroy them if they did not take delivery. Dr. Anis looks at me suddenly and says, "This is all I know, Hasan."

Why have I digressed to speak about the massacre in Shatila and the neighboring areas? Certainly I do not intend to make a crude comparison between plundered books and martyrs, or to equate plundering the Center with the massacre; but I wanted to give some indication, even tacit, of the context in which this Center grew and collected its documents, maps, manuscripts, and rare books. To set up a research center of this value in the context of the slaughter and in spite of it (and here I am not limiting myself to the slaughter of Shatila and the neighboring areas on Thursday, Friday, and Saturday, the 16th, 17th, and 18th of September 1982, but rather I mean Palestinian history over half a century, the continuous slaughter from 1947 up to the massacre in Hebron days ago)—to create this edifice in the context of slaughter is something of singular value, rare in human history. Thus participating in violating or scattering it is a compound crime, which includes among other offenses scorning the Palestinian name and the blood which has given it its identity and its meaning.

48

The Girls' Lathe

YES, "SHE'S BEEN TURNED ON the girls' lathe." Where did I get that expression? I heard it from my Uncle Abu Jamil's wife; it floated away, as forgotten things will, only for us to discover suddenly that they have been preserved, unaffected by being hidden away in some nook or cranny. Did Umm Jamil repeat the expression from time to time, or did she say it once, on noticing that I had become a young woman? I see Maryam growing day after day; the spring is doing its work, I know. And yet I notice suddenly, as if I did not know, and I say, "She's been turned on the girls' lathe." I think about Amin and look closely, as if I wanted to look for him too. Would his eyes have glistened to see his daughter such a beautiful young woman? I smile suddenly, and think, "Like a willow branch," her stature the more beautiful for its curves. Amin had said, "Look, Ruqayya, how beautiful her face is!" She was a nursing baby with a round face, her hair intensely black and her eyes dark blue, her skin soft, tender, and fragile, as if it were made of rose petals, the color between white and transparent pink. She's become a young woman, Amin, beautiful as she always was. And now her beauty is enhanced by a sharp tongue. She chatters, Amin, and talks a lot of nonsense like her brother Abed, loving bickering even more than he does, with a ready answer always at the tip of her tongue. And she sings. You liked her voice when she would sing, a child's voice; it's different, now. Yesterday she sang me a song she said she had learned from a class-mate of hers in school, a song about Alexandria:

> O Alexandria, how wondrous your sea,
>   Ah, if only I had some of your love!
> I'm tossed about from wave to wave,
>   As the fishing's good and the tide is high.
> I wash my clothes and hang out my cares
>   For the climbing sun, where I dissolve,
> Like a peasant in Urabi's army,
>   Cut down on the castle and gone to the sea,
> Like a breeze that floats above the hills,
>   Come from the sea to subside in your charm.
> O Alexandria, O lady born of Egypt,
>   Flashing a smile and starting to laugh,
> The sea is a window and a lattice,
>   And you are the princess overlooking the world.

I've missed you, Amin. I've missed you because you've been with us yet absent, because the pain of your absence seems like a thin thread braided with another, of pride perhaps, and of gratitude to you. She's no longer a child, Amin. It's a woman's voice, released by the melody and the words. Maryam has surprised me. It's surprised me that at fifteen, she's no longer a child; she's become a woman, a strong woman.

When we were alone in our suite at night I asked her to sing me the song again. She said, "No, it's better for you to wish for it," and she laughed. Then when I was in bed I found her standing next to me and singing me some of the lines of the song in a soft voice, as if she were rocking me to sleep. She changed some of the words, and the delivery and the voice; even the rhythm was altered:

> O Tantouriya,
> How wondrous your sea,

Ah, if only I had
Some of your love!
I am tossed
From wave to wave,
As the fishing's good
And the tide is high.
I wash my clothes
And hang out my cares
For the climbing sun,
Where I dissolve.

Then:

O Tantouriya,
O lady born of Haifa,
Flashing a smile
And starting to laugh,
The sea is a window
And a lattice,
And you are the princess
Overlooking the world.

She was smiling as she sang, scanning the words in a playful rhythm, caressing me with the singing. I resisted the sudden tears that sprang to my eyes; I didn't want the joy to turn into something sad. I said, "Good night, Maryuma."

She laughed. "'Maryuma' is only for Abed, the patent is recorded in his name."

I smiled. "It's legal to use it without infringing his patent."

"It's not legal!" She kissed me and went to bed.

It's strange. I slept and I saw you in a dream, Amin. You were receiving a large family who had come to ask for your daughter's hand. You were wearing your navy suit and light blue shirt and the dark, wine-colored tie. You seemed pleased;

you were smiling. Suddenly I asked, "Where is the young man who wants Maryam?" and I woke up.

Then I dreamed another dream, a longer one. I saw the young man who had been cast ashore. I saw him exactly as I had seen him in the sea of Tantoura, under the brilliant sun, his legs taut and his chest bare, approaching with deliberate steps on the wet sand. Even the drops of moisture on his shoulders were clear in the dream. He seemed very handsome, perhaps more handsome than when I had seen him previously, over forty years earlier. But the one sitting on the shore was not Ruqayya, but rather Maryam. I told her that his name was Yahya and that he was from Ain Ghazal. She was looking at him and nodded her head as she repeated, "I know . . . I know."

It's strange; it's as if the dream were a vision, Amin. One of the neighbors spoke to me, saying that she wanted to ask for Maryam for her son. She was speaking of the son who was studying in Cairo; she showed me his picture. I said, "Maryam is young, and she will go to the university after she finishes high school." The neighbor, who is a very nice woman, said, "Let's not talk about marriage now. When he comes during the vacation you will meet him, and he will meet Maryam and she him. If she likes him we would be honored by the relationship, Sitt Ruqayya." I told Sadiq and he laughed as if I had told a joke. When I steered the conversation back to seriousness, he refused decisively. He said, "No one now commits himself at fifteen nor even at seventeen. Maryam is young, why would you tie her down with marriage and children and responsibilities! She has responsibilities of another kind, her studies and her professional future." I spoke to Maryam and she reacted just like Sadiq, and since she has a sharper tongue, she began to comment on the young man who was asking for her hand without having seen her, relying on his mother's eyes. "Am I going to marry his mother?" Then she and Sadiq began to make jokes about it, twisting and turning it until it became a laughingstock.

Maryam has decided to study medicine, Amin. She doesn't miss an opportunity to announce her decision. Sadiq seems worried; he's not certain she wants it, he thinks she wants to be like you. He told me that privately, and he also told Abed on his second visit to us, in Abu Dhabi. Abed has not changed; just like the first time, he came for a week with the same small leather bag hung from his shoulder, in pants and a shirt and rubber-soled shoes. He announced on his arrival that he had only used the suit once, and that the suit, the shirt and the tie were all new, just as they had been. "This is a forewarning, Mr. Sadiq, so you don't do anything stupid again!" Just as he had before, he only remembered the gifts on the day he left. We laughed, and Sadiq said, "I think Abed is deceiving us, claiming that he forgot in order to make us laugh when we are seeing him off." Abed laughed and jokingly quoted an old film, "You wrong me, Sir!" So we laughed more. During his visit he sat down with Maryam to discuss her studies with her. He said, "Maryam, when you choose a field, don't pay a lot of attention to which academic subjects you like and which you don't; take a longer view. Think about what you want to do with your life. Are you with me? For example, if you decided to dig a ditch, it would be important for you to know how, I mean for you to acquire the skills needed to know the nature of the soil and the styles of digging and of shoring up the sides, etc. Isn't that so?"

She said, "Yes, it is."

He laughed, and said, "No it's not. The most important thing is to know where to put the ditch, from where to where and why, I mean why you are digging this ditch here precisely and not in another place, what its function is, and what your goal for it is."

I intervened: "I don't understand anything you're saying, Abed, and Maryam doesn't understand either."

Maryam looked at me and said, "Mama, wait a little. Go on, Abed."

Abed said, "In short, think about what you want to do with your life. It takes thought for all of us to choose who we want to be, what we will be, where we will stand, and why."

She interrupted him, "I want to be a doctor."

"You want to be like Father?"

"Maybe!"

"I was studying architecture. Perhaps I wanted to be like Sadiq because he was the eldest, and because Mother and Father were always praising his outstanding achievement. Perhaps because I was infatuated with building, infatuated with architecture books. After 1982 I looked up one day, as I was looking around me at the ruins and the destruction in the city and the camps, and I thought: what use is it to build beautiful houses and to plan cities if they are going to bring them down on our heads, what's the use? I said to myself, you have two choices, boy, and only two: that you specialize in military science and become a well-qualified resistance fighter—I mean, able to plan on the basis of real knowledge—or that you specialize in law. Protect the place first and secure it, and then let your imagination run wild, if you want to plan cities as beautiful as dreams. The first choice was not possible, so I went for the second. Do you understand, Maryuma?"

"I understand, Abud."

"And you understand, Mother?"

I did not answer his question. I was thinking about the day when he told me that he was going to leave the College of Engineering, and we had an argument. I was angry at his decision to leave a subject on which he had spent three years, in order to start all over again. I told myself that the boy had answered my question, nine years later. Is it a convincing answer, Amin?

He said, "Where do you want to study, Beirut?"

"I don't want Beirut."

"Where, then?"

"Egypt."

"Why?"

338

"Because it's Egypt. Because the expense will be less for Sadiq, I mean less than Europe, for example, and less than Beirut too."

"In Cairo?"

"In Alexandria, if my scores allow it—they require very high scores. If not Alexandria then one of the provincial universities."

"Why Alexandria? Because you love Fairuz's song?"

She sang the beginning to him: "Alexandrian shore, O you shore of love, We went to Alexandria, and it cast its spell on us." She laughed. "No, because of Sheikh Imam's song." She sang,

O Alexandria, how wondrous your sea,
    Ah, if only I had some of your love!
I'm tossed about from wave to wave,
    As the fishing's good and the tide is high.

She said, "Frankly, it's Alexandria for Mama's sake."

"Will you take Mama with you?"

"Naturally."

"How will you learn when you're snuggled in your mother's arms?"

"I'll snuggle, then I'll get up and go to the university and learn a little, then come back and snuggle. Every day a little learning, and a little plus a little will make a lot, even if I do snuggle!"

He laughed at the image. She became serious, "Mama wants to go with me; she's not happy here. When she came back from Beirut she was sick for a whole month. Mama loves the sea, and so I chose Alexandria and not Cairo."

Abed looked at me, "Do you agree to Alexandria, Mama?"

I didn't answer; I didn't know.

49

Beirut (III)

"BIRDS OF A FEATHER FLOCK together." The proverb came to me between waking and sleep, as I was preoccupied with the thought of going to a city we didn't know, where we didn't know anyone. Why not go back to Lebanon and live in Beirut, or return to Sidon and live like the rest of our people there, come what may? Sadiq said that the situation of the Palestinians in Lebanon was getting more difficult by the day. He said that a friend of his visited Beirut recently and met a young man who suddenly lifted his eyes and whispered, "I'm a Palestinian!" as if he were telling him something secret or embarrassing, calling for an explanation or an apology. He said that society there has come to reject the Palestinians, telling them in a thousand ways, we don't want you. Young men don't find work and the government doesn't permit them to hold dozens of jobs, not to mention the daily insults in casual words here and there about the foreigners who demolished the city and brought on its devastation.

We will not go back to Lebanon, we will go to Alexandria. A new beginning, at sixty. Who begins all over again at sixty? I would rather go back to Lebanon and flock together with birds of my feather. I heard that proverb from my uncle Abu Jamil's wife; it's strange, how she comes to me after a long absence. Not a day goes by but that I remember a proverb she quoted or a scene she was part of. I can no longer recall her face, though I remember that her complexion was the color of wheat, that her hair had a real curl, and that she was very articulate. I remember one day when she invited us to have musakhan at her house. As we approached we were greeted by the aroma of the oven-baked bread and the mixture of onions, sumac, and olive oil, and suddenly I said, "I'm hungry!" My brothers laughed and said that it was the aroma that made me salivate. "That's right," I said. "When I left the house I didn't feel hungry, and when I inhaled the odor I imagined the roasted chicken on the fresh bread and became hungry." They laughed more. There was no better musakhan than Umm Jamil's, nor any better maqlouba than hers. "Nor any better mulukhiya," adds Ezz.

Did Umm Jamil invite us often or was her food so good that that it stayed in the memory, as if we had eaten it with her dozens of times? The day we had the musakhan, or perhaps another day, Umm Jamil said that her father's grandfather had told her that many of the people of Tantoura came from Egypt in the days of Ibrahim Pasha, the son of Muhammad Ali, and settled there. My uncle Abu Amin laughed and said, "Maybe your grandfather loved Egypt, so he said that we come from there. Did he study in al-Azhar, Umm Jamil?"

"He studied in al-Azhar. He used to visit Egypt every year; he would mount his horse, say 'By your leave,' and come back loaded down with gifts of every shape and color. I was little, no higher than five hand spans."

My uncle Abu Jamil intervened, waving his hand, "In the Turkish era in the time of the Ottomans, the world was completely open. People would go and live wherever they wanted, since it was all Arab Muslim land."

Uncle Abu Amin laughed again and said, "Or everyone would choose to trace his origins to the place he loved best. One would say, 'We're descendants of the Prophet, we came from Mecca,' and another would say 'We're of Turkish origin,' as long as the Turks ruled the country. Someone would say he came from Aleppo, the administrative center in the old days. We can't tell the strand of truth apart from imagination."

Uncle Abu Jamil suddenly tensed, "Be careful, everyone, that's enough of this talk. If the Jews heard us they would say, 'Go to Egypt, that's where you come from.' That would be all we need!"

I no longer remember what Uncle Abu Jamil looked like. I only remember that he was old, that he carried a large rosary in his hand, that he prayed a lot, and that he was with us in the truck that took us to al-Furaydis. I don't remember him in al-Furaydis or al-Maskubiya in Hebron, but my mother said that he and his wife went to their daughter, who was married and living in Syria.

Maryam said that she would not study in Lebanon; was that her wish, or did she imagine that I did not want to go back to live in Beirut? When I returned from my visit to Beirut, the one visit after we left Lebanon, I was sick and stayed in bed for two months. Sadiq said that the visit was the reason; perhaps Maryam was influenced by what her brother said.

Yes, I visited Beirut. I went back after five years away, and stayed in a hotel. I lost my way in the camp; I couldn't find the houses I used to go to or the school where I taught, and I became disoriented in the lanes. I couldn't find anyone I knew, not Haniya nor anyone else. Where had they gone? I was so upset that I didn't leave my hotel room for two days. Then I tried again to bring back the city, to connect the memories I carried in my body with what was new in it. I walked, and looked closely; I thought, "It was here." I delved, as if I were looking for a city submerged in another city, sunk under a weighty pile. No, that's foolish writing, it wasn't like that, or at least not completely. The sea was in its place, Beirut's familiar sea. The mountains were its eastern border, as usual, and Bliss Street was also the same, and the American University. I pick my way carefully through the streets, looking closely, and I find—what do I find? Damage that convulses me, as if I had not been aware of it or had not seen it before. In the Tariq al-Jadida, the Fakahani, Hamra Street, the market area, the Demarcation Line. Is it because I'm seeing it now for the first time as a whole, from the outside? Acre Hospital is standing, people go to it and there are doctors and workers inside. The Gaza Hospital building is also standing, with immigrants living in it. But the camp has changed; all of Beirut has changed.

I'm letting my mind drift, Amin, and confusing things. I haven't told you why I left Beirut. I had decided that I would not leave, though Sadiq insisted and pressured me, saying that I was imposing a burden on him that he could not bear. He quarreled with me and said, "I have nightmares because I'm so worried about you and Maryam. I don't understand what's tying you to Beirut." I said I would not leave; then I did leave, because of Maryam. She was afraid whenever she heard any loud noise, thinking it was an explosion, and her face would be pale for days afterward. I told myself that she would bear up, like the others; not every child in the country has a brother working in the Gulf, where he can flee from the explosions. I decided to leave one day when Maryam came to me with her face wan and obviously upset. She asked me, "Mama, have you heard of Abu Arz, the Father of the Cedars?"

"Abu Arz, no. Who is he?"

"My friend in school told me about him. She said he's like the Phalange, but worse. He and his men kidnap Palestinians and slaughter them, then they tie them to their cars and drive them fast, dragging the dead body in the street and tearing it apart. She told me that he and his men cut off the ears of the people they kill and hang them on key chains."

I scolded her, "Don't associate with that girl. These are fantasies, sick fantasies. No one does that."

Maryam looked at me and said, "They're not fantasies, Mama, because she's a nice girl, and smart, and she's been my friend for three years and never lied to me once. I didn't believe what she said either, and I told her that whoever told her that was a liar. She said, 'No one told me. I heard my father telling my mother. My uncle disappeared two months ago and we were looking for him, then my father found out what happened to him. He told my mother, and cried. He didn't know I heard him, he thought I was asleep.' When she told me that, I believed her. Mama, what will we do?"

I decided to leave.

In Beirut they talk about the foreigners, Amin, and about the devastation we caused in Lebanon. It's the same old song from 1983, when the Phalange ruled. But the strange thing is that when I visited Beirut I heard it from others, who aren't in the Phalange party or among its supporters.

In Beirut I also met Abed, Wisal's brother. He had returned from Amman and was working in another think tank. He had five children. He talked to me a long time about general conditions in Lebanon, and about the situation of the Palestinians in it. He knows all the details because he lives with the situation, and also because his work obliges him to keep up and to research it. I asked him about Ain al-Helwa, and he spent a whole day telling me what neither Ezz nor Karima had told me. I understood then why Ezz decided to move to Tunis and stay in the PLO, despite his anger with the leaders and their performance during the invasion. You wouldn't know Ezz, Amin. Forget the white hair, white as a tuft of cotton, without a single black strand; he's been like that for more than ten years now. When I saw him in Beirut after the invasion and then two years later, he was roaring, hurling insults and curses as if he were Abed the younger, not our laughing Ezz. I understood many things because Wisal's brother Abed knows, and I would ask him and he would always answer. I've seen Ezz only twice since then, the day of Hasan's marriage in Greece, and one other time here in Abu Dhabi; he came for some purpose, and we met. I did not gasp or shout when I saw him the last time; God helped me remain calm.

I embraced him and spoke with him normally, as if how he looked had not shaken the very ground under my feet. That night I cried, by God, I cried. Not because he had gotten old; he had already aged when you left us, when the events of Ain al-Helwa occurred, during the invasion and afterward. Before that Ezz had always looked younger than his years, because he's thin or maybe because he's merry, because of his liveliness or because our Lord gave him a sweet disposition, like what you find in children. When he sneaked out of Sidon after the Shatila massacre to check on us, it seemed as if he had aged ten years in a few months; he already seemed like an old man then. But when he visited us in Abu Dhabi, Amin, he looked like an eighty-year-old, older than Uncle Abu Amin at the end of his days. It was as if old age had settled on his spirit and spread throughout his body, like a malignant tumor. He was silent, distant, and frail, and he even walked like an old man, slowly and with caution.

50

Egypt, Where . . .

WE LEFT ABU DHABI FOR Cairo the first week of September, 1993. No sooner had we stowed the bags and the plane taken off than I closed my eyes. I was on my way to Egypt for the first time in my life; Egypt, where my mother said that Sadiq and Hasan had gone. She lived and died repeating that and believing it. As soon as Cairo appeared at a distance of a three-hour flight, my mother came to me, she possessed me, her deranged mind stuck to mine. Sadiq and Hasan are over there, in the earth of Tantoura, I know; so why am I associating myself with my mother's fantasies, so that it seems as if no sooner than the plane lands on Egyptian soil and I stamp my passport, I must go out into the streets to search for them? As if what my mother's imagination had created had become a plant that grew with the passing years, clinging to the earth with a heavy growth of roots. I tell myself, my mother died forty-three years ago; we buried her in Sidon and her tomb is known. I tell myself, Sadiq and Hasan and my father died forty-five years ago; the young men buried them under the threat of arms, in the earth of Tantoura, with no marker for the grave, or sign. Perhaps their bodies have worked free, becoming part of the sand and Indian figs in the village. But my mother, strange, she has come with me. I shoo her away, I push her, or I speak reasonably and say to her, "You're dead, there in Sidon, what's brought you here? Why did you bring them? They are back there, leave them to the almond trees in the village, leave them to the olives, they're enduring, they live a thousand years."

"Are you sleeping, Mother?"

I open my eyes and shake my head.

"I thought you were asleep."

"I'm not asleep, Maryam."

I close my eyes and see my mother, all of her. I hear her repeating, "Sadiq and Hasan fled to Egypt," repeating, "I will go to Egypt and not come back until they are with me." Why are you coming to Egypt with me, Mother?

I had never seen a city the size of Cairo. I had seen it time and again in films, and before the films I was familiar with the name and some of its features. My father would say, "I heard that on Radio Cairo," or Umm Jamil would sing:

O Egypt, with all my beloved,
You are so far from me!
If my horses cannot reach you,
I'll go to you on my own two feet.

It was a song I use to sing to myself secretly, when I became engaged to the boy from Ain Ghazal. I told myself that I would not find anything there strange, that I knew it; but I did find it strange. The crowds alarmed me and the chaos confused me. Life there struck me, in its strength and its vitality. Maryam wanted to see a thousand things. I said, "We're moving to Alexandria in five days, you can come back a second time and a third and a fourth, just look at the most important things now." But Maryam wanted intensive tourism, she wanted to see the pyramids and the Citadel and al-Azhar, she wanted to visit the Egyptian Museum and the Islamic Museum and the Coptic Museum. She wanted to go to the tomb of Gamal Abd al-Nasser, she wanted to see Cairo University where Hasan studied, she wanted to ride a boat on the Nile at sunset. "I can't, Maryam, I'm dying!" She drags me with her and goes on with her touring. I follow her despite the exhaustion, pleased by her joy in what she sees. Maryam doesn't walk, she flies. I've never entered a museum before in my life, nor taken a tour. I repeat, Cairo is big. If my mother had visited it, she would never have imagined that she could find her two boys in it. Did she think it was a little bigger than Tantoura, or than Sidon? My mother never visited Haifa or Beirut, and saw no more of Damascus than a mosque she stayed in and a neighboring medical clinic. Maybe she had seen an old film with Abd al-Wahab or Asmahan and saw two or three streets, with no more people in them than you could count on your fingers. I was fatigued by Cairo, by Maryam's reckless program, by the clamor and the crowding. But I loved the Nile. I loved it and was amazed: as large as a sea, and calm, with no noise, no waves, no air filled with its smells to announce its presence before you see it. It doesn't seem to need it, for it inspires awe in abundance, in and of itself.

When we took the train to Alexandria I watched the land spread out like the palm of a hand, in neatly drawn rectangles and squares of cultivated land. No olives or almonds, fewer trees and a lot of planting. I thought, the land of Egypt goes with the river, a carpet beside a carpet; even its wildness has order and logic. She said, "They went to Egypt." Like every mother, she wanted every step her boys took to be safe. Her imagination rushed to her aid, with land like a carpet.

On the outskirts of Alexandria Maryam began to sing "O Alexandria, how wondrous your sea" in a whisper, so I laughed and followed her, distractedly. I was looking at my watch. I had never taken a train before in my life, and Sadiq had warned me: "The Sidi Gaber Station is not the last one on the line. The train stops there only five minutes or maybe ten, and then goes on to the last station. The trip takes two hours and ten minutes; get ready before you arrive. Pick up the things you've put near you, you and Maryam, and ask a worker to get down the large bags you've given him; he'll set them down for you as soon as the train arrives. At the station you'll find the friend I told you about. I told him to make sure to be there waiting for you; he'll take you and Maryam to the apartment. Here's his telephone number; if you want anything, call him. Assuming that for any reason you don't find him, then ask one of the porters to take your things on his cart and go with you to the taxi stand, outside the station. You'll give the driver the address, and you have the key to the apartment. The building has seven floors and our apartment is on the fourth. As soon as you arrive call to let me know."

Sadiq was laying out what we would and would not do. Maryam said that he was treating us as if we were children; he scolded her with a look and went on speaking.

When I got up from my seat in the train, Maryam said, "Mama, everyone is still seated in their places, they'll laugh at us." But I got up and she followed me. She was right, because we stood near the door of the carriage for a quarter of an hour before it was announced over the loudspeaker, "Sidi Gaber Station." Five minutes later the train stopped. Maryam was laughing.

51

Household Gardens

HOW DO THE YEARS PASS, how did they pass? In a flash or slowly, like a camel crossing a desert that stretches endlessly toward the horizon, before you, behind you, and on the left and right? What brings the desert to mind when I'm in Alexandria, living on a street where the buildings crowd together, and each one has several floors, with apartments and residents? The pedestrians and the cars in the street move in three lanes, one for the cars heading east, another for the opposite direction, and between the two, tramlines. I hear the friction of their wheels against the iron and the hissing of their brakes when they approach the station and stop, or begin to move again. Clamor all day long, beginning at daybreak and not subsiding until the wee hours of the night, when it leaves the city to the sea. I inhale the aroma of the sea even in the dark, without seeing it. I don't see it; I hear its roar and the impact of its waves on the stone breakwaters along the shore. Where did the desert come from?

Maryam is engrossed in her study; she leaves in the morning and returns only in the afternoon, or sometimes in the evening. I wait for her return, I wait for her to complete her education so we can go back. Go back where? I don't know; maybe to Sidon, if the children accept that. I don't know anyone in Alexandria. No, that's not so, I do—a nice neighbor here or there, the grocer, the butcher, the vegetable seller, and all the boys who work for them. Maryam's friends, and sometimes their mothers; I invite the women to have coffee in my house, or I go to them. It may be the only visit, or it may be repeated from time to time. I make a pretext of any occasion or none at all, and invite Maryam's classmates, boys and girls, to lunch or supper. Cleaning the house, shopping, and preparing the food is all done by an hour before noon, or sometimes two. What do I do with the rest of the hours of my day? I walk along the Corniche sometimes, then I become annoyed with the traffic, the clamor of the cars, their horns and their exhaust, and I go back home. Sometimes I go down to the beach; I take off my sandals and plunge into the sand with my bare feet, crossing it in a straight line toward the water. Then I stop, and give myself to the scent of the sea, to the splashing of the waves, to the salt and spray they scatter over my face and body, which somehow steal onto the tip of my tongue. I stay standing like that, watching; or else I go back a step or two and crouch down, or I don't go back, I simply squat down as I used to do when I was only three, not yet daring to jump in the water. I squat at the door of the sea, or I walk, wandering, unaware, not thinking of anything. Just the damp sand refreshing my feet, the blueness with its embroidery of foam, the air laden with a familiar scent that steals through my dress and onto my body.

One morning I asked the building doorman if he knew the way to a nursery nearby. He said, "A nursery for decorative plants?" I found the expression odd, and said, "For plants." He told me the way, and I went on foot. I came back by taxi, because I had bought seedlings, plastic pots, dirt, and extra fertilizer. When Maryam came home from school and saw what I'd bought she laughed and said, "Is the garden free, or is there a charge to go in?"

Sometimes I reflect on it and I think I am trying to deceive myself, to beguile the solitude and the wait; sometimes I forget to reflect, and become absorbed in the work of my little garden. I remember that my mother used to say that my uncle Abu Jamil's wife had a green thumb. I was four or five when I heard the expression, so I began to look closely at Umm Jamil's hands, every time I met her, searching for her green thumb. Her hands were wheat colored, a little darker than my own, so I thought that perhaps the thumb had been green and then returned to its natural color; or maybe it was green during times of the day when I didn't see her, or at night when she was sleeping.

Would my mother have said I had a green thumb if she had seen my little garden? It was not a single garden, but rather three small ones; what had begun as a thought, the day I asked the doorman about a nearby nursery, had turned into a daily preoccupation. I planted geraniums in seven oblong containers that I hung on the railing of the balcony. Mallow flowers are suited to the climate in Alexandria, to its sun, and even in the winter they keep their leaves and their colors, a fiery red or a soft violet or a third color, somewhere between the other two. The mallow flowers were the first plants I bought, and the game attracted me. Later on I put two deep pots on one side of the balcony, where I planted two kinds of jasmine. Jasmine is like a girl, it grows quickly and then fills out. That was the first garden (I have loved that word for garden, *jeneina*, ever since I became aware that it's the diminutive of *janna*, Paradise). The second garden was small: on the marble countertop in the kitchen, under the large window, were a pot of mint, one of basil, and one of sage (I thought they wouldn't grow inside the house in a little pot, but they surprised me). There was also a sweet potato in a cup of water, which rooted and then produced leaves; I tied up the canes with string attached to small nails, and it climbed and spread with its green leaves over the wooden window frame. The third garden was at the entrance of the apartment just outside the door, to your left as you come in. It was all cactus, in seven pots of different sizes, large and small. There were different kinds, and they flowered once a year.

I wanted to occupy myself with the plants; they enticed me, and I gave in to temptation. I would water them, turn over the dirt, feed them with fertilizer, clean their leaves, and think about them. I missed the almond tree, and in the spring I missed it more. Sometimes I would think about what I was doing and mock myself; then I would murmur, "It's not bad, not bad at all."

Sometimes I would be gripped by flower fever; I would look for stores and buy, arranging them in vases and distributing them throughout the house. There are beautiful flowers in Egypt. There was a strange, elegantly shaped flower I had never seen before: its long stalk ended in something that looked like the head of a swallow, with a crest on the head made of upstanding petals, yellow and orange, surrounding one or two petals of violet color. I asked about its name, and when the salesman said, "bird of paradise," I loved it more. I take the bird of paradise home with me, in season, and sometimes the damask rose, which I prefer red. Sometimes carnations catch my eye, and I buy them. I do not buy lilies; they aren't like the lilies in Tantoura, their scent is different, and I don't like them. I don't like expensive vases, either, nor vases of colored or decorated pottery. I avoid vases that attract the eye; what would be the point of the flowers, then? I put them in glass containers, ordinary jars like the ones where I put olives or coffee beans or sugar.

When I'm engaged in tending the plants I think of nothing else. I water them, I turn over the dirt, I wipe the dust from their leaves. I transfer a plant that has outgrown its pot to another, bigger one, where it can grow comfortably. I talk to the plants, I always talk to them, encouraging them in their behavior or scolding them for it. "Just look at you, what's all this, don't tempt the evil eye!" Or I scold the sluggish one for her laziness: "You silly thing, look at your neighbor, it's grown leaves and flowered and become twice your height!" Maryam comments that I'm behaving like a

354

schoolteacher with young pupils. I find the comparison odd, and ask, "How so?" She laughs.

The plants preoccupy me. When I go to bed I think about them and about my relationship to them, and say to myself, "A garden in prison, why not? No harm done."

Less than a week after we arrived in Alexandria I saw Abu Ammar at the White House shaking hands with Rabin and Perez, with Mahmoud Abbas on his left and the American president in the center. They had signed the Oslo Accords. Moments after the end of the live television broadcast of the White House event Sadiq telephoned. He said, "What has the old one done? The sole legal representative eliminated the coast from the agreement. Who represents Tantoura, then? Who represents Safad and Tiberias and Galilee and Haifa and Jaffa and Ramla and the Negev? Who represents Acre and Nazareth? Who represents us?" He was angry. He commented bitterly about Abu Ammar's insistence on shaking hands with Rabin and Perez, and their avoidance, as if they were condescending to shake hands. "What a farce, what an insult!" No sooner had I hung up than the telephone rang again. This time it was Abed on the other end. He swore and cursed, and as usual he spared no obscene expression, he used them all. Hasan did not call, and I knew that he was nursing his grief in his own way, shrinking like a wet dove chick. I called him. "What do you think, Hasan?" I asked. "It will take a long time, Mother. It will take a long time."

Hasan was right. In Alexandria, over the same telephone, from the very same seat and over the same television set I would follow the news of the Hebron massacre, the killing of Rabin and his funeral, and Abu Ammar's insistence on offering his condolences. He bent over the widow's hand and kissed it; I saw him. Then the events of the new Israeli incursion into South Lebanon, the Cana massacre, the funeral of the martyrs. I followed in silence, repeating Hasan's expression. "It will take a long time," I mutter.

I called Wisal in Jenin. Her voice comes over the phone and dispels some loneliness, or some lump in the throat that was about to choke me.

I continue to write because Hasan asks how far I've gotten, how much I've accomplished. He asks every time we speak. Sometimes the telling seems simple, it flows easily and the words are written as if of their own accord. Or it's a pleasure, as I relive some intimate or lovely moment with the children or Uncle Abu Amin. It's as if I summon them and they come, and fill the house for me. Then I stop; the writing is hard, and weighs me down. It seems like a weight of iron that I've placed on my chest of my own free will. Why, Hasan? I don't have to obey you, I can stop; why do I obey? I sit in front of the notebook and look at an empty page, open like an abyss. The writing will kill me, I told you that, Hasan. He said, "Writing does not kill." Why does he seem so confident?

I flee to the plants, to the sea. I suddenly decide that the window glass is dirty and makes the house dark, separating me from the sky. I bring the ladder and a rubber squeegee and both the short-handled scrub brush and the other one with a long handle, and a bucket of water and soap. I wipe the glass with the cleaning liquid and rub it well, polishing it. I dry it with the squeegee. I don't look up until Maryam comes home. She says, "Oh no, just a week ago you cleaned all the windows in the house and washed the glass." I say, "Just a moment, by the time you heat supper I'll have finished."

52

New Jersey

HASAN CALLED ME AND TOLD me that he was sending me
two copies of his new book, "one for you and the other for
Maryam."

A moment of silence, and then: "It's not a study or a
research work, Mother. It's a novel."

"A story?"

"Yes, a story."

I was amazed, and even more amazed when the book
arrived. Unlike his previous books, it was small in format
and size, ninety pages at most. He said that it was about the
attack on Lebanon. How? Is it possible to tell what happened
in these few pages? How could a small book, or a large one,
bear thousands of corpses, the extent of the blood, the quantity of rubble, the panic. Our running for our lives, wishing
for death. Anyway, *New Jersey*, what was this strange title?
What relationship did it have to what happened in Lebanon?
Does he speak about his father in his novel? Does he set aside
a larger place for Acre Hospital, or does the whole novel center on what happened in Acre Hospital? Does he talk about
Beirut, or write about Sidon and Ain al-Helwa, did he listen
to the details from his uncle Ezz? I don't know much about
stories and novels; before that I had only read the two stories
by Ghassan Kanafani that Ezz lent me in Sidon. I no longer remember more than the title of the short story: "The
Land of Sad Oranges." The longer story was about three

357

Palestinians who wanted to be smuggled into Kuwait, so they hid in the empty tank of a water truck. The border employees delayed the driver so the three died of suffocation, without daring to knock on the sides of the tank.

I was preoccupied with Hasan's book all day long, but I did not try to page through it or read any of its paragraphs. At night I sat in the seat next to the bed and opened the book, and read. I did not sleep until I had finished it.

The novel centers on a battleship named *New Jersey*. It was an amazing seagoing vessel, the size of three soccer fields put together, 887 feet long, forty-five tons, and as high as a seven-story building. Its main battery had nine canons, all sixteen inch, and its secondary battery had twenty smaller canons. Each of the large ones shoots missiles weighing 1,200 kilograms, with a range of thirty-seven kilometers. As for the smaller canons, they can reach fourteen kilometers.

The battleship is the heroine of the story. We follow the history of its birth, even its prehistory: it was one of six vessels that surpassed everything that went before. The United States decided to build them at the beginning of the Second World War, to support its forces in the probable theater of operations in the Pacific Ocean. On December 7, 1942, it was commissioned and christened, and its name was recorded on the rolls of the American Navy. Its official birthday was not celebrated until it was delivered for duty and assigned its first task in the war, on May 23 of the following year. The battleship took part in all US wars from the middle of the twentieth century on: the Second World War in Japan and the Philippines, in the forties; the Korean War in the fifties; Vietnam during the years 1968 and 1969, after an overhaul. Then at the beginning of the eighties there was another overhaul with the addition of launchers for long-range Harpoon and Tomahawk missiles, and afterward it went to the Mediterranean, bound for Lebanon. In 1991 it headed for the Gulf.

The account of the life of the battleship is gripping. We follow its movements, a floating structure wandering the high seas with more than two thousand men on board. It carries them to the Pacific Ocean, to the Atlantic, to the Caribbean, to the Mediterranean, and to the Gulf, clear under the sun, foggy and cloud-covered in the rain, shining with lights in the dark of night. We observe it closely as it carries out its task with zeal, precision, and competence: it points its guns and fires. It hits. Its crew—officers and soldiers, sailors and doctors, mechanics and janitors, those in charge of the food service and cooks—is a lively crew. All of them work. In the kitchen, for example, they produce 1,800 loaves of bread daily and 250 gallons of ice cream.

At the end of its service the *New Jersey* was retired, its record filled with the decorations it had collected, more than any other American battleship: nineteen medals. Two stars for its outstanding role in the Second World War, four stars for its performance in the Korean War, two stars for its accomplishments in the Vietnam War and four stars for its services in the Lebanese War and the Second Gulf War.

In the second part of the story we come to know the battleship better. In the next stage it was decommissioned and turned into a museum in Camden, New Jersey, where it's anchored on the shore of the river. The visitors are men and women, young and old, school excursions meant to give the pupils patriotic knowledge and education. Families with their children tour all parts of the ship, going down into its depths, passing through its corridors in files. They see the officers' rooms and the soldiers' beds, the steering and control rooms, the admiral's and the captain's quarters. The dining rooms, small, comfortable rooms where the officers had their meals and the large mess where the soldiers and sailors ate. The engine room, the clinic, the repair shop. They go up to the deck and climb the towers, looking down from windows here and there. They look out at the waters of the river, at the

Seaport Museum nearby, at the sky. They return to the deck and stand in front of the guns, raising their heads, dazzled by their hard steel and wide mouths. They listen carefully to the explanations of the tour guide or to the recordings they hear via small earphones. They chatter and laugh, or someone records observations in his notebook, or takes pictures of his family and friends.

It's not only a museum open for visits after purchasing a ticket, more costly for individuals and less expensive for school trips or tour groups. Part of it can also be rented for a dinner party, a small one in the captain's room for no more than twenty guests, or a big one on the deck of the ship, with dinner for four hundred people seated or a reception for eight hundred, most of them standing. A wedding can be held, or a hotel stay can be arranged on the weekend for young people who want to spend the night in the soldiers' beds. School groups and individuals can buy inexpensive, prepared meals from the canteen. Anyone who wants to can bring a little brown bag, with a sandwich he's prepared at home or bought from a grocer; when he enters the battleship he hands over the brown bag, and at the end of his tour he takes it back to eat whatever is in it.

After that comes the third part of the book: three pages. The battleship, refitted to add sixteen Harpoon rockets and thirty-two long-range Tomahawks, enters the Mediterranean in 1983. It approaches the Lebanese shore and joins the American fleet, which can be seen from the beach in Beirut. The task this time is not war but peace, supporting the multinational peacekeeping forces. Because the war in Lebanon has ended, because there is a ceasefire, because Israel, after the aerial bombardment and the invasion and the siege, can depend on an allied Lebanese government and an allied army. The Druze are not its allies, so how will they take control of the mountains, Jabal al-Druze, where they live? These are details the leaders will decide. The *New Jersey* executes its tasks as always: its lively crew loads the missile into the launcher and closes it carefully, then boom. The missile is fired, leaving an enormous block of dark red flame in the sky over the sea, which quickly becomes mixed with orange and yellow, then a thick black devours the colors and gradually changes into smoke. Afterward there's silence, crossed by clouds like tufts of white cotton, without any thickness, dispersing near the ship and disappearing. The sailors put another missile in the launcher and close it carefully. Boom.

In the mountains, in the piled-up houses of the Banu Maarouf, are the residents of Jabal al-Druze: old men with their traditional turbans; farmers who resemble their grandfathers because they never changed the look of their shirts and trousers; young men who, unlike their fathers and grandfathers, wear shirts or tee shirts and running shoes; grandmothers; mothers; girls with braids or childish short hair; the very young, who cannot yet walk or talk; the toddlers who have learned to walk and talk. The walls cave in on them and burn. They die, burned or bleeding or because something in the body suddenly failed, so they die even though their form is intact.

53

The Visit

MARYAM SAID, "YOU'RE BEING RIDICULOUS, Mother! You have money!"

I said, "What I have is sent by Sadiq for your school fees and our living expenses. I won't invite my friend to come at Sadiq's expense."

She laughed, "The bracelet you sold was bought by Sadiq; it's his money in both cases!"

I nearly said that he gave me the bracelet, so it had become mine, to do with it or its value as I pleased, but I did not speak. I called Wisal again to set the date for her trip. She said, "We'll harvest the olives and press them, then I'll come to visit you."

I bought the airplane ticket and sent it to her, and began to count the days and wait.

Maryam said with a laugh, "The tutor's in luck."

I said, "I don't understand Egyptian proverbs."

She said, "The tutor, that's the Qur'an teacher, is in luck when he has two completions of the Qur'an on the same night. That means he's invited to recite the Qur'an twice and he's given two feasts on the same night."

I laughed. Maryam amazes me with how fast she picks up the Egyptian dialect, with its proverbs and idioms. Yes, it was two completions in one night; as I was waiting for Wisal, Fatima called and said, "I'm in the country," adding that she would come to visit us for three days.

"Only?"

"I have to get back to Canada, to my work and the kids and Hasan."

"Fatima, can I ask a favor of you?"

"Please do."

"Can you visit Tantoura and take some pictures?"

"Hasan asked me that, and I did it."

"You visited it?"

"I did."

I nearly asked her to tell me what she saw, but I refrained. What would I ask about?

Maryam remarked on my absorption in preparing for the visits of Wisal and Hasan's wife, "Are they coming to us from a famine?" She laughs; I answer, "This is our way to honor a guest!"

I buy meat and chicken, and clean it, season it, and put it in the freezer. I think, the leg of lamb for the first day, and I'll stuff the breast for the second day. The chicken for the following day. I think, Wisal likes mulukhiya soup and okra; I buy them. I pull the leaves off the mulukhiya and remove the stems of the okra, and wash them. I let them dry two hours and then I put them in the refrigerator. I buy grape leaves and summer squash; I roll the grape leaves, and put off the squash until later. I make bread dough, form it into a ball, and let it rise, while I prepare the spinach stuffing; I fill the discs and put them into the oven. Every time I finish baking one set of the tarts Maryam eats a quarter of them. I scold her: "You'll finish them off before the guests come!" She pays no attention, and I shoo her away, and she comes back. I think, Fatima likes pickled eggplant. I buy small black eggplants and stuff them with walnuts and pepper, then I put them with lemon juice and olive oil in two large glass containers. "And the kubbeh?" asks Maryam. "For sure the guests will like kubbeh!" I laugh; for sure Maryam likes kubbeh! I soak the cracked wheat kernels, grind the meat and season it; I form the meatballs and stuff them, and put them in a plastic bag in the freezer. I go to the grocer, thinking I've forgotten such-and-such, then I go again. I go to the fruit seller and buy, then I buy again. I mutter, "What's missing?"

As soon as we entered the house I asked Maryam to make us coffee, but Wisal said, "Put off the coffee, Ruqayya, let's put the things away first." She rolled up her sleeves and took one of the two suitcases she had brought to the kitchen, the larger one. She squatted down beside it and started to take out the food she had brought. She handed me three plastic bottles, tightly sealed, containing olive oil, and three others in which she had put olives. She said, "I have a neighbor in the camp with a daughter-in-law from Egypt. I tell you, I went to visit her and have coffee with her, to ask her. I said, 'What do they lack in Egypt? Should I take okra and mulukhiya?' The Egyptian laughed and said, 'There's nothing more plentiful than okra and mulukhiya in Egypt.' I said to her, 'Oil and olives from our trees, I would take that to Ruqayya even if she were living in an oil press!' Then I asked her about the things that aren't available and she told me." She brought out a big plastic jar: "Naboulsi cheese." It was hard, molded pieces of cheese lined up in a jar, in three layers. I began to wrap up each set of pieces and put them in a plastic bag in the freezer, leaving out six to soak in water, to remove some of the salt. Then the bags: domestic thyme, dried and mixed with sesame and sumac; green thyme; sage; sumac; dried wheat grains. Last there was a large bag; Wisal laughed jovially. "I would have made musakhan, if it weren't for the distance—the bridge, then Amman, then Cairo, then Alexandria; I thought it would spoil. My neighbor's Egyptian daughter-in-law told me, 'Take sumac; in Egypt they don't know it and don't use it.' I asked, 'How do they make musakhan?' She said, 'We don't know it.' So I decided to buy you some bread from our ovens."

Wisal had even brought bread from the old ovens with her from Jenin.

Maryam laughed and said again, "It's obvious we're in a famine, Auntie Wisal!"

I said, "We aren't in a famine, but we love the food from home. If you don't want it, leave it for me."

She retreated hurriedly, "I want it and then some! When will you make us musakhan, Auntie Wisal?"

"Now, if you like."

"No, now you'll drink coffee."

We sat on the balcony. Wisal said suddenly, "Ruqayya, I haven't seen the sea of Jaffa since we left Tantoura!"

54

By Donkey

A PASSING STORY, ONE OF thousands of little anecdotes that
pass by every day, only to fall into the crowd. Suddenly it surfaced; I recalled it, and then I ruminated on it, saying why
not? The man was over a hundred and I haven't even reached
seventy. The story gave me ideas; I would have liked to hear
it again from Karima, in case she could add other details that
had escaped her.

It was the story of her father's uncle, Abu Khalil. He left
for Lebanon with them, and stopped like them in Rumaysh.
He went back across the border with them, heading for Saffuriya, and was arrested with them and put in prison in Acre.
From prison they sent them to Lebanon, and the Lebanese
authorities put them in Qaroun, taking them from there to
Ain al-Helwa. Karima said, "We were in Ain al-Helwa when
Abu Khalil announced that he was going back. My grandfather said, 'How will you go back? They'll kill you on the
borders, or imprison you and send you back again.' He said
that he was determined: 'If you want to come with me you're
welcome, but if you decide to stay, then I'm going.' 'Will you
go alone?' He said, 'My father and mother are there, and my
first son and his daughter.' He was referring to the dead in
his family, so the adults thought he had lost his mind. Then
one day we woke up and couldn't find him. We thought he
had lost his way to the camp—I said he was over one hundred, and he might even have been 110. We looked for him

in Ain al-Helwa and in Sidon, there was no one we didn't ask. A week went by with no news, not a thing. Then we heard that he had bought a donkey and gone back. We didn't rest until we found the man who had sold him the donkey and the person who showed him the way out of Sidon. We nearly accepted that the Israelis had killed him on the borders or that he had died; how could a man over a hundred cross the border alone, sleeping under an olive tree, with no provisions and not even a drink of water? He didn't have a penny to his name, because he had paid everything he had for the donkey, and everything his wife had, too (she discovered after he left that he had taken the few liras she had hidden in the mattress). His wife said, 'Don't worry, he'll manage.' My grandmother condemned her sister-in-law's words when she was alone with my mother, and said she had a heart of stone. 'How can she sleep all through the long night when her husband is wandering among the hyenas and the soldiers of that state? For shame, a man of a hundred, and his wife just lets him do as he pleases! If I were in her shoes I would go to him.' We little ones began to make jokes about what she said, imitating my grandmother's words mockingly, because the woman she wanted to take care of her husband was over eighty and toothless; she had to lean on our shoulders when she wanted to go from her house in the camp to our house next door. The family gave up on Grandfather Abu Khalil, and accepted that he must have died on the way or been killed. Four years later, when new refugees thrown out by Israel began to come to Lebanon, we learned that Grandfather Abu Khalil was still among the living. Someone from around our village said that he had seen him, and that he lived in the cemetery of Saffurya and said that he was the cemetery watchman. We asked how he managed, and they said, 'We don't know, but he was in good health, smoking and insisting on inviting anyone who visited the cemetery to a cup of tea!' My grandmother talked it over with my mother, and said, 'For sure Abu Khalil went back to get rid of his wife, because she's spiteful and miserly and no one can put up with her.'"

Karima was laughing as she told the story. It's strange, I remember everything she said that night, even though at the time it seemed like fleeting words, just like the rest of the talk. Then the story surfaced and became insistent. I thought, I'll tell it to Maryam; then I wondered suddenly, am I preparing her? Perhaps, I thought to myself.

Maryam can snatch a thought from the air. When I told her the story, she commented, "You intend to do the same? You think that if a man over a hundred was able to do it, then I must be able to! Remember, Mama, that Karima was a child of five, and her grandfather who she thought was over a hundred might have been a man of sixty or even fifty-five; kids think like that, that old people are really, really old. Anyway wait until I graduate and I'll go with you. We'll buy two donkeys and just take off." She said it and burst out laughing; I couldn't take her laughter, I was furious.

At sixty or over a hundred or at Noah's age, Noah who reached nine hundred, the man took his age in his hand, or on the back of a donkey, and did what he wanted. Neither the Israeli state nor its soldiers not the barbed wire on the border broke his will.

I'll go back, like him. Not on the back of a donkey but by the logic of birds.

Fatima said, "The residents of al-Furaydis know the locations of the cemeteries."

Yes, locations; the plural, not the singular. The old cemetery and the mass grave, and perhaps a third cemetery. If one of them went there with you he would point to part of the asphalt and say, "This is the mass grave, under the lot for cars, at the 'parking.'" Ruqayya would put up a tent for herself at the parking lot. Oh my God, hold on, Ruqayya! A refugee, in a tent, in Tantoura? Where will I go then, to one of the tourist chalets on the seashore? Yes, the village has become a resort.

Fatima gave me pictures and a CD that Maryam put into the computer, and I saw Tantoura, its sea and its islands and its palms and its Indian figs. Just as they were. What's new? The chalets, the sailboats, fishing, fishing for pleasure and not for sustenance, and God only knows what else besides.

Fatima said, "At the entry of the school there's a sign with the names of those who were killed."

"The names of the martyrs?"

The ghost of a smile; I realized that the question was foolish.

"No, a sign with the names of their dead, killed the day of the battle. I did not take a picture of the sign or of the school, for fear that one of them would appear before me suddenly and confiscate the camera. The school has become a center for agricultural research."

The pictures: the tomb of al-Jereini has stayed the same. Fatima said, "I found a woman praying. When she finished she greeted me and said, 'They have no power over the sheikh or his tomb. No one can budge it.'"

I looked up and pointed, explaining to Maryam, "This was the glass factory."

Fatima said, "Yes. They say that one of the Rothschilds, I don't know which one, one of the Rothschilds visited the town in the forties and saw the vines. He said, 'There's a lot of value here, it must be put to work.' He founded a glass factory, probably to bottle alcoholic beverages."

"In my time it was an abandoned plant."

"Now it's a museum for glass. Then there's this building, that has Arabic writing on it establishing the date when it was built."

"This is the Yahya house, the most prominent family in Tantoura. Is anyone living there?"

"It's dilapidated, just a façade and two or three rooms. Some of the young men from al-Furaydis use it to store their fishing equipment."

"And the rest of the houses?"

Fatima was silent. I repeated the question.

"They were torn down."

I look at the pictures, I look at them intently. Do the pictures nourish the logic of the birds? They transport me in a flash, with no checkpoints, no barbed wire, no armored soldiers; I just go. Then what—will I put up a tent, erecting it next to my family, in the parking lot, or will I live next to the Indian figs, each of us keeping the other company? When the guests leave I will scrutinize the pictures at length; while they're with me I just look at them once, once only, then I take them and put them away in a drawer among Amin's shirts. I know, I'm behaving oddly, I mean in keeping three of Amin's shirts. I wash them from time to time, and iron them and fold them and put them back in their place in the clothes chest. Maryam noticed them some time ago, and then again when we moved to Alexandria. She was on the verge of asking about them, and then her face flushed and she left the room.

Abed said, as he welcomed Wisal by telephone, "On the news yesterday they announced an earthquake in Alexandria."

"There wasn't any earthquake. Or maybe a very small one—none of us felt it."

"Auntie Wisal, you and my mother and Maryam and Fatima are all together in one place, and there's no earthquake? How can that be?"

She understood the teasing and laughed.

We have coffee together in the morning, we go to the sea, we sit in a café overlooking it. Fatima talks about Lid, about her childhood and her parents. I ask her about Hasan and she tells me. Wisal makes us laugh, telling us about the Intifada and her children.

"They arrested all five of them. Even the girl, they picked her up too. This one they arrested for two days, that one two weeks or a month, the other one six months, then they arrest him again. A knock on the door at dawn has become familiar. They knock on the door and I open it and shout at them: 'What's your hurry? Are we going to run away—how? There's only one door, and you're standing under the windows. And where's your shame? My daughter and I are in our nightgowns, can I open the door for you when we're in our nightgowns? You should be ashamed!'"

"You talk to them like that?"

"Yes. The first time I thought I went too far, but then I learned that they're usually young, and they blush. They already feel guilty, and when I scold them they feel it more. Of course, those are the kids; the officers and the special forces are another matter. They come to arrest a leader or one of the fedayeen, and they're really violent. They hit you with the rifle butt right away, and that's if they don't fire first."

"And the day they came to arrest you?"

"They came to arrest me. I said 'Okay, but I won't ride in an Israeli car.' They yelled at me and I yelled at them. They were young conscripts, I wouldn't have dared if they had been officers. I said, 'Maybe in a taxi.' They laughed, and said 'Madwoman!' I said, 'Mad or not, I won't ride in an Israeli car through the streets of Jenin, it would ruin my reputation! If my father were alive he would kill you and kill me, and say you're eloping with my daughter.' They didn't understand 'eloping.' I was laughing at them, and I enjoyed it more because they didn't know I was making fun of them. I said it again, 'I will not ride in an Israeli car unless you tie me up and put me in it by force.' Thank God I'm tall and heavy, no three of them would be able to lift me. I let myself go. They said, 'Then walk.' I went the whole way from the camp to the police station, walking calmly and with my head up, just like a queen. They were guarding me on both sides and the military car was coming behind me, slowly. I was laughing inside. I didn't let it show because I didn't want to get into real trouble, but it nearly got away from me when I saw some people I knew standing in the street. I saw the laughter in their eyes, and we understood each other perfectly. But I didn't laugh."

"Once on the night before Eid some young men from the camp climbed up and hung flags on the electricity wires. On the morning of Eid Palestinian flags were flying over the camp, as if it was a holiday for independence, and not for the end of Ramadan. It was like they were possessed, they came into the camp and swore and cursed. 'Take down the flags!' But the young guys had disappeared like salt in water, and the women said, 'We can't climb, you climb up.' We stood watching while they climbed up and took down the flags, with every one of us praying secretly that they would fall and break their necks. God didn't answer our prayers, except in one case. A soldier got clumsy on the pole and fell and landed on his snout, may God not help him. Who told him to oppress people and serve in an army of occupation?"

55

The Return to Lebanon

MARYAM IS TALKING ABOUT THE trip, she's burning to join
Abed in France. She's arranged all the details with him: she'll
be an intern during the first year and then start her specialty
training. I do not comment. She thinks I'm worried because
I want her to get married; she's twenty-two, when will she
marry? Abed is thirty-five; will she be like him? I put my concern into words, but I do not speak about the other topic, not
about where to go from here. Abu Dhabi? I don't want that.
Maryam says, 'Come with me.' Abed also says to come, that
he wants me to live with him, but I won't go. There's a lump
in my throat, just a lump that doesn't go away, maybe because
I don't talk about it with anyone. Sadiq is no longer satisfied
with calling once a week, instead he calls twice and sometimes
three times. He gathers what's bothering me, and assures me
that they're waiting impatiently for me. I say, "God willing";
the expression worries him, or maybe my way of saying it, and
he insists more: "You won't stay in Alexandria one day after
Maryam leaves. What's tying you to Alexandria?" I don't say,
a house, even though it's temporary. I hang up and explode at
Maryam, as if she were Sadiq or represented him: "Children
are strange, they think their mother is a suitcase they can take
with them wherever they go. They pick it up here and put it
down there. My God!" I was angry. Maryam kissed me and
said, "The boys, not the girls. I for example would like to be a
suitcase. You would carry me and take me with you wherever

you went. Imagine what would happen if you left me! A poor, abandoned suitcase, belonging to no one, crying bitterly. Then a kind passerby would notice and say, 'What's wrong, Suitcase?' She would say, 'My mother left me,' and the kind man would take me around the streets looking for my mother." She wants to make me laugh, but I don't laugh. I exclaimed, in a voice that seemed to me louder than it should be, "Damn exile, and damn Palestine!" The air was tense; Maryam disappeared. She came back carrying a tray with two cups of coffee; she put it on the balcony and said, "Come on, let's have coffee. You'll look at the sea and drink coffee with the apple of your eye, by which I mean Dr. Maryam, in person." I laughed, not because of her words but because as she was dragging me to the balcony by one hand, she was using the other to tickle me on the side, on my shoulder, and under the arm.

"Sadiq, I'm going back to Sidon."

"On a visit?"

"No, I'll rent an apartment and live there. In the summer we'll all get together there."

"God bless you, Mother, can't you find anywhere but south Lebanon, with the Israelis as your neighbors?"

"They'll leave."

"General Giap has spoken. He said they would leave, and they left!"

"Who's General Giap?"

"A leader of the Vietnamese liberation forces in the fifties and sixties. Now General Ruqayya has decided."

I did not lose my temper over his sarcasm. I repeated coldly, "They'll leave!"

"Even if they left, every time there's friction or at every little crisis they'll shell the south and storm in. Anyway Hasan and Abed won't be able to visit you in Lebanon."

"There's no problem for Abed, he has a French passport."

"And Hasan?"

I did not answer.

"Mother . . ." He marshaled his arguments and the call lasted half an hour before I hung up. In the evening I asked Maryam, "How much time will you stay in Alexandria after the exam?"

She said, "I'll wait for the results, and then to get my certificates from the university and have them notarized, then I'll leave. Maybe I'll need a couple of months. Why do you ask?"

"I don't want to start getting ready for the trip while you're studying for the exams. As soon as you finish your exams I'll begin to pack up the household."

"You've decided?"

"I've decided."

"Sidon?"

"Yes."

"Did Sadiq agree?"

"He didn't agree, but I've decided."

From Alexandria I followed the liberation of the south. Maryam was in her bachelor's exams, either in the college taking an exam or in her room studying. I would almost call her to see what I saw, and then stifle the call. But I did not stifle the tears. Maybe if she had been sitting beside me I would have stifled them out of embarrassment. It's strange; where did all these tears come from? Why are tears linked to sadness and care? Were they tears of joy, then? No, neither sadness nor joy, but something larger, with greater depth, ambiguous, like the look in your eyes when someone holds the newborn that has just slipped out of you. The newborn is wet with your water and blood, and whoever holds him, doctor or midwife or your mother, holds him upside down, by his feet. He's warm, about to open his eyes, about to announce with a cry that he has opened the airway in his throat to live. You're weary, maybe suspended between life and death; you look up weakly and tears flow from your eyes, not in sadness or in joy but rather . . . rather what? It's beyond my ability to put into words. Maybe it's a spring in some obscure place inside the body or the spirit or the earth, like the spring in the southern cave, east of town. My mother says that its water is sweet, like the water of Kawthar. "What's Kawthar, Mother?" She says it's a river in Paradise. I find that strange—how does she know the taste of a river in Paradise, had she ever visited it? Later I heard someone say that "Paradise lies at the feet of our mothers." I was seven and I thought, "then she did visit it; why didn't she tell me?" Television broadcasts scenes of the liberation live, and the mothers on television, who look like my mother and my aunt, trill and rejoice. They throw rice and rose petals on those who are returning to their villages. I'll live there, I'll live beside the tomb of my mother and my uncle Abu Amin, and when the time comes I'll settle beside them. One day maybe they'll take us all there. To the parking lot? Fatima said that they are under the 'parking,' there; that's the expression she used. But why move us? Maybe it would be better for us to stay where we are, like guards at the gate, between our old camp and the country that has become ours once again.

I'll cut out everything I've just written; if Hasan read it he would say that there's no call for that kind of talk, it's emotional and exaggerated and spoils the writing. People followed the liberation of 2000 on their television screens and it was described in thousands of reports and newspapers, and written about by specialists and non-specialists alike. I want you to write about what you witnessed. Isn't this a part of the testimony, Hasan? My fast heartbeat, the box of tissues, blowing my nose again and again as I watch the residents return to their villages twenty years later? God keep you, Sadiq, what's left of life is less than what's passed; let me do what I want.

Yes, I will live in the seventh and last house. I suddenly sit up in bed, after lying there between sleep and waking. I count on my fingers: our house in Tantoura; my uncle Abu Amin's old house in Sidon; the marital home, in Sidon also; the house on the Tariq al-Jadida in Beirut; then Abu Dhabi, then Alexandria. The seventh will be there in Sidon, at the gate. I like the number seven, maybe it's a blessing. I feel the key hung on my neck and Abed's gift, the silver piece made by the Kurd, carrying on the trade of his teacher, the Sabian smith.

I got up and began to pack a suitcase for travel. Maryam knocked on the door, saying "I thought you were asleep."

"Are you still studying?"

"I'm about to finish and go to bed. What are you doing, is this the time to pack?

"I'm getting ready to go."

56

The Gate

"GOD BLESS YOU, AS LONG as you were going to accept my move to Sidon anyway, why did we spend all these months arguing?" I was talking about Sadiq's determination to rent an apartment in Sidon. He asks and inquires and inspects and compares: an apartment on the fourth floor with a balcony overlooking the sea and big windows open to the sky and the sunlight? "It's great! What do you think, Sadiq?" "How will it hold us all when we come in the summer?" Another, bigger apartment, five rooms. "It's far from the sea, and the building is old." A third one, new, and overlooking the sea. "The building has no guard." Finally we find an apartment that meets all of Sadiq's conditions: it's new, large, sunny, near the sea, and has a guard with a strong build and a kind face. Sadiq checked everything about him, and announced with delight, "The guard's grandfather knew my grandfather Abu Amin, and his grandfather's brother worked in Acre in the days of Palestine; I visited his village two years ago. Now I can rest assured, as if I were the one guarding the building. Fine, I'll sign the contract tomorrow." Then Sadiq meets the neighbors: "I'm not comfortable with them. Neighbors are family, closer than family—you'll be alone for months at a time, and I won't be able to rest easy having you among them." Sadiq wasn't the only one looking, either: he brought in his friends old and new, and the young men of Ain al-Helwa, some whose relatives he had employed or whose education he had paid for, and their friends and their friends' friends, until it seemed as if all of Sidon was preoccupied with Sadiq's search for an apartment for his mother.

At last we rented an apartment, we furnished it, and he left.

God bless you, Sadiq, what have you done? It's as if I were a pupil in a strange town: before he left he appointed not just one guardian but a whole host of guardians for me, young and old. As I told Maryam on the phone, I had imagined that I would be alone for a few months at least, gradually meeting a neighbor here or there or finding some of my old acquaintances in Sidon, and reconnecting with Karima's family. I figured wrong, as if I didn't know Sadiq: one week in Sidon and he rented an apartment, furnished it, and turned it into a madafa. He introduced his friends to the house and to me, "And I don't have to tell you, guys . . . ." The young men living in Sidon would ask after me daily, and those who lived in Ain al-Helwa would come all the way into Sidon to ask. Sometimes they would be too embarrassed to come in and have a cup of coffee; sometimes they would come with their mothers or wives and children, and invite me to their homes. My God, how much Sidon has changed, and how much the camp has changed!

Hasan asks me on the phone, and I say, "It's the same, the sea, the castle, the Khan al-Afranj, the old quarter, and the vegetable market." A moment of silence, and then I add, "There are new buildings, with many floors."

"And the camp?"

I keep silent; he repeats the question.

"The situation there is difficult."

He asks about the site of our new house; I tell him the name of the street and the number of the building.

"How far is it from the old city? Tell me the way, Mother."

I laugh, and say, "Are you going to surprise me with a visit? You won't get lost in Sidon, Hasan. As soon as you arrive ask for the street and not one but a thousand people will tell you the way."

"Tell me where it is from the Jad Building."

I can't find an answer that satisfies him. The buildings that were destroyed, were destroyed, and new buildings were put up in their place. Why does he remember the Jad Building specifically? I no long remember where it was. What does Hasan want, to imagine the site of our new house or to redraw the city on paper, in a map like the many maps he excelled at drawing when he was little? How will he combine the city that was destroyed and the new city that was built on the ruins in one map?

He can't come to Lebanon to visit me, Sadiq was right about that; he had caused a huge commotion. Sadiq had called me in Alexandria, and said, "Call Hasan and try to talk him out of this stupidity. We don't need to add complications to our lives, by our own free will. He doesn't want to listen to me, but maybe he'll listen to you." Hasan had decided to travel with his wife, saying he would visit Palestine. Sadiq went crazy, and said, "You're visiting Israel. Yes it's Palestine, but officially it's Israel, and once they put the state stamp on your Canadian passport in their airport you won't be able to visit most of the Arab countries. You're not Canadian, even if you have a Canadian passport. Your name is Hasan and you were born in Sidon. Go convince the passport officer in Syria or in Lebanon that you just wanted to visit your country! Use your head, Brother, that's just the way it is, there's nothing you can do! Your visiting Palestine is a luxury we can't afford. How will you visit me, how will you visit your mother? And if Maryam got married in Syria or Lebanon, how would you visit her?" Sadiq was repeating to me the conversation he had with his brother on the phone. "He told me, 'Mama lives in Alexandria, and I can visit Egypt with no problem.' I didn't tell him that you're living there temporarily, and that as soon as Maryam graduates you'll come back to live with me in Abu

Dhabi. I didn't tell him because my blood pressure was sky high, so I ended the call.'"

Now Hasan asks me to describe our house; he can't come to Lebanon, and my heart aches for him. I think, Sadiq was right; then I take it back. Hasan had wanted to visit Palestine; how did it look to him? He did not call me in Alexandria during his visit, he did not telephone me to say, "I'm in Tantoura, Mother, I'm standing on the seashore there." He did not write a letter about his trip, and he didn't even talk about the trip when he visited me later in Alexandria. He didn't tell me about Tantoura, or al-Furaydis or Haifa or Lid, even though Fatima told me that he spent a month going everywhere. She said, "He visited the coast from Acre to Gaza, the West Bank from Nablus to Hebron. He spent three weeks in Jerusalem, and visited Wisal in Jenin. He went to Randa's family in Nablus, and met relatives in al-Furaydis, and met friends he had met in Canada, going to meet them in Nazareth. He visited the Negev."

But Hasan did not tell me. Strange! As if he were stricken with the same silence that once struck me.

57

Light and Shadow

THE DOORBELL WOKE ME. I looked at my watch, it was one a.m. Who can be knocking on the door at this hour? I open, and I scream—Abed and Maryam are standing before me! Abed laughs and Maryam says, "The jack-in-the-box only pops up in the middle of the night!" After hugs and laughter and flying half sentences and a quick tour of the house, "because we want to get to know our new home," we move to the kitchen.

"I'll make supper for you."

"We ate on the plane."

"We want coffee."

Maryam insists that she make the coffee: "Where's the coffee, where's the sugar, where do you keep the cups?"

The talk takes us far and wide, and the coffee boils over. We make another pot and take it to the living room.

Abed says, "Now we have a problem, and we want a solution."

Is he joking? He's speaking seriously; what's wrong? I'm apprehensive.

"Maryam resents me!"

So they're joking. Maryam says, "There are well-founded reasons for resentment, and also for fear. My vacation is five days, I'll take off and leave Abed with you for a whole month. First, that's not fair, second . . . ."

I began to laugh.

"Second, there are real reasons to fear that he will take advantage of my absence to occupy my place, even though it's known, proven, and confirmed by your very own words, that the three boys are one thing and Maryam is something entirely different. I'm alerting you to his evil intentions."

Abed jumps up and sits on the back of my chair, putting his arms around me.

"I will begin immediately to execute my evil intentions. I believe that Sitt Maryam has occupied the throne long enough, and the time has come to depose her. I'm a democrat! What do you say, shall we smuggle her out like kittens? We'll get rid of her and live without a nagging censor."

We didn't go to sleep until the break of dawn.

When they went to bed I made myself another cup of coffee and waited for daylight, then I left for the market. A boy helped me carry everything I bought to the house. Maryam was sleeping; as for Abed, he had bathed and changed his clothes. We had breakfast together, and then, "By your leave, Mother."

"Where to?"

"I have work, I'll see you at lunch."

Maryam doesn't know Sidon, she never lived there like her brothers. Maybe she only visited it once or twice, when she was less than five. She says she doesn't remember it.

I take her to old Sidon, to the Bab al-Serail Square, I say, "It was here . . . ."

I point to the Bab al-Sarail Mosque, to the Khan, to an old sign on the closed door of an apartment on the ground floor, which says: al-Irfan Printers, Ahmad Arif al-Zain, Proprietor, Founded 1910. "Your grandfather knew Sheikh Ahmad Arif al-Zain personally. He told me about him, and he said . . . ."

We go down a few steps and walk through a dark archway. This is the Abu Nakhla neighborhood. I point to the Abu Nakhla Mosque on my left and the oven on my right; I say, "When your grandmother made a vow she would inform the

Abu Nakhla oven, and they would make as much bread as she asked for and distribute it in the mosque."

A few steps under the arches that connect the two sides of the lane. "Here is the Sabil neighborhood, and this house on your right is where your grandmother and grandfather lived."

We keep walking. "This is what's left of the public bath where your uncle Ezz bathed the day of his wedding. It was destroyed by the Israeli shelling in '82."

I take her to the Great Omari Mosque, and say that the men gathered here on the day of . . . here was the funeral of . . . .

Then the Maqasid Islamic School next to the great mosque. Maryam tries to convince the guard to let us in, but he says he's sorry, it's not allowed; school is in session and the students are studying. Maryam looks through the gate at the school buildings to the right and left of the courtyard. I point to the sea behind the courtyard: "This is where the boats carrying the weapons would anchor at night, and . . . ."

I take her to the carpenters' market, to the shoemakers' market, to the perfumers' market. I take her to the castle on the sea and to the Khan al-Afranj.

We sit in a café overlooking the sea, divided from it by the highway. I say, "We used to call it 'the holiday sea'; now it has become 'the waterfront.'" She doesn't catch what I mean to say, and I don't explain.

Maryam said that Hasan was right. "He told me, 'Old Sidon is a sequence of light and shadow. The lane will be dark because it's narrow and there are houses and shops on both sides, with arches above and bridges that also might have houses suspended on them, but before you get used to the shadow you're surprised by a long, sunny open space. Because we were kids we didn't walk but rather flew, so we would move in the blink of an eye from the light to the dark and from the dark to the light, as if we were playing with the sun and it was playing with us. And not only the lanes but the houses too:

you step into a dark place where you nearly trip, because you can't see where you step, or because the ghoul is lurking there, waiting for you. Then suddenly you're on stairs flaming with daylight. You jump up the steps and stop a moment to lean over a tin basin planted with mint or jasmine, or you find yourself in front of the sea, lit up as if there were a fire under it.'"

"Hasan wrote me that in his letter. But he didn't tell me anything about the poverty, the run-down houses, and the tired faces."

It's strange; Maryam didn't buy sweets as visitors usually do, nor the bars of soap for which the city is famous. From the carpenters' market she bought a small chest and a sieve and a pair of clogs. I said, "As long as you want the clogs for decoration, let's look for some Syrian ones, inlaid with shell." Then laughing, "You've become like the foreigners, Maryam—you hang the sieve on the wall and put the clogs on the living room table. Souvenirs from life in the old days. I hope you don't ask me for an embroidered peasant dress so you can hang it on the wall of your apartment in France!"

She said, laughing hard, "'You wrong me, Sir!' As for the chest, I'll put your picture in it, and my father's picture, and the love letters that will definitely come to me some day! I'll close the chest and keep it in my dresser."

"And the sieve?"

"I'll put it next to my bed so I don't forget to sift my thoughts and feelings every night before I go to sleep."

I laughed. "And the clogs?"

"Here we have the main thing. I'll be sure to use them every day, if only for an hour. I'll stomp on the ground with them and hear the sound, and it will reassure me that I'm here, here and then some!"

"What an imagination you have, Maryam!"

"Mama, sometimes we keep things without being able to sum up their value in one meaning. Do you remember the marble that the boy in Shatila gave me?"

"What marble, what boy?"

"The one the boy bought from Mustafa Umda's shop."

"Who's Mustafa Umda?"

She reminded me of the story, and then said, "I still have it. Not because I think it will bring luck or it's an amulet or a charm, but just for some reason. A small glass marble for kids to play with. When I get it out of the place where I keep it, I put it in the palm of my hand and stare at it, and recall moments and places and faces. I see the boy who gave it to me; he was very handsome, astonishing. I was five; can a child of five fall in love? I wonder where he is now, if he left the camp and life took him to a new exile, or if he stayed there, and has been buried under the rubble since the fall of '82. I look into his marble and see things, I see myself and maybe the past and the future. I close my hand around it carefully and put it away again."

In the house we sit together, or we stand in the kitchen, sharing in preparing a meal or a cup of coffee to have on the balcony. We talk, endlessly. We laugh. She tells me things and I tell her. We barely see Abed, who leaves the house early and rarely comes back for lunch, though we usually have supper together. He's preparing to file suit in the Belgian courts. Why Belgium, Abed? He gives a lengthy, involved answer about binding international laws and regulations, the Treaty of Rome and the decisions that followed it, and the European countries that had adopted it. At the end of the detailed talk comes the specific answer: "Because Belgium is the one country in the world that allows individuals to file suits of this kind. They present their complaint to the investigating magistrate, and if the basis of the claim is present then he is required to look into it. This is the first reason; second, because immunity is not considered an impediment in the criminal courts in Belgium. Third, because the Belgian courts accept the principle of trying the accused in absentia, meaning that someone accused of torture or war crimes or crimes against humanity can be tried even if he is not present, or not a Belgian citizen, or not living in the country. Two weeks ago a group of my colleagues filed a suit in the name of twenty-three plaintiffs against Ariel Sharon, Amos Yaron, and other Israelis and Lebanese, for the massacre in Sabra and Shatila. They presented the documents to the investigating magistrate in the Belgian criminal court; now we're preparing other suits, about the Sidon elementary school and the Jad Building."

"Abed, where is the Jad Building?"

"It was destroyed. I'll take you to the site; why do you ask?"

"Every time Hasan called, he asked, 'Where is the building you live in from the Jad Building? How do you get there from the Jad Building?'"

"Don't you know the story of the Jad Building?"

"I know, it was shelled at the beginning of the invasion and everyone who was in the shelter was killed."

"And Hasan?"

"What about Hasan?"

"I mean Hasan's story, didn't he tell you?"

"About . . . ?"

Abed changed the subject; I found it strange.

Maryam is the one who told me, when Abed went out. She said, "Hasan was in love with a girl who lived in that building. He had loved her since he was in middle school, and he kept going back to Sidon to see her when you moved to Beirut. Abed told me that when Hasan came to Beirut in '82 he sneaked into Sidon to check on her. He went to Sidon two days before he left Lebanon."

"And so . . . ?"

"So, nothing. He knew what had happed to the Jad Building, but he was still hoping. The girl died, with her mother and father and grandfather and sisters and brothers and neighbors and everyone who came from elsewhere to take shelter in the basement of the building."

I found nothing to say. That night I asked Abed, "Did you see the girl Hasan was in love with?"

"Yes, I saw her."

"What was her name?"

"Mira."

"Describe her for me."

"She was small. Her hair was very black, and her eyes too. She was short and a little plump and had two braids, and dimples in her cheeks. Her face was usually bright and smiling."

"Was she much younger than he was?"

"No, I'm describing her to you the way I remember her from our time in Sidon. She was the same age as Hasan, or a year younger. Maybe she was thirteen or fourteen. I didn't see her after we moved to Beirut. By the time of the invasion she had finished school and was working."

"Why didn't Hasan ask to marry her after he graduated?"

"I think she was trying to convince her family to let her marry him."

Hasan had named his daughter after her, years after she died. He never told me about her. His brothers and sister knew, why didn't he tell me? I recall the details: Hasan's constant visits to Sidon, his sudden appearance in Lebanon during the invasion, his sudden departure. One morning he said, "I'm going back to Cairo today, Mother." "Today, this very day?" Had Hasan told Amin? I doubt it; if he had, Amin would have told me. He didn't say anything to his father out of shyness; Hasan was reticent and very shy. Strange; you think you know your son better than any other creature, you don't miss a single thing that concerns him. You put your trust in the thought that you are holding him under your wing and keeping him safe from all harm, even when he flies away and lands far from you. Strange!

Is Abed living in a fantasy? These suits that he's immersed himself in preparing for years, will they reclaim any rights for someone who was killed? Will they bring him back to life, so that he moves in his grave and rises up, shaking the dust from his body, wiping his face and stretching out his hand to his little sister, smiling? Abed is living in a fantasy; but I don't give him my opinion. He says there are many ways to reclaim rights, and this is one of them. Is he trying to convince me, or is he answering an internal voice that makes him doubt what he's doing? He works tirelessly; he says, "Today I met the director of the school, I mean the one who was the director in '82. He said, 'I was the one who permitted the women and children to spend the night in the school, when they arrived that night from Tyre, on the first day of the invasion, thinking it would be a small incursion that wouldn't get as far as Sidon. They walked from Tyre, on foot; there were 120, almost all of them women and children. There were a small number of old men and three young men. I brought the keys and opened the school for them, and told them to please go in. I sheltered them—would that I hadn't! We carried some of them to the mass grave. Have you visited Martyrs' Square, at the end of Riyad al-Solh Street? Yes, they're there. No, not all of them; some stayed in the school. To be exact, half of them stayed in the school, buried under the basketball court. Come, I'll show you. Yes, here, under the basket. We rebuilt the school, we repaired it and repainted it, and we paved the court. I didn't tell the children; I lied and told them we took them all over there. They're kids, how would they come to the school or care about it if they knew that kids like them, and mothers like their mothers, are buried under the court they're playing on? Yes, I lied to them.'"

Abed says, "I met the official in charge of civil defense. He has files in which he recorded everything, immediately after the shelling. He asserts that the number who disappeared in the Jad Building across from the school was 125. He said that he gathered their bones. 'I couldn't specify the number exactly because the corpses were burned and dismembered; but seven residents of the building happened to be outside it when it was shelled, and they helped me ascertain the number. Yes, 125. I suggest you meet them, I mean the seven who were far from the building when the planes shelled it. They all lost their families. You must meet Ahmad Shams al-Din; he lost his wife and four children and his sister and her five children. I'm not sure if he can participate in the suit; maybe he can be a witness. I haven't seen him for a while, maybe he's regained some of his balance. He couldn't believe he had lost them all; for weeks or maybe months he would look for them in the hospitals, asking and repeating their names and descriptions. He would go up to the Israeli soldiers barricaded here and there and ask them, while they were sitting on their tanks eating oranges or standing at the barriers brandishing their arms. He would go to their headquarters and ask them to look for his children. Then he got a permit from them and went to Nahariya, over there; they had taken some Lebanese there for treatment. He went around the Nahariya hospitals. Maybe he's regained some of his balance now, God help him. You must meet him.

"'There's another man, who isn't in a position to share in bringing suit or to be a witness. He completely lost his mind. But it would be useful to see him and record his name, and for his condition to be included. He was outside the building when it was shelled, and when he returned and saw what he saw, he began to walk the streets completely naked. He didn't go either here or there, he didn't approach the Israelis. Whenever some good person would help him and give him something to cover his body with, we would find him walking naked in the streets.'"

Abed meets with the residents daily, with the officials and the others, listening to them. He says, "We have plenty of witnesses, we have documents, we have reports that were published at the time in the Arab and foreign newspapers, and we have books documenting what happened. We're going to sue.

58

Across Barbed Wire

I CALLED MARYAM AND THE boys. "The day after tomorrow,"
I said, "I'm going with Karima's sisters," I said. Abed and
Maryam said, "You're lucky. I wish we had known about that
possibility when we were in Sidon." Sadiq said, "If you had
told me two days ago, I would have made arrangements and
gone with you." Hasan asked, "Where exactly? At what location, at what time?"

At six in the morning on the appointed day, I was in Ain
al-Helwa. I knocked on Karima's family's door, I drank coffee with them, and then we went to the collection point.
Seven large buses will take us there. The women of the
camp have dressed up as if it were the morning of Eid, and
the boys and girls as well. Everyone has bathed and put on
the best clothes he owns; the women are carrying things, as
if they were going on a picnic. I thought, they will put down
mats and their woolen wraps and sit with their children,
having lunch and drinking coffee and tea. It's a strange trip.
I imagined young men standing near the wire, smoking and
maybe thinking about tomorrow and what will happen. I
imagined elders in their white head cloths, looking out at
the land spread below them and contemplating what was,
and what might be. I was anticipating the day in my imagination, but my imagination fell short.

The buses took us over the hills of the south. If only my
uncle Abu Amin were with me, he knows the land in the

south as if it were Palestine. He knows the roads and the names and the hill here and the one there, the river and the stream, the villages and the little towns, and for each one he has a story or a memory. God have mercy on you, Uncle Abu Amin. If my father had seen the future, would he have said, "You've left my back exposed," and been so angry with him and shouted at him? He did not leave him exposed, he covered him: he left him two and took care of the other five.

I become aware of the sound of ahazij singing; young men were standing in the bus leading the singing, and everyone joined in, the elders, men, and women, and the girls, and the boys. The bus driver honked, not because of something on the road; the songs seem to have delighted him, so he joined the passengers in the celebration. He sounds the horn in a regular rhythm, speeding up and slowing down according to the mood. He passes the bus in front of us or lets another bus pass us, and everyone waves to everyone, everyone laughs together. An elderly woman suddenly sprang from her seat and cried, "God protect al-Sayyid Hasan, if it wasn't for him and for the resistance we wouldn't be able to set foot on any of this land. Twenty-three years of occupation, and they're gone for good." Voices rose praying for al-Sayyid: "God protect him, God keep him for us, he's brought us good luck, God grant the same for Palestine." One of the young men standing at the front of the bus cut in: "Our leader is Abu Ammar, pray for Abu Ammar, people." A moment of tension, that seemed as if it would go on; then it was suddenly broken by the voice of an old woman wearing a long peasant dress. She stood up and let loose a long *aweeeha*, as if she were in a wedding, followed by trills of joy. Trills rose in the bus and harmony was restored with more songs, dal'una, ataba, aliyadi, and zarif al-tul.

It wasn't yet eight-thirty in the morning when the buses stopped with us; they lined up beside each other and we got off. The young men in charge said, "The road is here, follow us." We went behind them on a climbing dirt road. "There's Palestine!" shouted a woman who was a little ahead of me. Two steps later I saw what she had seen, the land spreading out beneath us, red in color, with houses like blocks scattered at a little distance from the barbed wire. They looked more like pre-fabricated chalets in tourist resorts, painted white with blue wooden shutters at the windows. Was it a settlement or only a military post? On the other side of the barbed wire were a number of Israeli conscripts, arms on their shoulders and iron helmets on their heads.

One of the young men said, "Rest a little, they will come."

"Who will come?"

"Our relatives from inside. Also we'll be joined by some buses coming from Tyre."

After less than half an hour seven other buses arrived from Tyre. We saw them line up and the passengers get off, carrying signs and flags. In the flash of an eye it was as if the barbed wire had disappeared from view, covered by the bodies of the residents on both sides. They were greeting each other, shyly at first, and then speaking easily. People were meeting each other:

"We are from Haifa . . ."

"We came from Ain al-Helwa; originally we're from Saffu-rya. From al-Zeeb. From Amqa. From Safsaf. From al-Tira. From . . ."

"We're from Umm al-Fahm . . ."

"We came from the Mieh Mieh Camp . . ."

"We're from Shafa Amr . . ."

"We came from the Rashidiya Camp . . ."

"We're from Acre . . ."

"We came from the Burj al-Shamali Camp . . ."

"We're from Arraba . . ."

"We came from al-Bass Camp . . ."

"We're from Nazareth . . ."

"We came from Sidon . . ."

"We're from al-Bi'na . . ."

"We came from Tyre . . ."

"We're from Jaffa . . ."

"We came from Jezzin . . ."

"We're from Sekhnin . . ."

"We came from Ghaziya . . ."

"We're from Lid . . ."

"We're from Deir al-Qasi . . ."

"We came from al-Bazuriya . . ."

"We're from al-Jdayda. We're from al-Rama. We're from . . ."

"And the lady is . . .?'"

"From Tantoura."

A young man shouted at the top of his voice: "Here's a lady from Tantoura. Is there anyone from Tantoura?"

A girl of maybe ten jumped up. She slipped through the rows and climbed on a rock, and extended her hand to me across the barbed wire: "I'm from Tantoura."

"Do you live there?"

"No, it's not permitted, I live with my family in al-Furaydis. My name is Maryam. When they occupied our town my grandfather was five years old. They fled to Lebanon and then sneaked back. Don't move from this spot, I'll be right back."

She disappeared, and I stood waiting. The women were exchanging what they had brought. Stupid Ruqayya, the women of the camp were smarter and had more imagination; they wanted to feed their relatives on the other side with something they had prepared with their own hands. On the other side a woman was laughing and saying, "I'm from Umm al-Fahm, I made you musakhan."

"We're from Ain Ghazal."

I looked up at the woman standing near me. I said to her, "Ain Ghazal is on our town's line. They would walk to it, on foot. I'm from Tantoura." I laughed. "A young man from Ain

Ghazal asked for me before they threw us out of the town. We came to Lebanon and each of us went his own way."

The woman said, "From what family?"

I told her. I added, "His name was Yahya, and his uncle was the sheikh of the village."

She said "Dr. Yahya?"

"He became a doctor?"

"No, he became a university professor. He lives in Amman. He was late in getting married, then he married his cousin, not the daughter of the sheikh of Ain Ghazal but the daughter of his other uncle, the younger one. He had five children with her."

The girl came back with her grandfather. He introduced himself to me, and greeted me, saying, "Welcome, welcome to . . ."

I stammered; I said, "Umm Sadiq."

Where did all these balloons come from? In the blink of an eye hundreds of balloons were rising, here and there. They were flying from here to there. "Palestine" was written on some of them, and on some were written the names of towns and villages. The flag was drawn on some in color, and some were sets of four balloons whose strings were tied together so they flew together, each in one of the colors of the flag: black, white, green, and red. A woman with more imagination than anyone else had brought a cage of doves; she released them and the doves flew off. The sky above us was flocks of doves and a holiday of colored balloons. I went down to one side and sat on a rock; is joy exhausting? Is it joy or something deeper, coming from afar? I hear Hasan's voice. Strange, why does my imagination take me to Hasan rather than to the rest of the children? Why don't I hear Sadiq's voice, or Abed's, or Maryam's? Why hasn't my imagination brought me Uncle Abu Amin, or his son Amin? I hear the voice again, and jump from my place. It's not my imagination, this is Hasan's voice! I run to the barbed wire and call out at the top of my lungs. Have you lost your mind, Ruqayya, have you completely lost your mind?

What a surprise, what a surprise! Hasan was standing on the other side of the wire, waving and smiling and coming closer, making his way through the crowd. "I'm here, Mother, here, here." He walks toward me, and I walk toward him; we're face to face, on either side of the wire. I extend my hand and he extends his, and the hands grasp. He bends down and sticks his head through the wire, to kiss me. I say, "Hasan, oh Hasan, the wire will injure you, it will injure your face." He doesn't listen to me, he propels his whole body until he can reach me and put his arms around me, clinging to me. "When did you arrive from Canada, you didn't tell me?" He laughs and points. I become aware that Fatima is with him, and the children. Mira and Anis are standing next to their mother, and she is carrying the baby she had four months earlier. Hasan takes her from Fatima and lifts her high. A tall man extends his arms and takes her from him. He looks at the little one: "How beautiful, God protect her." He plants a kiss on her forehead and gives her to me. "Little Ruqayya," says Hasan, in a loud voice. What will I give Ruqayya? I give the baby to a woman standing next to me, and put my hand to my chest, intending to give her the silver piece that bears her name, made by Abed's Kurdish friend. I touch the silver and feel it, and then I touch the key. I lift the cord from around my neck, and put it around the little one's neck. I kiss her forehead, and give her to the tall man to give her back to Hasan across the wire, so her mother can take her from him. I say in a loud voice, "The key to our house, Hasan. It's my gift to little Ruqayya."

I see Hasan's tears, and I hear the woman next to me trill for joy.

The buses move off, taking us back. The disc of the sun is gradually falling into the sea, which we smell though it's hidden from view. Silence enfolds us; I think, the holiday is over, in the blink of an eye. Everyone is going back to where he came from. Strange! It's as if we were returning from a long trip. The silence is broken by a strong voice, belonging to a young man sitting on the left, in front, and singing a song of Fairuz:

> Back from far deserts, by tents of their own,
> The night fires are happy, and shadows are thrown.
> There's none to tell them of a wound deep as bone.
> The tents move on, and I'm left alone, alone,
> Yabaa oof, yabaa oof, aoof.

Where does a young man get all this sadness, from what deep well does he raise it? Who . . . the thought remains incomplete. The voice is possessed by the end of the mournful mawwal, rising and leaping as if to the sky above. Or as if a demon had possessed him, from among the dabka dancers who shake the earth with the stamp of their feet. The young men join in the singing:

> Strike the mortars, grind coffee for the guests,
> Strike the mortars, and let the south wind blow,
> My love will hear the pounding of the pestles.
> The black wind rises, strike the mortars now.

Once again the solo voice rose alone:

> Take down the tents, the bird has flown away,
> The tents' winds call: let us be on our way!
> The black wind rises, strike the mortars now.
> At the edge of the night the wolf sends forth his cry,
> The night breeze carries our complaints far and wide.
> The black wind rises, strike the mortars now.

The others answer the singer:

> Al-lala, we-lala, al-lala, we-lala, we-lala
> al-lala, we-lala, we-lala.

I close my eyes, following the colorings of the voice:

> The noonday sun starts to sink, O my love, my desire,
> They have gone to the heights, gone west in the moonlight,
> While I sit alone, waiting for them by night,
> Waiting by night.
> I look down on the valley, and say to the sun, flee,
> I fear your light will burn, so my love won't know me.
> I watch from the trees, forcing open my eyes,
> Afraid to sleep lest you leave me, and forget where I lie.

Was I fighting off sleep, or falling into it without realizing? Did I doze off? Did I see him in a dream, or was the boy sitting beside me and looking up at me? Can a person see what's around him with his eyes closed? The young man was still singing; the solo voice went back to the sadness of the mawwal, nearing the end:

> They took my love and went north, far away,
> Oh woe, oh woe, oh woe be the day!
> They took my love and went north, far away.

Where did the woman go who was sitting next to me? When did this boy sit down in her place? He was looking up at me, with his eyes wide. I noticed, and looked at him. He opened a large drawing pad, and said, "I wanted to show you your picture."

"A picture of me?"

"I drew it while we were there."

"Are you an artist?"

"I draw. I'm still in the second year of middle school." He fell silent, then continued, "I also work."

"What do you do?"

"I pick oranges in season, and I pick olives in season. I help builders sometimes, and sometimes I sell cakes on the sidewalk."

"You help your parents?"

"I could help them more. I give them some of what I earn; I need some of the money to buy drawing pads. They're expensive. I don't draw with colors, I draw in charcoal and black ink. Charcoal pencils aren't cheap, and ink is also expensive.

"Sometimes I give in and buy a piece or two of chocolate, and divide them with my brothers and sisters. I crave it, so I tell myself that it's not really wrong to do what you want, sometimes. What do you think?"

I smile, and say, "It's completely reasonable."

He opened the pad. In the drawing there was barbed wire and a crowd of people on both sides. At the front was a woman wearing a long peasant dress lifting her hands high, holding an infant in diapers that she was about to give to a young man on the other side of the wire, who was lifting his hands toward the infant. On the child's chest was a large, old key, covering a third of her body. The people on both sides of the wire were all tall, lofty lines, each leaning slightly toward the other side, as if they met in a trellis that nearly made an arch.

He turned the page. "This is another drawing I made of you now, while you were sleeping."

A few lines of charcoal summon the likeness. The tattoo under the nose is clear, as if the Gypsy woman had made it a day or two earlier. The hair fastened behind the head had become two plaits, in the picture. Here also, the boy had put me in a long peasant dress. I said, "Why did you draw me twice in a peasant dress, and why do I have two braids?"

He shrugged his shoulders. "I don't know, that's how I saw you."

"You didn't tell me your name."

"Naji."

"Where are you from, Naji?"

"From Ain al-Helwa."

"I know, but where are you from originally?"

"From Upper Galilee."

I heard someone say, "We've arrived." I opened my eyes; the bus was stopping and the passengers had started to get out. I got off and took leave of Karima's sisters, and of the people I had met on the trip, promising we would get together again soon. I stopped a taxi and it took me home.

In bed, between sleep and waking, I became confused. I thought, was Naji sitting beside me, or was it a vision in a dream? Would I find him the next morning in Ain al-Helwa? Would we meet and would he allow me to get to know him better, and to watch him day after day, as he grew up? Would Naji meet little Ruqayya, one day, across the wire, or without it?

I will sleep. The eventful day has exhausted me.

I will sleep so I can get up early and go to the camp, to look for Naji and make sure that he's there.

Notes

TANTOURA, QISARYA, SAFFURYA, AIN GHAZAL, Balad al-Sheikh, and the other villages and cities mentioned in this novel are real and can be found on any map. They are part of Palestine and its history.

The massacres depicted in the novel are documented events: the massacres of Tantoura, of Sabra and Shatila, of the shelter in the children's school in Sidon, of the Jad Building, and others.

With the exception of some historical figures and some proper names mentioned in the text, all the characters of the novel, with their careers, their relationships and their fates, are fictional.

Abd al-Qadir al-Husayni: a Palestinian nationalist leader and the founder of an organization that fought during the Arab Revolt, 1936–39, and in the war of 1948.

Abu Ammar: Yassir Arafat (1929–2004), chairman of the Palestine Liberation Organization (PLO).

Amal: A movement representing the Shia in Lebanon, founded in 1974.

Bashir Gemayel: Leader of the Phalange party and commander of the Lebanese Forces; elected president of Lebanon August 23, 1982 and assassinated September 14 of that year.

Fairuz: An extremely popular Lebanese singer (b. 1935).

Fatah: An acronym for the Palestinian National Liberation Movement, founded in 1959 by Yasser Arafat and others, and dedicated to the armed struggle for the liberation of Palestine. It joined with the Palestine Liberation Organization in 1969.

al-Hunayti: A captain in the Arab Legion and commander of the Arab Forces in Haifa.

Naji al-Ali: Palestinian cartoonist, sharply critical of Israel and Arab regimes (1938–1987).

Phalange: A right-wing, ultranationalist political and paramilitary organization in Lebanon, drawing most of its supporters from among the country's Maronite Christians.

The Popular Front for the Liberation of Palestine (PFLP): A secular, leftist revolutionary organization formed in 1967 from three smaller organizations, under the leadership of Dr. George Habbash, and known for airline hijackings and other high-profile acts in support of the Palestinian cause. It has been part of the umbrella organization of the PLO since 1968.

Saad Haddad: Founder and head of the South Lebanon Army, allied with Israel (1936–84).

Sabian, or Mandaean: A member of one of two groups living in Iraq, remnants of an ancient religious community following the teachings of John the Baptist.

Sayyid Hasan (Nasrallah): Secretary General of the Shii organization Hezbollah after 1992, and leader of the Lebanese resistance.

Second Bureau: Lebanese intelligence service.

Shatir Hasan: A hero of traditional tales.

Umm Kulthum: An enormously popular Egyptian singer (ca. 1900–75).

Translator's Acknowledgments

I WOULD LIKE TO THANK Radwa Ashour, Wendy Munyon, Kelly Zaug, and Mutiah Diab for their generous contributions to this translation. I would also like to thank Neil Hewison and Nadine El-Hadi, of the American University in Cairo Press, for their unfailing kindness in support of the work.

I would like to dedicate this translation to the memory of Farouk Abdel Wahab.